FIRE SPIRIT

Graham Masterton

This first world edition published 2010
in Great Britain and in the USA by
SEVERN HOUSE PUBLISHERS LTD of
9–15 High Street, Sutton, Surrey, England, SM1 1DF.
Trade paperback edition published
in Great Britain and the USA 2010 by
SEVERN HOUSE PUBLISHERS LTD

British Library Cataloguing in Publication Data

Masterton, Graham.
  Fire Spirit.
  1. Arson investigation–Fiction. 2. Genetic disorders in
  children–Fiction. 3. Horror tales.
  I. Title
  823.9'14-dc22

ISBN-13: 978-0-7278-6875-6   (cased)
ISBN-13: 978-1-84751-239-0   (trade paper)

All Severn House titles are printed on acid-free paper.

Severn House Publishers support The Forest Stewardship Council [FSC],
the leading international forest certification organisation. All our titles that
are printed on Greenpeace-approved FSC-certified paper carry the FSC logo.

Mixed Sources
Product group from well-managed
forests and other controlled sources
www.fsc.org Cert no. SA-COC-1565
© 1996 Forest Stewardship Council

Typeset by Palimpsest Book Production Ltd.,
Grangemouth, Stirlingshire, Scotland.
Printed and bound in Great Britain by
MPG Books Ltd., Bodmin, Cornwall.

ONE

They caught her in the parking lot of Casey's General Store, as she was stowing her shopping in the trunk of her car. It was dark, and raining, and a blustery wind was blowing, so she didn't hear them coming up behind her.

One of them seized her around the neck and clamped his hand over her mouth. She let out a muffled whinny of shock, like a young antelope being pulled down by a lion, but then he dragged her violently backward, away from her car, so that she dropped her bag and her shopping scattered across the ground.

She twisted and struggled, but he was much too strong for her. He forced her across the asphalt, her feet dancing through the puddles, until they reached a black panel van that was parked in the darkest corner of the parking lot, under a broken floodlight.

Another man banged open the van's rear doors. He was wearing a mask, bone-white and totally expressionless. Then yet another man came into her line of sight. He, too, was wearing the same kind of mask, except that his mask was scowling. He held up what looked like a twisted black bandanna in front of her face.

'Listen to me, young lady,' said the man who was holding her around the neck. His voice was thick and breathy, as if he had asthma, or a heavy cold. 'We're going to gag you. While we do that, I recommend that you don't try screaming, OK? If you do, we'll hurt you, and that's a promise.'

She tried to jerk her head from side to side, but the man's hand was gripping her jaw so hard that she could barely move it. He was wearing a leather glove and it tasted new and sour.

'Are you going to keep still?' he asked her. 'We don't want to hurt you, but we will if we have to.'

'*Mmfh!*' she protested. She could only breathe in short, shallow snorts and her heart was thumping painfully hard against her ribcage. But she remembered what she had been taught at self-defense classes: if you stand no chance of fighting your way out, it's always safer to give in. The man lifted his hand an inch away from her mouth, let it hover for a moment, and when she didn't scream he said, 'Good girl, excellent.'

The scowling man immediately pulled the bandanna between her jaws and tied it in two knots behind the back of her head. She swallowed saliva and almost choked herself.

'Is that hurting you?' asked the first man. She nodded, and made a mewling noise, to tell him that it was, but all he said was, 'Good. Excellent.'

The expressionless man produced a pair of black nylon handcuffs and looped them around her wrists, zipping them tight. Then the three of them took hold of her together and heaved her bodily on to a blanket in the back of the van. She kicked out at them, catching the scowling man hard in the left hip. He didn't say a word, but roughly pushed her flat on to the floor and seized her ankles, so that the expressionless man could fasten them together with another pair of nylon restraints. The two of them pulled the blanket right over her, and slammed the doors shut. Seconds later, the van's engine started up and it slewed backward out of its parking space. She felt it jolt over the speed-hump across the entrance to the parking lot, and then veer sharply to the left.

She lay in darkness, half-stifled by the blanket, swallowing and swallowing because of the gag. At first she was too shocked to cry. She found it almost impossible to believe that this was actually happening. When she had walked out of Casey's she had been worrying if she had enough crunchy peanut butter at home. Now she didn't know if she was going to live or die.

The van swerved right, and then left, and then right again, and each time she was rolled from one side of the floor to the other.

She couldn't help thinking about her car, with its trunk still wide open and her keys dangling in the door. And then she thought about Heidi and Joanna, who would be home from school in less than twenty minutes. How were they going to get into the house? And who would take care of them if anything happened to her?

How would Daniel take the news? Maybe Daniel didn't love her any more, but they had been married for seven-and-a-half years, and they were still close friends.

The van drove on and on, bumping and swaying, and she began to grow increasingly panicky and claustrophobic. The blanket was coarse and heavy and reeked of cigarette smoke and she found it difficult to breathe. Her jaws ached from the gag, and the nylon restraints were cutting into her wrists and ankles. Her right shoulder was bruised from hitting one of the wheel-arches when she rolled over, and every time the van took a left turn she hit it again.

Now her eyes filled up with tears, and she started to make a thin, repetitive squeaking sound in the back of her throat. She couldn't think why these three men had taken her, or what they could possibly want. It couldn't be for money. Daniel had his own insurance business, but he wasn't wealthy, and neither were her parents.

She closed her eyes so that her wet eyelashes stuck together and she thought of a prayer. *Dear Virgin Mary please please protect me from harm. Dear Virgin Mary please don't let these men hurt me. I don't want to die. Dear Virgin Mary all I want is to go home and hold my children close to me.*

The van slowed, and turned, and jolted up and down, and then came to a stop. She lay under the blanket, listening. She heard men's voices, although she couldn't distinguish what they were saying to each other. Then she heard the van's front doors open, and felt the suspension rocking as the men climbed out.

There was more conversation, and then the rear doors opened. One of the men leaned over her and pulled the blanket away from her face. It was the expressionless man.

'So sorry for the bumpy ride,' he said, but his mouth was only a horizontal slit cut into his mask and so she couldn't tell if he meant it. The only distinctive sound she heard was the way he said 'sho shorry', with a strong South Philly accent.

'Hurry it up for Chrissakes,' said the thick-voiced man who had first grabbed hold of her. They pulled her by her ankle restraints out of the back of the van and stood her up on her feet, holding her upper arms to keep her from falling over. Now she saw the thick-voiced man face-to-face for the first time. He was wearing a mask, too, but his mask was laughing. A mad, hysterical laugh, like The Joker.

She twisted her head around, trying to see where she was. The van had parked in the front driveway of a pale green two-story house on some long, straight suburban street which she didn't recognize. There was nobody else in sight. The glistening-wet sidewalks were deserted and the trees were thrashing in the wind with a noise like the ocean.

The scowling man dug his hands under her armpits, while the

expressionless man grasped her ankles. Together they lifted her up and carried her toward the house, both of them shuffling crab-wise. They climbed the front steps on to the porch, while the laughing man took out his keys and opened the front door.

'Welcome,' he said, then coughed, and had to stand still for a moment with his fist pressed against his mouth. When he had recovered, he said, 'Come along in.'

Inside, the house was gloomy and smelled of damp. The laughing man held the front door open while his companions carried her into the hallway and stood her up on her feet again. He went across to an ugly little plywood side-table and switched on a lamp with a naked bulb in it, so that the hallway was filled with harsh white light. Then he closed the front door, and bolted it, top and bottom.

She stared up at him, her eyes wide. He came close to her and tilted up her chin with his leather-gloved hand.

'Hey, are you *afraid*?' he asked her, in his catarrhal voice. 'There's nothing worse than feeling helpless, is there? Nothing worse than not knowing what's going to happen to you, neither.'

She looked around, trying to see if there was any other way out. There was a half-open door on her right-hand side, but that looked as if it led only to a living-room. At the far end of the hallway there was another door, blocked with a stack of dining chairs and an ironing-board.

'Come on through,' said the laughing man. He opened the living-room door and went inside, and the other two men gripped her upper arms and forced her to hop and stumble after him. The living-room was at least thirty feet long, with one wall painted maroon and the other three cream. The smell of damp was just as strong as it had been in the hallway, only there were other smells, too – a *brown* smell, like dried blood; and Raid fly-spray; and curdled milk; and stale cigarette smoke.

On the opposite side of the room there was a rough stone fire-place, its grate clogged with half-burned newspaper and cigarette butts. Above it hung a framed print of a forest in fall. What she found most disturbing, though, was the furniture, what there was of it. Four mismatched armchairs with deeply-soiled upholstery were arranged in each of the four corners of the room, around a stringy, worn-out rug. But in the center of the rug lay a large mattress with striped ticking, and countless stains in the middle of it, some dark, some pale, some that were no more than spatters, others that looked like aerial photographs of dried lake-beds.

The laughing man laid a hand on her shoulder and gave her a pat. 'It all comes down to this, in the end. Sooner or later, we all end up in hell.'

He nodded to the scowling man, who reached up and loosened the knots at the back of her head. The laughing man tugged the bandanna out of her mouth and dropped it on to the floor. She didn't scream, although she felt like it. She realized that if he had taken the gag off, there was no chance that anybody could hear her. She had seen the empty streets outside. On a wild, wet evening like this, everybody would be sitting indoors in their La-Z-Boys, with a can of beer and a pepperoni pizza and their TV turned up loud.

The expressionless man came forward and took out a pair of electrician's pliers. He knelt in front of her and cut the nylon restraints around her ankles, and then cut her wrists free. This was even more frightening. If they were prepared to take off her restraints, they must be completely confident that she couldn't escape.

She wiped her mouth on the sleeve of her cable-knit sweater. She looked at the three men in turn, trying to see their eyes through the holes in their masks, trying to detect some humanity. But all she could see in each of them was a glitter, like the glitter of cockroaches underneath a sink.

'You need to let me go,' she told them, with a catch in her throat.

The laughing man slowly shook his head from side to side.

'That isn't an option, I'm afraid. It's almost five already and we're running right out of time.'

'You can't keep me here! What do you want me for? My neighbor's expecting me back at five. If I don't show up, she'll call the police!'

'Well, yes, I expect she will. But the police won't never find you.' He sniffed behind his mask. 'Not until it's too late, anyhow.'

'Please,' she said, 'you have to let me go. I don't have very much money, but if it's money you want . . .'

The laughing man kept on shaking his head. 'What you can give us, it's worth much more than money, let me reassure you of that. It's priceless.'

'What is it then?' she demanded, more shrilly than she had meant to. 'Is it sex you want? Do you want to rape me?'

'Is that an invitation?' put in the scowling man. The expressionless man turned his face away, and let out a grunting noise that could have been a laugh.

'Ever hear of *ex*-orcism?' asked the laughing man.

'Of course I've heard of exorcism,' she retorted. Her voice was trembling but she was beginning to grow angry. 'What the hell does exorcism have to do with me? I'm just an ordinary woman and a mother and all I want to do is go home and cook my children's supper for them. If you want a damned exorcism, why don't you call for a priest?'

'Because it ain't no demon that needs to be exorcized, which is what priests do.'

'Then what? And why do you need *me*?'

'Because you're an ordinary woman and a mother and all you want to do is go home and cook your children's supper for them. You have all of the right qualifications. More than that, though, you *look* just right. Or nearly right, anyhow. Near as dammit.'

He crossed the room and picked up a red piece of cloth that had been hanging over the back of one of the armchairs. He held it up in both hands and she could see that it was a cheap red sleeveless dress.

'Why are you showing me that?'

'Because I want you to put it on.'

'What? *Why*?'

'Because it's part of the exorcism. Can't have an exorcism without all the required accoutry-ments, can we?'

She stayed where she was, breathing deeply, with her arms by her sides. 'You really need to let me go,' she repeated.

The laughing man walked back toward her. He stood so close that she could hear the phlegm crackling in his sinuses as he breathed.

'We don't want to hurt you, but I assure you we will, unless you do what we tell you.' He held out the dress. 'There you are. It should fit you, pretty much.'

She looked up at him and then glanced at the other two men. 'Where can I change?'

'Right here. Right in front of us. That's part of the proceedings, too.'

She took the dress and hung it over the arm of the chair that was next to her. Then, very slowly, she pulled down the zipper of her quilted navy-blue squall. The three men stood quite still, watching her. She took off her squall and hung it on the chair next to the dress.

'You don't have to take for ever,' said the laughing man.

'*What do you want?*' she screamed at him. '*Just tell me what you want!*'

'Hey, don't get your panties in a bunch. You're already doing it. You're already doing what we want. We wouldn't object if you did it a little quicker, that's all.'

In spite of her determination not to be intimidated, tears began to slide freely down her cheeks. She bent over and pulled down the zippers at the sides of her brown leather boots, and took them off. Then she crossed her arms and lifted her oatmeal-colored sweater over her head.

'Keep going,' said the laughing man. 'Brassiere off, too.' The lisping old-fashioned way he said 'brassiere' only increased her feeling of dread.

She shook her head. 'No.'

'Brassiere off, too, or we'll cut it off, and we won't be too careful.'

She reached behind her and unfastened the catch of her bra. She closed her eyes as she took it off, and tried to imagine that this was nothing but a bad dream, and that she wasn't here at all.

'Come on. Skirt, too,' the laughing man ordered her.

She opened her eyes and she was still in the gloomy living-room, with the three masked men still watching her. With shaking fingers, she unbuttoned her skirt at the side, and pulled down the zipper of that, too. She stepped out of it, so that she was wearing nothing now but her pantyhose and her white lace panties. Although the room was so cold, she suddenly felt hot with fear and embarrassment.

'We're waiting,' said the laughing man. 'We don't have the patience of Job, you know.'

'Please,' she wept. 'I'll do anything.'

'You bet your sweet bippy you will. Now come on, get on with it. Get them pantyhose off, and those pretty little panties, too.'

She did as she was told, and now she was naked.

'Nicely trimmed topiary there,' said the laughing man, and the expressionless man let out another grunt of amusement. 'Now how about putting on that dress?'

The dress was cheap, with stray threads and no lining, and it was too tight across her bust, but she managed to put it on and tug the hemline down to her knees.

'Well, look at you! Excellent! You look so much like her, I could've sworn she'd come back from the cemetery.'

She said nothing. She was shivering, and she had no idea what the three masked men were going to do next.

The scowling man trampled across the mattress and stood very close to her, on her left-hand side. He smelled faintly of camphor, like pain-relief liniment. 'You're right,' he said. 'She could be her double, almost. But – you know – *prettier*, if anything. Not so goddamned *blotchy*.'

The expressionless man crossed over the mattress, too, and stood on her right. She looked from one to the other. They were both staring at her, but of course their masks were giving nothing away. She was so frightened that she was close to wetting herself.

'Well, now, the next thing you need is a drink,' said the laughing man. He reached into the pocket of his coat and took out a plastic bottle of Sobieski vodka. He unscrewed the cap and held it up. 'Same brand *she* always favored. Only eleven bucks the bottle, that's why. Bring her here, fellas.'

The scowling man and the expressionless man took hold of her arms and frogmarched her into the middle of the mattress. They all found it hard to keep their balance, so that they looked as if they were trying to stand upright on the pitching deck of a ship. The laughing man said, 'Come on, now. Think you can do what *she* used to do? Think you can match up?'

She couldn't find the words to answer him.

'OK, then,' he said. 'Let's have you down on your knees, shall we? Then we can see what you're good for, or what you ain't.'

The scowling man and the expressionless man forced her arms so high up behind her back that the tendons audibly crackled and she had no choice but to kneel. Under her bare knees, the mattress felt damp and lumpy, and it stank of stale urine and dried blood.

The laughing man came right up to her and held out the bottle of vodka. 'Here . . . help yourself. *She* always did.'

'I don't drink,' she whispered.

He cupped his hand to his papier mâché ear. 'What? What did

you say? You don't drink? But you *have* to drink! That's all part of the exorcism. Everything has to be played out exactly the way it was, right down to the very last detail. She never wore no underwear so you can't wear no underwear. She always wore a red dress like that, or some other dress that was very much like it, so you have to wear one, too.

He paused for breath, gasping behind his mask. 'She *drank*. I mean, that was almost the whole reason it ever happened. She drank from morning till night. Sometimes she was so drunk she didn't even know who anybody was. Sometimes she didn't even know who *she* was.'

He held out the bottle again, prodding it against her lips. 'Come on, be a good girl, drink.' But she closed her mouth tightly and turned her head away.

'Well – sorry about this,' he told her, and nodded to his two companions. The expressionless man took hold of her hair and pulled her head back, while the scowling man squeezed her jaw so hard that she was forced to open her mouth, like a freshly-landed fish.

The laughing man poured vodka straight down her throat. It blazed all the way down her esophagus into her stomach, and when she tried to cry out, she breathed some of it into her lungs, so that she felt as if she were choking. The laughing man stood over her, waiting for her to finish coughing, but when she didn't, he nodded to his companions again and he splashed even more into her mouth, regardless of her coughing and her spluttering.

'You may look just like her,' he told her, 'but you sure can't take your booze the way she used to, and that's a fact.'

She retched and gasped for air, but he forced her to go on swallowing until the bottle was empty. He tossed it on to the floor, reached into his other coat pocket, and took out another bottle.

'*No!*' she screamed at him. '*I can't! You're killing me!*'

'Killing you? We're not killing you. All we're trying to do is show you a good time!'

Scowling and Expressionless pulled her hair again and opened her mouth, and Laughing splashed almost half a bottle more down her throat.

Eventually, however, they let her go, and she crouched on the mattress on her hands and knees, her stomach heaving, wheezing for breath. The men stood around her, watching her, saying nothing.

'Why are you doing this?' she sobbed. 'What have I ever done to you?' She raised her head.

The laughing man shrugged and said, 'You never did nothing, sweetheart, except to be in the wrong location at the wrong time. For *you*, that is, anyhow.'

He reached into his coat again, and this time he took out a pack of Marlboro cigarettes. He shook one out, tucked it into the slit in his mask, and lit it. When he blew smoke, it leaked out of his eyeholes as well as his mouth, so that it looked as if his head was on fire.

He hunkered down in front of her and held out the lighted cigarette. 'Here you are, take a drag on this. That should calm your nerves.'

She shook her head. 'I don't smoke.'

'You're still not getting it, are you? *She* smoked, so *you* got to smoke. This is an exorcism, don't you understand? Everything that she did, you have to do. You have to be her. What's the word . . . it's symbolical.'

He held the cigarette up to her mouth. She stared defiantly into his cockroach eyes, but he prodded it up against her lips again and again.

'You know you're going to have to smoke it, don't you?' he told her. 'Because if you don't, I'm going to be obliged to stub it out in your eye, and you wouldn't enjoy that too much, would you?'

'I hate you,' she whispered.

The laughing man nodded in appreciation. 'That's good,' he said. 'That's *excellent*. That's exactly the way that *she* used to talk. You'd be right on top of her, giving it everything you got, and she'd look you straight in the eye and say, "you scumbag, I wish you'd have a heart seizure, right here and now, so I could feel you die inside of me".'

He prodded her lips again, and this time she opened them a little so that he could insert the cigarette. The smoke drifted up into her eyes and stung them, and she started coughing again.

He watched her for a while, and then he said, 'Come on now, sweetheart, you got to *inhale*. Otherwise you don't get that hit.'

She hesitated, and then she breathed in. She managed to hold the smoke in her lungs for only a second before she exploded into another coughing fit. She coughed so hard that she bent forward and pressed her forehead against the mattress, as filthy and evil-smelling as it was.

'I'd say she needed a little more practice at that, wouldn't you?' said Scowling. '*She* used to get through two packs a day, no trouble at all. Sometimes three.'

The laughing man sat down in one of the armchairs and lit another cigarette. The expressionless man sat down, too, but the scowling man went to the window and parted the dark brown linen curtains so that he could look outside.

'Still raining,' he said.

'Close the goddamned drapes, will you?' the laughing man ordered him. 'You want half the goddamned neighborhood to see that there's somebody in here?'

'There's nobody out there, man.'

'You never know. Just close the goddamned drapes.'

Ten minutes went by, while the laughing man smoked and the expressionless man jiggled one leg as if he needed to go to the bathroom, and the scowling man paced around the living-room asking irrelevant questions, which neither of the other two men bothered to answer.

'Got to get that alternator fixed, you know that.'

'Did you ever try the roadhouse steak sandwich at Quizno's? Now that's what I call tasty. Or you can have the chicken with chipotle mayo. I never know which to choose.'

'Think it's going to rain all night?'

She stayed on her knees in the middle of the mattress. She was beginning to feel woozy, and she found it hard to keep her balance. She closed her eyes and prayed that when she opened them she would be back at home, and that none of this would have happened, but even with her eyes closed she could smell the laughing man's cigarette smoke, and hear the scowling man prowling around the room, talking to himself.

Please please dear Virgin Mary let this all be over. Please.

Suddenly, however, without a word, the laughing man flicked his cigarette butt into the fireplace and stood up. The expressionless man stood up, too. All three men approached the mattress and stood over her.

'You look pretty goddamned drunk to me,' said the laughing man.

'I feel sick,' she said, and her voice didn't even sound like hers.

'You don't want to be barfing, sweetheart, believe me. Barfing can put a fellow off, if you know what I mean.'

'No,' she said, 'I don't know what you mean.'

'Well, in that case, let's *show* you, shall we?'

With that, he pushed her in the face with the flat of his hand, hard, so that she fell over backward. She cried out, 'No! What are you doing? *No!*' and tried to roll on to her side, but he pushed her again, with both hands this time, and clambered on to the mattress on top of her.

He was big and he was heavy and he was very strong. He gripped her neck with his right hand, half-throttling her, while he used his left hand to reach down and tug open his pants.

'No!' she screamed at him, right into his leering white mask. 'No, you bastard, get off me! *Get off me!*'

He pulled up the hem of the cheap red dress and then forced her thighs apart with his knees. She kept on screaming, high and hoarse, but she knew that nobody could hear her and nobody was going to come and rescue her.

The laughing man turned around to his two companions. 'Come on, guys, what are you waiting for? She's drooling for it. No holes barred.'

She saw them unbuckling their belts, but that was all she saw because she closed her eyes tight and kept them closed. When the laughing man grunted and pushed his way into her, and the other two climbed on to the mattress beside her, she tried to think of that sunny fall day in Lafayette when she and Daniel had taken a walk in the woods and he had proposed to her, and she had never realized that it was humanly possible to be so happy.

She opened her eyes. She was lying on her right side, and she was shuddering with cold. The living-room was in darkness, except for a narrow line of street light that fell diagonally across the mattress from the gap between the drapes. She coughed, and sat up, and looked around.

The three masked men were no longer around, although she could still smell their sweat and their cigarette smoke and the faint pungency of liniment. She listened, but the house was silent, apart from the pattering of rain against the living-room window.

Her dress had been pulled right up under her breasts, and when she pulled it down again she felt the cold slime between her thighs and between the cheeks of her bottom. She felt sore and swollen, and even though the living-room was so gloomy, she could see that the insides of her thighs were covered in patterns of plum-colored bruises. Her lips felt dry, and when she licked them they tasted like bleach.

She didn't cry. She was too shocked to cry, and she was still drunk, too. All she could think of was the jostling, and the pushing, and the panting, and the pain. She had never felt pain like that before. It had been worse than giving birth.

She sat there for over a minute, trying to find the strength and the will to stand up and get dressed in her own clothes. In a strange way, she felt relieved. In spite of what the three masked men had done to her, it was all over, and she was still alive, and she hadn't been seriously injured. The Virgin Mary had protected her, after all, as much as She could.

She caught hold of one of the arms of the nearest chair, and was about to climb to her feet when a voice said, '*Mommy?*'

She said, '*Ah!*' in surprise, and looked around. A boy of about twelve was standing in the shadow of the open door. He was thin and pale, with a shock of wiry black hair, and he was wearing red-striped pajamas.

'Who are you?' she asked him. Her throat was so sore that she could hardly speak. 'What are you doing here? You're nothing to do with those men, are you?'

The boy stepped out from behind the door. He was an odd-looking child, with large dark eyes that were spaced wide apart, and a long skull, almost like an alien. His lips were a cupid's bow, and unnaturally red for a boy.

'Mommy, can *I* sleep with you, too?'

'I'm not your mommy, son, and I have to leave now. Where are your parents?'

'You never let me sleep with you.'

She had to clear her throat again. 'I'm sorry, but I'm not your mommy, and I really have to go.'

The boy crossed the room and climbed on to the mattress. He sat down next to her and looked up at her with those large dark eyes. He reached up and touched her cheek with his fingertips, and he was very cold.

'But you *never* let me sleep with you,' he repeated.

'Listen,' she said, 'I'm not your mommy and I'm going now.
Do you live in this house? Who's taking care of you?'

To her surprise, the boy wrapped his arms around her, and
pressed his head hard against her breasts. 'You do love me,
Mommy, don't you?' His hair smelled musty, as if it needed a
wash.

She took hold of his arm and tried to pry him away from her.
'For the last time, I am not your mommy. So, *please*, let go
of me.'

'I'm not going to let go. I'm going to stay here for ever. You
let *them* sleep with you but you never let *me* sleep with you.'

'Please get off me,' she told him. She tried to pull herself away
from him but he clung on to her dress, and when she tried to stand
up she lost her balance and she toppled down on to the mattress
again.

'Let go of me!' she shouted at him. 'Just let go of me!'

'I'm not *going* to let go,' he insisted. 'I'm not *going* to let go.'

She swung her arm around and slapped him hard on the ear.
He held on to her even tighter, so she slapped him again, and then
again.

'*Get away from me, you little bastard!*' she screamed at him.

'You never let me sleep with you! You never let me sleep with
you!'

'*Get the fuck away from me! Get off!*'

The boy raised his head, although he didn't release his grip on
her dress. He stared at her, his face so close that she couldn't
focus on him.

'Do you remember what happened, Mommy?' he asked her, in
a low, conspiratorial voice.

'I'm not your mommy and I don't remember what happened,
whatever it was. All I want you to do is to let go of me.'

'*You* remember what happened.' The way he said it, it sounded
as if it was something extremely lewd.

She grasped his shoulders and tried to shove him away from
her, but he held on to her like a monkey that couldn't be pulled
off a tree.

'*Get off me! Let me go!*'

In desperation and fear, she seized his ears and shook his head
backward and forward, as hard as she could.

'Get-off-me-get-off-me-get-off-me!'

At that instant, the boy burst into flames. Not just his hair, or his pajamas. He exploded into a mass of roaring fire, as if he had been doused in gasoline and set alight. He screamed, his mouth stretched wide open, and she screamed, too, because the flames seared her face and her arms and her hair flared up like a Roman candle.

She tried to wrench herself away from him, but the fiercer he burned, the tighter he held her. She felt her ears twisting into little charred knots, and her eyelids shrivel, and then her eyeballs popped in the heat and she was blinded.

The pain was unbearable. She burned and burned from her feet to the top of her head, and after her red dress had been reduced to blackened tatters, the skin on her back turned bright red, too, and then that became blackened in turn. Then she could smell her own flesh roasting, and it smelled just like roasting meat.

The flames died down, and she lay on her side on the smoldering mattress, quivering with shock, in the fetal position that burns victims almost always adopt as their tendons tighten. She was only seconds away from oblivion, but even though she was blind and deaf and her fingers were nothing more than charred twigs, and she couldn't have felt the boy even if he was there, she was sure that she was quite alone.

TWO

Ruth was woken up by Amelia whispering in her ear, a hot thunder that she could barely understand.

'I made you breakfast.'

She opened her eyes, and blinked. Amelia was leaning over her, her dark blonde hair pulled back into a lopsided ponytail. Her elf-like face was so close that Ruth couldn't focus on her.

'*What*?' she said.

'I made you breakfast. I even wrote you a menu.'

Ruth sat up. Next to her, all that she could see of Craig was the fingertips of one hand, sticking out from underneath the comforter, like a man crushed below a collapsed building. He was breathing so quietly that he could have been dead.

'Look. Here's your menu,' said Amelia, and she held up a sheet of notepaper – again, so close that it was too blurry for her to read.

Ruth twisted around and looked at her bedside clock. Five fifteen a.m. Her alarm was set for five thirty a.m. in any case, so Amelia had woken her only fifteen minutes earlier than usual.

'Shh,' she said. 'Don't wake your daddy. He hasn't been sleeping too good lately.'

It all came out in a breathy gabble. 'Daddy said you never had a proper breakfast, but *you* said that you never had time for a proper breakfast so I made you a proper breakfast myself.'

'*Shh*!' Ruth repeated, touching her finger to her lips. 'I'll see you in the kitchen.' She went into the bathroom and took her pink flannelette robe from the back of the door. Then she looked in the mirror over the basin. Her eyes were puffy and her short blonde hair looked as if she had been standing on the poop-deck of the *Pequod* all night. She splashed her face with cold water, bashed at her hair with a hairbrush, and gave herself an exaggerated scowl. She was still pretty, in a bruised-angel kind of way, still slim, although she was quite big-breasted, but she was beginning to feel her age.

Halfway along the landing she stopped at Jeff's bedroom door and opened it. Jeff was sprawled across his quilt in his jeans and his green Morbid Angel T-shirt, with his iPod still in his ears, fast asleep and snoring. Ruth quietly closed the door again and went downstairs to the kitchen.

'Good morning, madam and welcome to your breakfast,' said Amelia. She was already dressed in her favorite white sweater with brown knitted puppies on it, and jeans. She had set two place mats on the breakfast counter, with knives and forks and spoons and red gingham napkins folded into flowers. Outside the window the yard was just beginning to grow light, and a blue jay was squawking on the bare branches of their single apple tree.

Ruth climbed up on to her stool and tried to smile. 'Ammy, this is such a wonderful surprise. What time did you get up to do this?'

'Three fifty-three,' Amelia told her. 'Would madam care for some coffee?'

'Oh, yes please. What's that smell?'

'That's your eggs. They'll be ready in a minute.'

Ruth frowned at the range on the other side of the kitchen. Something lumpy and yellow was sizzling in a skillet, but she couldn't make out what it was. Amelia poured coffee into her mug, and then said, 'Here's your menu.'

The menu was written in red, green and purple crayons. It read:

Tuna lime refreshment
Egg and orange omelet
Pancakes with baked beans and crunchy topping
Mexican energy juice

Ruth read it carefully, and then nodded. 'It sure sounds *different*, I have to admit that.'

Amelia had been watching her, her eyes wide with anticipation. 'You're really going to enjoy it, I promise.'

While Amelia went to the fridge, Ruth tried her coffee. It was scalding hot, but very weak, and it tasted strongly of maple syrup.

'What do you think of the coffee?' asked Amelia. 'You always say how much you like those coffee and maple candies, so I thought it would be a great idea to make them into a drink.'

She set two glass bowls on the table, each of them filled with a pale beige mixture with grated lime peel on top. 'This is the first course. It's meant to wake you up. Try it.'

Ruth glanced at the menu. 'This is . . . "tuna lime refreshment"?'

'That's right. I made it with flaked tuna, vanilla ice cream and lime juice. You mush them all together and chill them.'

Ruth poked at the mixture with her spoon. 'Amelia, honey . . .'

'You have to try it. You'll like it when you try it.'

Ruth took a tiny spoonful and put it in her mouth. Amelia didn't take her eyes off her as she slowly chewed and swallowed.

'What do you think?'

Ruth pursed her lips tightly, but only to stop her eyes from filling up with tears. She loved Amelia so much, she could never bear to hurt her. She was so loving, and so vulnerable, and so enthusiastic about everything. But she had spent more than an hour making a breakfast which Ruth couldn't possibly eat.

'You don't like it, do you?' said Amelia.

Ruth put down her spoon. 'I'm sorry, sweetheart. There's nothing wrong with your breakfast. It all looks lovely. But I guess I never eat much in the morning because I'm never very hungry.'

'It's not lovely, is it? It's all horrible.'

'Sweetheart, I didn't say that. Listen, put the tuna back in the fridge and maybe I'll eat some this afternoon, when I get back home.'

'No, you won't. You'll throw it away and *pretend* you've eaten it.'

'Ammy—'

Amelia went across to the range, took off the skillet and emptied it with a sharp bang into the pedal-bin. 'Don't worry about clearing up,' she said. 'I'll do it when you're gone.'

'Ammy, please – listen to me!'

But Amelia flounced out of the kitchen and ran noisily upstairs to her room, slamming the door.

Ruth stood in the middle of the kitchen wondering if she ought to go after her. But from experience she would probably make things worse. Amelia's condition meant that she didn't see the world the way that other people saw it. She didn't understand lies. She didn't understand why some people were cruel and some people were untrustworthy. She didn't understand why, at fifteen years old, she couldn't take off all of her clothes to sunbathe. She didn't even understand the consequences of crossing a busy road without looking.

She couldn't see why tuna tasted delicious and vanilla ice cream tasted delicious but if you mushed them up together, that didn't make them twice as delicious, that made them inedible.

Ruth emptied her coffee mug into the sink, and as she did so she heard whining and scratching at the back door. She opened it, and Tyson came trotting in, with his long pink tongue hanging out like a facecloth.

'Hi, Tyson!' she greeted him, and knelt down on one knee to stroke him and tug at his ears, which he adored. 'Did Amelia let you out to do your business? Look – she cooked me breakfast! Wasn't that sweet of her? Would you like some? I'd hate to see it all go to waste.'

She set down the plate of tuna lime refreshment in front of him. He sniffed at it, and snuffled, and then he let out a sharp bark, as if she had deliberately tried to poison him.

'OK, boy, sorry,' she said. She picked up the plate and scraped the tuna lime refreshment into the pedal-bin. When she looked inside, she saw that Amelia had made her omelet with eggs all scrambled up with whole segments of orange. She couldn't begin to imagine what was to be put into the 'Mexican energy juice', but she could see that she had already taken a bottle of green Tabasco sauce out of the cupboard.

Tyson followed her around the kitchen as she cleared up the table mats and the cutlery, nudging her repeatedly with his nose.

'*Tyson*!' she complained, as she almost tripped over him. 'You know what your problem is? You should stop thinking you're a human being. You're not. You're a Labrador retriever, and it doesn't matter how clever you are you will never be able to drive a car or take me out to dinner or even have a half-decent conversation about the economy. It's a bummer, I know, but there it is.'

Tyson looked up at her with his sad amber eyes. She tugged at his ears again, and he growled in the back of his throat, as if she had given him hope that he did have a chance with her, after all.

The phone warbled. She picked it up and said, 'Cutter residence. Hallo?'

'Boss? It's Jack Morrow here. We've got ourselves a suspicious fire – corner of South McCann and West Maple. And I mean *highly* suspicious. I'd say you'd want to get over here as quick as you like.'

'OK. What's the scenario?'

'You'll see when you get here. It's pretty darn weird, to tell
you the truth. No major property damage, but one fatality.'

'On our way then.'

She knew that Tyson could tell they were going out on a call
because his tail began to beat frantically against the kitchen units
and he kept on licking his lips and snuffling, the way he always
did when he was excited.

'Come on, boy,' Ruth said. 'Give me a couple of minutes to
get ready and then we're on our way.'

Back in the bedroom, she lifted her dark blue uniform off the
coat hanger behind the door and dressed as quietly as she could.
Before she left, she went around to the other side of the bed and
tugged down the blue-striped comforter. Craig snorted, but he
didn't open his eyes. Most nights, he spent hour after hour wrestling
with the bedcover, but when morning came he could never wake
up. Ruth suspected that he didn't *want* to wake up, the way things
were.

'Craig, honey?'

'Whuh?'

'Craig, honey, I have to go to work. I'll call you later.'

He opened his eyes and blinked at her as if he didn't know
who she was. '*Whuh?*'

'I'm going now. I'll call you later, OK? Don't forget that Ammy
has to be at school by eight.'

'Urgggh. OK.'

'Are you going out today?'

'What day is it?'

'Tuesday.'

'Tuesday? Damn it. I have to go over to the Mayfield Drive
development. Meet those assholes from Kraussman Brothers. I
doubt I'll get back to the studio till gone twelve.'

'OK. That's OK. I'll call you then, OK?'

She kissed him on the forehead, and then kissed the faint scar
on his left cheek. When she and Craig had first met at college,
he had told her that he had been cut across the face when he was
fighting with a local gang, but his mother had later told her that
he had fallen off his bicycle when he was six, the first time his
father had taken off his training-wheels. He dragged up the
comforter to cover his face.

She stood beside the bed for a moment, looking at his dark

hair sprouting out. 'I love you, you daydreamer, you,' she said, although she probably said it too quietly for him to hear her.

As she went back along the landing, she saw that Amelia's bedroom door was an inch ajar, and that Amelia was watching her. She decided to say nothing. Amelia could never sulk for very long; it wasn't in her nature.

'Bye, Ammy,' she called out. 'I'll see you after school, OK?'

Amelia didn't answer right away, but as Ruth went down the stairs, she suddenly came out of her room and leaned over the banister rail.

'Mom – don't go.'

'What? I have to go. Bill Docherty's off sick so there's only Jack Morrow and me.'

'You shouldn't go, Mom. Please. Something's not right.'

Ruth hesitated. Amelia was looking genuinely worried.

'What do you mean, something's not right?'

'I don't know. I can't explain it.'

'Sweetheart, I *have* to go. It's my job. But I promise I'll be careful, OK?'

Amelia bit her lip, but didn't say anything else. Ruth blew her a kiss and then whistled for Tyson, who came careering out of the kitchen with his leash in his mouth.

Ruth looked upstairs again, but Amelia had gone back into her room and closed the door.

THREE

L ast night's storm had blown over to the north-east and it was
a dry, gusty morning. The sky was a strong artificial blue,
like a hand-colored postcard, and rusty-colored leaves were
rattling along the streets as if they were warning Ruth that winter
wasn't far away.

Six emergency vehicles were already parked outside the pale
green house on the corner of South McCann and West Maple: an
engine, an ambulance, the arson investigation truck and two vans,
including the battalion chief's new red-and-white Dodge, and a
police squad car. Ruth parked up behind them and climbed out
of her battered white Windstar. She lifted the tailgate to let Tyson
jump out, and to drag out the heavy metal case which contained
her investigator's tool kit.

This was a neat, tree-lined neighborhood, shabby-genteel, and
it was usually so quiet that it looked as if nobody lived here. Ruth
had been called out here only once, about three years ago, when
an irascible old woman had complained that her neighbor had
deliberately used paint-thinner to set fire to her conifer hedge,
because it was blocking the sunlight to his patio. This morning,
however, there was a crowd of more than thirty local residents
gathered on the sidewalk, as well as a reporter and a photographer
from the *Kokomo Tribune*.

Jack Morrow and Bob Kowalski, the battalion chief, were
waiting for her on the porch. Jack was a lean, serious man with
a thinning white pompadour and permanently narrowed eyes. He
was a much more experienced arson investigator than Ruth, with
almost twenty-five years on the job, but for various unexplained
reasons he had always resisted promotion. He spoke in a slow,
grinding growl, so that it was always hard to tell if he was excited
about what he had discovered or not.

By complete contrast, Bob Kowalski was tall and broad-
shouldered, big-bellied and bluff, with flaming-red cheeks and
a gingery-white buzz cut, and every one of his sentences
sounded as if it had an exclamation point after it. He liked a

beer and a joke and he always played Santa at the Fire Department's Christmas party.

'Morning, Ruthie!' he welcomed her. 'Sorry to drag you out at such a goddarn unsociable hour!'

'Hey, that's OK, sir. Tyson always enjoys an early morning run, don't you, Tyson?'

Jack Morrow nodded to her, cleared his throat and said, 'What we have here appears on first impression to be a Class B fire that was very limited in area and probably of very short duration, no more than five or ten minutes, but at the same time it was very intense. To tell you the truth I never saw nothing exactly like it.'

'Do we know when it happened?' Ruth asked him.

'Round about five thirty a.m.,' said Bob Kowalski. 'A delivery truck driver was taking a short cut to the Top Banana Farm Market, and as he passed the house here he happened to see flames leaping up behind the drapes. We dispatched Engine Number Three and it arrived within less than seven minutes, but the fire had pretty much extinguished itself by then.'

'Did the truck driver see anybody else in the vicinity? Any other vehicles?'

'Whole street was plumb deserted, as far as he could see.'

'And what color were the flames? Did he tell you that?'

'Yellow. And real fierce! That's what he said. Right up to the ceiling. We let him leave about twenty minutes ago to deliver his load of apples, but I took his cell number if you need to talk to him some more.'

Ruth took off her pink-tinted Ray-Bans and took a long look at the sightseers on the sidewalk. Six-and-a-half years with the fire/arson investigation unit had given her an eye for anybody who appeared overexcited, or anybody who was trying to keep themselves hidden behind the rest of the crowd. This morning, however, nobody immediately caught her attention, except for a dark-haired boy of about twelve who should have been getting ready for school by now.

'OK,' she said. 'Tyson and me had better take a look.'

Jack Morrow led her through the hallway to the living-room. There were three firefighters and two KPD detectives there already, as well as Val Minelli from the police crime lab. They all greeted her with 'hi's and 'how're you doing, Ruth?', but they were unusually subdued.

Ruth immediately saw why. In the center of the living-room lay a charred mattress, burned right down to the springs, and lying on the mattress was an incinerated human body. The fire that had engulfed it had been so fierce that it had been reduced to a blackened monkey, with grinning brown teeth, and it was impossible to tell if it had been a man or a woman.

The whole room stank of burned cotton batting and that distinctive bitterness of carbonized human flesh.

Tyson gave the body a tentative sniff. He let out a whine and looked up at Ruth with a questioning expression in his eyes. They rarely came across a cadaver as seriously burned as this, even in some of the worst fires they attended. Tyson strained at his leash, impatient to start searching the room for any lingering smell of accelerants, but Ruth said, '*Heel*, Tyson,' and he stayed where he was, although he didn't stop trembling and licking his lips and keening in the back of his throat.

Ruth hunkered down and inspected the body more closely. 'You're not wrong, Jack. This is one very unusual fire. Like you say, it must have been very short-lived, but while it lasted it must have burned hotter than hell.'

Jack said, in his expressionless voice, 'Your average commercial crematorium runs at more than a thousand degrees Celsius. Even then, it would usually take over a half-hour to reduce a cadaver to this condition.'

'Was the front door locked when the firefighters arrived?'

'Yes,' Jack told her. 'But only with the regular mortise lock. It wasn't bolted, or obstructed in any other way. They were able to break in right away.'

'OK.' Preventing firefighters from gaining easy access to a fire was a tell-tale indication of arson, but it didn't appear to Ruth as if that had happened here.

She circled the room. The walls were decorated with a frieze of V-shaped plumes of soot, from which grayish-yellow runnels of human fat had slid down to the floor. In spite of the intensity of the fire, however, the upholstery of the four armchairs that were arranged around the mattress had only been slightly scorched. If the fire had been hot enough to reduce a human body to bones and ashes in only a matter of minutes, she would have expected a flameover, and the air temperature to have risen so high that everything in it would have ignited spontaneously: chairs, cushions, carpet and drapes. And yet there was a plastic snow-dome from Chicago on top of the fireplace, and that had only been dimpled by the heat.

'Do we know the victim's identity?' she asked.

Detective Ron Magruder shook his head. He had a bristly little brown moustache and a cheap tan three-piece suit, with three cheap ballpens in his breast pocket. 'The house is currently un-occupied. The owner is a Mrs Evaline Van Kley, but she moved into the Paradise Valley sunset home about three months ago and the property has been up for sale ever since.'

'Who has access?'

'Apart from the realtors, both Mrs Van Kley's son and daughter have keys, but the son lives and works in Gary and the daughter works for some investment bank in London, England. The state police are double-checking the son's whereabouts for us, and we've already contacted all the staff at Sycamore Realty. But so far, zip.'

Val Minelli came over. She was a petite girl, with a long dark ponytail and an oval face like an Italian Madonna, and she did everything gracefully, even taking samples of burned human flesh. 'Whoever this is, man or woman, they were probably married, because they were wearing a gold wedding band. So it's possible that we'll get a missing persons call within the next twenty-four to forty-eight hours.'

'Unless, of course, it was their spouse who set them on fire,' said Ruth.

'Well, that's always one alternative,' Val admitted. 'But if this was deliberate, the perpetrator must have been seriously pissed. This isn't just a homicide. This is a *sacrifice*.'

'OK,' said Ruth. She set down her metal case, flipped open the catches and took out a pair of latex gloves. 'If I can have the room cleared now, please, except for Val. Jack, you want to check the utilities? Tyson – how about doing your stuff now, boy? Go on, boy. Go seek.'

The firefighters and the detectives made their way out of the door, treading as delicately as dancers so that they didn't disturb any latent evidence. Tyson ducked his head down and criss-crossed the living-room, enthusiastically sniffing at the floorboards and all along the skirting. Ruth took out her Leica camera and started to take flash pictures, dozens of them, not only of the incinerated body and the mattress it was lying on, but the floor all around it, and the walls, and the doors, and the windows.

The smoke and scorch patterns would show her if the fire had been deliberately started by the use of an accelerant, and how quickly it had burned, and what its rate of heat release might have been. To Ruth's eyes, every pattern formed part of a narrative, like a series of prehistoric cave paintings: how the fire had started, how it had become so intense. How the hot gases might have risen to the ceiling and then returned to the lower levels by thermal radiation, leaving those V-shaped plumes.

'How's Amelia?' asked Val, as she delicately tweezered a triangular piece of crisp black skin from the victim's shoulder and dropped it into an evidence bag.

'She's good,' said Ruth. 'Better than ever. Do you know something, she even cooked me breakfast this morning, and she got up at the crack of dawn to do it.'

'Amelia is *such* a sweet girl,' said Val, although Ruth couldn't help hearing the unspoken words, 'in spite of the fact that she has William's Syndrome.'

'She did great,' Ruth lied. 'Made me an omelet and everything. She's really growing up.'

Val slightly raised the body's left hand, being careful not to break it off at the wrist. 'You see this wedding band? What temperature does gold melt at?'

Ruth peered at it. The ring had lost its shape and had even started to form a teardrop drip at one side. 'Over one thousand degrees Celsius,' she said. She took five photographs of the ring, all from different angles. Then she prodded the mattress springs. 'See? Most of these springs have collapsed, which means that the temperature must have been well over seven hundred, but I can't say that I've ever seen any gold jewelry melt before, even at that temperature. It's a pretty good size, isn't it? Hard to tell if it's a man's or a woman's.'

She packed away her camera. She was surprised to see that Tyson was still whuffling around the room in obvious frustration.

'How's it going, boy?' she called out. Tyson looked across at her and gave a single sharp bark.

'He's annoyed at himself,' she told Val. 'If he can't find anything, he thinks he's let me down. He's also worried I won't give him his dog-choc.'

She took her hydrocarbon detector out of her case, switched it on, and started to probe the ruins of the mattress with it. The detector was like a wand attached to a tiny vacuum-cleaner. It sucked up any residual vapors or gases and it would buzz like an irritated blowfly if it sensed the presence of any accelerants.

All the same, she was already beginning to question whether this fire had been started with accelerants at all. If there were any traces of fuels to be found, Tyson would always head for them like a rocket and sit on the area of strongest concentration first, panting proudly, to show her where they were. Tyson's nose was ten times more sensitive than her detector; he could locate a thousandth of a drop of half-evaporated gasoline in a room twice this volume.

Jack Morrow came back into the living-room. 'All of the utilities check out,' he told her. 'Electricity is still on, but the wiring looks sound, even the cables that run right beneath this room. Gas is still connected, too, but nobody's tampered with the meter or any of the piping. No wrench-marks, no disconnected joints, no leaks.'

He sniffed, and added, 'No windows are broken, but the kitchen door could have been jimmied. Ron Magruder's taking a look at it. There's no damage to any other room in the house. No signs of lightning-strike. How's Tyson doing?'

'He hasn't found anything so far, and neither have I.'

'Could've been a cigarette, I guess,' Jack suggested. 'Maybe this was a vagrant, using the house as someplace to crash. Got drunk, dropped his smoke on the mattress, Bob's your uncle.'

'I don't know. It's old-fashioned cotton padding, this mattress, not polyfoam. If it had been smoldering for any length of time, the walls and the ceiling would have been much more heavily stained with smoke. Like, this has all the hallmarks of a Class B fire, but so far there's absolutely no evidence to show what started it.'

'Maybe it was spontaneous human combustion.'

'Oh, *sure* it was.'

'You shouldn't be so skeptical,' said Jack. 'Back in nineteen eighty-two I was called out to a fire up in Cassville, and I still reckon that was SHC.'

'Oh, come on.'

'No – a fifty-seven-year-old woman was sitting in her kitchen chair and she spontaneously burst into flames. Whoomph, just like that. That's what her husband and her son said, anyhow, at the inquest. The husband tried to put her out by dragging her over to the sink and splashing water on her but the flames were too fierce. He burned his own hands pretty bad.

'I saw the woman's body for myself. Apparently she didn't burn for no longer than five or six minutes, but all the clothes were burned off of her and her skin was charred all over like a hamburger.'

'Get out of here, Jack,' Ruth told him. He was always telling stories about bizarre fires and she never knew whether to believe him or not. 'Go bring me some evidence cans from the truck. And some cellophane envelopes, too.'

She turned back to the blackened body lying on the mattress. Maybe Jack hadn't been so far away from the truth after all. Maybe this man or woman *had* spontaneously caught fire. There was no conclusive evidence to support any of the six or seven alleged cases of spontaneous human combustion, but in the most recent incident, in 1980, a farmer called Henry Thomas had been so severely burned while sitting in his armchair that only his skull and the lower part of his legs had remained. Maybe something similar had happened here.

Tyson came up to her and nudged her knee. She tugged at his ears and gave him a dog-choc. 'I know, boy, you couldn't find anything. It wasn't your fault. If somebody set this fire on purpose, they must have been some kind of black magician.'

Ruth remained at the house for the better part of the day, taking samples of fibers and ash and frizzled hair and carbonized flesh. At about three thirty in the afternoon, two technicians from the Howard County Coroner's office arrived, wearing white Tyvek coveralls. They carefully lifted the burned cadaver into a body-bag, and carried it away to the morgue. Ruth and Jack wrapped up the mattress in plastic sheeting so that it could be taken back to their Fire and Arson Laboratory for further tests.

'How about a beer?' Bob Kowalski suggested as he and Ruth finally stepped out of the front door. The wind had dropped, and there was a high hazy covering of white cloud.

'I'd love to, sir, but I have to pick up Ammy from school.'

'What's your gut feeling about this?' he asked her, nodding back toward the house.

'I'm not sure. But I don't think that any kind of known accelerant was used. Jack suggested that it might be SHC, but frankly I don't believe in it.'

'Oh, he told you about that woman in Cassville? You don't want to set any store by *that*. What happened was, that woman was wearing all nylon clothing and a spark of static set her ablaze. Very rare occurrence, but it has been known.'

Ruth said, 'It looks to me like the victim here was in close contact with an intense source of heat, but I can't understand what it was.'

'Blowtorch, maybe? Or a cutting torch? That's at least three-and-a-half thousand degrees Celsius.'

'Even so, that would have taken *hours*, and the pattern of burning would have been totally different. The flames would have been a different color, too, not yellow. Apart from which, whoever did the blowtorching would have left footprints.'

'So what was it, do you think, this intense source of heat?'

'I have absolutely no idea. I've seen similar charring on victims who have fallen into furnaces or barbecue pits or open fires. You remember that old man last year, out on Water Works Road, who fell into that hog roaster? All of the subcutaneous fat evaporated from his head and his shoulders, just like this. But in this case the victim's entire body surface was carbonized, head to toe, and right now I can't think how that could have happened, not without an accelerant.'

They had reached the sidewalk, where a police tape had been strung across the front of the property to keep out the crowd of onlookers. As Bob lifted it up for her, Ruth saw the dark-haired boy again. He was standing by himself about twenty feet away from the rest of the crowd, with his hands in his pockets. His face was so pale that it was almost white, and his eyes were as dark as holes burned into a sheet of paper. His hair was badly cut, so that it stuck up at the back. He was wearing a faded black T-shirt and a pair of worn-out red jeans.

'See that kid?' Ruth asked Bob. 'He was here when I arrived this morning, and he's still here.'

Bob frowned in the boy's direction. 'He's not wearing a Smokey Bear hat, I'll grant you. But he doesn't look like much of an arsonist to me.'

'Oh, come on, Bob. You know better than that. No two arsonists ever look alike. Here – hold this.'

She handed him her metal case, opened it, and took out her camera. She took more than a dozen pictures of the crowd, panning slowly from right to left so that the boy wouldn't think that she was focusing her camera only on him.

'There,' she said, putting the camera away again. 'Now I'm going to go over and ask him who he is, and what he's doing here.'

She said, 'Pardon me, excuse me,' and pushed her way through the crowd. When she reached the place where the boy had been standing, however, he had gone.

She looked around, puzzled. The only place for him to have hidden was behind a large white oak at the side of the next-door yard, but she couldn't understand how he could have crossed the sidewalk to reach it, not without her seeing him. She circled the oak twice, but there was nobody there. She shaded her eyes and peered along the street, but it was totally straight all the way down to West Park Avenue, a distance of more than half a mile, and there was no sign of the boy anywhere.

She went back and rejoined Bob Kowalski, and now Jack Morrow and Detective Ron Magruder came out, too.

Detective Magruder said, 'We've made a thorough search of the yard and the woods immediately in back, but there's no sign of any discarded cans or bottles that might have contained accelerant, or any other evidence of arson for that matter. The kitchen door was forced open, for sure, but there are no fingerprints and no fibers. No footprints, neither, apart from our own. Whoever set this fire, they left the house before any carbon deposit fell on the floor.'

'What about witnesses?' asked Ruth.

'Apart from our fruit-truck driver, none. The elderly couple who live next door, they're both deaf as doorposts and they didn't *see* nothing, neither. The family who live right opposite, they've been in Muncie for three days, visiting the husband's mother, and they got back only about two hours ago.'

He tucked his pen into his breast-pocket and said, 'Any of you people have any wild theories?'

'Sorry, Ron,' Jack told him. 'We arson investigators don't deal in wild theories – only forensic evidence. But we'll keep you up to date with how things are progressing.'

Jack walked Ruth back to her car. 'I'll see you tomorrow,' Ruth told him. 'Maybe we'll know the victim's identity by then.'

Jack said, 'Maybe. But I have a strange feeling that's not going to help much. There's something real weird about this fire.'

'Hey, I thought we arson investigators only dealt in forensic evidence. Where do strange feelings come into it?'

'I only said that for Ron Magruder's benefit, because I don't have the least notion how this fire was started, or how it reached such a high RHR so rapidly, or why it suddenly extinguished itself before the rest of the house went up in flames. We're missing something here. It's probably going to be downright obvious when we find out what it is, but right now it's making me feel like there's a gaggle of geese walking up and down on my grave.'

'You still think that it might have been spontaneous human combustion? Bob said that woman in Cassville caught fire because of her nylon clothing. You know, static.'

'That's what Bob likes to think, because Bob doesn't want to acknowledge that some fires can't be completely explained by scientific facts. Listen, Ruth, I've been investigating fires for half of my life, and if I've learned anything at all, it's that every fire is a hungry beast with a will of its own. This here was no ordinary fire, believe me. This fire had an appetite for this particular victim, for some reason or another. It *ate* this person, like a wild animal, but it didn't eat nothing else, because once it had done that, it was satisfied and it snuffed itself out. Before anything else, we need to find out what this particular fire wanted, and why it wanted it. Until we do, we won't understand what happened here, or if it might happen again.'

FOUR

Amelia was late coming out of school, so Ruth had to wait outside for over ten minutes. As she sat in her car, watching the last few stragglers emerge, she suddenly felt very tired, and isolated, as if she couldn't carry on any longer.

She felt as if everybody depended on her: Ammy, and Jeff, and Craig, and now the anonymous blackened victim who had been burned to death on that mattress. *Why me?* she thought. *Why can't they all take care of themselves, and sort out their own problems?* But she knew the answer to that. They needed her, and they had nobody else.

When Amelia eventually appeared, in her red beret and her red plaid coat, she stopped on the steps outside the school's main entrance to send a text message on her cellphone. Ruth gave her an impatient toot on her horn.

'Hey, don't worry about me,' she said, as Amelia climbed into the passenger seat. 'I have all the time in the world.'

Amelia said, 'I had to text Sandra. I'm going round to her place this evening, so that we can do our homework together.'

'Oh, yes. Who says?'

'Me. *I* say. Somebody has to help me, don't they?'

'*I* always help you.'

'Well, you don't have to bother any more. Sandra said *she* can do it.'

'Sandra knows how to deal with William's Syndrome? I don't think so.'

'At least Sandra doesn't treat me like a retard.'

Ruth pulled away from the curb and drove toward Jefferson Street. 'Ammy, you're not still mad at me about breakfast, are you?'

'Of course not. I wish I hadn't bothered, that's all.'

'It was a lovely thought. You don't know how much I appreciated it.'

'Don't lie. You hated it.'

They stopped at the next red traffic signal. Ruth turned to Amelia

and said, 'Listen, sometimes you can try to do nice things for
people and for one reason or another it doesn't work out. Once I
organized a surprise party for Dad's birthday, and I invited some
of his old classmates from school, but what I didn't realize was
that he couldn't stand the sight of them – any of them. What a
disaster *that* was! Ten men with their arms folded, glaring at each
other for four hours. They almost came to blows.'

Amelia said nothing, but sat with her arms tightly folded and
her lips pouting. Ruth reached across and stroked a stray lock of
her hair, winding it around her finger.

'Ammy, you know you're different. But that's what makes you
who you are, and I *love* who you are. I wouldn't want you any
other way.'

'Signal's green,' said Ammy. The car behind them blew its horn
and Ruth lifted her hand in apology.

While their meat feast pizzas were heating up in the oven, Ruth
took her camera out of its case and looked through the photographs she had taken at the house on South McCann Street. She
skipped quickly past the flash-lit images of the victim lying on
the mattress, and the victim's black-charred hand with its wedding-
band, and the smoke-stained walls, until she reached the series of
pictures she had taken of the crowd outside.

The very last photograph should have shown the dark-haired
boy in the faded T-shirt and the worn-out red jeans, standing in
the middle of the sidewalk. But there was nobody there, only the
empty street, lined with trees.

She frowned, and went through the pictures again to see if she
had missed one. She was sure that she had caught the boy in her
viewfinder, but he simply wasn't there. She switched off her camera
and put it away.

Amelia came into the kitchen. '*You* look serious,' she said, in
a high-pitched voice. 'Is everything all right?'

'Yes, of course. Supper's going to be ready in a minute.'

'That fire you went to today . . .'

'Yes?'

'Did somebody die?'

Ruth nodded. 'Yes. We don't know who yet. It was probably
some down-and-out.'

'I had such a horrible feeling about it.'

'Yes. I was going to ask you about that. What kind of horrible feeling?'

Ammy thought for a moment, and then she made a pulling gesture with her right hand as if she were opening an invisible door. 'I don't know. I felt like people were coming in. People who should have stayed where they were.'

'What people? I don't really understand what you mean.'

'There's lots of them. Some of them are very faint so you can hardly see them. But others have very white faces.'

'Was this a *dream* you had?' Ruth asked her. She was used to Amelia describing her feelings in unusual ways. When she had a migraine, she said that somebody had smashed a mirror in her head.

'No, it wasn't a dream. It was when Uncle Jack called you. I had a feeling that all these people had started to come in. That's why I didn't want you to go.'

Ruth said, 'Come here,' and gave Amelia a hug. 'It wasn't very nice. I mean, whoever it was who died, they were very badly burned. But there were no faint people there, or people with white faces.'

But then she thought about the dark-haired boy, who had been so faint that he hadn't even appeared in her photograph.

Craig didn't arrive home until well past eight o'clock. He stood in the kitchen doorway with a frown on his face, as if he wasn't at all sure that he was in the right house.

Ruth was wiping the place mats. 'You want pizza?' she asked him. 'Ammy and I, we've had ours. God knows what time Jeff's going to be home.'

'I, ah – I'm not too hungry at the moment. I'll wait for Jeff.'

He dragged out a chair from under the kitchen table and sat down heavily.

'You've been drinking,' said Ruth.

'You think? Oh – I forgot. You're an arson investigator. You have a nose for flammable liquids. Gasoline, methanol, vodka Martinis, you name it.'

'And what good will drinking do, exactly?'

He raised one finger, as if he were about to impart the greatest gem of wisdom since Moses. 'Drinking stops you thinking. That's what good it does.'

'I see. Drinking stops you thinking. Well, I'm not drinking because I still have a full-time job to do and a house to run and two teenage kids and a husband to look after. A *drunken* husband, as it happens.'

'You're a saint, Ruth. I always said that. That's why I married you. Saint Ruth of the Smoothly Running Household.'

'So,' she asked him, 'how did it go with the Kraussmans?'

'The Kraussmans?' he grimaced. 'Not exactly great, to tell you the truth.'

'What does that mean?' asked Ruth.

'It means that the Kraussman Brothers have been pretty badly hit by the credit crunch, like everybody else. They're drawing in their horns, that's the way they put it.'

'And what does *that* mean – "drawing in their horns"?'

'In a nutshell, it means they're putting a temporary hold on any future housing development.'

'So they won't be giving you any more contracts?'

'Not for the foreseeable future, no.'

'But the Kraussmans – they supply you with more than half of your gross income.'

Craig nodded. 'Correct. They do. But right now it looks like we'll just have to find somebody else to fit kitchens for.'

'Like who, for instance? If the Kraussmans are drawing in their horns, then everybody else will be drawing in their horns, too.'

'I don't know yet,' said Craig. 'I'm working on it.'

There was a long silence between them. Then Craig said, 'Ammy . . . she was pretty upset about that breakfast she cooked for you.'

'I know. But we've made up now. Where are you going to find more contracts?'

Craig looked up, and for the first time ever his gray eyes looked hooded and defensive. 'I don't know, sweetheart,' he told her. 'I truly and honestly don't know.'

'But you have about three months' grace, don't you? They're still going to finish the Mayfield Drive development?'

'I don't think so. In fact I very much doubt it.'

'*What?*'

Craig took a deep breath. 'That's what this morning's meeting was all about, honey. The Kraussmans have run out of credit at the bank and they've had to stop all building work at Mayfield

Drive and Wildcat Creek West, and lay everybody off. They didn't
want to, but they didn't have the choice.'

'So where does that leave you? Where does that leave *us*?'

'Struggling for survival, I guess.'

'But they will pay you for the work you've done already? Come
on, Craig, you've laid out thousands of dollars for worktops and
sinks and floor tiles and God knows what else.'

Craig shook his head. 'They're flat-busted. Eugene Kraussman
said he was very sorry, he's been doing everything he can to keep
the company's head above water, but even if he manages to finish
the development, he won't be able to sell any of the houses at a
profit, not at today's prices, if at all.'

'But they *have* to pay you! You have a contract!'

Craig reached across the table and held her hands. 'If they don't
have the money, sweetheart, they don't have the money, contract
or not. You can't get blood out of a cinder block.'

Ruth didn't know what to say. She had been conscious for the
past few months that Craig was growing increasingly worried
about cash flow, and that new orders for fitted kitchens had been
few and far between. He had not only been sleeping badly, he had
been drinking much more than usual, and his elbows were reddened
with eczema.

'How are you going to pay any wages?' she asked.

'I can pay Randy and Carlos for this week, and Cora, too. But
after that – well, I have five working days to find next week's pay.'

'And if you can't?'

Craig gripped her hands tight. 'No such word as "can't", sweetheart. One way or another, Cutter's Kitchens is going to stay in
business. Even if I have to rob a bank.'

Ruth took off her red checkered apron and hung it up. 'Why
don't you go upstairs and take a very cold shower? I can make
you some coffee if you like.'

Craig shook his head. 'Cold showers and coffee, they won't
help. Nothing's going to help. It's finally arrived, the end of the
world. Armageddon, just like it says in the Bible.'

At that moment, Ruth heard the burble of a car engine outside.
It stopped abruptly, and then the front door opened. Jeff came into
the kitchen, his black hair all spiked up, wearing his black leather
jacket and his black jeans.

'That crappy car, I swear to God.'

'Good evening, Jeff,' said Ruth. 'Nice to see you, too.'

'Yeah, whatever. I'm driving along West Sycamore, right, and this dork's right in front of me driving real slow, but when I pull out to overtake, he puts his foot down and he's going faster and faster and I can't get past him and he's only driving a frigging *Taurus*, right, but even when I put my foot flat down on the floor I still can't get past him and then I see this semi coming the other way toward me and I have to drop back or else it's going to be a head-on collision, right, and do you know what he does, this dork in the Taurus? He's about a hundred years old, right, but he gives me the finger. Can you believe that?'

Craig looked across at Ruth as if Jeff had been speaking a foreign language. Ruth said, 'Did you get his license number, this hundred-year-old dork in the Taurus?'

'What do you think? I was too busy trying not to get killed.'

'Well, you didn't get killed, and I have to say that I'm pleased about that.'

'Yeah, but if I had a decent car, instead of that junker...'

'I told you to get a job.'

'Yeah, like what job? Stacking shelves or something? Flipping burgers?'

'Nothing wrong with either of those. It's all money, after all. I think Dean Huntley at the Red Lobster is looking for a dish-washer.'

'Oh, great. How come Dan Collins' parents have just bought him a brand-new Honda, and they don't expect *him* to wash dishes?'

'Because the Collins are rolling in it,' Craig retorted. 'And right now, this family is very much *not* rolling in it. It's called a recession.'

'Oh, great. Thanks a lot. Trust me to get born into the wrong frigging family.'

'Wash your mouth out,' said Craig.

Jeff said, 'I'm out of here. I'm going to Lennie's.'

'Back by eleven!' Ruth called after him as he slammed the front door.

Craig sat at the table with his head bowed and his eyes closed. At last, he looked up and said, 'He's right, of course. We should be able to buy him a new car. I really don't like him driving around in that beaten-up Pinto.'

'Your parents never bought *you* a new car,' said Ruth. 'You had to work for it. So should he.'

'But that was the whole point, wasn't it? We were always going to be better off than our parents. We were always going to give our kids everything.'

'Yes, we were. Maybe that's where we went wrong.'

Craig looked around the kitchen and frowned. 'Did you say pizza?'

'Yes. Do you want it?'

'I don't know. I don't know what I want. I'm sorry. I've let you down, haven't I? I never thought that it would ever come to this.'

Ruth sat down beside him and took hold of his hand. 'It's not your fault, Craig. Everybody's suffering, just the same. We'll get through it. We have to.'

Craig nodded. 'Do you know what Ammy said to me today, when I was taking her to school? I was trying to explain to her that business wasn't going too well, and she said, "Whatever you've done, no matter how long ago it was, even if you've forgotten all about it, in the end you always have to pay for it."'

'*Ammy* said that? That was very deep. For Ammy, anyhow.'

'I don't know. It was the way she was looking at me when she said it. I really got the feeling that she wasn't talking about the credit crunch at all. It was like she was talking about something else altogether, but I'm damned if I know what.'

Ruth stroked his cheek. 'Craig,' she said, 'the only thing that you have ever done is try to take care of us. You can't blame yourself for a worldwide recession.'

He stared at her, and his eyes were glistening with tears. 'I love you, Ruth. You know that, don't you?'

'Yes,' she said. 'I know that. I love you, too. Now how about that pizza?'

As Ruth came upstairs, she could hear Amelia singing in her bedroom. Her voice was high and very clear, and she had almost faultless pitch. It was one of the peculiarities of William's Syndrome that she had highly sensitive hearing and had only to listen to a piece of music once and she could sing it or hum it note-perfect.

Ruth stopped outside Amelia's bedroom door. It was about a

half-inch open, and she could see one corner of Amelia's desk, with her homework spread out on it, and a collection of family photographs, and three toy frogs sitting on top of her PC.

'*I wonder where he's going*
With that smile upon his face.
I wonder if he knows it's going to rain.
I wonder if he knows she doesn't live there, any more
And he'll never see or hear from her again.'

Ruth knocked and opened the door wider. Amelia was sitting cross-legged on the end of her bed, wearing her pajamas with the big pink flowers on them.

'Hi. I heard you singing. That was a very sad song.'

'I made it up myself.'

'It's sad, but it's very good, too.' She nodded toward Amelia's desk. 'Did you finish your homework?'

'Most of it.'

Ruth looked at the photographs. There was a picture of Amelia sitting in her playpen, hugging a tatty pink rabbit; and a picture of Amelia walking hand-in-hand with her father, on the shores of Lake Michigan; and another picture of a blonde woman with curly hair and a pearl necklace, smiling vaguely at the camera as if she wasn't enjoying having her photograph taken. This woman looked remarkably like Ruth. She could have been Ruth's mother or her sister. But Amelia had found the picture in the bottom of her closet when they first moved into this house, and she could only guess that the woman was the wife of the previous owner.

'I don't know why you keep this picture,' said Ruth. 'You don't even know who she is.'

'I *like* her. She's you, if you were my friend, instead of my mother.'

'I hope that I am your friend.'

Amelia smiled, and then stopped smiling abruptly. 'There was something I wanted to ask you.'

'Oh, yes?'

She looked uncomfortable. 'I'm glad I didn't go to Sandra's. I'm sorry about being so sulky. I knew all the time I was cooking your breakfast that you wouldn't like it.'

Ruth sat down next to her. 'Hey . . . you don't have to be sorry. I thought it was a lovely idea. You can't blame yourself because you don't think the same way as most other people. Blame *me*, if you're going to blame anybody.'

Amelia laid her head in Ruth's lap. 'But I'm always saying things and doing things even when I *know* that people aren't going to like them.'

'We all do that, sweetheart. It's called being human.' She stroked Amelia's hair and they were silent together for a moment.

Then Amelia said, 'You will be careful, won't you?'

'Hey, I'm always careful. I have people who depend on me. Whenever I have to go into a burned-out building, I always make all of the safety checks first. I don't want any floors collapsing or ceilings falling on top of me.'

Amelia raised her head and looked at her seriously. 'I don't mean that. I mean those people I was talking about. Now that they've found out how to come through, they're going to keep on coming.'

'Do you know who they are?'

'I'm not sure. They're not all the same. Like I said, some of them are very faint but some of them have white faces. I can sort of hear them talking but I don't know what they're talking about.'

'Where do they come from? I mean, when you say that they've found a way to get through – through from *where*?'

Amelia closed her eyes and repeated the door-opening gesture she had made in the kitchen, only more slowly. 'I don't know. There's a whole crowd of them in the doorway and there's too many of them and I can't see past them.'

'Do you have any idea what they want?'

Amelia shook her head.

Ruth gave her a kiss. 'You know what I think? I think you need to stop worrying about these people. They're all up here, inside of your mind, that's all. Just like those imaginary pets you used to tell me about when you were little. You remember Puffy, your imaginary poodle? Just like him. Just like the man in your song.'

'*He's* real, but he's not a man. He's only a boy.'

'Oh, yes. Who is he? Somebody from school?'

'No,' said Amelia. 'I don't know his name. But I saw him in the street.'

'Which street?'

'*This* street, of course! He was standing right outside.'

'When?'

'This evening,' said Amelia. She was beginning to grow impatient. 'That's why I made up the song.'

'The boy in your song was standing outside our house this evening?'

'*Yes*. He was there for ages.'

Ruth took hold of Amelia's hands. 'What did he look like?'

'He looked sad.'

'You should have told me. Maybe he was looking for a lost dog or something.'

'He was just standing there, staring. He had black hair and a black T-shirt and red jeans.'

Ruth stared at her. She felt a tingling sensation in her wrists. 'Are you sure? A black T-shirt and red jeans?'

'*Yes.*'

Ruth stood up and went over to the window. She drew back the flowery cotton drapes and looked down into the street. Her view of the sidewalk was mostly obscured by the huge old basswood tree beside the driveway, but she couldn't see any boy standing out there.

'What's wrong?' Amelia asked her, after a while.

Ruth pulled the drapes together, making sure that she closed them tight. 'Nothing, sweetheart. There's nobody there now. It's time you thought about washing your teeth and going to bed, isn't it? It's school again tomorrow. By the way, what were you going to ask me?'

Amelia said, 'If I write a song on a piece of paper, but then I burn it, what happens to the song?'

'I'm not sure. So long as *you* can remember it, it won't be gone for ever, will it? And even when you've forgotten it, maybe the smoke will go on singing it.'

FIVE

Tilda was just about to climb into the bathtub when the doorbell rang. She stopped, one heavy leg still raised. Who was
calling on her at this time of the evening? More to the
point, who was calling on her at all? She had only one really close
friend – Rosemary Shulman at the office – and Rosemary wouldn't
come around to her apartment to see her, quite apart from the fact
that she didn't drive.

She waited. Maybe somebody had made a mistake and pressed
the wrong button. It happened now and again, especially at night,
because the neighborhood kids were continually breaking the light
over the porch. Once she had opened the door to be confronted
by a handsome black man holding out a huge bouquet of yellow
roses, but it had turned out that he was looking for Etta, the skinny
black salesgirl who lived next door.

She dipped her toes into the foam to check how hot the water
was. She had been paid on Friday, so she had indulged herself
this evening with a chicken-dinner-for-two which she had pre-
prepared at the Dream Dining franchise down on East Markland
Avenue. She always made a dinner-for-two because it filled her
up and stopped her snacking so much during the evening, and so
that the kitchen helpers at Dream Dining wouldn't realize that she
always ate alone, on her lap, in front of the TV.

The doorbell rang again, twice, as if the caller was growing
impatient. She took her foot out of the water and bent over to dry
between her toes, the way that her mother had always told her.
She tugged at her straggly brown curls to make sure that she
looked presentable, and then she took down the pink candlewick
robe that was hanging on the back of the bathroom door, and put
it on, grunting with the effort.

She crossed the living-room and went to the intercom beside
the front door.

'Who is it?' she asked.

'Pizza guy.'

'You have the wrong apartment. I didn't order pizza.'

'I know. But this is *free* pizza. Complimentary, on the house.'
The pizza guy's voice sounded hoarse, as if he had asthma.

'What do you mean?'

'You order pizza from Papa Joey's, don't you?'

'Yes.'

'Well, this is your reward for being a loyal customer. Tonight every loyal customer gets free pizza.'

Tilda frowned. Somehow this didn't sound right. But on the other hand, she *did* regularly order pizza online from Papa Joey's, and if this wasn't a legitimate promotion, how did they know where she lived?

The hoarse voice said, 'Listen, ma'am, I don't want to rush you or nothing, but I have twenty other deliveries to make. Do you want the free pizza or not?'

Tilda bit her lip in indecision. 'The problem is I ate tonight already. Can I have the pizza some other night? Like tomorrow night, maybe?'

'Sorry, ma'am. The offer is good for tonight only.'

'What topping is it?'

'Same as you always order. Hawaiian Barbecue Chicken.'

'OK, then,' she said. 'I'll take it.' If the pizza guy knew what she regularly ordered, he must be legitimate. And even if she wasn't hungry now, she might be later, before she went to bed, and she could always save any uneaten slices for tomorrow morning. She enjoyed cold pizza for breakfast, just as much as she enjoyed cold fried chicken and cold cheeseburgers.

She pressed the entrance buzzer and after a moment she heard the elevator whining. She heard the doors jolt, too, as the elevator reached the second floor. But then there was a long silence, almost half a minute, and she inclined her head toward her front door, listening for footsteps. Nothing. Maybe this was a hoax. Some of the neighborhood kids shouted insults at her when she arrived home in the evening, calling her 'lardass' and 'porky' and 'thunderthighs'. But the pizza guy on the intercom hadn't sounded like a kid.

Without warning, there was a sharp knock on the door, which made her jump.

'Pizza guy!'

'OK, OK. Wait up a second!' She squinted through the peephole. All she could see was a man wearing a white Papa Joey's cap and a red T-shirt. He was holding up a Papa Joey's pizza box. Normally, she would ask the delivery boy to show his order number, but of course this pizza had arrived unordered.

For three slow heartbeats, she wondered if it was safe for her to open the door. But the man was wearing the proper Papa Joey's uniform, and where would any of the neighborhood kids have found one of those?

She unfastened the deadlocks, and opened the door, although she left the safety-chain on. 'Thanks,' she said. 'You can pass it through here.'

'Sorry, ma'am, have to keep it flat. Company policy. If I tilt it sideways, all of your pineapple's going to fall off, right?'

'Oh, OK.'

She drew back the safety-chain. Immediately, the man slammed the door wide open, and collided with Tilda so hard that she fell over backward, on to her glass-topped coffee table, which collapsed underneath her and shattered. He swung the apartment door shut behind him and slung his pizza box across the room. He pulled off his Papa Joey's cap, too, and threw that aside.

Tilda was winded at first, but then she sat up and screamed out, '*Help! Somebody help me! Etta!*'

The man barked, 'Shut up, you fat bitch!' and forced her back on to the wreckage of her coffee table. He gripped her by the neck, half-strangling her, and at the same time he dug his right knee deep into her stomach, so that she sicked up undigested chicken and onion strings, some of it through her nostrils, and almost choked.

She was shaking with shock and dread. What terrified her the most was the man's face, which was covered by a dead-white mask. Whatever his real expression was, his mask was fixed into an expression of maniacal glee, as if he couldn't wait to make more mischief, and humiliate her even more.

She spat out chicken and gravy-colored mucus. 'Please . . .' she begged him. 'I'm going to puke again. Please.'

The man stayed where he was, with his knee buried in her stomach, and she could see his eyes behind the slits in his mask.

'You have to swear on your life that you're not going to scream.'

'Please, I can't breathe.'

'Did you hear me? You have to swear on your greedy, bloated life that you're not going to scream!'

'I swear,' coughed Tilda. Her stomach was going into nauseous convulsions, and her mouth was filling up with bile. 'Please, get off me. I swear to God I won't scream.'

The man hesitated for a few seconds, and then released his grip on her neck and stood up. Tilda rolled over on to her side and vomited up the rest of her chicken-dinner-for-two. After that, she stayed where she was, sniffing miserably.

'Look at you,' said the man, with complete contempt. 'You're just like *she* was, you miserable lump of suet.' He spat on her, and then he wiped his mouth with the back of his hand.

'What do you—' Tilda began, but she had to cough up more chicken before she could get her words out. 'What do you want?'

'What do I want? What do I want? I don't want nothing at all, ma'am. Not from you, especially. But what *I* want, that's beside the point.'

'Please don't hurt me. I have to take care of my mother.'

'You think I give a shit about your mother? Why should I give a shit about your mother? This is human destiny we're talking about here. This is *history*. Things have gone wrong and now they have to be put right.'

Tilda looked up at him. He was highly agitated, and he kept pacing from one side of the room to the other. On the opposite side of the room, he kicked the pizza box, which was obviously empty.

Her telephone was fixed to the wall, in the kitchenette area. She wondered if she could reach it in time to dial 911, but she doubted it. She turned around and looked at her bookshelves, which were filled with romance novels and diet books, but also with books about travel in the Far East. She had left her floppy beige purse on top of them, and in the side-pocket of her purse lay her cellphone. But again she knew that she had almost no chance of crossing the room and taking it out before the man knocked her down a second time.

'I'm not saying it's your fault,' the man told her. He cleared his throat, and paused to get his breath back. 'The problem is, it has to be fixed somehow, and so far as I know this is the only way.'

'I don't understand what you're talking about,' said Tilda. '*What* has to be fixed?'

'The . . .' the man began, but then he seemed to be lost for words, and all he could do was throw up his hands. '*Everything*. Everything has to be fixed, that's what.'

'Please, you won't hurt me, will you?' said Tilda.

But at that moment there was a soft, quick knock at the door and two more men came into the apartment. Still sitting on the floor, Tilda humped herself away from them, toward the couch, and she couldn't stop herself from letting out a muted squeal of fear. Both men were dressed in black sweatshirts and black pants, but one of them wore a mask that was totally expressionless, while the other wore a mask of scowling anger. The laughing man closed the door and locked it.

'You're right,' said the expressionless man. 'She looks exactly like her. Gives you the willies, don't it?'

The scowling man came up to Tilda and hunkered down close to her. He took hold of her face in his hand and squodged her cheeks together. 'How much do you weigh, sweetheart?' he asked her. 'Two-twenty? Two-thirty? More?'

Tilda couldn't speak. The scowling man said, 'Never mind. You look the part, that's all that matters. You're a dead ringer.'

The expressionless man came up close to her, too, and between the two of them they heaved her up from the floor. She clutched her bathrobe around her, and looked from one of the men to the other, trying to understand what they wanted from her.

'You have a boyfriend, Tilda?' asked the laughing man.

She shook her head. Her throat hurt and her eyes were filled with tears.

'That's good. That makes it more authentic. She didn't have no boyfriend neither. Well, she was such a tub of lard. Just like you.'

'Please don't hurt me,' Tilda whined. 'Please, I'll do anything.'

'Well, we know you will,' said the laughing man. 'But that don't change nothing. Take off the robe.'

'What?'

'You heard me, sweet cheeks. Take off the robe.'

Tilda gripped the lapels of her bathrobe and crossed her arms tightly over her bosom. 'I can't.'

'No, Tilda. You don't get it. You *can* take it off, and you will, and you'll do it right now. We're none too patient, none of us.'

'I can't! I can't! I've never—'

The laughing man leaned over her, so that his white papier

mâché nose was almost touching hers. 'You've never *what*, darling?'

Tilda was feeling faint, and she couldn't stop herself from swaying. 'I've never . . . *showed* myself. To a man.'

The scowling man came up close to her, too. 'You've never been naked in front of a man? Like, you've always turned the lights off?'

Tilda closed her eyes. *Please let this not be happening. Please.* 'I've never been with a man. Ever.'

'Well, stick a feather up my ass and call me a peacock. You were never with a man, *ever*? How old are you, Tilda?'

'Twenty-three. Twenty-four, nearly. My birthday's next week.'

'In that case, you're in luck, because we're going to bust your cherry before you get a single day older.'

Tilda swayed sideways and almost fell over, but the scowling man caught her arm. 'Hey – I know this is kind of thrilling for you, but there's no need for you to pass out on us.'

'Please,' Tilda mumbled. 'What am I going to tell my mother?'

'Who gives a shit? Tell her you enjoyed it. Tell her anything you want. It's none of *her* business anyhow. It's personal.'

Tilda suddenly wrenched herself away from him and screamed in his face, '*Go away! Go away all of you and leave me alone! Get out of my apartment! Get out!*'

The laughing man waited patiently until she had finished her outburst, and then he said, in that breathless, asthmatic voice, 'You want to calm down, Tilda. You really do. Think of your blood pressure. Look at yourself, you've gone all purple in the face. That can't be good for you.'

Tilda's chest was rising and falling with the effort. 'Please get out,' she panted. 'Please leave me alone.'

'If only we could, sweet cheeks. But we have to do this, other-wise we're going to be in deeper trouble than you could ever imagine. Sometimes, in this life, it's a question of doing what you have to, regardless of the consequences, and no matter who gets hurt in the process.' He paused for a moment, and then he said, 'Take off the robe, Tilda. If you don't take off the robe, we'll have to hurt you, and we don't want to do that. No more than neces-sary, anyhow.'

Tilda looked up at him. If only she could see his face. If only she could tell what he was thinking. But all she could see was that maniacally laughing mask, a frozen reaction to a long-forgotten joke.

'Come on, Tilda,' he coaxed her.

She loosened her sash, and then she let her arms drop to her sides, so that the robe slid off her shoulders by itself, and dropped on to the floor.

'My God,' said the scowling man. 'You're one whale of a woman, I'll have to grant you that.'

Tilda could see herself reflected in the mirror beside the front door. She hated looking at herself naked. Her breasts were enormous, and her stomach bulged as if she had just walked out of the ocean with a half-deflated lifebelt hanging around her hips. Her massive thighs were already dimpled with cellulite, and her ankles were so swollen that the straps of her shoes left indentations in her flesh.

The laughing man looked around the apartment. His eyes lighted on the wooden bowl of fruit on the kitchenette counter. He went over to it and picked out an apple.

'Get yourself down on all fours,' he told Tilda.

'What?' She was trying to cover her breasts with her left arm and keep her right hand cupped between her thighs.

'You heard me. Get yourself down on all fours.'

'No,' she retorted, although her voice was so weak that the laughing man pretended not to hear her at first, and mockingly cupped his hand to his papier mâché ear.

'*No,*' she repeated.

The laughing man returned to the kitchenette and noisily pulled open the drawers, one by one, until he found a six-inch boning knife. He came back and held it up in front of Tilda's face. 'Don't get argumentative, OK? That's all I'm asking. You look like a pig already, but I can make you look even more like a pig if I cut your nose off.'

Tilda stared at him, breathing faster and faster. He hesitated for a few seconds, and then he jabbed the end of her nose with the tip of the knife. She said, '*Ah!*' and lifted her hand to her face, but then she realized that she was exposing herself and quickly put it down again.

The laughing man polished the apple on his sleeve, and then he said, 'Here . . . stick this in your mouth. Go on.'

Tilda began to weep, but when the laughing man pushed the

apple hard against her lips she opened her mouth wide and took
a bite into it and held it there.

'Good girl. Excellent. Now get yourself down on all fours.'

Sobbing, Tilda lowered herself on to her hands and knees. Her
breasts and her stomach hung down, and she felt overwhelmed
with shame. Keeping the apple between her teeth made her drool,
but she didn't dare to let it drop out in case the laughing man did
what he had threatened and cut off her nose.

'What a cute little piggy,' said the laughing man. 'Got an apple
in its mouth and everything. All it needs now is some stuffing.'

He tugged down his zipper and dug his hand into his pants. He
levered out his penis and brandished it in front of Tilda's face, so
close that she could smell it.

'See this, Tilda? This is the finest pork stuffing. You'll love it,
same way that *she* always loved it.'

Tilda closed her eyes. The apple was beginning to make her
jaws ache. But the laughing man said, 'Come on now, Tilda. You
keep your eyes open. Otherwise I'll have to cut off your eyelids
so you don't have no choice in the matter.'

He went around and knelt down behind her. 'Wish me luck,
boys!' he said. He had a short coughing spasm, and then he added,
'I'm boldly going where no man has gone before!'

He used both hands to pry apart the cheeks of Tilda's huge
buttocks, and then he raised himself up a little and forced himself
into her, all the way, hard, even though she was dry. Tilda bit
harder into the apple, because he was hurting her so much, but
she thought to herself: *Pretend this is a movie you're watching,
and it isn't happening to you at all. You came home, you ate your
dinner, and then you had your bath. Now you're watching some
violent movie on TV.*

The laughing man pushed harder and harder. He reached around
her with both hands and dug his fingers deep into her pendulous
belly, and kneaded it, as if it were dough. He coughed, and she
could feel his coughing right inside her, but he didn't stop. And
now the scowling man and the expressionless man both opened
up their pants, too, and stood in front of her, holding themselves
in their hands.

'We can save you the trouble of taking a bath, Tilda,' said the
expressionless man. 'How about we give you a shower?'

The scowling man started giggling behind his mask, and that

giggling made it impossible for Tilda to pretend any longer that this wasn't real, and that these three men were going to do whatever they wanted to her, and that when they were finished with her, they would probably kill her. She let the apple drop from her mouth on to the floor.

She was woken by the *meep-meep-meep* of her alarm-clock. She opened her eyes and saw sunlight, shining on the carpet. She was lying on her side in the middle of her living-room, completely naked. The three masked men appeared to have gone, but when she raised her head she saw they had left her covered in scores of dark crimson bruises. She had bruises on her breasts, bruises on her stomach, bruises on her thighs. They made her look as if she were covered with fallen leaves, like one of the Babes in the Wood. Her lips were swollen and her left eye was puffed up, too. Her hair and her skin were sticky and she reeked of urine. She breathed in, and retched.

She managed to sit up, and as she did so she felt a hard, uncomfortable sensation between her legs. She reached down and felt herself and discovered that they had pushed the apple up inside her, with her own teeth marks in it.

'*Oh God*,' she whispered. '*Oh God oh God*.'

She reached out for the arm of the couch and managed to heave herself on to her feet. The first thing she did was hobble over to the bedroom door and look inside, to make sure that none of the masked men was hiding in there. The alarm-clock was still beeping so she switched it off, and listened, but all she could hear was the muted rumbling of plumbing as the residents of her apartment block started to fill kettles and run showers and flush toilets.

She went to the closet and opened it, but there was nothing inside except her 1X dresses and her size forty-two sweaters. She went back into the living-room and locked the front door, and double-locked it, and fastened the safety-chain.

'*Oh God*,' she kept whispering. '*Oh God*.'

The bathroom door was half-open and she could see that the tub was still filled, even though the foam had all disappeared and the water must be stone-cold. But she had to wash off the stench of those terrible men. Her mind was crowded with jumbled images of what they had done to her, but she made a deliberate effort not to think about them. First of all she needed to get herself clean.

She lowered herself into the bathwater, her teeth chattering with cold and shock. She lay back and pinched her nose between finger and thumb, and completely immersed herself. She stayed under the surface for as long as she could, and then she reared up again, gasping for breath.

Oh God oh God. As if I haven't been humiliated all my life. Teased and bullied at school, ever since I was three years old. Ignored by boys. Pitied by my girlfriends. And now I've been raped and beaten and defiled, as if I'm nothing but a dumb farm animal. And this is the first time that any man has ever touched me.

She turned on the hot water, full, and then she stood up and lathered herself all over, washing her hair and her face and her breasts and furiously soaping herself between her legs, even though she was so sore and swollen.

I will not let them, she repeated. *I will not let them break me. I will not.* But at the same time the tears were pouring down her cheeks, and her mouth was dragged down in a silent howl of anguish and distress.

She was still soaping herself when a voice said, '*Belinda*?'

She twisted around, lost her balance, and dropped down into the bathwater with a catastrophic splash. A boy of about twelve years old was standing in the bathroom doorway, staring at her. He had dark tousled hair and a very pale face and he was wearing a faded black T-shirt and a pair of worn-out red jeans.

Tilda grabbed her big brown bath-towel from the stool beside the tub and covered her breasts with it. '*Who are you*?' She was so frightened that she was hyperventilating. '*What are you doing in here? How did you get in*?'

The boy took a step nearer. 'I've been trying to find you for *days*,' he said. His voice was very flat and bland, but with a strong local accent, so that his words came out as 'ahbin tryna fahnjew'.

'Get out! *Go away*! I'm going to call nine-one-one!'

But the boy ignored her. He came nearer, until he was standing close beside the tub. Tilda dragged the bath-towel into the water and stuffed it protectively down between her thighs.

'Why didn't you never come back, Belinda?' the boy asked her. 'You coulda saved me.'

'Just get out of here,' Tilda quivered. 'I don't know who you are or what you want but you have to leave now.'

'I looked everywhere trying to find you but I never could. Where did you go, Belinda? Why didn't you never come back?'

'My name isn't Belinda,' Tilda told him. 'Now, I don't know how you managed to get in here, but I'm calling the police right now and you're going to be in big trouble, believe me.'

The boy looked bewildered. 'Why can't you hug me, Belinda, like you used to? You went away and I never knew where you went, and Mommy was always sleeping or drunk or else she had the screaming meemies. You coulda saved me.'

Tilda gripped the handle at the side of the bath, and started to lift herself out of the water, still holding the heavy wet towel in front of her to protect her modesty. But without warning the boy pushed her back down again. He didn't have to push her very hard, because she was bruised and exhausted and still in shock, and in any case she always found it an effort to climb out of the bath.

Then, to her horror, he stepped into the bath and climbed on top of her, fully dressed, still wearing his sneakers. He wrapped his arms around her and pressed his head against the towel that covered her breasts.

'*Get off me!*' screamed Tilda, trying to lever him upward. She rolled sideways and thrashed at him, dragging at his T-shirt, but his fingers were digging deep into the flesh that girdled her hips and she found it impossible to get herself free. His clothes were sodden and he was panting with effort, but he kept his grip on her, even when she seized his wet brown hair and forced his head back as far as it would go.

'Just like it used to be, Belinda!' he said. His white face was shining with elation. 'You and me together in the tub! Remember that? And then afterward, when we cuddled together, and you sang me that song?'

'Get off me!' Tilda babbled. 'Oh God, just get off me!'

'But it's just like it used to be!' the boy repeated. 'It's wonderful! It's just like it used to be!'

Tilda let go of the boy's hair and attempted to seize him by the throat, but he butted her with his forehead on the bridge of her nose, so hard that she felt her cartilage crack. She slipped backward and downward into the bath, with a riotous splash and a ribald squeak of bare skin against enamel.

Spluttering, half-choking, she reared up and went for his throat again. '*Kill you!*' she shrieked. '*I'll kill you!*'

'Don't *hafta!*' crowed the boy, triumphantly. 'Didn't you know that, Belinda? Don't *hafta!*'

With that, he exploded into a fireball. The flames that enveloped him were instantly fierce, and actually *roared*. His hair blazed, his face blazed, his whole body blazed, and for one terrible second Tilda could see him staring at her through the fire, his eyes wide, his mouth stretched open in a high-pitched scream.

Tilda screamed, too. She struggled wildly to get out from under him, but the flames overwhelmed her. She felt a scorching blast of heat, as if somebody had suddenly opened up a furnace door. Her curly hair frizzled and her eyebrows were burned off, and the skin on her cheeks tightened and shriveled, layer by layer, quicker and quicker, until her face was charred black.

The boy burned so ferociously that the bathwater started to bubble, and within seconds it had reached boiling-point. Tilda jerked and shuddered, her arms and legs moving as stiffly as a giant puppet. She had never known that human beings could feel such excruciating levels of pain. Surely it wasn't possible. Surely she ought to be dead. Her face and her shoulders and her breasts were being seared by fire, while at the same time her back and her thighs and her buttocks were being boiled.

Oh Mommy, she thought, *oh please Mommy, help me.*

Then she screamed out, '*Help me!*' and her heart stopped.

The boy continued to burn until his skeleton dropped apart, and even his skull collapsed into fragments. The last of the bathwater crackled dry, leaving the bathroom foggy with steam. Tilda's blackened body lay on its back, with both arms raised as if she were still trying to fight the boy off; her legs raised, too. The plastic shower-curtain drooped from its hooks in long melted strings.

The morning passed. Nobody rang. Nobody knocked at Tilda's door. For a while, a Hoover droned in the corridor outside, and the cleaner sang 'Baby, Don't Change Your Mind', but then there was silence.

SIX

Ruth was twenty minutes late arriving at the Fire Department headquarters on West Superior Street. She pushed open the door to the Fire & Arson Laboratory with her elbow, because she was carrying a cappuccino in one hand and a raspberry espresso and a bag of donuts in the other. Jack was bent over the burned-out mattress from South McCann Street, wearing his white lab coat and magnifying eyeglasses, so that he looked like a studious insect. The whole laboratory was filled with the sour reek of charred cotton.

'Sorry I'm so late,' said Ruth. 'I had to do the school run this morning and the traffic was a nightmare.'

'I thought you had good old Craig trained to do that,' said Jack, without looking up.

'He usually does it, yes. But when Ammy came down to breakfast this morning she was acting kind of fretful, so I thought that I ought to take her.'

'She's OK, though?' Jack was Amelia's godfather and always took a special interest in how she was doing.

Ruth put down the two cups of coffee and the bag of donuts. 'She was much more settled by the time I got her to school. But she kept on saying that she felt worried.'

'*Worried*? She's only fifteen! I know she's kind of special, but what does *she* have to worry about?'

'Believe me, Jack, even ordinary fifteen-year-olds have just as much to worry about as we do, if not more. But she couldn't say *why* she was worried. She said she felt like a storm was on its way. You know her. She says things like that.'

Jack came over, pushing his magnifying eyeglasses on to the top of his head and snapping off his latex gloves. He took the espresso and removed the lid. 'Thanks. I've been gasping for this. What flavor donuts did you buy? Right at the moment, everything tastes like charred mattress.'

'Apple spice cake.'

'My favorite. Why are you so good to me, boss?' He said it so dryly that he was right on the edge of sounding sarcastic.

Ruth patted him on the shoulder. 'Because a good boss has to show the people who work for her that she appreciates their skill and their expertise, and apart from that, apple spice cake is *my* favorite too, so don't eat them all, *capiche*?'

Jack sipped his coffee and then he put his cup down. 'I've found something passing strange,' he said. He walked over to the mattress and Ruth followed him. Most of the interior of the mattress had been burned out, leaving only the springs, and heaps of blackened fiber.

'You can see here the remains of the cotton batting, and the springs, which have been annealed by the heat. Of course there are still a few bits and pieces of human residue, too, which originated from the cadaver we found. I'd say that on the Crow-Glassman scale, the cadaver burned to a little over CGS level two. Unrecognizable as to sex and identity, of course, but not totally destroyed.'

'OK,' said Ruth. 'So what's so strange?'

'*This,*' Jack told her, holding up a test-tube. It was half-filled with very fine gray powder. 'When I sieved through the ashes, I picked out five or six sizeable skin fragments from the cadaver as well as the distal and middle phalanges from the cadaver's left little toe. But *these* remains were mingled in with them, too. They're human, but they come from somebody else – another victim, maybe, but a victim who was burned well beyond CGS level five.'

'So we have *two* victims?'

'I can't say for sure, not yet. However this other person died, it looks likely that he or she was cremated in a professional crematorium. Not particularly well, because we still have a scattering of larger bone fragments, but I'd still say that after the body was incinerated the remains were put through a cremulator, which is not a piece of equipment you can readily obtain from your local Handy Hardware.'

Ruth took the test-tube, put on her half-glasses and examined it closely. The gray powder looked exactly like the human remains that undertakers hand to relatives after a funeral – not technically ashes, although that was what they were commonly called, but very finely crushed bone. Some undertakers called them 'cremains' – a portfolio word for 'cremated remains'.

'How much of this did you find?'

'By weight? Less than a kilo, so it could have been a child. On the other hand, I can't tell you if what I found was all of that individual's remains. It depends where they came from and how they got there.'

'But you think this second person was cremated sometime well before the first person was burned, and most likely at a crematorium?'

'That's right,' said Jack. 'Which means, of course, that we have no way of knowing how he or she died. Not yet, anyhow. Not unless we can find out who it is. Could have been a homicide victim. Could have died in any kind of accident. Could have died of natural causes. Who knows?'

'But how did their remains get into the mattress?'

'That's the sixty-four-thousand-dollar-and-ten-cent question. Maybe, when the first person was burned, they were holding a box containing the second person's remains. Or maybe the remains were scattered on to the mattress *before* the fire started, either by the first person themselves or by a third person unknown.' Jack picked an apple spice donut out of the bag and took a bite. 'I'll send a sample to Aaron Scheinman for a DNA test,' he said, with his mouth full. 'You never know your luck.'

'Hell of a long shot,' said Ruth.

'It's worth trying. There are several larger fragments which could be bits of tooth. At least we may be able to find out if it's a male or a female.'

Ruth went to the closet and took out a starched white lab coat. She was still buttoning it up, however, when her cellphone buzzed against her hip. She took it out and saw that she had received a text from Amelia. '*Sumthin BADS hpn.*'

She tried to call Amelia, but she didn't answer. She must be in class, texting under cover of her desk. So Ruth texted her back. '*Call me*!!'

Less than five minutes later, her cellphone buzzed again. It was Amelia, and her voice echoed, as if she were in the restroom. Ruth stepped outside the laboratory door so that she could get a clearer signal.

'Mommy? I was right in the middle of math and I suddenly had this really terrible feeling.'

'What kind of a feeling? It's not your period, is it?'

'It was like I was burning. I got so hot that I nearly fainted.'

'Maybe you're pining for that Asian flu. You didn't feel too good this morning, did you? Listen, I'll come right over and take you out of school.'

'You don't have to, really. I know you're real busy.'

'No, no. Jack can cover for me. I'll be there in ten minutes.'

She drove to Kokomo High and found Amelia waiting for her on the front steps, with one of her classmates, Rita Dunning, beside her. Rita had a snub nose and a ponytail and braces on her teeth and a very short kilt.

'Thanks, Rita,' said Ruth, as Amelia climbed into the car.

'That's OK, Mrs Cutter. Wish *I* could have a day off, just for being weird.'

Ruth was about to say something sharp, but Amelia said, 'Forget it, Mom. I'm used to it. She doesn't mean any harm.'

They drove off. Tyson was standing up in the back, panting hoarsely and thumping his tail against the back of the seat. He always got excited when Ruth picked up Amelia.

'How do you feel now?' asked Ruth.

'Not hot any more. But so thirsty. My throat's so dry that I can hardly swallow.'

'I really think you need to see Doctor Feldstein. There are all kinds of bugs going around right now.'

'I felt like I was on fire,' Amelia told her. 'But it wasn't like having a fever or anything. It was more like my skin was burning. You know when we went to Florida that time and I sat in the sun too long and got in the shower? It was exactly like that.'

When they reached the next stop signal, Ruth turned and pressed her hand to Amelia's forehead. 'You *look* OK. I mean, you're not flushed, are you? If anything, you're kind of pale.'

'But there's *this*, too,' said Amelia. She reached into her school bag and took out her math work book. It was dog-eared and covered in masses of elaborate doodles, because Amelia was always drawing over all of her books – flowers and fairies and princesses and cats. She opened it up in the middle and held it up so that Ruth could see it.

Ruth was driving, but she managed to glance at it. On the lower half of the right-hand page there were three parallel scorch marks, about an inch-and-a-half long, and one of them was so deep that it had burned right through to the next page, and the page after that.

'What on earth did *that*?' asked Ruth.

'My fingers.'

'What?' Ruth slowed down for another stop signal.

'My *fingers* did it. I was writing with my left hand and I had my right hand resting on my book and when I lifted my hand up the paper was all burned.'

'How could that happen?'

'I don't know, Mommy. But it did. Rita saw it, too.'

Ruth turned into the driveway in front of their house and parked. She took the math book from Amelia and examined it. She even sniffed it, but it smelled of nothing more than burned paper. The scorch marks were soft and smudged, and they were shaped exactly like fingerprints, but how was it possible that Amelia's fingers had made them? Yet Amelia never lied. She didn't know how to.

'This doesn't make any kind of sense,' said Ruth. She took hold of Amelia's hand and turned it over. 'Look – your fingers aren't blistered, are they?'

'I'm only telling you how it happened. I felt like I was on fire and then my book was burned and I heard somebody say, "Andie".'

'"*Andie*",' Ruth repeated. 'Who said "Andie"?'

'Inside my head somebody said "Andie", but it wasn't me. It sounded like a boy's voice.'

Ruth climbed out of the car and Amelia followed her up to the front door, with Tyson snuffling right behind her. Ruth said, 'You definitely have to see Doctor Feldstein. It could be you need your medication reassessed.'

'But he did that only about a month ago.'

'I know, sweetheart, but you're growing up, your hormones are all running wild. Maybe you need to cut down on your beta blockers. Who knows? But you shouldn't be feeling worried all the time, and hearing voices inside of your head, and burning up like that, should you? You're my precious girl, Ammy.'

Amelia hugged her. 'You're my precious mommy, Mom.'

They went inside. Ruth went through to the kitchen, took a bottle of Gatorade out of the fridge and poured Amelia a large glass, with ice in it. As she put it down in front of her, the phone rang.

'Ruth? It's Ron Magruder. Jack Morrow told me I'd probably catch you at home.'

'How's it going, Ron?'

'Well, we seem to be making some progress. The coroner has

finished his preliminary report, and he says that the cadaver is that of a woman aged between thirty and thirty-five. She's given natural birth to a child or children, too.'

'Still no idea how she got burned up so bad? Because Jack and me haven't, not yet.'

'Nope. No evidence that any accelerant was used, just like you said. But we think we may have a pretty good idea who she is.'

'Go on.'

'We've had three missing persons reports in the past two weeks, but only one of them comes close to the coroner's description. Julie Benfield, thirty-four years old. She's a personal assistant at the Harris Bank. She was supposed to be home by six p.m. Tuesday evening but she never showed. Her Land Cruiser was found at seven fifteen p.m. at Casey's General Store on South Dixon Road with the keys still hanging in the door and all of her shopping scattered across the parking lot.'

'Sounds like she was abducted. Any witnesses?'

'None. Nobody saw nothing. Nobody *heard* nothing. Her ex-husband Daniel Benfield is a partner in a local law firm – Jones, Hagerty and Benfield. He was working late at the office on North Washington Street until eight thirty p.m. so we've ruled him out as a suspect. Poor guy wanted to identify the body, but of course it was out of the question. We showed him the wedding band we found on the cadaver and he thinks it's hers but he's not one hundred per cent sure. Val Minelli took a mitochondrial DNA sample from one of their kids so we should know soon if it's her or not.'

'Does her husband know why anybody should have wanted to kill her?'

'Nope. Everybody loved her, that's what he said. The divorce was amicable and there was no trouble over access to the children. She was a leading light in the PTA and a member of the Grace United Methodist choir.'

'This is so strange, isn't it? Because whoever killed her, they really wanted her burned to ashes. Like Val said, it was more of a sacrifice than a homicide.'

'Well, we still have a lot of questions to answer,' said Ron. 'We're conducting a house-to-house all the way along South McCann and West Maple Streets, and we're checking through the CCTV footage from Casey's store, to see if there was anybody paying Mrs Benfield any undue attention.'

'Did Jack tell you about the second remains?' asked Ruth.

'Yes, he did. He's going to send me the DNA results just as soon as he gets them. But he doesn't expect them for a couple of days and so far I'm trying to keep an open mind.'

'You mean you're as baffled as we are.'

'That's not the way I'm going to put it to the media, and I hope the Fire Department doesn't, either.'

Ruth called the Walters Clinic and made an appointment for Amelia to have a check-up with Doctor Feldstein the following morning. As she hung up the phone, she could see Amelia in the living-room, sitting cross-legged on the couch watching *The Simpsons* and laughing. She loved Amelia so much she would have done anything for her. If Amelia had been suffering from a kidney disease, she would happily have given her one of her kidneys. But there was no way to give her the twenty-six genes she was missing.

She called Craig but his assistant said that he had already left the office for a meeting with the bank. She tried his cell but he had switched it off.

'Mommy,' said Amelia, turning around. 'Come sit here and watch this with me. It's so funny!'

'Sure,' smiled Ruth, and walked into the living-room. As she did so, she glanced out of the window. The boy in the faded black T-shirt and the red jeans was standing beside the basswood tree in their front yard, staring at the house. Ruth felt an unpleasant jolt of alarm, as if she had touched a bare electric wire. She stood and stared back at the boy, and there was no doubt that he must have seen her, but he stayed where he was, his arms by his sides, frowning slightly, as if he were trying to make up his mind to come nearer.

'Sit down, Mommy!' said Amelia. 'This is a really funny bit!'

Ruth continued to stare back at the boy. He was only about twelve years old, and very thin, but for some reason he made her feel deeply unsettled.

'Mommy?' said Amelia, and then, 'What are you looking at?'

'It's that boy,' Ruth told her. 'That boy you saw yesterday evening. He's come back.'

Amelia stood up and looked out of the window. 'I wonder what he's doing here. He looks like he wants something, doesn't he?'

'Yes, he does. Let's go ask him, shall we?'

'I don't know. Maybe we shouldn't.'

'Ammy, he's only a boy.'

'I know he is, but he makes me feel scared.'

'Oh, come on. Why does he make you feel scared?'

'I don't know. But it feels like the door's open. It feels like they're all trying to come through.'

'Well, you stay here and *I'll* go,' said Ruth. 'He could be lost, or maybe he's run away from home. He's still wearing the same clothes as yesterday, isn't he?'

'Mommy, *don't.*'

Ruth laid her hands on Amelia's shoulders and gave her a re-assuring squeeze. 'Don't worry, honestly. I'm sure that he's perfectly harmless. We can't leave him standing outside like that, can we, if he doesn't have anyplace to go? We'll have to call Children's Services, so that somebody can take care of him.'

She opened the front door, but as she did so, Amelia let out a peculiar little moan of dread. Ruth turned back. Amelia was standing in the hallway with her face cupped in her hands, her eyes wide, like Edvard Munch's painting of *The Scream*.

Ruth went back and gave her a hug. 'Sweetheart, there's no need for you to be scared of him. He's only a boy.'

Amelia looked up at her. 'Don't let him come close to you,' she said.

'Why not?'

'*Please,* Mommy, just don't.'

'OK, if you don't want me to, I won't.'

'He doesn't know who you are. That's why he's come here. He thinks you're somebody else.'

'Who? And how do you know that?'

'I don't know. But he wouldn't be here, otherwise.'

'OK, then. I promise you I won't let him come close. Now you just stay there, if he scares you so much. I won't be a minute.'

With that, Ruth opened the door and stepped out. The sun was shining and the front yard was so bright that at first she had to shield her eyes with her hand. The boy had been standing right beside the trunk of the basswood tree, but now that she was outside she couldn't see him.

She crossed the lawn until she reached the tree, but the boy had gone. She went further, on to the sidewalk, but there was no sign of him, not in either direction. She looked back toward the house. The front door was open, and Amelia was peering out apprehensively, but the boy had completely disappeared, as if he had been nothing but a trick of the mid-morning shadows.

She was still standing on the sidewalk when she saw Craig's silver Explorer coming along the road. He turned into the driveway and parked behind her Ford.

'Hey, you waiting for me?' he asked her as he climbed out.

Ruth shook her head. 'There was a boy here . . . standing outside the house.'

Craig looked up and down the street. 'I don't see any boy. What did he look like?'

'Dark hair, very pale face. He was wearing a black T-shirt and red jeans. The funny thing is, he was out here last night, too, and I saw him in the crowd outside that house on South McCann Street – you know, where we found that burned body on the mattress.'

'Maybe he's stalking you,' said Craig.

'Why would he be stalking me?'

'Maybe he's got a crush on you.'

'Oh, get serious. He's only about twelve.'

'I used to get crushes on women when I was twelve. I was desperately in love with Jane Fonda for about six months.'

He looked toward the house and saw Amelia behind the front door. 'What's Ammy doing home? And come to that, what are *you* doing home?'

Ruth told him. He went inside and put his arm around Amelia and asked her if she was feeling better.

'I am now that boy's gone.'

'What's the poor kid ever done to you?' Craig asked her.

'He's not a poor kid. He's a *creepy* kid.'

'Well, we can't have any creepy kids giving you the willies, can we? If you see him again, just you tell me, and I'll chase him away.'

They went through to the living-room. Craig immediately went to the drinks table and poured himself a large glass of Jack Daniel's.

'*Craig*,' Ruth admonished him.

He raised his glass to her in salute. 'I know. But after the morning I've had . . .'

'Martin wouldn't lend you the money?'

'He didn't even say he was sorry,' Craig told her. 'He just said no. And how long have he and I been friends?'

'What did he think of your business plan?'

'He said it was great. Well thought-out, carefully costed. A year ago, he would have given me as much as I wanted, if not more.'

'So what happens next?' Ruth asked him.

'Well, I think I have three options. I could either hang myself, shoot myself, or lie down on the railroad tracks and wait for the next Norfolk Southern freight train to come along.'

'Things can't be that bad.'

'Why do you think I haven't gone back to the studio? Miller Homes called me this morning, from Fort Wayne. I was talking to them last month about a new housing development out on Orchard Ridge. Seventy-five houses, seventy-five custom-fitted kitchens.'

'And?'

'Canceled. Same as Muncie Properties and Keiller Housing and Davis Nugent. I've been cold-calling developers all day. I even called Kanakee Homes in Peoria.'

'We'll get through this somehow,' said Ruth. 'We're not the only family that's suffering.'

The Simpsons finished and Amelia went upstairs. When Ruth was sure that she was out of earshot, she went over to her school bag and took out her math book. She opened it and held it up so that Craig could see the scorch marks.

'What's this?' asked Craig. 'Don't tell me Ammy's been smoking.'

Ruth said, 'No. These aren't cigarette burns. A cigarette tip has a mean temperature of six hundred degrees Celsius and it would have created much darker and narrower marks. Besides, I may not have a nose as sensitive as Tyson's but I would have smelled the tobacco tar.'

'So . . . what caused them?'

'Ammy's fingers. That's what she told me, anyhow. She says that when she was burning up, she had her hand resting on the page, and when she lifted it up the paper was scorched.'

Craig frowned. 'That's not possible.' Then he said, 'Is it? I mean, you're the fire expert.'

'Jack was talking yesterday about spontaneous human combustion. You know, when people catch alight for no explicable reason.'

'You don't think—'

'No, I don't. I don't believe in it. Well, I *shouldn't* believe in it.

But, you know, Ammy's so different. Maybe her fingers can give out intense localized heat, just for a second or two. Some people are natural conductors. But her fingertips weren't blistered. They're not even red.'

Craig looked at the marks even more intently. 'There has to be some explanation. You could take this book into the lab, couldn't you, and run some tests on it?'

At that moment Amelia came back downstairs again. Ruth hid the math book behind her back but Amelia said, 'It's all right, Mom. I know what you've been talking about. I really don't mind. I get it all the time at school.'

'I'm sorry, sweetheart,' said Ruth. 'We're worried about you, that's all.'

'I heard the voice again,' Amelia told her.

'When?'

'Only a minute ago, in my room. It was the same voice, inside my head. It said, "*Andie's ashes*".'

'"Andie's ashes?" Are you sure?'

Amelia nodded, and kept on nodding, like a dipping duck. 'It was him. I know it was. The Creepy Kid. I don't think he means me to hear him, but I do.'

Ruth went to the living-room window and looked out at the front yard, and Craig came up close behind her and laid his hand on her shoulder.

'I can't see him,' she said. There was nobody out on the street except for an elderly man in dark glasses and flappy gray shorts, walking an overweight spaniel.

'That's because he doesn't want you to see him. But he hasn't gone away.'

The phone suddenly warbled, right next to her, and it made Ruth start. Craig picked it up and said, 'Cutter's Kitchens. Craig Cutter here. How can I help you?'

He listened, and then he passed the receiver over to Ruth. 'It's Jack. He says they've found another one.'

SEVEN

S he lugged her heavy metal case along the corridor and into the open door of the victim's apartment. Tyson trotted close to heel behind her, but already he was sniffing and snuffling and letting out little sneezes of excitement.

Bob Kowalski was standing in the living-room talking to a young woman detective, Sandra Garnet. Detective Garnet was red-haired and freckly, with upswept eyeglasses and an olive green suit that was a little too tight across the rump, but she was very pretty and chatty and Bob Kowalski always said that he would have asked her to marry him if he hadn't been married already, and she hadn't been fifteen years too young for him.

'The vic's in the bathroom,' said Bob. 'Just as badly burned as yesterday's unfortunate young lady, but at least we're pretty sure who she is.'

Ruth looked around. She knew that this apartment complex on West Rainbow Drive, on the south-east side of Kokomo, had been built less than four-and-a-half years ago. Craig had been contracted to fit the kitchens, and it had been one of his first really big contracts.

It was poignantly obvious that the victim had lived here alone. A single pair of worn pink slippers was peeping out from under the couch, and on the kitchen counter stood a single yellow coffee mug with the name *Tilda* painted on it. Along the window sill there was an arrangement of framed photographs of a chubby, smiling young woman, some taken with a grumpy gray-haired woman who looked like her mother, and others with a group of girls in blue blazers and white blouses. No photographs with men.

Detective Garnet said, 'The deceased is too badly burned to identify one hundred per cent, but it's almost certain that it's Tilda Frieburg, who rents this apartment. She's a twenty-three-year-old tele-salesperson who works for Allstate Insurance, 452 West King Street.'

'What the hell happened in here?' asked Ruth. The glass-topped coffee table was shattered, with two of its legs splayed out, and the rug underneath it was rucked up. Several colorful cushions were scattered on the floor, all of them spattered with blood. In the far corner of the room, beside the door that led to the bathroom, rested an apple with teeth-marks in it. The beige carpet was stained with damp, and there was a strong, acrid odor in the room.

'It looks like Ms Frieburg was attacked by one or more assailants,' said Detective Garnet. 'And that funky smell you can smell, that's pee. At some point somebody urinated on the floor, either Ms Frieburg or the person or persons who assaulted her, so we have copious amounts of DNA. We don't yet know who the blood belongs to, but that won't be too difficult to identify. We have Ms Frieburg's hair from her hairbrush and we're contacting her doctor for her blood group. We've located her orthodontist, too.'

Jack came out of the bathroom, wearing a rustling blue Tyvek suit and latex gloves. 'Hi, boss. Come and get an eyeful of this.'

Tyson was inhaling the smell from the carpet enthusiastically, but Ruth said, 'Come on, boy. Heel.'

Val Minelli was still taking pictures in the bathroom, so the room kept flickering with photographic flash. It made the body in the bath look as if it were jolting and jerking in a vain attempt to jump out.

'Ever see anything like this?' said Jack. The young woman had been charred all over, and she was crouched in the same pugilistic position as the cadaver on the mattress on South McCann Street. Unusually, her eyes were open, although both eyeballs were amber. Her face was blackened and her lips were scarlet and raw, so that with her eyes wide open she looked like a hideous parody of a minstrel.

Ruth knelt down on the bath mat. There was a dirty gray tidemark all around the tub, which showed her that it must have been filled with water when the fire first ignited, to a depth of at least seventeen inches. The bath was empty now, except for some thick gray sludge at the bottom, underneath the cadaver. But down the sides there was a succession of streaky gray rings, like geological strata, and this told her that the water had not been emptied out through the waste pipe, but had *boiled* – and boiled with such ferocity that it had all evaporated. When she leaned forward she saw that the plug was still in.

Ruth stood up, opened her case, and took out her camera, too.

She took pictures of the cadaver, and the bath, and the entire bathroom. The tiled walls were thickly coated with smoke and human
grease, and so was the floor.

'Any footprints?' Ruth asked Val.

'Only three, by the door, and they were made by the super who
found her. Ms Frieburg had complained about her fridge rattling,
and he came in this afternoon to fix it for her. Thought she'd be
at work.'

Ruth stood staring at the cadaver and the filthy bathtub in which
it lay, and she felt totally baffled.

'How do you cremate somebody in a tubful of water?' she asked
Jack. 'How do you raise the water up to such a temperature that
it all boils away and you're left with nothing but a barbecued
body? This is an American standard bath so there must have been
at least forty-five gallons of water in here, even if the victim *was*
a little on the chubby side.'

'Maybe the perp found a way to use magnesium in some form,
or sodium. Both of those react violently with water when they
combust, don't they, and cleave all of the oxygen out of it? Your
famous exothermic reaction.'

'Well, we'll soon see when we analyze the residue,' said Ruth.
'But I still can't imagine how it was done. And how did this poor
young woman get herself so thoroughly broiled, as well as boiled?'

She let Tyson go sniffing around the bathroom, but he could
find no trace of any accelerants. Eventually he lay on the floor,
looking disconsolate, while Ruth and Jack finished taking photographs and samples.

Detective Garnet came in. 'Some goddamned conundrum, ain't
it?' she said. 'Do you think it could have been the same perpetrator as yesterday?'

'Wouldn't like to say for sure,' Jack said, dryly. 'I mean, you
don't often get two incinerations one after the other, only a few
miles apart from each other. But stranger things have happened.
Could be that some nut job saw yesterday's burning on the news,
and thought that this poor young lady deserved the same fate.'

'So far as we know, Tilda Frieburg was pretty well liked,' said
Detective Garnet. 'She had no ongoing relationships with any
men, or women for that matter. In fact, one of her friends said
that she had never had any relationships with anybody.'

'That's sad,' said Ruth.

'Yep,' added Jack. 'Just like the virgin postmistress. Returned unopened.'

Detective Garnet said, 'It also makes this whole case even more difficult to understand. It looks like she was chosen at random, just like Mrs Benfield was.'

'Well, you folks concentrate on *why* it happened,' Jack told her. 'We'll do our darndest to tell you how.'

While Val Minelli dusted the door and the tiled walls for fingerprints, Ruth and Jack took dozens of samples from the rings around the tub and scooped up all of the dark gray sludge at the bottom. They also cut pieces from the shower curtains, since the pale turquoise vinyl would have undergone various chemical changes, depending on the rate of heat release, and that would give them a measure of how intensely the fire had burned, and how fast.

Ruth talked to the super, a squinty-eyed man with an elaborate comb-over and a straggly gray moustache. She asked him if he had seen anybody around the apartment complex, not necessarily acting suspiciously, but anybody who looked as if they didn't really have any legitimate business there. No, he hadn't.

She asked him what he had smelled when he first opened Tilda Frieburg's apartment door.

'Barbecue.'

No chemical smell? No metallic smell? No smell like gasoline or varnish or paint-thinner?

'No, ma'am. Just barbecue. And piss.'

It was past seven thirty p.m. when Ruth eventually arrived home. She had called Craig and asked him to defrost a chili that she had made two weeks ago, and when she came in through the front door she could smell it.

Craig was sitting on the couch with his laptop open on the coffee table. He looked tired and harassed, and his hair was sticking up at the back.

'How's it going?' she asked him, standing behind the couch and massaging his shoulders.

'Crap. Eagle Estates have asked me to quote for a twelve-unit housing development out at Frankfort.'

'Well, that's hopeful, isn't it?'

'It would be, if they hadn't warned me that there are five other kitchen-fitting companies putting in bids, and that I need to trim my price right down to the bone. As it is, I'm practically cutting my legs off to save on shoe leather.'

'I'll go check the chili.'

She went through to the kitchen, with Tyson following her. She opened the oven and took out the glass casserole dish with the chili in it. She stirred it and tasted it. It was almost ready, but she had to try hard not to think about Tilda Frieburg's body, lying in the bathtub, with her charred minstrel face and her little black fists, as if she wanted to fight the whole world.

'How was your fire?' Craig called out. 'Eastwood Apartments, of all places. That seems like a lifetime ago.'

Ruth was opening up a can of Ol' Roy Hearty Cuts in Gravy Country Stew Flavor, for Tyson, who was licking his lips and doing a clickety little dance on the kitchen floor.

'It was . . . *weird*,' she called back. She spooned the dog food into Tyson's bowl and then went back into the living-room. 'The victim was burned in her bathtub. But when the fire first ignited, the tub was actually filled up with water.'

Craig did an exaggerated double-take. 'Huh? How do you set fire to somebody in a tubful of water?'

'Yes, that's what I'd like to know. Not only that, the water had all boiled away.'

'It wasn't that spontaneous what's-it's-name, was it? That spontaneous combustion thing that Jack was talking about.'

'SHC?' Ruth shook her head. 'I told you. I don't believe in it. The adult human body is made up of seventy per cent water. Can you think of anything less likely to burst into flame?'

Craig called Amelia downstairs and they sat around the kitchen table for supper, while *Old Christine* flickered on the TV in the living-room, with the sound turned down. Ruth forced herself to eat, although she found each mouthful increasingly difficult to swallow. But Amelia didn't seem to have any appetite at all, and sat slumped in her chair, prodding at the beans in her chili with her fork.

'Don't you like your chili, Ammy?' asked Ruth, at last. 'Did I make it too hot for you?'

'I think it's terrific,' said Craig. He had almost finished his meal, and was wiping his bowl with a torn-off piece of tortilla. 'Best one you've made in a long time. *Muy picante,* just the way I like it!'

'Actually, I'm not really hungry,' said Amelia, and put down her fork. 'Is it all right if I leave the table?'

'Hey, sweetheart, are you feeling OK? You're not feeling worried again, are you?'

'I'm fine. I'm not hungry is all.'

Craig was about to say something but Ruth touched her finger to her lips and gave him a look which meant: *don't*.

Amelia went upstairs to her room, while Ruth and Craig cleared the table and stacked the dishwasher.

'Maybe she's in love,' Craig suggested. 'That hot flush she had in school today. Maybe it's hormones.'

'I don't know. I never knew hormones burn paper before.'

'I'll bet you anything she's in love. Maybe she has a crush on her math teacher.'

'Have you *seen* her math teacher? He looks like PeeWee Herman.'

Ruth allowed Amelia twenty minutes on her own, and then she went upstairs. As she approached Amelia's door she could hear her singing that song again.

'*I wonder where he's going*
With that smile upon his face.
I wonder if he knows it's going to rain.'

She knocked, and waited, and then Amelia said, 'It's OK. You can come in if you want to.'

Inside Amelia's bedroom, it was dark, except for the orange street light that flickered behind the basswood tree. Amelia was standing at the window, staring out.

Ruth went up to her and said, 'What is it?'

'I told you. The door's open and people are trying to come through.'

'I know you told me, Ammy, but I still don't quite understand what you mean.'

Amelia turned and looked at her. The shadows of the leaves danced on her face and made it appear as if her expression kept altering: from laughing to angry, from angry to indifferent, and then laughing again. Ruth found it strangely unnerving.

Amelia made a complicated beckoning gesture with both hands. 'It's the same as you coming into my bedroom from downstairs. That's where they're coming from, downstairs.'

'Downstairs where? You mean *here*? Downstairs in our house?'

Amelia shook her head. 'Downstairs everywhere. Downstairs where it's *hot*. That's where they always have to go. But now they want to come back up. Somebody's opened up the door and come through and now they *all* want to come through.'

Ruth said nothing. She still couldn't understand what Amelia was talking about, but whatever it was it seemed to be disturbing her deeply, and Ruth didn't want to make her feel even more anxious by asking her *which* door, and *what* people, and what did these people want?

She would ask Doctor Feldstein about it tomorrow. Doctor Feldstein had suggested a course of psychotherapy late last year, when Amelia had developed a phobia for going outside in traffic, but at the time Ruth had argued against it. Amelia was already undergoing a strict physical regime for the genetic weakness in her heart and the difficulty she had in swallowing food, and Ruth hadn't wanted her to feel even more different than she already did. She knew that many young people with William's Syndrome displayed signs of acute anxiety, but this was mostly because of their hyperacusis, their heightened sense of hearing – hence her fear of going out in traffic. Most of the time Amelia was loving, sociable and confident. It was only in the past two or three days that she had started to say that she felt worried.

Apart from that, with Craig's business in so much financial trouble, Ruth doubted if they could afford a psychotherapist.

'These people,' she told Amelia, 'they're not really real.'

'Yes they are. They *were*, anyhow.'

'What do you mean, they *were*? You're not talking about ghosts, are you?'

'Sort of, some of them. It depends.'

'Ammy, there is no such thing as ghosts. They're just stories that people make up to frighten themselves. And it sounds like this is what *you're* doing. Making up a story about people coming through some imaginary door, people from downstairs. I don't know why you're doing it. Maybe you need to change your medication. But it's all in your mind, I promise you.'

'Then what about *him*?' asked Amelia, pointing out of the window.

Ruth looked out. The boy in the black T-shirt and the red jeans was standing next to the basswood tree, staring up at her.

'Him? He's not a ghost, Ammy. He's just an ordinary boy, and I'm getting pretty tired of him hanging around our house.'

She pushed her way out of Amelia's bedroom and ran down-stairs. She crossed the hallway and pulled open the front door. Craig was watching TV in the living-room and he called out, 'Hey! Ruth? Ruthie – what the hell's going on?'

She didn't stop to answer him. She ran down the steps and across the front lawn until she reached the tree. And again, just like the last time, and the time she had tried to catch up with him on South McCann Street, he wasn't there. She stopped, and looked around, and listened, but she couldn't even hear the sound of sneakers slapping along the sidewalk as the boy ran away.

She was still standing there when an old black Buick Riviera came softly burbling along the street. It slowed down as it passed her, and she could see three men inside it, who seemed to be staring at her. The Buick's windows were coated in brown dust, but she could see that their faces were very white, as if they were wearing masks.

She stepped backward, away from the curb, but as she did so the Buick gunned its engine and drove away. She saw its red brake lights as it stopped at the intersection with North Courtland Avenue, but then it took a right and disappeared.

Craig came out of the house. Ruth looked up at Amelia's bedroom window and she could see her staring down. She waved, but Amelia didn't wave back.

'What the hell are you doing?' Craig asked her. 'You haven't seen the Creepy Kid again?'

'He was here, I swear it.'

Craig looked up and down the street. 'So where is he now?'

'I don't know. It must have been a trick of the light, that's all.'

'Maybe I should call the cops?'

'No, don't do that. We'd only be wasting their time.'

'OK. But if you see him again . . .'

They walked back to the house. Before she closed the front door, however, Ruth took a quick look back at the street. She was sure that she could see a figure standing close to the trunk of the basswood tree, but then it might have been nothing more than a complicated shadow, or an optical illusion, an imaginary boy made out of their mailbox and the next-door hedge.

Upstairs, she went back into Amelia's bedroom. Amelia had

drawn the drapes now, and was taking out her clothes, ready for the morning: her bobbly red sweater, her long brown skirt.

'He wasn't there,' Ruth told her. 'By the time I got there, he'd gone.'

'You shouldn't go near him, in any case,' said Amelia.

'Why not? Do you think he's dangerous?'

'It's all because of him. That's why the door's open. That's why all of these people want to come through.'

'Ammy—'

Amelia came up to her and there were tears in her eyes. 'Mommy, I can't explain it. I know it's happening, but I don't know why.' She pressed her hands over her ears and said, 'There's so much noise! So many people talking and shouting and crying and trying to get through.'

Ruth held her tight. 'Don't you worry, sweetheart. Whatever it is, we'll find a way to close that door again.'

She glanced toward the bedroom door. Craig was standing in the corridor outside. All he could do was raise his eyebrows and give her a sympathetic shake of his head.

EIGHT

They went to bed early, with two large glasses of Shiraz. Craig watched *CSI: Miami*, while Ruth tried to finish the cryptic crossword in the *Kokomo Tribune*. During a commercial break, Craig said, 'So, like – even Ammy herself doesn't know why she's feeling so anxious?'

Ruth took off her reading glasses. 'Maybe it's her meds. But she's growing up, Craig, and Dr Feldstein always warned us that girls with William's Syndrome grow up quicker than other girls. Apart from that, she's so different, and when you're that age, you never want to be the odd one out.'

'Maybe you should talk to Dr Feldstein about that therapy.'

'Well, I can *talk* to him about it, for sure. Whether we can afford it is another question altogether.'

She went back to her crossword. Craig sat and looked at her for a while without saying anything.

'What?' she said, taking off her glasses again.

'Nothing. It's just that I hate to see her so fretful. She's not being bullied, is she?'

'Not so far as I know. Come on, Craig, we always knew this was going to be difficult. All we can do is support her, and listen to her, and teach her to turn her disadvantages into assets.'

Craig thought about that, and then shrugged. 'I guess God has His reasons for everything, even William's Syndrome.'

'Yes,' said Ruth. 'But sometimes I wish I knew what the hell His reasons were.'

'*Ruth*!' said Craig. His father had been a Methodist minister, and he was still sensitive to blasphemy.

She picked up the remote, switched the sound on again, and returned to seventeen across. *Dead body in a vehicle*.

After a minute or two, Craig said, 'Why does he always pose like that?'

'Who?'

'David Caruso. The guy who plays Horatio. Why does he always pose like that, with his sunglasses on top of his head and his hands on his hips? How would you like it if I went around posing like that?'

'You can go around posing like that if you want to. It's a free country. But I can't guarantee that I wouldn't choke myself laughing.'

Craig was about to retaliate when the phone rang. Ruth picked it up, and a voice said, 'Ms Cutter? This is Trooper Kelly Farjeon, ISP. Sorry to tell you there's been a ten-fifty on the Davis Road at the intersection with Jewel Road, involving your son Jeffrey.'

'Oh my God, what's happened? Is he hurt?'

'No, ma'am, I'm happy to say. He's pretty damp, though. Looks like a steering-link broke and his car went off the highway and ended up in a lake.'

'Where is he now?'

'The tow truck's just arrived to pull the car out. Soon as we've supervised that, we'll bring him home to you.'

'Thank you, Trooper. You're sure he's OK?'

'Nothing hurt apart from his pride, ma'am.'

Jeff was brought home about twenty-five minutes later, wrapped in a thick brown blanket. He had an angry crimson bruise across the bridge of his nose, and a face like thunder, but apart from that he appeared to be unscathed. He handed the blanket back to the State Trooper who had given him a ride, and then stamped upstairs to his bedroom.

'How about his car?' asked Craig.

'I'm afraid that's headed for the Carter Street parking facility,' said the trooper. He meant the thirty-acre scrap metal site on the east side of Kokomo, by the railroad spur. 'You should go out there tomorrow, talk to the foreman. If you're lucky he'll give you twenty bucks for it.'

'Thank you, anyhow,' said Ruth. 'I'm relieved Jeff wasn't injured, that's all.'

'So are we, ma'am. But there's a few ducks out there suffering from shock.'

When the trooper had gone, Craig and Ruth locked up the house again and went upstairs. Craig knocked on Jeff's door and said, 'Jeff? Everything OK?'

Jeff didn't answer so he opened the door and they stepped inside. Jeff was lying on his bed in his crimson Indiana Hoosier hooded sweatshirt and scrub pants, with his iPod in his ears, texting furiously on his cellphone.

They waited until he had finished his message and then Craig made a lifting gesture to indicate that he should take out his earphones.

'I'm *OK*, OK?' Jeff protested.

'Glad to hear it,' said Craig. 'Do you mind telling us what exactly happened?'

'You really want to know? We were driving south on Davis and I was hanging a right on to Jewel when there was this, like, *bang*!, and we went clear off the highway and straight through all of these bushes and, like, ker-*sploosh*!, we drove right into this frigging lake that somebody had left there.'

'*Language*,' said Ruth, sharply.

'You want to hear language?' Jeff retorted. 'You should of heard what Lennie and me were shouting out when we started to sink. If that lake'd been any deeper than four feet we would of drowned.'

'The lake was only four feet deep?' Ruth asked him.

'It was still wet, Mom, and I still drove my car right into it.'

Ruth looked at Craig and she was trying very hard not to laugh. But Craig's expression was serious. He sat down on the end of Jeff's bed and said, 'Listen, we're sorry for what happened to you, and we're really glad that you and Lennie didn't get hurt. We should have made sure that you had a decent car to drive.'

Jeff said, 'Forget it, Dad. I know you don't have the money. I'll just have to get a job, like you said.'

'Believe me, Jeff, if we *did* have the money—'

'I know, Dad. I know. You'd buy me a brand-new Mustang Bullitt, in midnight black, with black-tinted windows and a Magnaflow exhaust, right? But you don't have the money, so you can't, so forget it.'

Craig continued to sit there for a little while longer, while Jeff replaced his earphones and closed his eyes. Ruth could see how hurt Craig was, how inadequate he felt, and she stroked the fine gray hair at the back of his neck.

'Come on,' she coaxed him. 'Let's go back to bed. You don't want to miss *Special Victims Unit*, do you?'

Shortly before dawn, Craig shifted himself closer to her and slid his hand up her thigh, underneath her nightshirt. He gently stroked her with his fingertip, and then slipped his finger inside her. She felt herself becoming slippery, and a warm sensation began to rise between her legs.

'*Craig,*' she whispered, and kissed his eyelids and his lips and his ears.

He tugged her nightshirt up around her waist, and she lifted her hips to help him. Then he climbed on top of her, kissing her in that hungry way he used to kiss her when they first went out together.

'*You're so beautiful,*' he breathed. '*I love you so much.*'

When he tried to put himself inside her, however, he was still too soft. She reached down and took hold of him and stroked his penis up and down, harder and harder, but it still refused to stiffen.

After a few moments he rolled off her and fell back on to his pillow. 'Sorry,' he said. 'Guess I'm not such a love god after all.'

She snuggled up close to him and gave him an intimate squeeze. 'You need to stop worrying, that's all. It's the stress. We can try again later.'

'I'm no damn good at anything, am I?' he told her. 'Can't keep my business going. Can't pay the mortgage. Can't even make love to my wife.'

Ruth stroked his chest. 'You're the best man that any woman could wish for. You're the best husband. You're the best father. You're the best lover, too.'

'Oh, really? I can't make any money, I give you one daughter with a chromosome disorder, and a son who thinks he's a latter-day Fonzie. I can't even get my dick up.'

'Shh,' said Ruth. 'You're beginning to depress me.'

Craig had been very close to tears, but now he let out a burst of laughter. 'You're right,' he said. 'It *is* pretty depressing, isn't it? Thank God I'm an optimist.'

NINE

The next morning, it was still so dark at eight a.m. that it looked like the end of the world, and as though they would never see the sun again. A furious gale was blowing from the south-west, and rain was sweeping across the road and flooding the gutters. The basswood tree was thrashing its branches as if it had gone berserk and was trying to uproot itself.

Ruth had arranged to take two hours off so that she could take Amelia to see Doctor Feldstein. Before she left the house, however, she called Jack to find out how his tests on Tilda Frieburg's bathtub were progressing.

'Pretty good,' he told her. 'I've started to analyze the sludge we found at the bottom of the bath, and I should know what its principal constituents are in a couple of hours. And by the way, the shower curtains are telling me a very contradictory story. If that fire was intense enough to boil away that bathwater and cremate that unfortunate young lady, it should have melted the curtains completely.'

'I thought that, too. Do you have any theories about that?'

'I can only guess that the seat of the fire was highly concentrated, and that there was very little radiant heat outside of the bathtub itself. How that could have occurred, I have no idea whatsoever, apart from my original thought that maybe it was an exochemical reaction, set off by magnesium or sodium. But my tests on the sludge will probably tell us.'

'OK, Jack. I should be into the lab by lunchtime.'

'You take your time. Amelia always comes first. Oh – and by the way, I had a call from Detective Magruder. The ME has confirmed the vic's identity. It *was* Tilda Frieburg. The cops are round at her place of work now, interviewing her colleagues.'

'Thanks, Jack. I'll see you later. I have some strawberry short-cake left over from dinner last night. Do you want me to bring you a slice?'

'When you die, boss, they're going to make you an honorary angel.'

Ruth helped Amelia to button up her bright yellow waterproof, and then she put on her own black raincoat and pulled up the hood. The two of them ran hand-in-hand across the front yard through the clattering rain, with Tyson bounding after them. Just as they climbed into Ruth's car, there was a devastating cannonade of thunder, which almost seemed to split the air apart. Amelia screamed and clung on to Ruth's arm, and even Tyson started to bark.

'They're coming closer!' Amelia panted. 'I know they are! They're coming closer!'

'Hush, Ammy. It's only an old electric storm. It'll pass over in a while.'

'But something bad is going to happen. Something *worse*.'

'Ammy, sweetheart, you mustn't allow yourself to get hysterical. Just remember that everything sounds much louder to you than it does to everybody else. It's part of your condition.'

'It's not just the noise. I can *feel* them.'

'Come on, sweetheart. Let's get you to Doctor Feldstein. I'm sure he'll be able to tell you that everything's fine.'

Amelia stared at her, her green eyes wide. 'They never knew that they could come back. They thought they had to stay downstairs. But now they've found out that they don't have to.'

Ruth leaned across and held Amelia close. She was shaking, as if she were suffering from hypothermia. Ruth didn't know what to say to her. It was obviously no use trying to convince her that 'they' were only a delusion. All she could do was try to reassure Amelia that she wasn't in any real danger.

After a while Ruth gave her a kiss on the forehead, and said, 'OK? You ready to go now?'

Amelia nodded. But as Ruth backed out of the driveway and into the street, there was another deafening barrage of thunder, and Amelia cowered down in her seat with her hands clamped over her ears.

At the same time, over on North Jay Street, opposite Bon Air Park, Neville Ferris was pushing Mrs Ida Mae Lutz along the pathway from her house to the white Spirit of Kokomo bus that was waiting at the curb.

Mrs Lutz could walk unaided, but the morning was so wet and windy that Neville was using the wheelchair to pick up all of his passengers. He had collected seven of them so far. Three of them were headed for St Joseph's Hospital, two for the Fewell Eye Clinic, one for the Grace United Methodist Church, and one for lunch at the Senior Citizens' Center.

'One hell of a day, isn't it?' shouted Mrs Lutz. She was one of the feistiest of Neville's regular pick-ups – a handsome seventy-seven-year-old who had once been a minor TV actress. She was always smartly dressed, although today she was wearing a bright red vinyl raincoat and a matching sou'wester.

'Wasn't forecast, this storm,' said Neville. 'Don't think those weather people got the first idea.'

He parked the wheelchair beside the bus and opened up the door. Then he helped Mrs Lutz to climb the steps and find her usual seat right behind his.

'Morning, everybody!' said Mrs Lutz, taking off her sou'wester and shaking her white bouffant hair. 'One hell of a day today, isn't it?'

'Morning, Ida!' the rest of the passengers chorused, all except for Mr Thorson, who had throat cancer, and could only croak.

Neville folded up the wheelchair and locked it in place in the wheel-well. Then he started up the bus and called out, 'Hold tight, everybody! First stop, Fewell Eye Clinic!'

He pulled away from the curb, but the rain was lashing so hard against his windshield that he didn't see the Buick Riviera until it overtook him and slewed across in front of him, at an angle. He stamped on his brake pedal and the bus jolted to a halt. Mrs Betty Petersen, who was eighty-four years old, was thrown on to the floor, and Mr Carradine knocked his teeth against the seat in front of him.

Neville said, 'What in the name of—?' Then he twisted around in his seat and said, 'Everybody OK? Anybody hurt? Mrs Petersen – are you all right?'

He made his way to the back of the bus and helped Mrs Petersen back up on to her seat. He found her eyeglasses on the floor and carefully placed them back on her nose.

'I'm fine,' she told him. 'I just hit my knee.'

'Mr Carradine? Your lip's bleeding.'

'Don't you worry, Neville. I bit myself, that's all. If I need any fixing, they can fix me up at St Joseph's.'

Neville went back to the front of the bus, opened the door and stepped down on to the road. The rain was hammering down now, so hard that he had to shield his face with his hand. The Buick remained in front of the bus, its engine running. It was an old car, 1969 or 1970, with a boat-tail trunk, and its steeply-angled rear window made it impossible for Neville to see who was inside it.

He approached the driver's door and knocked on the window. 'What do you think you're doing, man? I got seniors here, two of them got hurt! Get this piece of junk out of my way before I call for the cops!'

At first there was no response. Raindrops continued to course down the Buick's window, and even when Neville wiped them away with his hand, he still couldn't clearly see the driver.

'Did you hear what I said? Get out my way, man! If you don't, I'm going to call for the cops right now!'

There was a huge barrage of thunder, and the trees in Bon Air Park all thrashed around in panic. Before the thunder had died away, the Buick's driver turned and stared at Neville through the window. His face was utterly white, and to Neville's horror he appeared to be screaming with laughter. Neville said, '*Shee*-it!' and took two stumbling steps backward in shock.

The car's door opened, and the driver climbed out. He was tall, and wearing a long black raincoat and black leather gloves, and now that he was standing outside the car Neville could see that his white face was a mask. The rain rattled against it, and ran down its cheeks, so that it seemed to be laughing so much that it was crying.

'I don't know what you want, man,' said Neville, 'but you'd better get the hell out of here. I got seniors here, and if anything happens to any of them, you're going to be in real deep shit, I warn you.'

The man in the laughing mask came closer, and Neville backed away.

'Calm down, Rastus,' said the laughing man, in a muffled, card-boardy voice. 'We're not here to cause you any trouble. We're here to perform us a little ceremony, that's all.'

'*Ceremony*? What in the *hell* you talking about? And who's "we"?'

At that moment, the Buick's passenger door opened and another two men climbed out. These two were also dressed in long black raincoats, and both wore white masks, except that one was utterly expressionless and the other was scowling in rage. They came around the back of the car and stood on either side of the laughing man, with their arms folded. Neville smeared the rain from his face with the back of his hand, but it was still raining so hard that water was running from his nose and his chin.

'We need to perform an *ex*-orcism,' said the laughing man.

'Say *what*?'

'An exorcism. You know what an exorcism is, don't you, Rastus? You must have seen the movie. Linda Blair's head rotating around and around, and jabbing herself in the muff with that crucifix.'

'You're nuts,' said Neville. 'Why don't you get out of here before you do something you are seriously going to regret.'

'Too late for regrets,' said the laughing man. 'Much too late for *any* regrets, serious or otherwise. Now, why don't you climb back on to your bus and announce to your geriatric flock that we intend to come aboard, and whatever we ask them to do, they had better cooperate, without any argument, or else it's going to be very much the worse for them.'

'I can't do that,' Neville retorted. 'I'm responsible for these people's welfare, and if you think I'm going to allow you anywhere near them, then you're a whole lot crazier than you look.'

'Well, that's very noble,' said the laughing man. He turned to the expressionless man and then to the scowling man. 'Don't you think that's very noble?'

The two of them nodded in agreement, and the scowling man said, 'Very, *very* noble,' and let out a high-pitched snort of amusement.

The laughing man took another step closer to Neville, and Neville took another step back, until he was standing with his back pressed against the bus.

The laughing man's voice was barely audible above the drumming of the rain on the bus's roof. 'You have one chance of survival, Rastus, and that is to do what we tell you, no questions asked. You got that?'

Neville swung at him, one of the southpaw punches that had won him the Indiana Golden Gloves Junior Championship. But he had been seventeen then, and now he was fifty-four, and nearly four decades slower. The laughing man whipped up his right forearm and deflected the blow before it was even halfway to hitting him.

Without hesitation, the laughing man punched Neville in the stomach, hard, just below his breastbone, and Neville let out a '*dah*!' of pain, colliding with the bus behind him and then dropping on one knee to the asphalt.

'Do I have to repeat myself?' said the laughing man. He coughed, and coughed again, and it was several seconds before he was able to continue. Neville was gasping, too, desperately trying to get his breath back.

Eventually, the laughing man said, 'If you don't do what I tell you, Rastus, then believe me I will make you wish on your mother's grave that you had.'

The scowling man came forward and shoved Neville's shoulder with the heel of his hand. 'You need to listen up, feller,' he put in. 'You wouldn't want to be wishing that wish in a falsetto voice, now, would you? Because that's what you'd be doing.'

'Now, up on your feet,' the laughing man ordered him. 'We need to get this exorcism started.'

A white panel van approached them, driving southward with its headlights on and its windshield wipers flapping at full speed. It slowed down as it came nearer, and the driver put down his window. Neville saw the words *Eli's Electrics* stenciled in red on the side. The driver looked as if he were about to call out to them and ask them if they needed any help, but then the scowling man and the expressionless man turned around and confronted him, and he obviously thought better of it, and accelerated away. Neville tried to shout out, 'Call the cops!', but he was too winded to get the words out, and all he could manage was an aspirate wheeze.

The scowling man and the expressionless man came up on either side of him and took hold of his arms. They dragged him up on to his feet, and then forced him up the steps into the bus. His eight elderly passengers all stared up at him anxiously, and Mrs Lutz said, 'What is it, Neville? Who are these men? What's happening? Are you all right?'

Mr Kaminsky said, 'Is this a stick-up?'

'No, sir,' said the laughing man. 'This isn't a stick-up.'

'Oh, no? If this isn't a stick-up, why are you wearing masks?'

'Neville, what's going on?' asked Miss Elwood, peering at him through her half-glasses. She reached into her purse and held up her cellphone. 'Do you want me to dial 911?'

'Nobody's going to dial nothing,' said the laughing man.

He jerked his head at the scowling man, and the scowling man made his way down the bus and tugged Miss Elwood's cellphone out of her hand.

'*Hey!*' she protested, but the scowling man slapped her hard on the side of the head.

'You leave her alone, you goddamned coward!' quavered Mr Kaminsky, rising from his seat, but the scowling man slapped him, too, and he fell backward and hit his head against the window, knocking one lens out of his spectacles.

'Give me your cells, all of them!' the scowling man demanded.

'I most certainly will *not*!' Mrs Tiplady retorted. Mrs Tiplady had been head teacher of a private girls' school, and although she wore a pink eyepatch on her right eye and her upper lip was whiskery, she still cut an imperious figure.

The scowling man punched her in the face, breaking the bridge of her nose with an audible crack. Blood spurted out of her nostrils and down her chin, spattering on to her raincoat. Mrs Tiplady cupped her hand over her nose, whimpering, while the scowling man wrenched open her pocketbook and tipped out the contents on to the seat next to her.

'Give me your cells, you dried-up bunch of old coots!' he barked. 'And I mean *now*!' The remaining passengers all fumbled in their pockets and their purses and brought out their phones. The scowling man snatched them one by one and then dropped them on to the floor of the bus with a clatter and stamped on them.

'You *pigs*!' cried Miss Elwood. 'You total *pigs*!'

The scowling man went back along the bus and slapped her again, twice. Miss Elwood started to weep.

The laughing man said, 'Anybody else have anything to say? If you have, you can say it, but it's going to make your life expectancy a whole lot shorter than it is already. You hear?'

He turned to Neville and said, 'Sit down, Rastus, and get this bus started. Drive us into the park.'

Neville was trembling with anger at his own impotence. He was supposed to take care of these old folks, supposed to protect them, but he couldn't.

'I'm not doing it, man,' he said. 'There is absolutely no way.'

'*Knife*,' said the laughing man. The expressionless man produced a large clasp knife from his raincoat pocket and passed it over. The laughing man pried it open, coughing as he did so. He held it up in front of Neville's face and said, 'If you defy me one more time, Rastus, I'm going to put out one of your eyes and I'm going to stick it on the end of this shank so that you can see it with your other eye. Then I'm going to put out that eye, too. And then I'm going to cut off your floppy black dick and I'm going to make you eat it. And if you don't think I'm deadly serious, here's a taster.'

With that, he turned the knife around, lifted his fist, and stabbed Neville right in the middle of his forehead. Neville shouted out, '*Ah!*' and clamped his hand to his head, and as he did so the laughing man stabbed him through the back of his hand, too.

'*Now* do you think I'm kidding?' asked the laughing man, in his thick, asthmatic voice.

'Go on, Neville!' called out Mr Kaminsky. 'Do like he says! *Please*! We don't want to see you getting hurt!'

The laughing man turned around and said, 'I thought I told you all to shut the fuck up! But that's good advice, grandpa. Wouldn't like to see this poor guy eyeless and dickless, would we, just on account of some misguided point of honor?'

The scowling man got off the bus and went over to the Buick. Meanwhile, Neville sat down in the driver's seat, with a runnel of blood dripping down the middle of his nose. He started up the bus's engine and closed the doors. It was raining even harder now, and he had to switch the windshield wipers on at full speed.

The scowling man started up the Buick, too, and drove it slowly over the curb, across the sidewalk, and on to the grass of Bon Air Park. Neville looked around, hoping that some passer-by would notice that something very unusual was going on, but there was nobody in sight.

'What are you waiting for, Rastus?' said the laughing man. 'Follow him, and stay real close.'

Neville steered the bus over the sidewalk and across the grass. His passengers were jostled from side to side as he drove over the curb, but none of them said a word. Mrs Tiplady was dabbing at her nose with a blood-soaked tissue and Miss Elwood was still quietly sobbing, while Mr Kaminsky was trying in vain to fit the right lens back into his spectacles.

The Buick slowly made its way between the trees, and Neville followed, making sure that he kept no more than ten feet behind it.

The rain continued to drum on the roof of the bus, with occa-
sional syncopated patters as they drove beneath the branches.

After a few minutes, when they were out of sight of the road,
the Buick stopped, and Neville stopped the bus, too. Through the
ribs of rain that were running down the windshield, Neville saw
the scowling man climb out of the Buick, open its trunk, and take
out a large gray laundry bag. He came up to the side of the bus
and the laughing man said to Neville, 'Open the door, Rastus.'

The scowling man climbed up into the bus. He tugged open
the cord of the laundry bag and tipped its contents on to the floor:
a crumpled assortment of hospital gowns, with pale green patterns
on them. They were all filthy, stained with what looked like dried
blood and excrement, and they smelled sweaty and sour.

The laughing man leaned down and picked one up. He held it
up so that everybody on the bus could see it, and said, 'We're
going to perform our ceremony now and these are your ceremonial
robes.'

'What?' said Mr Carradine. 'You don't expect us to put those
on? They're disgusting!'

'Hey, grandpa, did I give you permission to speak?' the laughing
man snapped at him. 'Did I say you could question what we're
doing here? No, I did not. So shut up and do as you're told. You
don't even deserve an explanation, but I'm going to be good enough
to give you one.'

The bus passengers turned and looked at each other and all of
their faces were drawn with fear. Even Mr Kaminsky's eyes were
filled with tears, and he hadn't cried since his wife died five years
ago.

'Now then,' said the laughing man, 'this is what you old coots
are going to do for me. You're going to pretend that you're dementia
patients, those of you who aren't half-demented already. You're
going to dress the part and you're going to act the part. Any one
of you who doesn't is going to be sorry.'

Neville said, 'Man, you can't do this! These people, they're
completely defenseless!'

The laughing man laid a hand on his shoulder. 'That's the point,
Rastus. That's entirely the point.'

TEN

Amelia stood at the window of Doctor Feldstein's consulting room, staring out at the rain. The thunder was further away now, rumbling in the distance, but it still appeared to unsettle her. She repeatedly twisted the pink ribbon in her hair, around and around, and whenever it thundered she started to pant, as if she were panicking.

Doctor Feldstein leaned forward in his chair and picked up Amelia's notes. 'I'll tell you, Ruth, I don't honestly think that these anxiety attacks are triggered by Amelia's meds. The benzo-thiazepine seems to be keeping her vascular dilation in check, without upsetting her digestion, and the dicycloverine has been working a treat for her colic. Is she still taking telcagepant capsules for her migraines?'

Ruth nodded. 'They're fine. They don't make her sick like that Zomig. But if it's not her meds, I can't think what else could have started this off.'

Doctor Feldstein stood up. He was very tall, over six-two, with wild black hair, thick horn-rimmed spectacles and a nose like a predatory hawk. He had taken an unfailing interest in Amelia's progress ever since she was born, and he had followed every development in the treatment of William's Syndrome so closely that he had become something of an expert on it.

He laid his large hairy hand on Amelia's shoulder, and looked down at her with a benevolent smile. 'It could be that you're simply growing up, Amelia. Lots of young women suffer from anxiety attacks when their hormones are out of whack, and you're more sensitive to any changes in your body chemistry than most.

'All the same,' he said, 'why don't you talk to Doctor Beech? She may be able to suggest a way in which you can handle this anxiety – put it in perspective for you.'

'Doctor Beech is a psychiatrist,' said Ruth. 'You don't really think that Ammy needs a *shrink*?'

'I don't know. Considering her condition, she seems to be in excellent health, so apart from a hormonal imbalance I can't see any *physical* cause for her anxiety. There's no harm in her talking to Doctor Beech, is there? And there might be some genuine benefit.'

The thunder grumbled again, out to the north-east, over the airport. It seemed to be prowling around the city like a junkyard dog. Amelia looked up at Doctor Feldstein wide-eyed, and her breathing quickened. 'Don't you worry, young lady,' he told her. 'We'll get to the bottom of this, and before long you'll be laughing about it, believe me.'

He went back to his desk, pressed his intercom and said, 'Zelda? Are you free right now? That's great. There's somebody I'd very much like you to meet.'

After a few minutes, the door to Doctor Feldstein's consulting room opened and Doctor Beech came in. She was mid-thirties, with a mass of brunette curls, and a heart-shaped face. She was wearing a tight black skirt and a gray silk blouse that was open at least two more buttons than Ruth would have worn it, but unlike Ruth she had very small breasts and she wasn't even wearing a bra.

'Zelda, this is Amelia. You remember we were talking about the bright young lady with WS? This is her, and this is her mother, Ruth.'

'Hey, I'm *so* pleased to know you,' said Doctor Beech. 'You work for the Fire Department, don't you, Ruth? I was reading about you in the *Trib* the other day. Such a fascinating job that must be.'

'Very dull, most of the time,' Ruth told her. 'Most of the time it's insurance fraud, especially these days. Bankrupt restaurateurs leaving the gas on, or realtors dropping lighted cigarettes into wastebaskets.'

'Our local dry-cleaner burned out last week,' said Doctor Beech. 'Sparkleen, on Home Avenue? I lost two dresses and my favorite white sweater. You didn't investigate that one, did you?'

'I shouldn't tell you this, but the Sparkleen fire was arson,' Ruth told her. 'The owner splashed perc around, but perc vapors never ignite spontaneously, so I knew at once that it was deliberate.'

'In that case, I shall definitely sue,' Doctor Beech smiled. 'And you can be my expert witness.'

Doctor Feldstein said, 'Amelia here has been having some worries, haven't you, Amelia?'

'OK,' said Doctor Beech. 'Why don't you sit down and tell me about them? You don't mind your mom being here, do you, or Doctor Feldstein?'

Amelia shook her head. She sat on the tapestry couch beside the window, holding an embroidered cushion on her lap, and Doctor Beech sat down next to her.

Doctor Beech said, 'So . . . what have you been worried about, Amelia?'

Amelia hesitated for a moment, and then she said, very quietly, 'People coming through.'

'I see. What people?'

'They come from downstairs. They didn't realize before now that they could come back through, but now they do.'

'When you say "downstairs", is that downstairs at your house?'

'No.' Amelia thought for a moment, and then she said, 'Actually, it's more like *underneath* than downstairs.'

'Underneath where? Underneath *here*? Underneath this floor?'

'Underneath everywhere. They had to go there but now they've found a way to come back up.'

'Do you know who they are? Have you seen them?'

'I've seen one of them. He's a boy. He was standing outside our house yesterday and the day before and he wears a black T-shirt and red jeans and he's creepy. I call him the Creepy Kid because he's so creepy.'

'I've seen him too,' Ruth put in. 'I saw him on Tuesday on South McCann Street, when I was attending that fire there, and I saw him on both occasions outside of our house. He wasn't doing anything. He was just standing there, staring.'

'So he's a real kid, this Creepy Kid?'

'Yes,' said Ruth. 'Except that each time I tried to confront him to ask him what he was doing there, he vanished. Like, totally without trace. I even took a photograph of him on South McCann Street – at least I *thought* I took a photograph of him – but he didn't appear in it.'

Doctor Beech turned back to Amelia. 'So the Creepy Kid is the only one of these people you've actually seen? You haven't seen any of the others?'

Amelia shook her head again.

'OK . . . but if you haven't seen them, how do you know for sure that they're there?'

'Because I *know* they are. Because I can feel them, and I can *hear* them.'

'What kind of feeling do they give you? Can you describe it?'

Amelia closed her eyes for a moment. Then she slowly rubbed her upper arms, and said, 'Some of them are rough.'

'I see. What do you mean by rough? They act rough?'

'No, not really. They push each other. They're all trying to get through, like when people go to a ball game and they're all trying to get to the best seats first. But their *skin* is rough. It's all dry and flaky.'

'Can you think why that is? Do they have some kind of skin disease?'

'I don't think so. I don't know. I can just feel it.'

Doctor Beech sat and looked at Amelia for a few moments, with a faint frown on her face, thinking. Then she said, 'You told me that only some of them are rough. Are there any others who aren't rough?'

Amelia nodded. 'Lots of them. They're more like dust than people. And they whisper. *Whisper-whisper-whisper.* It's like they're all whispering together. It's like sand, when the wind blows it.'

'Like sand, when the wind blows it,' Doctor Beech repeated, as if she were trying to understand what Amelia meant. Then, 'How long would you say you've been having these feelings?'

'Not very long. Only since Tuesday. Mom had to go to that fire on South McCann Street, and when Uncle Jack called her I just felt like she shouldn't go. I mean I really, *really* felt like she shouldn't go.'

'Why did you feel like that? Can you explain it?'

'Because they'd find out who she was, and I didn't want them to.'

'You thought they might be some kind of threat?'

'I don't know. Yes. They scare me. I don't know what they're trying to do, but I know that it's something terrible.'

'And since Tuesday? How many times have you had the feelings since then?'

'Two or three times a day. More. But I always know in the back of my mind that they're coming, all the time.'

Doctor Beech took hold of Amelia's hands and gave her a reassuring smile. 'I think we can find a way to help you,' she said.

Then she turned to Ruth. 'You may not agree to this, and if you have any qualms about it at all, please say so. But I met a young man at a psychiatric seminar in Chicago last fall, and he had experienced some strikingly similar feelings to your Amelia. "Men and women are coming through from underneath," that's what he said.'

'Really? He used those exact words?'

Doctor Beech nodded. 'Not only that, but he spoke of a boy who kept watching his house. He seemed very rational, this young man – very sincere – but I'm afraid to say that I dismissed him as some kind of oddball at the time. You get a whole lot of *very* strange people at those seminars, especially at the fringe meetings. People who believe that plants have a consciousness, people who think that Down's Syndrome sufferers can communicate with aliens. But now I've talked to Amelia . . . well, unless you're dead set against it, I really would like to get in touch with this young man and see if he can help her to understand exactly *why* she's experiencing this particular anxiety.'

Ruth said, 'I'm not at all sure. I mean, when you say young, how old is he? And what exactly did he tell you about this "coming through from underneath" thing? I don't want to make Ammy's condition any worse. Does he think that – *what*? – it's all some kind of delusion? Or does he believe that it's real?'

Doctor Beech shrugged. 'To tell you the truth, I only spoke to him for five minutes. Like I say, I thought at first that he was just another oddball. But he said that he'd written a book about it. I can't remember what the title was, The Nine Circles of Something. Wait just a moment. I have his name and his number in my diary.'

While Doctor Beech went back to her office, Ruth looked across at Doctor Feldstein. 'What do *you* think, Doctor?' she asked him. 'I don't want anybody telling Ammy that these people are all real, if they're not. She has enough problems already, doesn't she?'

Doctor Feldstein held up both hands. 'Ruth – I totally understand your concern. But Zelda Beech is a highly responsible psychiatrist. She would never do anything that put any of her patients under unnecessary stress, or jeopardize their mental stability. Besides, I wouldn't let her upset Amelia, you know that. Amelia's my special girl, aren't you, Amelia?'

'But if this man is having the same kind of delusions—'

'We don't know for sure that they *are* delusions, do we? You just said that you saw at least one of them for yourself. What did

Amelia call him? The Creepy Kid. Maybe this fellow can shed
some light on whatever it is that's making Amelia feel so anxious.
I don't see that there's any harm in your getting together and
comparing symptoms. And let's face it – Amelia may be dis-
advantaged in many ways, but she's not easily fooled, is she?
People who are congenitally incapable of telling lies always know
when other people are speaking with forked tongues.'

Doctor Beech came back with her diary. 'Here it is: Martin
Watchman, six-six-seven-four West Byron Street, Chicago. And
his telephone number, too.'

Ruth went over and sat on the couch next to Amelia. 'I think
this is your choice, Amelia. Do you want to meet a man who
thinks that people are coming through from underneath, just like
you do?'

Doctor Beech said, 'You don't have to, Amelia. I'm not putting
any pressure on you. But I do think that if you two meet, and talk
over your anxieties, it might enable me to see your condition from
another point of view. Give it another dimension, so to speak, like
a CT scan.'

Amelia thought for a long while, and then she said, 'Does
Martin Watchman have William's?'

'No, he doesn't.'

'He won't think I'm strange, will he?'

'Of course not, because you're not strange. You're just
distinctive.'

Amelia looked down at the cushion on her lap. It was embroidered with the words *Always Be True*. Outside, there was another
rumble of thunder, closer this time, and the rain suddenly began
to beat against the consulting-room window like a plague of
locusts.

It was raining harder in Bon Air Park, too, and because of that,
the park was deserted. No dog-walkers, no children playing on
the swing-sets, no police patrolmen, no park attendants. Only an
old black Buick Riviera with a sagging suspension, and the Spirit
of Kokomo senior citizens' bus, hidden amongst the trees.

The laughing man walked slowly up the aisle of the bus, and
tossed a filthy hospital gown at each passenger.

'You want to know where these came from?' he asked them.
'Saint Bartholomew's, Barrettstown, where they send dribbling,

babbling, incontinent geriatrics to spend their last miserable days, not knowing whether it's night or day, not recognizing any of their loved ones, not even knowing who *they* are, themselves.'

He pushed his mask into Mrs Tiplady's face, and said, 'Do you remember who *you* are, old lady? Or has it all melted away?'

Mrs Tiplady lifted up her blood-caked face in defiance. 'You go screw yourself, buster. I know who *I* am. How about you? At least I'm not so chickenshit that I have to hide my identity behind some stupid carnival mask.'

The laughing man hesitated for almost a quarter of a minute, breathing noisily in and out behind his mask. Then he punched Mrs Tiplady in the face again, and fresh blood burst out of her nostrils.

The laughing man looked at each of the bus passengers in turn.

'Anyone else want to get uppity? I truly don't mind. I enjoy it.'

He waited, and when nobody spoke up he said, 'These gowns we've just handed out to you, these are what you wear when you lose the last vestige of being human. These are what you wear when your brain has left the building, and all that's left is a zombie. Well, you know what happens in those zombie movies, don't you? They tear each other to pieces. That's what they do. They tear each other to pieces with their bare hands.'

He paced up and down the aisle with a jumpy, excited strut. He drummed black leather fingers on the luggage rack rail, and every now and then he let out a little 'yip, wow!'

Each time he passed, the elderly passengers turned fearfully away, and Mr Carradine even raised his scarf up over his face and put his eyeglasses on top of it, so that he resembled the invisible man.

'Now then,' said the laughing man, lifting his index fingers and spinning around on his heels, as if he were line-dancing. 'What you have to do now is take off all of your clothes and put on these gowns. You want to look authentically doolally, don't you?'

Miss Elwood said, 'You're asking us to *undress*? You mean here, now, in this bus?'

'You got it, ma'am. And as quick as you like.'

'I will not!' Miss Elwood protested. 'I am seventy-three years old and I have never undressed in public, ever!'

'In that case, you shriveled old crone, you have probably been doing the public a very great favor for all of these years,' said the laughing man, leaning over her so that his white papier mâché nose was almost touching hers. 'But today you're going to do what I tell you to do, and that means get bare-ass naked, and it means here, and now, and it means quick.'

'I would rather *die*!' Miss Elwood spat at him.

'You would? Okaly-doky-do, your choice.'

With that, he gripped her head and twisted it sharply to the right, so that her neck snapped. He did it with no hesitation whatsoever, so that although Miss Elwood's fellow passengers all heard the distinctive crackle of her upper vertebrae being broken apart, only Mr Kaminsky saw what happened, because he was sitting right behind her. The rest of them didn't realize that she had been killed until her head dropped sideways on to her shoulder and she toppled on to the floor, all arms and legs, like a marionette with the strings cut. There were gasps and cries of 'Alice! *No!*'

'What happens no-o-ow is entirely up to you,' said the laughing man. 'All I'm asking you to do is put on a little performance for us. A play, to propitiate the gods of ill fortune. If you choose *not* to – well, like I say, that's entirely up to you. But this is what will happen to you if you refuse. The gods of ill fortune, they don't take kindly to folks who deny them what they want.'

Mrs Lutz was the first to stand up. She unbuttoned her red vinyl raincoat and said, 'Come on, everybody. Survival is much more important than modesty. And most of us have seen it all before, haven't we?'

She took off her raincoat and dropped it on to the seat beside her. Then she crossed her arms and pulled her dark green sweater over her head, so that her bouffant white hair stood up like a parrot's plumage. Next, with arthritic fingers, she unfastened the pearl buttons of her blouse and took that off, too.

Neville rose up in his seat and said, 'Mrs Lutz – don't you go no further!' But the laughing man prodded him with the point of his knife.

'Hey, Rastus – you don't want this nice old lady put through the *highly* unpleasant experience of having to watch you masticate your own manhood, do you?' he asked, and then coughed.

Mrs Lutz said, 'It's OK, Neville. Sometimes it's braver to admit when you're licked than it is to fight back.'

'You're *sick*,' Neville told the laughing man. 'All three of you, you're worse than dogs.'

The laughing man feinted at him with the knife, and Neville jolted back in his seat, lifting up his left elbow to ward him off.

The scowling man laughed. 'Won't have to do much surgery on you, Rastus. Looks like you don't have no balls to begin with.'

Mrs Lutz tugged down the zipper of her charcoal-gray skirt and stepped out of it. Now she was wearing only a thin satin slip, and a bra, and thick black pantyhose. She took all of those off, and as she did so the bus fell silent, except for Mr Thorson, whistling through his tracheotomy tube.

'There,' she said, looking up at the laughing man in defiance. For a woman in her middle seventies she had an exceptionally good figure, even though her stomach was a little rounded and her full breasts had given up their fight with gravity. Her nipples crinkled like two walnuts.

'Do you know something, ma'am?' said the scowling man. 'If I was eighty years old, I think I could take a shot at you. In fact, if we had the time, and someplace to lie down, I think I could take a shot at you right now.'

The expressionless man handed Mrs Lutz her hospital gown. It had crusted yellow-and-green food stains on the front, and a wide brown bloodstain on the back, where its previous wearer had obviously suffered a severe rectal hemorrhage. Mrs Lutz took a deep breath, put her arms into the sleeves and awkwardly tied up the strings at the back.

'Now the rest of you!' the laughing man demanded. 'And you, too, Rastus! Let's see if you *really* don't have any stones!'

Grunting, shuffling, the six remaining passengers stood up and began to take off their clothes. Mrs Petersen had difficulty unlacing her tight pink corset, because her carer always helped her to take it on and off, so Mrs Lutz helped her. She also knelt down and helped Mr Carradine to remove his shoes and socks, because he suffered from lumbago and he couldn't bend forward and reach his feet. Mr Thorson, when he dropped his pants, revealed that he was wearing an adult-sized diaper.

'Take that fucking thing off,' ordered the scowling man.

Mr Thorson pressed his fingertips to his tracheotomy tube and croaked out, 'I can't. I'm incontinent.'

'I don't give a shit, grandpa. Ha-ha, even if you do. Take it off.'

Neville undressed, too, taking off his Spirit of Kokomo necktie and his khaki uniform shirt and pants. He stood at the front of the bus with tears filling his eyes and his lower lip puckered because he was so ashamed of himself. Not because of his own nakedness, but because his passengers all looked so vulnerable and frightened.

As if to remind him of his inability to save them, the laughing man pricked the glans of his penis with the point of his knife. 'See?' he said. 'It just isn't true what they say about you black guys, is it? I'd say that this one is average to bijou. Here, put this gown on. Don't want the ladies laughing at your shortcomings, do we?'

His voice shaking, Mr Kaminsky said, 'What do we have to do now? You've murdered poor Alice. You've made the rest of us dress up in these disgusting gowns. Don't you think you've humiliated us enough?'

'Oh, no,' said the laughing man. 'This is where the fun begins. Now that you *look* like dementia patients, it's time for you to *behave* like dementia patients.'

He pointed to Mrs Petersen and said, 'Hit her.'

'*What?*'

'You just asked me what it is that you have to do now. Well, that's what you have to do. Hit her.'

'I can't. Are you out of your mind?'

'No, and neither are you. But you're going to have to act as if you are. Hit her.'

'No. I won't.'

'OK then, I'll have to kill her, like that other old bag.'

He came down the aisle with his knife raised. Mr Kaminsky shouted, 'No! You can't do this! No!' He tried to seize the laughing man's arm, but the laughing man gave him a deep criss-cross cut on the side of his face, exposing his cheekbone. Fresh blood sprayed all the way down the front of his gown.

'*I told you to hit her!*' the laughing man shouted at him. '*What part of "hit her" do you not understand?*' He coughed, and coughed, and for a moment he had to hold on to one of the seats to steady himself. When he had recovered, he took a deep breath and repeated, 'I told you to hit her. If you don't hit her, I'm going to cut her throat so deep that her head is going to fall backward like a coffee-pot lid. You understand what I'm saying now?'

Mr Kaminsky had his hand pressed against his cheek. Blood was running between his fingers and dripping from his elbow. He was too shocked and terrified to answer.

'*Hit her*,' the laughing man insisted. 'This is your last chance, old man, because if you don't hit her, I'll have to kill her, and if she's dead then I'll have to ask you to hit somebody else instead. And if you don't hit *them*, I'll kill *them*, too, and so on and so on, etcetera.'

'You're out of your mind!' Neville shouted at him, his voice hoarse. 'You can't ask him to hit an elderly woman like that! She has angina, for God's sake!'

'You listen to me, Rastus!' the laughing man retorted. 'This is an exorcism, got it? Ex, Or, Sizzum. This is a ceremony that has to be played out, or else the goddamned gods don't get propitiated and then, believe me, there will be *hell* to pay!'

He paused, still holding up the knife, but he was clearly so angry that his chest was rising and falling and his hand was trembling.

'If you don't hit each other, then I'll have to kill all of you, and if I have to kill all of you then the goddamned gods won't be propitiated and we'll have to find another bus load of old coots and go through this whole goddamned performance all over again! You want to save lives? You want to save people's lives? Then do as you're damned well told and hit her!'

He had hardly finished speaking when Mr Kaminsky gave Mrs Petersen a half-hearted slap on her wobbly left cheek. Mrs Petersen let out a gasp, but it was obvious that she was more surprised than hurt.

'Well,' said the laughing man. 'That wasn't exactly a haymaker, but it was a start. Now, you hit him back.'

'What do you mean?' asked Mrs Petersen, breathlessly.

'What do you think I mean, fatty? I mean, hit him back, and make sure you hit him harder than he hit you.'

'I can't possibly do that.'

'Oh yes you can. Because if you don't, I'm going to cut his throat, just as deep as I was going to cut yours. Did you ever look down a man's neck before? Fascinating what you can see down there.'

'Come on, Margot,' said Mr Kaminsky. 'You can do it. Don't you worry about me. I'm tough as old boots. I was at Hofen with Butler's Blue Battlin' Bastards. Wounded twice.'

Mrs Petersen took a step toward him. Then she let out a high, piping scream and began to pummel his chest with her fists.

'That's more like it!' the laughing man encouraged them. 'Now you hit her back, grandpa, even harder!'

Mr Kaminsky slapped Mrs Petersen's face, twice. She retaliated by slapping his left cheek, where the laughing man had laid it open with his knife. He said '*gah!*' in pain and slapped her back. She staggered back and fell against her seat, losing her balance. Mr Kaminsky straddled her with his bony knees and started pulling at her hair. Mrs Petersen heaved her wallowing hips from side to side, but when she couldn't dislodge him she fumbled underneath his hospital gown, grasped him between his legs and squeezed him hard.

Mr Kaminsky shouted, '*Aaaahh!*' and punched Mrs Petersen's breast. Mrs Petersen released her claw-like grip on his scrotum, but then she dug her crimson-polished fingernails into the bone-deep cut underneath his eye and pulled downward, tearing furrows in his cheek. He punched her again.

While they were still struggling, the laughing man grasped Mrs Lutz by the shoulder and dragged her down the aisle. 'Now *you* can hit *her*!' he told Mr Thorson.

Right next to them, Mr Kaminsky and Mrs Petersen were rolling from side to side, hitting each other harder and harder, partly out of fear that one or other of them would have their throat cut open if they didn't, and partly out of rising hysterical rage. They might have been hurting each other because they had to, but that didn't make either of them any less angry, or make their punching and slapping any less painful.

Mr Thorson bubbled and wheezed through the stoma in his throat. 'You can't make me hit her,' he gargled.

'Oh, I think I can,' said the laughing man. 'How's about I cut her gazongas off, one after the other, and then I cut her throat? What do you think about that?'

'I think you're a diseased bastard,' said Mr Thorson.

'I'm diseased? *I'm* diseased? You should look at yourself in the mirror, throat cancer man. What was it, three packs a day? Go on, hit her!'

'Oh God in heaven forgive me,' said Mr Thorson, and gave Mrs Lutz an awkward backhand slap across the mouth.

Like a raging fire that feeds on its own ever-intensifying heat, their terror and their anger and their self-disgust turned into uncontrollable madness. They pushed and scratched and pulled at each other, tearing at each other's hair, knocking each other's heads against the seats and the window-frames, breaking each other's glasses. Even Neville joined in, punching Mr Kaminsky again and again, half in the hope that the old man would drop unconscious to the floor and not have to fight any more, and half in desperation, because he knew that the three masked men would blind him and mutilate him if he didn't.

All the time they were fighting with each other, the elderly passengers moaned and screamed and ululated, like a choir from hell. They struggled with each other for nearly ten minutes, and when the struggling was over, five of them lay unconscious or semi-conscious on the floor of the bus, bleeding and bruised. Neville was still standing, and so were Mrs Lutz and Mr Carradine, but Neville's face and arms were deeply scratched, as if he had been attacked by a mountain lion, while Mrs Lutz's lips were swollen and her eyes were half-closed, and Mr Carradine had blood dripping from his left ear and had also lost his upper teeth.

Neville turned around to the laughing man. 'What now?' he demanded, his voice shaking with strain. 'Are you satisfied? Look what you've made these people do to each other.'

'Please, we can't take any more,' said Mrs Lutz. 'I'm begging you, please go away now and leave us alone.'

The laughing man came up to her and pushed her so hard with the heel of his hand that she fell backward on to one of the seats.

'Leave you alone? Sorry, lady, we can't leave you alone. The gods of ill fortune won't allow it. They have to be propitiated, like I told you, and they're a long way from being propitiated yet.'

'*Go away!*' shouted Neville. '*Go away and let these poor people be! What have they ever done to you?*'

The laughing man coughed. 'They've done nothing except to be conveniently on hand when an exorcism was called for, that's all. Like I told you, I'm sorry. But the night has to follow the day, even if we don't want it to. Darkness always inevitably has to fall, brother. Darkness always inevitably has to fall.'

'Don't you go calling me your brother, you motherfucker. You're not my brother.'

'Oh, we're all brothers under the mask. And you go back to

the Bible, brother. You go back to the Good Book. What did the very first brother do to the second brother?'

The laughing man half-turned away, but then he swung around with his right elbow raised and Neville didn't even realize that he was holding his knife in his hand. With a single elegant sweep of his arm he cut Neville's throat wide open so that blood cascaded down the filthy hospital gown that he was wearing.

Neville's eyes bulged with shock. Instantly, he clamped both hands over his throat, but he could feel for himself that the laughing man had killed him. He took one staggering step backward, and then another, and then he tipped sideways over his driver's seat, trying to seize the steering wheel with one bloody hand to stop himself from falling.

'No!' screamed Mrs Lutz. '*No!*'

But the scowling man slapped her across the face, twice, and then ripped her hospital gown open.

Mrs Lutz said, 'God will punish you for this. You are going to burn in hell.'

The scowling man pulled her gown right off her, and kicked it away down the aisle. 'Lady,' he said, 'I already did.'

ELEVEN

Ruth arrived at the Fire & Arson Laboratory at lunchtime. It was still thundering and it was so dark outside that Jack had switched all the lights on. He was perched on a stool in his white lab coat, reading the sports pages in the *Tribune* and making a mess of eating a ham and provolone submarine from Jimmy John's.

'Hey – how did it go?' he asked her. 'Did the doc find out why Amelia's been feeling so antsy?'

Ruth took off her raincoat and hung it up. Then she took off her beret and slapped it to shake off the raindrops. 'He seems to think her meds are OK, so it could be nothing more than her hormones playing up. But we talked to a shrink, too – Doctor Beech? She wants Ammy to meet up with some guy who's been having the same kind of problems.'

Jack picked up a slice of tomato that had dropped on to a picture of Caleb Abbott, the big hitter from the Kokomo Knights. 'I know Zelda Beech, she's good. She used to treat Lois.'

He didn't say any more and Ruth didn't press him. She knew that Jack's first wife, Lois, had suffered a severe mental break-down, and that she had eventually committed suicide, but she didn't know all of the details and if Jack didn't want to tell her, that was his privilege.

'I just don't know if it's a good idea,' she said. 'You know – meeting up with somebody who's suffering from the same kind of anxiety. I don't want Ammy to get any worse.'

'Zelda Beech is good with people,' Jack reassured her. 'She's not your run-of-the-mill shrink, not by any means. She's very open-minded. If she thinks that her patient will respond to a certain kind of treatment, she'll try it, even if she doesn't necessarily agree with it. Like hypnosis. She was always very wary about hypnosis because she didn't like the after-effects. The nightmares, the sweats, the heebie-jeebies. But she hypnotized Lois when Lois was going through the worst, and it helped her to make some sense of the world. Not that the world has ever made *any* kind of sense.'

'You can say that again. How's it going with Tilda Frieburg?'

Jack put down his sandwich and smacked his hands together. 'I was going to call you, but I didn't want to interrupt you while you were talking to the doctor, and in any case I wanted to see your face in live action when I told you.'

He walked across the laboratory and came back with a test-tube half-filled with light gray powder.

'What's this?' Ruth asked him.

'Sludge from the bottom of Tilda Frieburg's bathtub. Filtered and dried, tested and analyzed.'

He waited, smiling, for Ruth to react.

'OK,' said Ruth. 'Why are you keeping me in suspense?'

'I enjoy being dramatic, that's all. This powder is in fact cremated remains. *Professionally* cremated remains, just like the cremated remains we found inside the mattress on which Julie Benfield was burned. What's more, they have minute bone fragments in them, exactly similar to the bone fragments we found in the first sample. If I was to give you an educated guess, I'd say that both samples came from the same not-terribly-efficient crematorium.'

'You're kidding me.'

'No, I'm not kidding you. But then I'm still waiting on the DNA analysis from the first sample, if any DNA survived the cremation, and I'll have to send away *this* sample, too.'

'Did you dry out *all* of that sludge?'

Jack nodded. 'Total weight after drying was a fraction under a kilo. A smidgin more than we got from the mattress.'

'So if we collected up all of it, or *most* of it, it could have been a child?'

'I couldn't say, boss. That's an educated guess too far.'

'If it *was* a child, though, that would mean that each of the two fires involved some cremated kid's remains. *Two* cremated kids' remains.'

'That's what I mean about the world not making any kind of sense.'

Jack spent the rest of the afternoon testing every item of evidence that they had taken from Tilda Frieburg's bathroom, including her sponge, her soap, her towels and her bathrobe. Meanwhile, Ruth fed into her computer the dozens of digital photographs she had taken, and used them to recreate the progression of the fire from the moment it had started.

It was nearly five p.m. when Jack's phone rang. He picked it up and said, 'Jack Morrow. Yes, it is. Yes. I see, thanks.' He hung up and then he turned to Ruth. 'That was Aaron Scheinman. I was right. There *were* pieces of tooth in that sample, and he was able to extract DNA. Our mystery remains were those of a male, of Northern European origin. Aaron's emailing the full report.'

Ruth was staring intently at her computer screen. She had fed in all the photographic evidence, as well as the chemical clues – the carbon particles which had penetrated Tilda Frieburg's sponge, and the hydrogen chloride gas which had contaminated her towels and her bathrobe – but still the fire made no sense at all. There were mineral traces in the sludge from the bottom of the bath, but not magnesium or sodium, which she would have expected from an exothermic reaction – only cadmium and lead.

Jack came over and peered at the screen over her shoulder. 'Well?' he asked her. 'What do you think?'

'I still can't work out how the fire first ignited. There were absolutely no accelerants involved. No chemicals that might have reacted with the bathwater. All we have are cadmium and lead, and since cadmium and lead are what you're left with when you burn PVC, and since we have cremated human remains here, my guess is that this was PVC varnish from a funeral casket.'

'Which still doesn't explain what happened here. Or what made the fire so intense. Or why it burned for such a short time. Or why the heat was confined to the bathtub and almost no place else.'

Ruth said, 'I'll run some simulations on the computer. If those don't tell us what happened here, we'll have to try some real-life tests with pig carcasses.'

Jack looked at her. 'What if it was SHC? How do you simulate that?'

'Jack, I've told you. I don't believe in SHC. People don't suddenly burst into flame for no reason at all. Especially if they're sitting in forty-five gallons of water.'

'Just remember what Sherlock Holmes said about eliminating the impossible. When you've eliminated the impossible, whatever remains, however improbable, must be the truth.'

'SHC is impossible.'

'Maybe. Maybe not. But right now I can't think of anything else that could have boiled and broiled Tilda Frieburg both at the same time.'

Mrs Lutz opened one eye. The other eye was so swollen that she couldn't see out of it at all. She was lying on her side on the floor of the bus, and Mr Kaminsky's face was so close to her that she couldn't focus on it.

She lay there, not moving, and listened. Somebody in the bus was sobbing softly. It sounded like Mrs Tiplady. Somebody else was groaning – Mr Kaminsky? But what Mrs Lutz was listening for was the laughing man, or the scowling man, or the man with no expression on his mask at all. She wasn't going to move if she suspected that all or any of those three was still around.

She felt bruised all over – her neck, her shoulders, her back, her knees. Her left wrist was tucked up under her ribs like a broken bird's wing, and it hurt so much that she was sure that it was fractured. She also felt a deep throbbing between her legs, where they had violated her, all three of those men.

Five minutes went by. She heard thunder booming in the distance, and the rain was still pattering on the roof of the bus, but apart from the sobbing and the groaning she heard nothing else. Maybe they had finally gone, those terrible monsters. To Mrs Lutz, as she lay there, the most appalling aspect of what they had done to her, and all of her fellow passengers, was that there seemed to have been no reason for it. It had been cruelty for its own sake. She couldn't even believe that they had taken any pleasure out of penetrating her, a skinny seventy-seven-year-old woman with sagging breasts and withered thighs.

She raised her head a little, and tried to shift her elbow so that she could sit up. But the bones in her wrist crunched audibly, and the pain that lanced up her arm was so intense that she cried out loud, a self-pitying wail that sounded more like a wounded animal than a woman.

She lay back, quivering. She couldn't do it. She couldn't move. All she could hope for was that some passer-by would see the Spirit of Kokomo bus standing under the trees in the park and call for the emergency services.

She whispered a prayer that she used to recite when she was a little girl. '*Dear Jesus, as you pass along, walking through the*

*adoring throng, please turn your head and see my tears, please
hold me close and soothe my fears . . .'*

It was then, though, that another voice joined in. A young boy's
voice, a little hoarse but still unbroken.

'*. . . oh dear Lord Jesus, give me light, and save me from the
fearful night.'*

Mrs Lutz raised her head again. 'Who's that?' she quavered.
'Who's there? Haven't you hurt us and mocked us enough?'

There was a moment's silence. Then somebody stepped into
her line of vision – a boy in faded red jeans, with scuffed brown
sneakers. She managed to raise her head a little further, and now
she could see his face. He looked very pale, with tousled black
hair and large brown eyes. He was frowning.

'Grandma?' he said, kneeling down beside her and gently
touching her shoulder. 'Grandma, what's happened?'

'Son, listen to me,' said Mrs Lutz. 'You need to go find us
some help.'

'But what happened, Grandma? Are you hurt?'

'Please . . . all I need you to do is find us some help. Go outside,
find a grown-up. Find anybody. Tell them we need the police and
an ambulance. You know where this is, don't you? Bon Air Park,
near the pavilion. Tell them it's very urgent. Tell them some people
have been killed.'

But the boy stayed where he was, stroking her shoulder. 'Don't
worry, Grandma. I'll look after you. Whatever they did to you, I
won't let them do it again.'

'Please,' said Mrs Lutz. 'Go find some help. Please do it now.
Please.'

'It's all right, Grandma. Remember that time when you fell
down the steps and broke your hip? Remember I made you those
brownies? You liked my brownies, didn't you, Grandma? You said
they tasted like the angels had baked them, in God's own kitchen.'

Mrs Lutz took three deep breaths to steady herself. Then she
said, 'What's your name, boy?'

The boy stared at her, as if he didn't understand what she meant.
'They shouldna took you away, Grandma. I won't let them do it
again.'

'Listen,' said Mrs Lutz. 'I am not your grandma. I am just an
old woman who has been attacked by some very evil men, and
I've been very badly hurt. All of these old people on this bus have

been badly hurt, too. At least two of them are dead, do you understand that? They're dead, they've been murdered, and everybody else needs urgent medical attention, right now.'

'They shouldn't have taken you away, Grandma. Nothing bad woulda happened if they hadn't took you away.'

For the love of God, thought Mrs Lutz. Of all the people who could have found us on this bus, it had to be some kid with an IQ of less than fifty.

'*Go find help!*' she shouted at him, even though her ribcage was bruised and the pain when she shouted was almost unbearable. '*Go find somebody to help us! Don't you understand me?*'

Mrs Tiplady let out a cry. She must have heard them talking and was calling out for help. Mr Kaminsky groaned, and Mr Thorson gave a hideous cackle from the stoma in his throat.

The boy smiled and started to stroke Mrs Lutz's hair. 'You're beautiful, Grandma. You always said you loved me, didn't you? They shouldna took you away. I'll look after you, I promise. *I* won't send you away.'

Mrs Lutz let her head sink back on to the floor. She felt utterly defeated.

'*Son*,' she whispered. '*Listen to me, son.*'

The boy bent his head close, still smiling at her. She looked into his eyes but she couldn't understand what she saw there. Was he really a retard? Or was he simply playing with her? Maybe the three masked men had brought him here for the sole purpose of giving them false hope. Maybe this was just another part of some sadistic and humiliating joke, some three-act torture.

'*Son*,' she repeated.

'What is it, Grandma?'

She took another deep breath, and then she said, 'Go get some help, son. Do it now.'

The boy ignored her. Instead he lay down on the floor of the bus right next to her, and put his arm around her. 'I'll help you, Grandma. I'm the only help you need. I love you, Grandma. I always will.'

'Go get some help,' she insisted. 'Go get some help.' Then she shrilled at him again: '*Go get some fucking help!*'

'You're so *cold*, Grandma,' the boy told her. 'I can warm you up.'

Mrs Lutz stared at him, helplessly and hopelessly. Maybe he

was deaf. Maybe he simply hadn't understood her – or worse still, maybe he hadn't *wanted* to understand her.

'We need help,' she intoned. 'We need help.'

'You're cold,' he repeated. 'But you don't have to be cold, ever again.'

He clung on to her tighter and tighter, so that she felt as if she were being crushed.

'Stop!' she gasped. 'Stop, you're hurting me! Oh God, you're hurting me! *Stop!*'

But then the boy detonated into flames – instantly, as if he had been doused in gasoline and set alight. He stared straight into Mrs Lutz's face, his eyes wide open, and he screamed at her in agony and terror.

Mrs Lutz screamed, too. Bruised and broken as she was, she struggled and kicked to get herself free, and she managed to roll over on to her back. But the blazing boy was holding on to her much too tight, and now he was burning so fiercely that her skin began to shrivel. Her hair caught alight, and turned from a white pompadour to a high plume of orange flame, as if she were a candle.

Mrs Lutz's face reddened, and then blackened. She began to shudder, her bare heels hammering on the floor of the bus as the fire seared her nerve-endings. But as her nerve-endings were burned away and she lost all sensation, she stopped shuddering, and both of her arms slowly rose up, to embrace the burning boy as if he really were her grandson, and both of them had been baked together in God's own kitchen.

She thought, *this doesn't hurt any more. Nothing will ever hurt me any more. I'm so happy.* She saw her late husband's face, turning toward her as they walked together beside Mississinewa Lake, with the sun shining so brightly off the water that she was dazzled. She said, *'Ted,'* or at least she thought she said it. Then she died.

By now, however, the bus seats next to them had caught fire, too. Within less than a minute, the interior of the bus was filling up with toxic black smoke, and the three passengers who were left conscious and alive began to cough and retch. Mr Thorson managed to stand up and beat at the window five or six times with the heel of his shoe, but he was far too weak to break the glass, and he collapsed, trying to cover his stoma with his hand so that he wouldn't breathe in smoke through his throat.

Mr Kaminsky managed to crawl on his elbows all the way along the aisle to the front door of the bus, but it was tightly closed and he had no idea how to open it. He lay with his head hanging down in the stairwell until he, too, succumbed to the smoke.

Now the fire raged hotter and hotter, until the entire bus was blazing like a funeral pyre. Flames leaped twenty feet up into the branches of the trees, and the rain crackled like sparklers on the Fourth of July. The burning bus was first seen by a dog-walker, who called the Fire Department on his cellphone while his brown spaniel stood and stared at the fire, transfixed, with the flames dancing in his eyes.

TWELVE

Craig tapped his knife on his wine-glass and said, 'Hush up, everybody! I have an announcement to make.'

They were sitting at the kitchen table, eating a supper of peanut-crusted chicken with creamed potatoes and collard greens. Ruth had decided that it was time they all ate supper together, even though Jeff had grumbled that he had arranged to go out bowling with his friend Lennie, and Amelia wanted to eat alone in her room, finishing another plaintive song about a boy who didn't know that it was going to rain and that his girlfriend had left him for ever.

Ruth wanted her family close to her because she could feel something in the air, something *wrong* – and it was a feeling she couldn't shake off. It was partly the inexplicable nature of the fires that she had been investigating. She couldn't stop thinking about them – how they could have started, how they could have burned so fiercely and yet caused so little peripheral damage. But it was also Ammy's persistent anxiety about 'people coming through from underneath,' and the repeated appearance of the Creepy Kid, although she couldn't understand why one dejected-looking boy should disturb her so much.

Craig tapped his glass again. 'Shush, will you, and listen up!'

'Don't tell me,' said Jeff. 'We've gone bankrupt and we have to go live in the Sycamore Stump.'

Even Craig couldn't help himself from smiling. The Sycamore Stump was the remains of a hollowed-out tree, supposedly more than one-and-a-half thousand years old, which was preserved as a tourist attraction in Highland Park.

'No,' he said. 'It's much better news than that. For all of us – but especially for you, Jeff. This morning, ladies and gentleman, I signed a contract to fit eight new kitchens out at Logansport.'

'Sweetheart, that's *wonderful* news,' said Ruth. 'Maybe things are starting to look up at last.'

'Well, let's hope so. Eight kitchens is only eight kitchens, but I guess it's better than no kitchens at all. But the main point is,

I was talking to Gus Probert, the project manager, and I told him about your accident, Jeff.'

'Great. I bet you both laughed your asses off.'

'I can't lie to you – we did, as a matter of fact. But when we stopped laughing, he said that he was just about to trade in his wife's car, and would I be interested if he threw it in as part of the kitchen-fitting contract. Seems like he can get some kind of a tax break if he does.'

Ruth passed the basket of cornbread across to Amelia. 'You mean, he'll give you the car as part of the deal?'

'That's right. He'll write it off as transportation expenses, something like that.'

'What kind of a car is it?' asked Jeff, suspiciously. 'Not some girly Toyota?'

'No . . . it's a 1999 Pontiac Grand Prix SE, white. Three-point-one-liter V6. Great condition, he says, for a car that's over ten years old, and only seventy-three thousand miles on the odometer.'

Jeff tossed the hair out of his eyes. 'What? And I can have it?'

'If you want it, sure.'

'If I *want* it? Are you *kidding* me? When?'

'I can go pick it up for you tomorrow evening.'

Jeff didn't know what to say. He looked from Craig to Ruth and back again and all he could do was shake his head in happy disbelief.

Amelia pulled one of her airy, who-cares faces and said, 'So long as you don't go driving *this* car into a lake.'

After supper, when they were clearing the table and stacking the dishwasher, Ruth said, 'You sure cheered somebody up tonight.'

'Hey,' said Craig, holding her close and kissing her forehead, 'what are dads for?'

'Well, you cheered me up, too. I am *so* pleased about that contract at Logansport.'

'That's what *husbands* are for.'

'What about lovers? What are they for?'

Craig kissed her again. 'Sometimes it seems like nothing is ever going to go right. You know what I mean? Sometimes you feel like you're stuck down the bottom of a well like that girl in *The Ring* and you're never going to be able to climb out of it. But I decided, that's it, I'm going to start climbing, no matter how difficult it is. I have you, and I have Jeff, and I have Ammy, and I'm never going to give up. Ever.'

Ruth reached up and touched the scar on his cheek. His eyes were as gray as rain clouds. 'I think fate was smiling on me when I met you,' she said. 'You mean everything to me, you know that?'

'How about another glass of wine?' he asked her. 'Maybe we could take it up to bed and watch TV. Or something.'

'Sure. "Or something" sounds highly tempting.'

While Ruth covered the remains of the chicken with Saran wrap and put it in the fridge, Craig opened a bottle of Zinfandel and poured out two large glasses. They were about to switch off the lights when Jeff came into the kitchen, already shrugging on his oversized gray windbreaker.

'OK if I go round to Lennie's? I just got to tell him all about my new ride.'

'Can't you phone him? Or text him? It's raining buckets out there.'

'No way. I need to see his jaw drop when I tell him it's a Grand Prix.'

Ruth said, 'All right. So long as you're back by eleven.' She couldn't help being reminded of what Jack had said that afternoon about the cremated remains in Tilda Frieburg's bathtub. *I wanted to see your face in live action when I told you.*

Jeff opened the front door, and as he did so a strong gust of wind blew into the hallway, almost as if a malevolent spirit had swept into the house. Then he slammed it shut, and he was gone, and the house was quiet again, except for Ammy singing upstairs in her room.

Craig said, 'Come on. Let's go upstairs.'

Ruth sat down in front of her dressing-table, staring at herself. She felt tired, but Craig's words had cheered her up, and renewed her determination. *I'm going to start climbing, no matter how difficult it is.* And now that he had managed to find more work, she felt that their life might come back together again, the way it used to be.

She was still sitting there, wiping off her eye make-up, when the phone warbled. Craig answered it, and said, 'Yes? Oh. OK, Jack. Sure.' He came into the dressing-room wearing only his shirt and his socks and handed the phone over to Ruth. 'It's Jack Morrow.'

'Jack?' said Ruth. 'What's happening?'

From the blustery noise in the background, she could tell that Jack was outdoors.

She could also hear the throbbing of diesel engines, and people shouting.

'Sorry to interrupt your evening, boss. There's been a bad one in Bon Air Park. A bus full of seniors has burnt right out. Multiple fatalities.'

Ruth closed her eyes for a moment. 'OK, Jack. Give me fifteen minutes.'

'Take as long as you like, boss. These people aren't going anyplace.'

When she arrived at Bon Air Park, she found it crowded with police cars, fire trucks, ambulances, Fire Department support vehicles, two panel vans from the Howard County coroner's department, TV trucks, press cars, and more than a hundred police, firefighters, paramedics, CSIs, reporters, cameramen and onlookers.

Smoke was still swirling between the trees, even though it was raining harder than ever. The raindrops sparkled red and blue in the flashing lights from the emergency vehicles, so that from a distance the crime scene looked like a funfair. Ruth parked on North Jay Street and walked across the wet grass, with Tyson loping close to heel.

She found Jack waiting for her by the police tape, in a glistening khaki waterproof, with only his nose protruding from his hood, so that he looked like some elvish character from *Lord of the Rings*. Detective Ron Magruder and two other detectives were there, too, shoulders hunched, all looking wet and miserable.

'Where's Bob?' asked Ruth.

'On his way here now. He was in Muncie, for a funeral.'

'Well, he's not the only one,' said Detective Magruder. 'So far as we can tell, we have at least six cadavers here, probably more.'

Ruth ducked under the police tape and walked up to the burned-out bus, followed by Jack and Detective Magruder. Tyson lifted his nose and started to sniff, but Ruth said, 'Stay.'

The blackened carcass of the bus had been draped in gray tarpaulins. Heavy rain could wash away critical evidence in a matter of minutes, especially smoke and ash and accelerant, and it could distort the patterns of carbon residue which were essential to understanding how a fire had spread. Jack said, 'The cops are bringing a forensic tent. Once they've done that, we'll be able to get in there for a really thorough check.'

Although it was partly covered, Ruth could see that the bus had been completely incinerated. Its tires were charred, right through to the reinforced steel belting, and the gas tank had exploded, so that the rear body-panel had been blown into a grotesque sculpture, like a shrieking woman flinging her arms above her head.

Detective Magruder said, 'This was the Spirit of Kokomo free bus service for seniors, on a regular run. I've sent an officer to City Hall to locate the list of reservations. That should give us all of the names and addresses of the passengers, as well as the route, so we can check who got picked up before the bus drove into the park, and who was lucky enough not to.'

'Can I take a look inside?' asked Ruth.

'Sure,' said Detective Magruder. He dragged over an aluminum stepladder and propped it up against the side of the bus. Then he dragged aside one corner of the tarpaulin, so that Ruth could climb up the ladder and shine her flashlight into the interior of the bus.

If the crime scene looked like a funfair, the inside of the bus was its ghost train. Four blackened figures were tilted at various angles in seats that had been burned right through to the springs. All four of them had their arms lifted like performing monkeys, and all four of them were grinning at Ruth as if they were delighted to see her, even though they were dead. Ruth didn't believe in an afterlife, not as fervently as Craig, anyhow, but she sometimes wondered if the dead took comfort in their cadavers being found, and their remains being treated with reverence. She had once come across the papery, mummified remains of a three-year-old girl. She had been hidden in a tiny closet under the stairs of a house near Houston Park, and her body had only been discovered when the house had burned down to first-floor level. Maybe she had been playing hide-and-go-seek, years and years ago, and nobody had ever found her. Ruth had thought how lonely she must have been, even after she had died of dehydration.

Jack said, 'You probably can't see them, but there are three or maybe four more victims on the floor of the bus. They've all been burned to pretty much the same degree, CGS level two. It looks as if the fire might have started in the second or third row of seats, that's where the damage to the floor and the upholstery is the most intense.'

'Any guesses?' Ruth asked him.

Jack glanced at Detective Magruder. 'Come on, boss, you know I don't go in for speculation.'

'How about an educated hypothesis, then?'

'OK . . . it doesn't look like an electrical fault or a fractured fuel-line or any mechanical failure like that. The fire started inside the passenger compartment of the bus, and I would estimate that it had already been burning for five or maybe ten minutes before the gas tank blew.'

Ruth climbed down and Detective Magruder hauled the tarpaulin back over the bus. 'This was no accident,' he said. 'I mean, what the hell were they doing here, in this bus, right in the middle of the goddamned park?'

'Suicide pact?' Jack suggested. 'Half-a-dozen old folks decided they wanted to go out with a bang?'

'Well, I'm not laughing,' said Detective Magruder. 'Right now, I'm willing to believe anything.'

A police department pick-up truck came jolting across the grass, carrying aluminum poles and sheets of folded PVC in the back. Police officers and firefighters unloaded it, and quickly began to erect a large white forensic tent around the bus, as well as laying aluminum stepping plates on the grass to preserve any footprints. The PVC flapped and rumbled in the squally wind.

Ruth stood back, holding on to Tyson's collar. He was growing increasingly restless and edgy, and he kept looking up at her and whining. 'What is it, boy? What can you smell?'

He let out a throaty bark and Jack said, 'Seems like he's gotten wind of something. Never seen him so jumpy.'

At first Ruth thought that Tyson might have picked up the scent of accelerant, carried on the wind from the burned-out bus. But he kept straining his head to the left, away from the bus, toward the trees. His tail was wagging furiously, and he was growling in the same way that he growled whenever strangers came up to the house.

Ruth strained her eyes. She couldn't see what might have excited his attention. It was dark beneath the trees, and dozens of people were ceaselessly passing to and fro between them like figures in a shadow-theater. But if the bus had been deliberately torched by an arsonist, maybe he had dropped his empty container of accelerant there, before making his escape, and it was the smell of that container that Tyson had picked up.

'I'm just going to check this out,' Ruth told Jack, and let go of Tyson's collar. 'Go on, boy! Go seek!'

Usually, when Tyson smelled accelerant, he headed for it like a bullet. But this time he stayed where he was, still growling, but seemingly reluctant to go any closer to the trees.

'Come on, Tyson,' Ruth coaxed him. 'Go seek. Show me what you can smell.'

Tyson took three or four paces forward, but then he stopped. He barked twice, and looked up at Ruth, and barked again. She had never heard him bark like that before. *My God, she thought, he's frightened. He's trying to tell me that he's scared.*

She walked slowly toward the trees. The rain was rattling through the leaves, and behind her she could hear the clanking of aluminum couplings as the tent was put up. But underneath the trees it was strangely hushed, almost as if she had walked into a chapel and closed the door behind her.

She lifted her flashlight and looked around. There was no sign of any container that might have been used to hold accelerant. No jerry can, no soda bottle. But even if there was no container, maybe the arsonist had emptied out the last of his accelerant here, and if she could find out what kind of accelerant it was, it might help her to identify its source. The problem was, only Tyson was capable of locating it. She couldn't go around on her hands and knees, sniffing the ground herself.

'Tyson!' she called, turning around, but Tyson was still standing where she had left him, his head lowered, his tail swinging. 'Here, Tyson! Come here, boy! Now!'

Tyson came a little closer, but then he stopped again, and barked.

'Tyson! Bad dog! Come here, boy! Now!'

She started to walk back toward him, but as she did so she became aware that a figure was standing between two trees, less than thirty feet to her right. She shone her flashlight toward it, and when she realized who it was, she actually shouted out in shock.

It was the Creepy Kid – the pale-faced boy in the faded black T-shirt and red jeans. The same boy she had seen on South McCann

Street, but hadn't been able to catch on camera. The same boy who had been keeping watch outside her house, beside the bass-wood tree.

She shone her flashlight directly into his face. He raised one hand to shield his eyes, but he didn't turn away, and he didn't move.

'Hey, you – *kid*!' she called out. 'Who are you? What are you doing here?' She tried to sound stern and authoritative, but her words came out much shriller than she had intended them to.

The boy didn't answer. He stayed where he was, between the trees, his hand half-covering his face. Ruth lowered her flashlight and he slowly lowered his hand, too.

'Who are you?' she repeated. 'What are you doing here? Have you been *stalking* me?'

Still the boy said nothing. Ruth walked up to him, until she was standing close enough to touch him. He looked up at her with an expression that Ruth could only think of as infinitely weary, tired of life. She had seen old people with that expression, but never a child. He was shivering slightly, too.

He was an odd-looking boy. His head was elongated, as if she were viewing a picture of him from a very acute angle. His hair was thick and dark and wiry, and it had been cut so badly that Ruth could only guess that his mother had done it for him, or he had tried to do it himself. His eyes were wide apart, like a flat-fish, and his lips were unusually red, and bow-shaped – a girl's lips, rather than a boy's.

'What's your name, kid?' Ruth asked him, much more gently this time.

The boy said nothing for almost twenty seconds, although the pupils of his eyes kept darting upward and to the left.

Ruth was just about to ask him again, when he suddenly said, in a croaky voice, 'Don't you *get* it? Don't you *get* it? You hafta leave me *alone*.'

'What? What do you mean?'

Again, there was a long pause and more eye-darting before the boy spoke again. 'If you don't leave me alone, there's gonna be trouble.'

'What are you talking about? What kind of trouble?'

'If you don't leave me alone, I'm telling you, there'll be *hell-tapay*.'

Ruth heard Jack call out, 'Boss! Boss? The tent's up and ready! You want to come inside and take a look?'

She didn't reply. Instead, she said to the boy, 'How can you ask me to leave you alone when I'm not doing anything to you? I don't even know who you are. As far as I can make out, it's *you* who's been following *me*.'

'I won't warn you again,' the boy told her. 'Less'n you want something rilly *hawble* to happen.'

'Boss!' Jack shouted.

Ruth turned and waved her flashlight. 'Won't be a minute, Jack!'

She turned back, but the Creepy Kid was gone.

'Hey!' she called out. '*Boy*, whatever your name is! Where are you? I need to talk to you!'

She shone her flashlight between the trees, but the boy had vanished. She listened, but all she could hear was the rain, and the blustering sound of the wind, and the shouts of the rescue workers as they set up floodlights inside the tent. Then a portable generator started throbbing and drowned out everything else. She waited for a few moments longer, and then she switched off her flashlight and walked back to rejoin Jack. Tyson trotted beside her, looking up at her as if he were trying to say sorry. She bent over and tugged at his ears to show him that he was forgiven. 'It's OK, boy. I know that you were frightened. I was pretty frightened myself, to tell you the God's honest truth.'

They climbed up into the starkly-lit interior of the bus. The tent billowed all around them in the wind, and rain continued to lash against the PVC. They counted eight cadavers altogether – four of them sitting in seats and four of them lying on the floor – all burned beyond recognition. But Ruth's attention was immediately caught by the heaps of charred clothing that were strewn across the seats.

She picked up the shriveled remains of Mrs Petersen's pink corset. 'Look at this. And look at this skirt. And these corduroy pants. And this bra. Before the fire started, they all undressed.'

Val Minelli held up some scorched tatters of blue cotton, with a lavender floral print on them. 'When they were burned, they were wearing only these, by the look of it. Hospital gowns. This is a standard pattern from BMH Supplies. All the local hospitals use them.'

'Now why the hell would they take off their clothes?' said Detective Magruder. 'These are seniors, for Christ's sakes, seventy and eighty years old. Not your average orgy-goers.'

'I can only guess that they were *forced* to,' said Val. She knelt down to focus her camera on a grinning, bristly-haired skull, which was still wearing a pair of spectacles, their lenses black with soot. Then she took a picture of another skull with a melted pink hearing-aid in its ear cavity. 'The Lord alone knows why.'

Ruth walked slowly up and down the aisle. Jack had been right: the fire appeared to have started in the second row of seats, where they found a cadaver that was much more seriously burned than all of the rest, at least CGS level three. Even though the lower part of its skeleton had fallen apart, Val was confident from the shape of its pelvis that it was a woman. 'Probably seventy-five to eighty years old, if this osteoporosis is anything to go by.'

Tyson trotted up and down the bus, too. It took him only seconds to sniff out the gasoline residue from the vehicle's own tank, but he could find no trace of any accelerants where the fire had first started. He looked up at Ruth as if he could guess what had happened here but couldn't explain it. Ruth said, 'Come on, Tyson. You've done your stuff. If you can't find anything more, that's OK.'

She helped him to jump back down the stepladder and led him into a corner of the tent. She reached into the pocket of her squall and gave him a Grrriller to chew, and affectionately slapped his flanks. 'Good dog,' she told him. 'I'm proud of you.' But when she climbed back up into the bus he sat with the untouched treat at his feet, looking deeply disconsolate, as if he felt that he had let her down.

'What's wrong with Tyson?' asked Jack, as he crawled along the floor of the bus on his hands and knees, taking samples of ash. 'He looks kind of depressed. I mean, do dogs get depressed? I had a macaw once, and he used to get so depressed that he dropped off his perch.'

'I was going to talk to you later,' said Ruth. She hesitated, and then she said, 'I just saw that Creepy Kid again.'

Jack sat up on his heels. 'You mean *here*?'

'Yes, here. In the trees. Tyson must have picked up his scent, but for some reason he wouldn't go near him. I think he was frightened.'

'*Frightened*? What of?'

'I don't know. But you know how sensitive Tyson is. Anyhow, I went up to the kid myself and asked him what he was doing here.'

'OK . . . what did he say?'

'He said we should leave him alone, or else there'd be trouble.'

'We should leave *him* alone? It's more like he's following *us* around.'

'That's what I told him. But he said that if we didn't leave him alone, there'd be hell to pay. Those were his exact words. "There'll be hell to pay."'

'Hey – you need to tell Ron Magruder about this. Like, what's he doing, this kid? This is the second fire he's turned up at. That's not a very healthy pastime for anybody, let alone somebody of his age.'

'I didn't tell you, but I've seen him outside my house a couple of times, too.'

Jack said, 'Your own home? That *is* serious. Like I say, tell Ron about it. It may be nothing, but on the other hand, who knows? Just because he's a kid, that doesn't mean he's no kind of threat. Remember that old guy out at Studebaker Park last year? Got himself stabbed to death by an eight-year-old because he wouldn't throw the kid's baseball back.'

'Don't worry. I'll tell Ron. But I don't want to get paranoid about it.'

Jack said, 'Paranoid? You're kidding me. I'd be plenty paranoid, if I were you. We have three separate cases of people being lighted on fire without any apparent use of accelerant – and at two of those fires, this kid shows up. Like I told you before, there's something really weird going on here, and maybe this kid could be involved. You know what they say about firebugs. They always like to come along and relish what they've done.'

'Well, maybe you're right, but I don't know. Whoever started these fires, they weren't amateurs. Let's talk about this later, OK? Right now, we have a major arson scene to process.'

'Whatever you say, boss. You're the boss, boss. But you mark my words. That Creepy Kid of yours, you need to keep a weather eye on him. He's creepy.'

Jack had now reached the carbonized body of the woman next to the second row of seats. Taking care not to disturb any of her crusted flesh or her dark brown bones, he lowered his head and shone his flashlight under the seats next to her.

'Boss,' he said, after a moment. 'Take a look at this.'

Ruth knelt awkwardly down beside him. The woman's hand was as fleshless and crooked as a buzzard's claw, and several of her finger-bones had dropped off, as Ruth would have expected. But it wasn't her hand that Jack was pointing out to her; it was the scattered heap of pale gray powder underneath it, as if a small bag of gray cement had been dropped on the floor.

Jack said, 'Is that what I think it is?' Using a cardboard scoop, he took out a sample of powder, and carefully brought it out from under the seat, so that they could examine it more closely. The powder was very soft, and fine, but when Ruth rubbed it between finger and thumb she could feel through her latex gloves that there were tiny fragments of bone in it.

'Cremated remains,' said Jack. 'I'll have to analyze them, of course. But these look pretty much the same as the remains we found next to Julie Benfield and Tilda Frieburg.'

Ruth looked at him seriously. 'Jack,' she said, 'what the hell is going on here?'

'I don't have any more idea than you do, boss. But you know what they say in the funeral ceremony. "Ashes to ashes, dust to dust." Maybe that's what happened on this bus – some kind of funeral ceremony. The only difference is, the people who got cremated didn't happen to be dead.'

THIRTEEN

Ruth was woken up the next morning by the phone warbling. 'Craig, sweetheart?' she said, blurrily. 'Craig, would you answer that, please?'

There was no reply and the phone went on warbling and warbling. 'For God's sake, Craig! Pick up the phone, will you, *please*?'

Eventually the phone stopped. Ruth opened her eyes and sat up, blinking. The bedroom was gloomy, but the digital clock on the nightstand told her that it was ten seventeen in the morning. Craig's side of the bed was empty, with only a punched-in pillow and a twist in the comforter to show that he had slept there.

Ruth eased herself out of bed. She felt stiff-jointed and bruised, as if she had spent too long in the gym. She picked up her pink toweling robe from the back of the bedroom chair and went downstairs.

'Craig! Jeff! Ammy!'

The house was deserted. Through the kitchen windows she could see that the sky was charcoal gray and that it was raining hard. The kitchen smelled of coffee and toast, and there was a note on the counter. *Thought you needed to sleep. I've taken Jeff & Ammy to school. CU l8er. XXCraig.*

Ruth sat down on one of the kitchen stools and plowed her fingers through her hair. God, she felt like death warmed over. She and Jack had spent over seven hours examining the burned-out bus, sustained only by lukewarm Dunkaccino and stale cinnamon donuts, and they hadn't left Bon Air Park until three thirty-five a.m. She had taken over 300 photographs, as well as countless samples of fabric and plastic and human remains, but by the time they had finished she still had no clear picture in her mind of how the fire could have started, or how it had spread.

Usually, she was able to visualize fires as soon as she arrived on the scene. She could tell almost immediately if they were accidental, or if they had been started on purpose. The nature of the premises was one of the first clues, especially now that local businesses were suffering such an economic downturn. Furniture stores, hi-fi outlets, real-estate offices, jewelers, specialist food suppliers, bookshops – they were all highly likely to have been set alight by their near-bankrupt owners. Other telltale clues were empty filing cabinets, with no business records in them, and the absence of any valuables or sentimental items, such as family photographs. Then Ruth only had to see where the blaze had actually started, and how quickly it had taken hold, and if any doors had been jammed to hamper the firefighters when they tried to gain access.

Somehow, the Julie Benfield fire and the Tilda Frieburg fire and now the Spirit of Kokomo fire all seemed to be connected, but they were more connected by what they *weren't* than what they were. There was no obvious motive for any of them – not revenge, not vandalism, not insurance fraud – and each in its own way was pyrotechnically inexplicable. The interior of the Spirit of Kokomo bus had reached a temperature of well over 1500 degrees Celsius, hot enough to melt steel, although there was no evidence that it had been started by any accelerant. With the exception of the near-cremated woman in the second row, every other victim had been burned very evenly, as if they were chickens roasted inside a fan oven.

Ruth checked inside the Pasquini espresso machine and saw that Craig had already spooned out fresh coffee for her, so all she had to do was switch it on. She was hungry but she didn't know what she felt like eating. She couldn't face leftover chicken from yesterday evening, not after tweezing skin samples all night from those eight flaking corpses. She took out a blueberry yogurt and peeled the lid back.

As soon as she had taken her first spoonful, the phone warbled again. She picked it up and it was Jack.

'Morning, boss. The rain it raineth every goddamned day. What time do you plan on coming in?'

'As soon as my pulse has restarted. Where are you?'

'Here in the lab already. I just had a call from Aaron Scheinman. You're not going to believe this. The cremated remains we retrieved from Tilda Frieburg's bathtub were a ninety-nine-point-nine per cent match for the cremated remains from Julie Benfield's mattress.'

'*What*?' Ruth had taken another spoonful of yogurt and she almost snorted it up her nose.

'That's right. Both of those two samples of remains originated from one and the same cremated individual.'

Ruth sat down slowly. 'I don't understand this at all. This means that our perpetrator must have divided up somebody's cremated remains and left them at two separate arson incidents. I mean, *why*? What the hell *for*?'

'Search me, boss. *Es un misterio.*'

Ruth thought for a moment, and then she said, 'We're not talking about a cremated child any longer, are we? We're talking about an adult male.'

'That's my guess.'

'Did you send Aaron the remains we took from the bus?'

'First thing. He promised to give me an analysis early this afternoon, if not sooner.'

'You're not thinking what I'm thinking, are you?'

'You mean – what if the remains from the bus match the other two? If they do, he wasn't just an adult male, he was a very big adult male.'

Ruth said, 'You're not kidding. We have at least two kilos of remains already, don't we? And when you cremate your average adult male, what do you get? About two-point-seven kilos, depending on his skeletal structure. Only somebody who was nearly a giant would produce *three* kilos. We're talking Primo Carnera.'

'You know what?' said Jack. 'This whole thing is hurting my head.'

'Come on, Jack. Think. Fires don't start for no reason at all. You remember that fire on South Locke Street, the one that was started by the sun shining through a glass flower-vase? It took me *months* to work out what had happened there, but I did it in the end.'

'I don't know, boss. Something tells me these particular fires aren't going to be as scientifically logical as that. Listen – I'm going to start testing the victims' clothes for residue and gases. What time do you think I'll see you?'

'I'm not sure exactly. Around twelve thirty.'

'OK, then. *Hasta luego.*'

She put down the phone and went over to pour herself a cup of espresso. As she did so, the phone warbled again.

'*Shit,*' she said, under her breath. She was almost tempted to ignore it, but it warbled on and on and in the end she picked up.

'Ruth? Hi, hallo there. This is Doctor Beech.'

'Oh, hi, Doctor Beech. I'm sorry I took so long to answer. I was up for most of the night and I haven't really woken up yet.'

'I'm sorry if I disturbed you. But I've had a call from Martin Watchman. He's driving down from Chicago and he should be here by mid-afternoon.'

'Wow. *He* sure didn't waste any time, did he?'

'I don't want to alarm you, Ruth. You understand that Watchman may be suffering from delusions, and that none of what he suggests may be real. Amelia's anxieties, they may be delusions, too. But the point is that she and Watchman are both suffering from almost identical delusions, and that may help us to understand what's going on here.'

'Sure, I realize that. But so long as Ammy's prepared to go along with it, and so long as this Martin Watchman character doesn't scare her any more than she's scared already, that's all I ask.'

'He said he needed to come down here as soon as possible because he considered the situation to be urgent. I don't know how seriously we need to take him, but he said that Amelia's feelings are indicative that something catastrophic is going to happen, and sooner rather than later.'

'Something catastrophic? Something catastrophic like what? A tornado? An earthquake?'

'He wouldn't explain in any detail. He said he needed to talk to Amelia first. But let me tell you this: he was very interested in the Creepy Kid. He said the Creepy Kid could be the key that unlocks everything.'

'Did he say how?' Ruth asked her. 'More to the point, did he say *why*?'

'To tell you the truth, when he said that I was beginning to wonder if I was making a mistake, asking him to come down to Kokomo. He definitely sounded as if he had a couple of screws loose.'

'So what changed your mind?'

'He asked me if there had been any unexplained fires in the area.'

'What?'

'He asked me point-blank. Out of the blue. We hadn't been talking about fires and he didn't even know that you're an arson investigator. But not only did he ask me about unexplained fires, he specifically said *fatal* fires. Well, I told him then who you were.'

Ruth could see her face reflected in the black glass of the oven door, like a ghost of herself. 'You're aware that I attended two fatal fires at the beginning of the week, aren't you? And there was another one last night. A Spirit of Kokomo bus was burned out in Bon Air Park, with eight seniors still in it. All dead, and so far we have no idea how it started. So, yes, it was fatal, and yes, it's unexplained.'

'I saw it on the TV news this morning,' said Doctor Beech. 'That was about five minutes before Watchman called me. I guess that was what convinced me that he was worth talking to, at the very least.'

'What time do you think he'll get here?'

'Three, three thirty. Maybe later, depending on the traffic on I-ninety. He said he's made himself a reservation at the Courtyard Hotel. He's going to call me when he arrives.'

Jack was analyzing charred seating fabric when she arrived at the Fire & Arson Laboratory.

'You look totally bushed, Jack,' she told him. 'You should take a couple of hours off.'

Jack massaged his forehead with his fingertips, as if he could feel a migraine coming on. 'You know something, the more I find out about these furshlugginer fires, the less I understand them. And the more they creep me out. Talking of that, did you talk to Ron Magruder about that Creepy Kid?'

'Not yet. But I intend to. Especially if I catch him stalking me again.'

'Well, I believe he might,' said Jack. 'I have a very strong feeling that we're going to see more of these attacks.'

Ruth was buttoning up her lab coat. 'What makes you think that?'

'Nothing scientific. Nothing logical. Just a feeling, that's all.' Jack turned away as if he didn't want Ruth to see the expression on his face.

'Jack?' she said. He didn't answer at first, so she said, 'Jack? What is it?'

'Nothing,' he told her. 'I'm tired, is all.'

'Tell me,' she insisted. 'You don't have to turn around. Just tell me.'

Jack hesitated, and she could hear him softly panting, as if he had been running upstairs. 'I never told you, In fact I hardly told anyone. But Lois took her own life by pouring gasoline all over herself and setting herself on fire.'

'Oh, Jack.'

'It doesn't matter. I guess however she did it, it would have been equally difficult to come to terms with it. Cutting your wrists, taking too many sleeping-pills, throwing yourself in front of a truck. What difference does it make?'

'I'm so sorry.'

Jack turned around to face her. His eyelashes were stuck together with tears, but he was trying to smile, too. 'I've gotten over it now, mostly, coming home and finding her like that. I knew what had happened even before I opened the kitchen door, because I know what an immolated human being smells like. But it's not that. It's what happened afterward.'

'Go on.'

'She was cremated. Leastways, Bluitt and Son, the funeral directors, finished what she'd started. I took her remains home in an urn and I placed her on the window sill in the sunroom, over-looking the yard, so that she was close to her flowers and she could hear the birds singing.'

Ruth said nothing. She had never heard Jack speak like this before, and she didn't want to interrupt him in case he decided not to carry on.

'About a month later I looked out of the window and, holy Jesus, there she was, standing in the yard. She was looking at the house. She was wearing the same purple dress she died in. Her hair was tied back and she was just looking at the house.' Jack paused for a few moments, and then he said, 'Strange – but I wasn't scared. It was only Lois, after all, and somehow I didn't register that she was dead and there was no possible *way* that she could be standing out there in the yard. It didn't even occur to me that I might be going out of my mind.'

He paused again, and wiped the tears away from his eyes with his knuckles, like a small boy.

'What did you do?' Ruth asked him at last.

'I went outside to talk to her. I guess I felt angry with her for leaving me. At the same time, I wanted to put my arms around her and tell her how much I'd missed her. When somebody you love kills themselves, there's so many questions that you don't know the answers to, and never will. That's what really makes it unbearable. You're forever asking yourself why they did it. You're forever thinking, was it *my* fault?'

'What happened when you went outside?'

Jack pulled a face. 'She wasn't there. Well, what did I expect? I walked around the house but there was no sign of her. But I couldn't believe that she was only some kind of mirage. The sun had been shining on her hair and she had cast a shadow across the decking. A mirage can't do that.'

Ruth said, 'Did you tell anyone that you'd seen her?'

'How could I? I'm supposed to be Mr Pragmatic. If the chief had gotten to hear about it, he probably would have suspended me and sent me off to the nuthouse.'

'Jack – lots of people think they see their loved ones after they've been bereaved. After my father died, I kept seeing men who looked exactly like him. In the street, in the supermarket. Once or twice I even called out to them, but then they'd turn around and they weren't him at all.'

Jack shook his head. 'Unh-hunh. This was different, believe me. This wasn't a woman who looked like Lois. This *was* Lois. Besides, there's no way in and out of my back yard except through the sunroom.'

'So what are you trying to tell me? How is this relevant to the Creepy Kid?'

'I saw her again,' Jack told her. 'It was, what, about a week later. She was standing in the same place, wearing the same dress, looking at the house in just the same way. It was foggy that morning, so she looked pretty ghostly. This time I didn't go outside as soon as I saw her. I stood there watching her to see what she would do. After about five minutes she walked off, crossed the grass and disappeared behind the yew tree. When I went out, she was gone. Vanished. *Desaparecido*. Same way you told me that the Creepy Kid had vanished.

'Two days after that, she turned up one more time. I came into the sunroom and she was outside the window, right up close, staring at the urn on the window sill – staring at her own remains as if she couldn't believe it was her. I could even see her breath on the glass, that's how close she was. I went up to the window and looked out at her, but she didn't look back at me, didn't lift her eyes toward me even once. Then she walked off again, like she had before, and disappeared behind the yew tree. I didn't follow her. What was the use?'

'So what did you do?' Ruth asked him.

'You won't believe this, but the first thing I did was talk to a pastor – Mike McConnell at St Luke's. Mike – well, he was very understanding, very sympathetic, even though he probably thought that I was bananas. But he said that I should forgive myself for Lois taking her own life, and that instead of keeping her remains in an urn, I should set her free. He said that was why most people commit suicide. Whatever it is about life that's getting them down, they want to be free of it.

'So, the same afternoon I took the urn to the community garden at Ivy Tech. Before she got sick, Lois used to love it there, growing her own fruit and vegetables. I walked around and emptied out the urn as I went. Discreetly, you know, between the rows of potatoes. I said a kind of a prayer for her, too, commending her soul to God. Lois was never religious, no more than I am, but I didn't want to limit my options – just in case there *is* a God and He was happy to take care of her for me.'

Ruth laid her hand gently on top of his, but said nothing, waiting for him to finish.

'Lois never appeared to me again. Sometimes I wish I hadn't scattered her remains, because at least I'd be able to see her now and again. But if Mike McConnell was right, I gave her what she was looking for, which was freedom.'

Ruth said, 'You really believe that something similar is happening here? You think the Creepy Kid may be dead, and cremated, and he keeps turning up because somebody is holding on to his remains?'

'Sounds insane when you say it like that, doesn't it?'

'Yes, it does.'

Jack thought about it for a while. 'You're right,' he told her. 'I need a couple of hours off. We'll figure this out, won't we? Maybe it won't be the sun shining through a glass flower-vase, but then again it won't be mirages, will it? Or ghosts, or dead kids looking for their ashes.'

FOURTEEN

Nadine was giving Bronze Star a final polish with a large rubber curry comb when she heard the stable door bang shut. The weather had been squally all morning so it didn't surprise her, but Bronze Star snorted and whinnied and pawed at the floor of his stall as if something had unsettled him.

'It's OK, boy,' Nadine reassured him, and patted his flanks. 'Nothing to be scared of.'

Bronze Star had always been a nervy horse, which made him unsuitable for children and inexperienced adults to ride, and last spring Nadine's father had talked about selling him and buying a more docile animal. After all, at Weatherfield Stables they made their living out of renting out horses and giving horseback riding lessons. A jittery creature like Bronze Star was a liability rather than an asset. If only a few people could handle him, he still needed feeding and veterinary care, as well as insurance. It was only because he was Nadine's favorite that her father had relented and allowed her to keep him. Nadine believed that Bronze Star could understand everything she said to him, and that he would have answered her, if he could, like a neurotic version of Mister Ed.

The stable door banged again, and then again. Nadine put away her curry comb and her dandy brush and buckled up her kitbag. She gave Bronze Star one last kiss on the nose, and then she let herself out of his stall and bolted the door.

It was then that she looked along the length of the stable and saw three men standing there, posed like gunfighters at the OK Corral. They were all dressed in black ankle-length coats and they were all wearing white masks – one of them fixed in hysterical laughter, one of them scowling, and the third one totally expressionless. Behind them, the stable door was swinging open in the wind, and outside it was dark and raining hard, with intermittent flickers of lightning. Raindrops were sparkling on the men's shoulders.

'Can I help you?' Nadine called out. The men's appearance

didn't unduly disturb her. Some of the people who came to
Weatherfield Stables to rent out horses were wearing the most
bizarre costumes, especially when they were out on a stag night
or celebrating a special birthday. Nadine had catered for Vulcans,
and X-Men, and Flintstones. Last month a party of Knights Templar
had turned up dressed as geisha girls.

'Help us?' the man in the laughing mask called back to her,
looking around. He coughed, and then he said, 'That depends.'

'I'm sorry?' said Nadine.

The laughing man slowly walked right up to her, a little too
close for comfort. She tried to see his eyes, but the slits in his
mask were totally black and empty.

'I said, that *depends*,' he repeated. His voice was coarse and
catarrhal, as if he were suffering from a heavy cold or asthma.
'What I need to know is, are you going to do what we want you
to do, without argufying, or are you going to give us trouble?'

'Why should I give you trouble?'

'I don't know. Think about it. You might scream, for instance.
You might complain. You might shout out for help.'

Nadine dug into the pocket of her padded vest and took out
her cell. 'Let me call my dad. Whatever you want, he can take
care of you better than me. I only do the cleaning up around here.'

But the laughing man gripped her wrist and forcefully pried
the cell from between her fingers. 'Now, come on. We won't be
needing your old man for this. This is something that only *you*
can help us with, honeybun.'

'So what do you want?' Nadine asked him. She was feeling
panicky now. 'Look – my dad will be here at any minute. He can
help you. He knows all of the rental charges and stuff like that.
He can work out discounts, too. You know, three rentals for the
price of two.'

'Ah,' said the laughing man. 'The thing of it is, we didn't come
here to rent no horses.'

'Then, I'm sorry, but what *did* you come for?' Nadine retorted.
'If I can help you with something, arranging some riding lessons,
I'll help you. But if not, I really think you'd better leave.'

The laughing man leaned toward her, although his feet remained
where they were, so that he was tilted at what seemed like an
impossible angle. 'Well, well,' he said, thickly. 'You *are* the feisty
one.' He coughed, but when he had finished coughing, he said,

'Look at you. Curly blonde hair, cute little turned-up nose, eyes as big as breakfast plates. I do declare you look good enough to eat, from the toes upward.'

'Please, go,' said Nadine. Her throat felt tight and her heart was beating so hard that her ribs hurt. She knew that her father had driven into the city to meet his tax accountant, and that he wouldn't return home for hours. Her mother was in Cleveland for three days, visiting her sister, and the only people left in the house were Cora, the maid, and Duncan, the odd-job man, who could fix anything that needed fixing, but who was no brighter than a mirror with its face to the wall.

'No, no, doll face, we're not going,' said the laughing man. 'Not until we get what we came here for. And the way it looks, what we came here for is *you*.'

'I don't even know who you are,' said Nadine. 'How could you possibly want me?'

'You're the stable girl, aren't you? Or rather, the *un*stable girl. Or a pretty good likeness, anyhow, except you're much better looking. And you *smell* a whole lot nicer than she did, too. You smell of talcum powder, and freshness, that's what you smell of. Much more desirable than sweat and horse-shit and unwashed hair.'

Nadine said, 'Really – I don't know what you're talking about or *who* you're talking about, but you really need to leave, right now.'

'Oh, we're not leaving, not yet awhile,' said the laughing man. He had an unusual accent which she couldn't exactly place. 'We have an ex-or-cism to perform, and we can't leave here until that's carried out, no sir, yip-a-dee-doodle. We have to put some souls at rest, and right some wrongs. Some terrible wrongs, the like of which you can scarcely imagine. So, no ma'am, we're not leaving.'

'Who are you?' Nadine demanded. She was feeling bolder now, because she was growing angry and frustrated, and her adrenaline level was rising. Bronze Star whinnied and kicked against the door of his stall, and he could obviously sense that something was wrong.

The laughing man said, 'It doesn't matter who we are, sweetheart. Not to you, anyhow. But the first thing I need you to do is to take off all of your clothes.'

'*What*?' said Nadine. 'Are you crazy? I'm not taking off my clothes! Just get out of here before my dad comes back!'

The laughing man shook his head. 'We know where your dad is, honeybun, and we know that there is absolutely zero chance of him arriving home for another five hours at the very outside. So why don't you behave like a good little girl, the sort of girl who's used to pleasing her visitors, and get yourself naked?'

'No way!' Nadine shouted at him. 'No damn way! Now, get the hell out of here!'

'OK,' said the laughing man, in his muffled, cardboardy voice. He lifted both hands as if in surrender. 'If you won't cooperate freely, out of your own goodwill, then I guess we'll have to try something else.'

He clicked his fingers, and when he did so, the expressionless man reached into his coat and drew out a thin-bladed kitchen knife, at least eight inches long.

Nadine screamed, '*No*! What are you going to do? *No*!'

She ducked left, and then right, and tried to dodge around him, but the laughing man effortlessly caught her sleeve and twisted her around. He pulled her up close to him and she could smell a strong medicated liniment.

'I'm really, truly sorry,' he told her, and then he coughed, and coughed again. 'Sometimes, we have no way of escaping what has to be done, and this is one of those times.'

The expressionless man walked across to one of the stalls on the opposite side of the stables, where a six-year-old chestnut mare called Maggie May was watching them. He took hold of Maggie May's plaited mane and pulled her head toward him. Maggie May snickered and resisted at first, and tried to back off, but the expressionless man pulled her harder. 'Come here, you fucking four-legged pain in the ass.' Then he held the kitchen knife close up to her windpipe.

'*No*!' Nadine screamed at him.

But the laughing man pushed his white mask right into her face, so that he was only two or three inches away from her, and whispered, '*Your* choice. I asked you to cooperate, did I not? I asked you to act real nice and I didn't ask for nothing more. Now let me ask you one more time. Please, cooperate. We won't harm you if you decide not to do what you're told, but this horse will die, in a way that you never saw a horse die before.'

Nadine was shaking all over. 'Are you cold?' the laughing man demanded. 'Don't tell me you're *cold*! We want you to take off all of your clothes, and we can't have you feeling the cold!'

'Please let me go,' Nadine pleaded with him.

'You want to give me one good reason why I should, when there's everything in it for me?'

'Please,' said Nadine, and now the tears were running down her cheeks and she couldn't stop herself from breathing in deep, panicky sobs. 'What have I ever done to you? Tell me, and I'll do it!'

'Oh, you'll do it all right,' the laughing man reassured her. 'Not only that, but a few other things you probably never heard of. Now, which is your favorite horse here?'

She couldn't stop herself from glancing across at the expressionless man. As soon as he saw that she was looking at him, he drew his kitchen knife slowly across Maggie May's throat, not deep enough to sever an artery, but enough to start blood sliding down to her shoulders, as if a shiny red scarf had been tied around her neck.

'*Don't hurt her*!' Nadine cried out. 'Please – whatever you want me to do, I'll do it! But don't hurt her any more!'

'I'm only asking you which is your favorite horse.'

'I can't tell you. These are working horses, not pets. I don't have any favorites.'

'Oh, come on, you must have a favorite. How about this one here?' He peered at the nameplate over the top of the stall. 'Bronze Star. That's a fine-looking animal, isn't it? Shiny as a salesman's shoes. And that's a fine-looking pecker he's got there, doesn't he just! Almost as big as mine, when I'm feeling in the mood for it!'

'I told you, I don't have any favorites,' Nadine repeated. She was terrified that if she revealed her feelings for Bronze Star, they would hurt him badly, or kill him.

'Still and all, he's a good-looking animal, ain't he?' said the laughing man. 'We could start with him, and work our way around the stables, until we find the horse you like the best.'

He beckoned to the expressionless man, who let go of Maggie May's mane and came across the stable to Bronze Star's stall. Bronze Star snorted and kicked as he approached, but the expressionless man stood in front of his stall, pointed his finger at him and said, 'Listen, horse! You're going to stop fretting now, you got me? You're going to quiet down and stay that way.'

Bronze Star whinnied again and rolled his eyes, but the expressionless man continued to point at him, as if he were a disobedient child, and after a while he stopped kicking and scuffing at the floor of his stall and stood completely still, with his head lowered. The expressionless man opened the door of his stall and stepped inside.

Nadine looked at the laughing man in alarm and bewilderment. She had never seen anybody who could pacify Bronze Star like that. Even experienced horse-wranglers usually had to whisper to him and cajole him and pat him and get him used to their smell.

'My friend, he has a real way with horses,' said the laughing man. 'Dogs, too, even Dobermanns and pit-bulls. You know what I think? When it comes down to it, he scares them. Shit, I know he scares me.'

The expressionless man lifted his kitchen knife again and held it up until the point was only an inch away from Bronze Star's left eye. But Bronze Star stayed where he was, his head still drooping, and didn't flinch.

'What I'm going to do is, I'm going to blind him first,' said the expressionless man. 'That will put him into a panic, and when he's in a panic his heart will beat that much faster, so that when I cut his carotid artery open, his blood's going to come pumping out like a goddamn fire hose.'

Nadine hesitated for a few seconds. Then she took off her padded vest and dropped it on to the floor. Next she started to unbutton her green-and-brown check shirt.

The laughing man watched her as she unfastened her cuffs, and then took her shirt off, too.

'Don't stop now,' he told her, with a cough. She reached behind her back and slid open the hooks of her white cotton bra. Barebreasted, she stood and faced him defiantly. 'Don't hurt any of my horses, that's all.'

'Oh, girly, you don't know the half of what we're going to do,' said the laughing man.

'Little tiny tits you got there,' said the scowling man. 'Nothing like *hers*. Hers was humongous.'

The laughing man lifted his hand as if to tell the scowling man to hold his tongue. He waited for a moment, and then he said, 'Go on, sweet thing. Get yourself stripped off.'

Nadine tugged off her green rubber boots and her riding-breeches and then her thong. She was seventeen and she had gone all the way with only one boy before, Peter Vandermeer, a twenty-one-year-old law student at Ivy Tech, with an incipient black moustache. Their relationship had lasted only two months, and she had never stood naked in front of any other man. She felt angry, and embarrassed, and utterly defenseless, and she had never felt so frightened in the whole of her life. The stable doors banged again and a chilly draft stirred the sawdust on the floor.

'What we're going to do now is a little cull,' the laughing man told her. 'You know what that is, a "cull"? Comes from the French "*cuillir*", to collect. In practice, it means weeding out your surplus livestock and putting them down.'

'Please don't hurt my horses,' Nadine begged him. 'You promised you wouldn't.'

'*Moi*? I'm not going to hurt your horses. *You* are. This is a re-enactment, sweet cheeks, an exorcism, and if it's going to work any good then it has to be done right, just the way it originally was. Here. Knife, please.'

He held out his black-gloved hand, palm upward. The expressionless man came away from Bronze Star and gave him his knife. The laughing man approached Nadine and held the blade up in front of her face, so that its point was only inches away from her nose. Nadine stared at him, gulping and trembling, convinced that he was going to cut her open, there and then. But instead he turned the knife around and offered her the handle.

'Take it,' the laughing man coaxed her. 'Go on, take it.'

Nadine took hold of the knife. She was shaking so much that she almost dropped it.

'How many horses do you have here?' the laughing man asked her.

'Eighteen.'

'Hmm. That sounds to me like about seven too many. So what I want you to do is, go around and pick out seven that you could do without, and slit their throats.'

'What? I *can't*! You can't ask me to do that? I *can't*!'

'If you don't, my darling, then you are surely going to die, in the slowest and unpleasantest way that me and my friends can conceive of. So that's your choice. The horses or you. Come on, they'll forgive you, these horses, once they get to horsey heaven. They'll understand that you didn't have a choice. Then again, maybe they won't. I never thought that your average horse was that intelligent, did you? Would *you* let any old lardass saddle you up and jump on your back? Or maybe you would. Depends what kind of a girl you are.'

He took Nadine's elbow and led her over to Bronze Star. 'There we are,' he said. 'All it takes is one deep cut. Quick and deep. No hesitation. He won't feel a thing.'

Bronze Star was still standing motionless, with his head lowered, as if the expressionless man had completely broken his spirit.

'I can't,' said Nadine, and started to sob.

'Go on. He won't hold it against you.'

'I can't!'

'So I was right. He *is* your favorite. In that case, I totally understand. Let's try another horse, shall we?'

The laughing man kept hold of her elbow and steered her along the stable to the next stall, with the scowling man and the expressionless man following close behind.

'Here, how about this old hack?'

The horse in the next stall was Nightlight, a black eight-year-old with a single white blaze on his nose. Most of the horses at Weatherfield Stables were five and over, because horses of that age were used to being ridden, and tended to be more obedient and less likely to throw their riders over the nearest split-rail fence.

Nadine shook her head. 'No.'

She deliberately dropped the knife on to the floor, but the laughing man immediately picked it up and held it out to her. 'You *have* to, don't you get it? The exorcism won't work, otherwise, and if the exorcism doesn't work then it's going to be your fault, and me and my friends, we won't like that, and neither will the gods of ill fortune. The gods of ill fortune, they have to be propitiated, or who knows what gruesome events are going to befall us.'

'I can't kill him,' wept Nadine. 'He's such a beautiful horse. I can't.'

Without warning the scowling man pushed himself right up behind her, so that his papier mâché nose jabbed the back of her head, and she could feel the buttons and the rough material of his overcoat against her bare shoulders. He reached around her and took hold of her breasts in both of his hands, and squeezed them so hard that she screamed.

'You listen to me,' he breathed, close to her ear. 'You're going to cut that horse's gizzard right here and now, because if you don't I'll slice your tits off and chop 'em up bite-size and make you eat them raw.'

Nadine turned in panic to the laughing man, but the laughing man simply nodded, as if he were assuring her that the scowling man would really do that, and that he wouldn't do anything to stop him.

'All right,' she heard herself saying, although it didn't sound like her at all. It sounded like another girl altogether.

The scowling man released his grip on her. She took the knife from the laughing man and held it behind her back. She approached Nightlight slowly, lifting her left hand and stroking the blaze on his nose. Nightlight snuffled and licked his lips, because Nadine always brought him a sugar-lump when she brought him out of his stall.

'I'm so sorry, Nightlight,' Nadine whispered. 'You know that I wouldn't do anything to hurt you, don't you?'

Nightlight looked at her, and she was sure that he understood what she was going to do to him, and why. She had been brought up with horses all of her life, and she was convinced that they were not only brave but intuitive, and that they were prepared to give everything to the people who loved them and looked after them. It was what people who knew about horses called 'heart'.

'You *will* be in heaven, Nightlight, I promise you,' said Nadine. 'You'll have sunshine, and sugar-lumps, and all the sweet hay you can eat.'

'For Christ's sake, shut up and get on with it, will you?' the laughing man demanded. 'You're making me nauseous.'

Nadine held Nightlight close, lifting herself up toward him so that his nose was over her left shoulder, and she could feel his warm breath down her back. She knew that she needed to be decisive, and quick, and that any hesitation would only prolong his pain. She closed her eyes for a moment and then she raised the knife to the side of his neck. Nightlight remained unnaturally still.

'Please forgive me,' said Nadine. She took a deep breath and then she drew the knife diagonally across Nightlight's jugular groove, severing his carotid artery and his jugular vein and the sympathetic trunk which carried his nerves from his brain to his spine. Nightlight let out an extraordinary noise, like a man shouting, and tilted forward, flooding Nadine with a bucketful of warm blood.

Nadine lost her balance and fell heavily backward, hitting her shoulder against the side of the stall. Nightlight nearly collapsed on top of her, but the scowling man seized her arm and dragged her clear. She stumbled on to the sawdust and rolled over on to her side.

She managed to stand up, quaking with shock. When she looked down at herself, she saw that she was smothered all over with blood, like some primitive woman warrior who had covered herself from head to foot in scarlet warpaint. Nightlight was lying in his stall, his legs still shivering. He gave a few spasmodic kicks, but Nadine knew what she had done to him. He was dead.

The laughing man stepped back, giving her a slow handclap. 'Well done, honeybun! Very well done! Wouldn't have guessed you had it in you!'

'See the way she dropped him?' the scowling man whooped, with obvious relish. 'That was something! Just like he'd been poleaxed! I never saw a horse go down like that before!'

'OK, OK,' the laughing man interrupted him. 'That's one down and six more to go. We'd best be hustling, before Ms Honeybun's pa gets back and tries to spoil our fun!'

Nadine shook her head from side to side. 'No,' she said. 'I can't kill any more. Please don't make me.'

'Oh, come on, now,' the laughing man cajoled her. 'Of course you can kill some more! You're a natural. You should have worked in an abattoir rather than a riding-stable. Besides, it's essential that seven horses die. It's essential and it's necessary. Got to mollify those gods of ill fortune, girl! Got to give 'em what they crave and desire.'

Nadine started sobbing again. 'I can't! I don't care if you hurt me! I don't care what you do! I can't!'

The laughing man stepped right up to her and slapped her face, twice, once each way. 'Shut the fuck up!' he barked at her. 'Shut the fuck up and do what you're told! You can't even imagine what the consequences are going to be, less'n you do! You want to see hell, in all its blazing glory? You want to see the whole world

burning up like a burning fiery furnace? Because that's what's
going to happen, less'n you do what you're told to do, and quit
that moaning and howling and constant complaining.'

He stood over her, breathing harshly. He suppressed a cough,
and then another. 'All right, then. Are we agreed? Yes? So let's
get down to it. Pick me another winner, doll! This is better than
an afternoon's racing at Indiana Downs!'

FIFTEEN

He arrived at the Walters Clinic a few minutes after four p.m. A battered silver Taurus drove into the parking-lot outside Doctor Beech's window, and Ammy immediately said, '*There he is*! *That's him*!' Ruth and Doctor Beech glanced at each other, but neither of them asked her why she was so sure. They didn't really understand Ammy's sensitivity, but they both respected it.

It was still raining, harder than ever, and the low clouds were billowing like a filthy gray circus tent with its guy ropes adrift. The door of the Taurus opened up, and a tall man in a brown wide-brimmed hat and a long white trench coat climbed out. He kept his hat clamped to his head to stop it from blowing away, so that as he crossed the parking lot his hand masked his face. He walked quickly toward the clinic entrance with his coat flapping in the wind.

After a few moments, Dora, the receptionist, knocked on the door. 'Mr Watchman's here, Doctor,' she announced. But Doctor Beech didn't have time to reply before Martin Watchman entered the room, lifting off his hat as he did so.

'Doctor Beech!' he said, in a low, hoarse voice, holding his hat over his heart and extending his hand. 'I can't tell you what a great pleasure it is to meet you again, in spite of the circumstances.'

Ruth would have guessed his age at thirty-five or thirty-six. He had dirty-blond hair – collar-length, and wildly messy, as if he had only just woken up – and he obviously hadn't shaved in three or four days. He was handsome, in a lean, hollow-cheeked way, with unusually pale green eyes, the color of a shallow sea, and he had a faint, faded tan, as if he had visited someplace exotic sometime in the spring.

He took off his white trench coat and handed it to Dora, who accepted it with a look of disdain. 'I'll hang this up for you, shall I?' she said.

'Thank you,' he told her. 'On the chain, please. It's a Burberry. Bought it in London. Oh – and here. My hat. Thanks.'

'This is Ruth Cutter, Amelia's mother,' said Doctor Beech. 'And this is Amelia.'

Martin Watchman came across the room and shook hands with both of them. 'So you're the arson investigator,' he said. 'I'm delighted to meet you. And I'm *very* pleased that Doctor Beech had the good sense to call me. I remember how skeptical you were when I talked to you in Chicago, Doctor Beech, but I believe that you have a critical situation here, and we need to deal with it as a matter of urgency. It could be too late already.'

Ruth couldn't quite place his accent. It was educated, and it certainly wasn't Chicago. He lifted up the ends of his words and said 'here' like a Bostonian: 'he-*yuh*'.

Doctor Beech said, 'Why don't you sit down, Mr Watchman? How about some coffee, or a soda? You've had a long drive down from Chicago.'

'A glass of mineral water will do for me, thank you. No ice.'

'Is that all? Anything to eat?'

'I'm good, thank you. And please – do call me Martin.'

He went over and lifted up an armchair, carrying it across the room and placing it close to Amelia. He sat down next to her, turning his head and staring at her unblinkingly with those sea-green eyes. Amelia gave him an uncomfortable smile and shifted in her chair.

In spite of his unruly hair and his stubbly chin, there was an old-school formality about the way that Martin Watchman was turned out. His suit was well-worn, but it had obviously been expensive when it was new. It was light gray, immaculately cut, but it was double-breasted, with wide lapels, and who wore double-breasted suits any more?

His tan loafers were the same: expensive, but with scuffed toes and worn-down heels. Ruth noticed that he wasn't wearing a wedding band, although he had a heavy gold signet ring on the third finger of his right hand.

'I've already told Ruth and Amelia about our meeting at the psychiatric convention,' Doctor Beech told him. 'What you said about "people coming through from underneath".'

Martin nodded, without taking his eyes away from Amelia. 'I'm flattered that you remembered me, Doctor. You meet so many goddamned fruit-loops at those conventions, don't you? Pardon my French.'

'Well, I won't deny that I thought *you* were a fruit-loop, too. To begin with, anyhow. I'm sorry.'

Martin smiled. 'You don't have to be. The things that I've found out, they're not at all easy to believe in. For a very long time, I didn't believe in them myself, even though all the evidence was right there in front of me, staring me in the face.'

'Personally, I'm still reserving judgment,' said Doctor Beech.

'I know, and I don't blame you,' Martin told her. 'But you have to admit that if Amelia here has been talking about people coming through from underneath, it's a coincidence at the very least.'

'But what exactly is so critical? Why did you think it was so urgent for you to come down here?'

Martin didn't answer her for so long that Doctor Beech said, '*Martin?*', but then he immediately turned away from Amelia and said, 'The fires. It was the fires that convinced me.'

'The fires?' Ruth asked him.

'That's right. Totally by chance, I caught a report about one of them on the TV news. It was the one where the girl was burned to death in her bathtub.'

'Go on,' said Ruth, cautiously.

'Fires like that, they have a very specific cause, unlike any other kind of fire, and they very rarely happen in isolation. Like, you'll almost always have a pattern of four or five consecutive fires, and sometimes many more. The highest number I've heard about is eighteen, in Indianapolis, about three years ago. I checked on the Internet and saw that you'd had a similar fire here in Kokomo only a couple of days before. And now all those seniors have been burned to death on that bus. I heard all the grisly details about that on the radio while I was driving down here.'

'That's all very well,' said Ruth. 'But I still don't understand how these fires can be connected to what Ammy's been saying about "men and women coming through from underneath". Or how they're connected with each other, even.'

'Listen to me: the same boy keeps showing up at every fire, doesn't he? And Doctor Beech told me that you've also seen him mooching around outside your own house.'

'That's right. Amelia calls him the Creepy Kid. But we have no idea who he is, or what he's looking for.'

'The Creepy Kid,' said Martin, and allowed himself a thin,

slanted smile. 'That's a really appropriate name for him, I have to tell you.'

'But what's the connection? We're still investigating these fires, but there's no obvious link between any of them. The first victim was a young mother, abducted from a supermarket parking lot, and burned on a mattress. The second was that poor girl who was cremated in her own bathtub. And the third one was all of those seniors in their bus. Each fire was *very* unusual. Each of them was started by an intense, highly-concentrated source of heat, but that's about all they had in common.'

Martin shook his head. 'You're wrong. They have the Creepy Kid in common. And the fact that he's been hanging around outside your house is the proof of that. He knows who you are, Ruth, and he knows that you're trying to discover the cause of these fires, but he doesn't want you to. Right now, you've been lucky, and he's only been threatening you. But you could be in very real danger, I warn you.'

Ruth said, 'I saw him in the woods at Bon Air Park, after the Spirit of Kokomo bus fire. He said that if I didn't leave him alone, something terrible would happen to me. But come on, when it comes down to it he's only a kid. *Creepy*, for sure, but still a kid.'

'No way. He's much more than that. He's a catalyst, don't you get it? He's the one who's been causing these fires.'

'All right,' said Ruth. 'You want to explain it to me?'

Martin got up. He went to the window and looked out, then he came back and stood directly behind Amelia's chair, with his hands on her shoulders. Amelia didn't seem to be at all disturbed by him doing this, and turned to look up at him with a smile.

Martin said, 'My mother was what you might call a psychic. She could tell fortunes and she could also clear disturbing vibrations from houses and apartments in which something traumatic had happened in the past – like a suicide or a murder or an accidental death.

'My gift has never compared to hers – that's if you can call it a gift. It's more of a curse, to tell you the truth. But I've always been sensitive to the resonance that remains in a room after a tragedy. I can even walk into a doctor's surgery like this and feel the pain that people have talked about while they've been here. Human distress, Ruth! It echoes, and it goes on echoing for years.'

Oh God, thought Ruth, *I hope we're not wasting our time here.*

This man is beginning to sound like a nut job. Or a charlatan. Or a Scientologist. Or all three.

'I first felt it when I was only five years old,' Martin went on. 'We went to stay with my grandparents in Maine, my mother and me. I woke up in the middle of the night and saw a young curly-haired boy in a white nightshirt hanging from the back of the door. I screamed and ran into my mother's bedroom. At the time she told me that it was only a bad dream. But years later, she said that her younger brother Thomas had accidentally hanged himself with the cord from his bathrobe, fifteen years before, and that my description of him fitted exactly.

'As I grew older, I had experiences like that more and more often. I very rarely *see* anybody, not like poor young Thomas. We were related, maybe that was why I saw him so clearly. But I can *feel* people, I can feel their presence, and sometimes I can hear them, too.'

'Same as me!' Amelia burst out, with sudden enthusiasm. 'I can walk into a room, and I can tell right away if people have been sad in there, or if somebody got hurt, or if somebody died. And those people coming through from underneath, I can hear them whispering. *Whisper-whisper-whisper*. It's like sand, when the wind blows it.'

Martin nodded. 'You see?' he said. 'Me and Amelia, we're pretty much the same. I used to think that being sensitive to human resonance was like being a medium, or a clairvoyant. But it isn't. It's nothing to do with the supernatural, it's a physical ability that you're born with – or a disability, depending on how you look at it. It's genetic. Me – I don't have William's Syndrome like Amelia here, but I do have a chromosome disorder which makes me aware of stuff that normal people simply can't pick up on. It's just like some people can hear dog-whistles, or see infrared light—'

'OK,' Ruth interrupted him, 'but what does any of this have to do with these fires?'

'I'm sorry, I'm getting around to that,' said Martin. 'As I grew older, I kind of learned to live with all of the voices that I could hear and all the pain that I could feel. It became like background noise, you know, like living in some crowded apartment where you can hear everybody's TV playing and people arguing and doors slamming.

'But then I met a girl called Susan and we fell in love. Susan was a very talented painter and she was funny and bright and pretty and we talked about getting married. But we had only been together for seven months and four days when we went swimming at Breakheart Reservation near Saugus and Susan just disappeared under the water. A beautiful summer's afternoon, a flawless blue sky, but she just disappeared. The lifeguard dived down and found her tangled up in weeds on the bottom of the lake. He tried to resuscitate her, but it was too late. To this day I still don't know what happened. Could have been a cramp, who can tell?'

'Breakheart Reservation,' said Doctor Beech. 'That was a sadly apt place to lose the love of your life.'

'This is the whole point, though,' Martin told them. 'I *didn't* lose her. Not completely, anyhow. About a month after the funeral, when I was taking a shower, I felt her put her arms around me. I practically jumped out of my skin, I can tell you, but when I turned around I couldn't see her. I could still *feel* her, though. Her face, her hair, her body. I stayed in that shower for almost twenty minutes, holding her, but when I turned off the water she was gone. How can I describe it? It was just like she *evaporated*.

'After that, almost every time I took a shower or a bath, I felt her clinging on to me, although I never saw her. I put my hands into the kitchen sink once, to pull out the plug, and under the water I felt her hand taking hold of my wrist, as if she didn't want me to empty it out.

'I was scared, I can tell you. But in a strange way I didn't want her to stop doing it. I didn't know if she was a spirit, or if I was gradually going mad, but at least I felt that I hadn't lost her for ever.'

He gently stroked Amelia's hair, as if he were giving her a blessing. Amelia closed her eyes. Ruth was sorely tempted to tell him to take his hand off her, but he seemed to calm Amelia down, and she didn't want to appear too prickly.

Martin said, 'One day I went back to Breakheart and I took a swim in the same lake that Susan had drowned in. I don't know why – just to kill my ghosts, I guess. But I was less than halfway across when I felt Susan pulling me down from under the water. She dragged me under five or six times before the lifeguard reached me and helped me back to the shore. I was about as close to drowning as you can get, but somehow I had felt for a few insane seconds that I *wanted* to drown.' He paused and looked away for a moment. 'At least Susan and me would have been together again.'

Doctor Beech slowly nodded. 'I can understand that,' she said. 'I've treated plenty of grief-stricken widows and widowers who have told me that they were looking to die in the same way as the loved ones they've lost: overdoses, hanging, throwing themselves in front of a train. Some of them have even prayed to get cancer. They think it's some kind of guarantee that they'll be reunited in the afterlife.'

'Well, they're right,' Martin told her.

'Excuse me?'

'I mean it. How you die, that's all-important. Not when, not why, but *how*. It affects everything that happens to you after you're dead. It can make all the difference between resting in eternal peace or having to suffer everlasting torment.'

'Please,' said Ruth. 'I don't mean to be rude or unappreciative, Martin, and I'm very sorry for your loss, but I don't think any of this is at all helpful. Ammy's had enough anxiety attacks, thank you, without causing her even more stress.'

She stood up and said, 'Come on, Ammy. Let's go. I'll take you to Crazy J's for a triple chocolate malt. I'm sorry, Doctor Beech. I know you meant well, but I really can't listen to any more of this.'

But Ammy clung on to her chair. 'No, Mommy. Martin's right. I know he is. I want to hear him out.'

'Ammy – it's nonsense. When you're dead, you're dead.'

'That's not what Daddy thinks.'

'I know. But Daddy . . . well, Daddy has different beliefs. I respect them, but I don't agree with them. We're all very lucky to have a life on this earth, but we should make the most of it, because when it's over, it's over.'

'You're not one hundred per cent sure of that, are you, Ruth?' Martin put in.

'I don't know what you mean.' Ruth was seriously beginning to dislike this man.

'I mean that when I was telling you about Susan, you reacted in a very interesting way. You started to blink very quickly and your breathing rate went up. You didn't want to believe me, did you? But I'll bet you money that you've heard something similar before. Somebody else has told you about a loved one coming back. Or maybe you've experienced it for yourself, but you didn't want to believe it was true.'

Ruth sat down again, but she stayed very straight-backed. 'All right. I was talking to one of my colleagues at the Fire Department this morning, and he told me that his dead wife came to visit him.'

'And after he had told you, what did you think?'

'I thought – I didn't really know *what* to think. I assumed that he had probably experienced some kind of hallucination, triggered by grief.'

'How did his wife die?'

'She committed suicide. She burned herself to death.'

'Is that Uncle Jack?' asked Amelia. 'Is that Uncle Jack and Aunt Lois you're talking about? Aunt Lois *killed* herself?'

'I'm sorry, sweetheart, yes, she did. I didn't see any point in telling you. I didn't know myself exactly how she died, until yesterday.'

'Oh my God, she *burned* herself. That's *terrible*.'

Ruth put her arm around Amelia and gave her a reassuring hug. 'It's OK now, Ammy. She hasn't come back any more. Uncle Jack scattered her remains over the Ivy Tech garden, and now she's at peace.'

'Intelligent man,' said Martin. 'That was exactly the right thing to do.'

Ruth looked up at him. 'Will you get to the point of what you're trying to tell us? I think we've all had quite enough distress for one day.'

Martin lifted both hands in mock-surrender. 'Of course, Ruth. I'm truly sorry. But like I said before, none of this is easy to believe, and there's still a whole lot that even I don't understand.'

He sat down next to Amelia, and looked at Ruth intently. 'After my experience with Susan, I did as much research as I could into post-mortem visitations, if only to prove to myself that I wasn't ready for the rubber room.

'I made contact with almost every paranormal investigation society in the USA, and believe me there are dozens of them. Most of them turned out to be overexcited nerds with raging acne and high-tech video cameras, or middle-aged moon-howlers with their spectacles held together with Band-Aids. But I found one professor at Madison University in Wisconsin, Frederick Solway, who's been looking into PMVs for over twenty years. He has degrees in physics and the history of science going way back to Greek and Roman times.'

'"Post-mortem visitations"?' Ruth challenged him. 'Isn't that just a fancy way of saying "ghosts"?'

'Unh-hunh. Because there's no such thing as ghosts.'

'So what are they, these "PMVs"?'

'The simplest way that I can describe them is to say that they are resonant reappearances of people who have died in violent or traumatic circumstances. They died, or they were killed, but they were never released. They all had unfinished business with the living, because of the way they died.'

'Unfinished business?'

'They couldn't move on, Ruth. They couldn't find peace. When you say that death is the end, you're absolutely right. If you die a quiet, natural death, it's just like being born in reverse. One minute you're conscious, and breathing, and part of the world around you. Then you're gone, back to the blackness where we all came from.

'But people who die an unnatural death, they have scores to settle, they have problems to sort out. They have all kinds of loose ends to tie up. And they can't go into that blackness until they have. They're physically dead, but they're not *spiritually* dead. That's why they come back. They need to exorcize the past.'

Ruth took a deep breath. She wanted to tell Martin that she didn't believe a word he was saying, but at the same time she couldn't help thinking of Jack. '*Holy Jesus, there she was, standing in the yard, wearing the same purple dress she died in.*' Why would a hard-nosed man like Jack Morrow tell her something like that, if it wasn't true?

'So what exactly are you trying to tell me?' she said. 'That these people coming through from underneath, they're like *zombies* or something?'

'No, not like zombies. Well, not like zombies in the George Romero movies, anyhow. But they do appear exactly like they looked on the day that they died.'

'My colleague's wife burned herself to death, but she didn't *look* burned. Not according to him.'

'She wouldn't have done, any more than somebody who died in an auto wreck would look all smashed up. It's not like that *Monkey's Paw* story, where the boy gets crushed in a mining accident and his father wishes him alive again, but when he comes knocking on the door he's still mutilated.

'All the same, if somebody got themselves severely burned, but they subsequently died from some other cause – infection, maybe – then they *would* look pretty gruesome.'

Ruth said, 'I still don't get it.'

'Then let me explain it to you the way that Professor Solway explained it to me. He showed me that if you die violently, you go through a period of transition. It's like a living person going into shock. In early Christianity, they called this period of transition "Purgatory" – a place where your sins could be washed away and you could be made ready for heaven. That's unless you were such an unrepentant sinner that you were beyond redemption, and you had to go kicking and screaming down to hell.

'And hell? What was that like? The concept of hell being a burning fiery furnace apparently came from medieval priests who had received post-mortem visitations from people who had died in fires. But Frederick Solway showed me documentary and scientific evidence that every single form of violent death has its own particular hell – not just fire alone. That's how I came to write my book about it, *The Nine Circles of Hell.*'

Doctor Beech said, 'That was it! I knew it was the Nine Circles of Something-or-Other. Was it ever published?'

Martin shook his head. 'I tried very hard to get it into print. But the scientific publishers said it was too superstitious, and the religious publishers said it wasn't inspirational enough, and the general publishers said it was badly-written mumbo-jumbo. Which it probably was. Not mumbo-jumbo, but badly-written. I never pretended to be Norman Mailer.'

'So tell us about these nine circles of hell,' said Ruth. She was growing increasingly impatient and irritated, but she was trying hard not to show it. Amelia was listening to Martin with such a rapt expression on her face, and after all she had brought Amelia here to the clinic to help her come to terms with the Creepy Kid and the people coming through from underneath, whatever they were, zombies or ghosts or PMVs.

Martin said, 'Frederick Solway is certain that the nine circles of hell actually exist, and that they have a definite location in time and space, in the same way that medieval theologians believed that Purgatory was a place that you could actually visit, if you could find out where it was.

'But Frederick Solway worked out that the nine circles of hell exist in our immediate future, always a split-second ahead of us. We can't go there until we die. After we're dead, however, we can take that split-second step back into the past and revisit the living – especially, like I say, if we have unfinished business, or we're looking for revenge.

'Frederick Solway tried to explain the physics to me. It's all to do with Einstein's theory of relativity and something called the Lorentz transformation of time, but don't ask me to explain it to you because I don't understand a goddamned word of it. Pardon my French.

'But there are literally hundreds of anecdotal accounts of dead people coming back to visit the living – right from the thirteenth century to the present day. Even John Hancock was visited by his dead mother, Mary Hawke, did you know that? In the winter of 1784 he saw her twice – once at the top of the staircase and once at the end of his bed. On the advice of his local minister he had her body secretly exhumed, and cremated, and her ashes scattered over Weymouth Fore River.'

'I don't believe this,' said Ruth. 'John Hancock, who signed the Declaration of Independence?'

But Martin ignored her. He said, 'Frederick Solway divided the residents of hell into nine different categories. Disease victims are probably the most populous, because they run into millions; followed by the victims of starving or dehydration. Then there's freezing victims, crushing or falling victims, victims of strangulation or suffocation, drowning victims, stabbing or shooting victims, poisoning victims and fire victims – which is of course what we're dealing with here.'

'But what do they *want*?' asked Ruth. 'They're dead, aren't they? Why can't they just *stay* dead?'

'Because they're suffering,' Martin told her. 'They want release. They're screaming in hell and they would do anything at all for the agony to stop. They want that all-enfolding darkness.'

'And that's how they get this "all-enfolding darkness" – by coming back and incinerating other people?'

'So far as we can tell, yes. They employ what you might call hit-men, or assassins, to act out the circumstances of their own burning. These fires – they're like exorcisms, or passion-plays. The hit-men pick out somebody who resembles the original fire victim. Usually it's somebody totally innocent. Then they recreate the original victim's death. It's a sacrifice, if you like.'

'A sacrifice? To whom, exactly?'

'Professor Solway has a theory about it. He thinks that there are various lesser gods that dead people can do deals with, so that they can rest in peace. But like I told you, there's a whole lot that I don't understand.'

'So where does this Creepy Kid fit in? You said that he caused the fires. You said that he was the catalyst.'

'He is. I guess you could call him the angel of death. He's dead himself.'

'How can that be? I've seen him standing outside my house. I've *talked* to him, for Chrissakes.'

'I know that. Amelia's seen him, too, haven't you, Amelia? But I warn you here and now, Ruth. Get away from here, as soon as you can, and take Amelia and the rest of your family with you – and maybe your colleague at the Fire Department, too. Get the hell out of here before hell comes looking for you.'

SIXTEEN

Nadine tried to open her eyes but her eyelashes were glued together. She felt bruised all over and her head was banging so hard that she felt as if somebody was hitting it against the concrete floor, again and again, with every beat of her heart.

She tried to sit up, but when she did so her ribs crackled and she screamed out in pain. She lay back, sobbing. She couldn't think where she was, or what had happened to her, or why she was hurting so much.

'*Daddy!*' she cried out. '*Daddy, where are you?*'

She raised her hands to her face. Her fingers were sticky, but she managed to rub her eyelashes until they became unglued. She peered at the crumbly red granules on her fingertips, and it was only then that she realized that her eyelids had been sealed together by dried blood.

Gasping with effort, she raised her head. She was still naked, but her bare skin was covered all over with a patchy varnish of dark red. She tried to sit up again but her broken ribs jabbed into her lungs and the pain was too much for her to bear. She had a hideous pain between her legs, too – a pain that made her muscles go into uncontrollable spasms, as if she had been impaled on a fence.

Whimpering, she reached down and felt herself, and with a flood of absolute dread she discovered that she had been penetrated by two long-handled brooms, the kind they used for sweeping out the stables, and that her attackers had left them inside her.

'*Daddy!*' she screamed. '*Daddy, help me! Daddy!*'

Weeping, she tugged the broom-handles out, one after the other. Then she rolled over on to her side and stayed there for three or four minutes, shuddering with shock. She could hear thunder, and rain drumming on the stable roof. She could hear horses, too, restlessly circling in their stalls. She tried to convince herself that she was lying in her bed asleep, and that this was a nightmare, but she knew that it wasn't. She was suffering too much pain, and she could remember the three men in white masks.

She could remember cutting the jugular grooves of seven horses, and gallons of warm blood bursting out all over her. She could remember sinking on to her hands and knees on the stable floor, bloodied all over, too traumatized by what she had done even to cry. She could remember the man in the laughing mask standing in front of her and tilting her chin upward.

'Eat me,' he had ordered her.

Thunder rumbled again, and she heard the stable door banging. She had to get out of here and find her father. Very slowly, she managed to turn herself over and crawl toward the nearest stall. She took hold of the bridle that was hanging beside it, and used it to pull herself up on to her feet. Three stalls further along, Bronze Star saw her, and whinnied.

'Good boy,' she whispered. She didn't turn her head and look behind her, because that was where the dead horses were lying, the horses that the laughing man had forced her to slaughter.

She hobbled stiffly along the stalls, holding in her breath because of her broken ribs. A tan horse-blanket was draped over the side of Bronze Star's stall, and she dragged it off and wrapped it around her shoulders. Then she began to make her way toward the stable doors, moaning with every step. Lightning flashed outside in the yard, and inside the stable the lights flickered and dimmed.

She was only ten yards away from the stable doors when a small figure appeared out of the rain – a young boy with a pale face and dark curly hair, dressed in a black T-shirt and red jeans. Nadine pulled the horse-blanket tighter around herself, and stopped to catch her breath.

'Freda?' the boy called out. His voice was high and unbroken, and when he spoke he almost sang. 'Freda, is that you there? Watcha done, Freda?'

'I need help,' said Nadine.

'What's that you say? I can't hear you, Freda. You'll have to speak up!'

Nadine slowly sank to her knees. 'I need help,' she wept. 'I really need help.'

The boy came closer. 'You look like some kind of mess, Freda. Watcha done here? You're all over red.'

'They made me kill my horses. Three men. They made me kill my horses and then they beat up on me.'

The boy came up to her and hunkered down right in front of her.

His head was strangely elongated and he had wide-apart eyes and
very red lips. He was like no child that Nadine had ever seen
before. But he cocked his head to one side and gave her a sympathetic smile. 'Warn't your fault, Freda. You just wigged out is all.
Not surprisin', what they put you through, those bastids.'

'My name's Nadine – Nadine Gardner. You have to help me.
Go to the house and find a woman called Cora. She's probably
in the kitchen. Tell her I'm here in the stables, and I'm hurt real
bad.'

'It warn't your fault,' the boy repeated, as if he hadn't heard
her at all. 'They was always givin' you such a hard time, those
bastids.'

'Please,' Nadine begged him. 'Please go to the house and find
Cora for me. Tell her to call my father, too.'

The boy leaned forward, peering into her eyes so intently that
she had to look away. His breath smelled of onions. 'Pa always
said you was cracked, but I never believed him and I don't believe
him now. What you did, Freda, that warn't your fault, and you
only did it to show them, didn't you? Well, good for you, that's
what I think. But now you've done it we can run off together,
can't we, and they're never going to know where to find us.'

'What are you talking about?' said Nadine, wretchedly. 'I don't
understand a word you're saying. I need help, that's all. I need
you to go to the house.'

'You always said that you loved me, didn't you, Freda? You
always said that you an' me, we should run away together and
don't never come back. Because none of those bastids understood
us, did they? They thought you was cracked, and they thought
you was taking advantage, but they didn't know how much we
loved each other, did they? They didn't know we was plannin' on
havin' a baby of our own.'

'Go away!' said Nadine. 'If you can't help me, then please just
go away!'

The boy slipped his hand under the horse-blanket and took hold
of her blood-sticky shoulder. She tried to push him away but he
gripped her even tighter. 'Come on, Freda! Don't chicken out on
me now! Let's do it, just the way we always planned to do it, you
an' me. Let's hightail it out of here, right now!'

She closed her eyes. She felt as if she were going mad. Or
maybe this boy was mad. But if he could help to get her out

of here, what did it really matter if he thought she was somebody called Freda, and that she had agreed to run away with him?

'All right,' she said. 'If you can help me up, please.'

'Surely can,' said the boy. He stood up and took hold of her hand, and pulled it, and he was surprisingly strong. She climbed to her feet and stood there for a moment, swaying. Sparkling dots of light swam in front of her eyes, and she felt the stable floor tilting.

'Hey, Freda, are you OK?' the boy asked her. 'You're not going to faint on me or nothin'?'

'No, no, I'm OK. Just take hold of my arm and help me to walk. It isn't too far.'

'*Walk*? We won't get hardly nowhere at all if we walk. We have to take one of these horses and *ride*.'

'No, no. There's no way I can ride. My ribs are broken. I don't have any clothes. I just need to get back to the house, that's all.'

'We have to ride,' the boy insisted. 'I'll help you, like I *always* helped you. Which horse are we going to take? How about that black one?'

'Don't you understand? I can't possibly ride. I'm hurt too bad.'

'I'll help you,' the boy told her. 'You always said we were goin' to go ridin' off together, into the sunset. You always said that, over and over. You *promised*. Turn around, touch the ground, that's what you said. You promised. You said that if things ever got too bad for us, if anybody ever tried to split us up, that's what we'd do. And now this is our chance to do it.'

'All right, I'll try,' said Nadine. 'But you'll have to help me. I'm hurt too bad to do this on my own.'

'I can help you. Don't you worry about that. Then we can go ridin' off together, can't we, just the way you always said.'

Nadine nodded. 'OK,' she whispered, and when it was clear by the expression on his face that he hadn't heard her, she repeated, '*OK*?' much louder.

'So which horse we goin' to pick? This black one? I really like this black one. He looks mean!'

'This one,' she said, pointing toward Bronze Star. She was badly concussed, but she was still capable of thinking that she was the only one who could make Bronze Star behave with complete docility. If the boy tried to make off with him on his own, Bronze Star would immediately toss him out of the saddle.

The boy took her arm and helped her to shuffle over to Bronze

Star's stall. She held Bronze Star's head while the boy lifted down his bridle and his dark blue saddle-cloth and walking saddle. Nadine told him how to make sure that the saddle was positioned properly, with the underflaps lying flat, and how to flex Bronze Star's forelegs to make sure that when the girth was tightened, it didn't pinch his skin.

Bronze Star looked at her solemnly, and Nadine felt that he could sense her distress and would have spoken to her, if only he could.

The boy adjusted the stirrup-irons, and then he said, 'Come on, Freda, you can climb aboard now.'

'I can't. Really I can't. I hurt too much.'

'Come on, Freda, you can't give up on me now. This is us, runnin' away together! This is you an' me, elopin'! We can go someplace where nobody don't know who we are, and we can raise a family and do whatever we damn well please!'

'Can't you just help me to walk to the house?'

Without warning, the boy seized a handful of her blood-encrusted hair and twisted it, hard, so that she screamed.

'You promised me, Freda, and a damned promise is a damned promise!'

'I can't!' Nadine sobbed. 'Just leave me alone! I can't!'

The boy dragged the horse-blanket away from her and threw it across the stall. Bronze Star snorted and took two or three steps to one side.

Nadine stood naked and shivering, still holding on to Bronze Star's bridle. 'Don't make me! Please don't make me!'

The boy looked around the stall. On a wooden rack on the wall hung horseshoe tongs and nail-pullers and a long blacksmith's file with a sharp-pointed end. He pulled out the file and went across to Bronze Star, holding it up so that its point was only inches away from his flank.

'Maybe you don't think you killed enough horses today, Freda? Maybe you want to see one more go down? I seen an automobile with a puncture, but I never saw a horse with a puncture. But there's always a first time for everythin', wouldn't you say?'

'Leave him alone!' Nadine screamed at him. 'You just leave him alone!'

'I will, for sure, if you do what I'm askin' of you, and climb up into that saddle.'

'Please, I'll try. But don't hurt my horse, OK?'

She managed to raise her left foot into the stirrup-iron, but she couldn't summon up the strength to mount.

'You should see yourself, Freda,' the boy grinned. 'You're a sight to behold, and no mistake!'

'Help me up,' said Nadine. 'I can't do this on my own.'

The boy came around behind her and grasped her buttocks. Nadine was in so much pain that she thought she was simply going to black out and fall backward, but the boy said, 'Come on, Freda, one-two-three!' and gave her a boost. She screamed as she managed to swing herself into the saddle, and when she was mounted she sat with her head tilted back and both hands pressed against her ribs, sobbing. Bronze Star shifted restlessly underneath her, and every movement he made hurt her more.

'Don't you howl, Freda,' the boy admonished her. 'We'll be out of here before you know it, and then we'll be happy ever after! You'll see if we ain't.'

He dragged across an upturned feed-bucket, and climbed up on it. Then he grasped Nadine's left thigh with one hand, and the back of the saddle with the other, and clambered up behind her. He made himself as comfortable as he could, and then he wrapped his arms around Nadine's waist.

'Not so tight!' she pleaded. 'Please! You don't know how much it hurts.'

'Don't you fret. I'll take care of you, I promise. Now, let's get out of here, shall we?'

Nadine took a series of quick, shallow breaths, which was all she could manage. Then she clicked her tongue and said, 'Walk on, Star. There's a good boy.'

Bronze Star seemed confused, and he hesitated. He had never been ridden with two up before, and he was obviously aware that something was wrong. Usually, Nadine spoke to him in a high, encouraging trill, but this evening her throat was choked with misery, and she was barely audible.

'Walk on, Star,' she told him. 'Go on, boy.'

Gently, she guided him out of his stall. She kept her head turned away so that she wouldn't see the bodies of all the horses she had killed and the glistening black blood that covered the floor. As they approached the stable doors she could see that it was still raining outside, but not so hard, and she was relieved to hear that the thunder had passed over to the north-east. The loudest noise was the clattering of water from the overflowing gutters around the roof. Bronze Star nudged one of the doors with his nose, and they stepped out into the rain.

Off to the right, less than 200 yards away, Nadine could see the Gardner family house. Her father wasn't back yet. There was no sign of his Explorer, anyhow. But the lights were shining in the kitchen window, and in two of the upstairs bedrooms. She saw Cora, standing in front of the sink in her pale blue apron, and she let out a low, thankful sob. She clicked her tongue again and tugged at Bronze Star's reins, directing him toward the driveway.

'*No!*' said the boy, in a shrill, panicky voice. 'Where the hell do you think you're going?'

'Back to the house, of course! Where do you think?'

'You can't do that! We're runnin' away! If we go back to the house, they'll punish us. They'll beat us black and blue, those bastids! They won't let you an' me stay together, not never again!'

Nadine twisted around in the saddle, although the boy clung on to her even tighter. 'I'm going back to the house and you're not going to stop me!' she screamed.

'You wanta bet?' the boy shouted back at her. 'You really want to *bet*?'

In spite of the pain in her ribs, Nadine reached down and took hold of his wrists and tried to pull his hands apart. 'Help!' she gasped. 'Help me! Cora! *Cora!* Help me!'

But at that instant, with a soft *whoomph!* like a gas boiler firing up, the boy exploded into flame. He let out an ear-piercing scream and Nadine screamed, too, and Bronze Star reared up and let out a terrible bray that was almost like laughter.

Within seconds, the boy was blazing from head to foot. Nadine felt the hair on the back of her head frizzling down to the scalp, and her shoulders scorching. She tried again and again to break the boy's relentless grip around her waist, but his arms were on fire, too, and her own hands started to blister.

'Help me!' she cried out. 'Oh, God, help me!'

Bronze Star bucked and kicked and screamed with pain, because the boy's fiery legs were clenched around his flanks and were searing his hide. Nadine tried to pitch herself sideways out of the saddle, on to the ground, but the boy was holding her so tightly that she couldn't break free of him. He blazed hotter and hotter, with a steadily-rising roar, and his temperature rose so rapidly that Nadine began to blaze, too, her skin shriveling and her body fat spitting and flaring. Within a few seconds, the whole of her upper body was seared, the skin cracked apart to expose raw red muscle, and her contorted face was a grotesque parody of Darth Maul, scarlet and black.

Maddened with fear and pain, Bronze Star went berserk. He bolted wildly through the rain and the darkness with Nadine and the boy on his back, both of them trailing flames behind them like burning flags. To begin with, he swerved left and right, kicking and rearing in a frantic attempt to dislodge them, but by the time he reached the driveway that led to the main road, he was burning as furiously as they were, and so he galloped hard and straight, as if he could run fast enough to leave his agony behind him. His mane was a crest of flames and his tail was a thick shower of whirling sparks. His shoes clattered on the asphalt in a sharp, hysterical drum pattern, and as he galloped he left a long trail of smoke behind him, which whipped and twisted in the wind.

Bronze Star had nearly reached the archway over the main entrance to Weatherfield Stables when Charles Gardner, Nadine's father, turned into the driveway in his dark green Explorer. He was singing along with the Bee Gees' 'Stayin' Alive'. '*Whether you're a brother or whether you're a mother you're stayin' alive, stayin' alive.*'

He saw a billowing mass of fire careering toward him and he stamped on his brake-pedal, but it was too late. Bronze Star and his two riders collided with the front of his SUV at a closing speed of over forty miles an hour, and burst apart in a whirling, blazing cascade of legs, arms, ribcages, cannon-bones and skulls.

The noise of the collision was deafening, and Charles Gardner was instantly punched in the face by his air bag, which broke his nose. He sat back, bruised and stunned, while pieces of burning flesh pattered on to the roof of his Explorer, and his daughter's smoking pelvis banged down on to the hood, right in front of him, and rocked from side to side.

SEVENTEEN

Ruth said, 'I'm sorry, Martin, I don't believe a word of what you're saying.'

'*Mommy—*' Amelia protested, but Ruth shook her head emphatically.

'I'll admit these three fires are totally unlike any fires that I've ever come across before,' she said.

'You don't know how much,' Martin told her.

Ruth shook her head again. 'In the past five years I've investigated hundreds of fires, and some of them have started in really weird ways. Chemical fires from non-combustible chemicals, electrical fires after the power was switched off, freak lightning strikes, gas leaks. I've even had spontaneous combustion in stores of pistachio nuts. But, come on, Martin. Dead people coming back from hell?'

'All right,' said Martin, raising his hand. 'I can't say that I blame you for being skeptical. But why don't we forget about the technicalities for the moment and concentrate on why Zelda asked me to come down here? Your daughter and I share a common feeling that people are coming into this world from someplace underneath, and I think that's too much of a coincidence for us to ignore.'

'It *is* a coincidence, I agree. But you said yourself that you suffer from a chromosome deficiency, just like Amelia. Maybe that deficiency makes you both suffer the same kind of delusion.'

'What about Susan?' asked Martin. 'I saw Susan after she was drowned, and your colleague saw his wife after she had burned herself. How do you account for that?'

'I don't know. Grief can play some pretty strange tricks on us, can't it? Maybe there are times when we want to see somebody so much that we think we can.'

'And the Creepy Kid?'

'I don't know about him, either. But, like I said, he's probably just a kid who happens to be creepy. We'll find out who he is, given time – same as we'll find out how these fires were started.'

'I'm sure you will,' Martin told her. 'Except that in my opinion, solving one conundrum will solve them both. Cause and effect. Or *vice versa.*'

'What do you think, Doctor Beech?' asked Ruth.

'I think Martin's right,' said Doctor Beech. 'We need to find out more about this feeling that he and Amelia have both been experiencing – these "people coming through from underneath". We need to know why they're having it, and what it symbolizes.'

'So how do we do that?'

'I'm proposing a kind of hypnosis. But before we talk more about that, does anybody want coffee, or a soda? How about you, Amelia?'

'Yes, please.'

Doctor Beech went to the door and asked Dora to bring them three cups of coffee and a can of Dr Pepper. Then she sat down again and said, 'I've never been very happy about using hypnosis. After some people have been hypnotized, they can suffer some very undesirable after-effects, some of which can last for years: delusions, paranoia, personality disorders.

'But there's a method of suggestion which I sometimes use in cases of severe psychological trauma, especially when there are two or more people involved. It's called the Liébault Technique, and it was devised by Ambroise-Auguste Liébault, who was a very respected nineteenth-century hypnotherapist. It encourages patients to share their thoughts not only with their therapist but with each other. It makes it possible for them to see whatever it is that's been disturbing them in three dimensions, so to speak, and also to see themselves as other people see them.'

'OK . . .' said Ruth, cautiously. 'How does it work?'

'Simply by encouraging patients to play back the images that they already have stored in their minds. You know, like playing back the tape from a CCTV. The last time I used it was for five people who had been involved in a serious auto accident on Route Thirty-Five. Four people had died, and both of the surviving drivers each thought they were responsible for what had happened, while two of their surviving passengers blamed one of them and the third surviving passenger blamed the other.

'As you can imagine, the drivers' families had both been torn apart by what had happened. How can you live with a man when you blame him for killing your mother and three young girls and permanently crippling your baby daughter? But I persuaded them all to sit down together and recreate the accident in their minds, and it was only *then* that they remembered the girl who had suddenly fallen from an overpass, right in front of them.

'One car had swerved to avoid her, but had hit her all the same, as well as the car that was traveling next to it. Both cars had collided with a third vehicle, a bus carrying seven Girl Scouts, and then an SUV, and all of the vehicles had caught fire. Most of the occupants of the vehicles had managed to get out unhurt, but five people had died.

'The police had assumed that the body of the girl who had fallen from the overpass was a passenger in the SUV, but the Liébault session showed us where she had really come from, and that neither of the drivers were guilty of dangerous driving.'

Dora came into the room with the coffees and the soda, and set them down on the table, along with a plate of Oreos.

'I shouldn't eat these goddamned things,' said Martin, taking three cookies at once. 'Once I start, I can't stop. Pardon my French.'

Doctor Beech said, 'If you agree to my using the Liébault Technique today, we can at least find out if these "people coming through from underneath" are really real. Or really *not* real.'

'How can you do that?'

'Because the Liébault Technique shows me in my mind's eye what all of my patients are seeing, simultaneously. It assembles all of their differing viewpoints into one picture – a picture which is much more objective than the memory of any individual patient on their own. It's as near as any therapist can get to the truth. It's as near as *anybody* can get to the truth.'

'Is there any danger?' Ruth asked her. 'You said that hypnotism can have serious after-effects.'

Doctor Beech said, 'I know. But in this case – with Amelia and Martin here – I can't see that there's any substantive risk. They're not suffering from any psychological trauma like those road-accident survivors. They've been experiencing anxieties, for sure. They've been hearing things and seeing things. But in my professional opinion I think they'll both feel a whole lot better if we can find out once and for all whether the things that they've been seeing and hearing have any basis in reality.'

'What if they do? I mean, what if they *are* real? How do we deal with that?'

Martin unexpectedly laid his hand on top of Ruth's hand, and gave it a reassuring squeeze. 'If they are real, we'll just have to find ourselves a way of sending them back where they came from, won't we?'

'Supposing they don't want to go?'

'But they *do* want to go. That's the whole point. They want peace. They want oblivion. All we have to do is find out how to give it to them, but without losing any more innocent lives.'

Ruth exchanged glances with Doctor Beech, but Doctor Beech could only give her a resigned shrug which seemed to mean 'we won't know for sure until we try it out.'

'OK, then – how do you do this What's-his-name Technique?' asked Martin.

'We have to sit in a circle facing each other,' said Doctor Beech. 'Then I'll lightly press my fingertips against Martin's right temple on the one side and Amelia's right temple on the other. Amelia in turn will press her fingertips against Ruth's left temple, while Martin will raise his left hand and press his fingertips against Ruth's *right* temple. In that way, we will all be physically and psychologically connected to each other's thoughts, and the images in our minds will go round and around between us, faster and faster, like a fairground carousel.'

Martin dragged the coffee table to one side and they arranged their chairs so that they were facing each other. Doctor Beech went across to her desk, opened her drawer, and took out a multi-faceted glass ball. It was mounted on a small plastic base, and when she switched it on, it lit up and began to rotate, refracting the light and splitting up its colors like a diamond. She set it down on the dark-green carpet at their feet.

'This will help you to bring your remembered images back to life. Now, let's make ourselves comfortable, shall we, and make contact?'

They sat down and lifted their arms, pressing their fingertips to each other's foreheads. Amelia smiled at Ruth and then started to giggle.

Doctor Beech said, 'Don't worry. I know it seems funny, but I promise you it's going to work. I want you all to stare at the glass ball down on the floor. Try to blink as little as you can, so that it gradually goes out of focus.'

Ruth couldn't help smiling, either. She had always had an

irreverent streak, and when she was a young girl she had always found it impossible to keep a straight face when she was in chapel, or when a teacher had been scolding her. Even at her grandfather's funeral she had been forced to bite the inside of her cheek to stop herself from laughing. She had loved her grandfather dearly, and she had cried for hours when he died, but she had known that he was gone, and that there was nobody lying in that casket which her family were treating with such solemnity, only a dead body in a three-piece suit.

All the same, she stared unblinkingly down at the rotating glass ball, as Doctor Beech had asked them to do. Its facets sparkled red, and emerald green, and sapphire blue, and Ruth had been staring at it for less than half a minute before its reflections seemed to be dancing in the air, like tiny colored butterflies.

'Each of those colors that you can see is part of a picture,' said Doctor Beech. 'Keep on staring at them, and you will gradually see that picture come together. Keep on staring at them, look at the way they mix and mingle. Think of the people who are coming through from underneath. Think of what they look like. Take those colors as your palette and make them come alive.'

She repeated herself, over and over. '*Think of what they look like. Watch them come together. Think of the people who are coming through from underneath.*'

Ruth wanted to look up and see if Ammy was all right, but she found that she was unable to take her eyes away from the twinkling colored lights. Doctor Beech was right: they did seem to dance together in a particular rhythm, so that they formed a pointillistic picture. Orange flickered with yellow, and yellow flickered with scarlet, and then she suddenly realized that she was looking at *flames*.

With a huge effort she managed to turn her head a half-inch toward Amelia. Flames were flickering across Amelia's face, but they were more like a projection of flames from a movie rather than real flames. They were only a picture, after all, a picture that Amelia was seeing in her mind.

Suddenly, the fire jumped up higher and higher, and Ruth was sure that she could hear the flames roaring. She turned toward Martin, and saw that his face, too, appeared to be crawling with flames. The fire was growing fiercer because *his* visualization of it had now joined Amelia's, and the two of them were sharing their vision of the same inferno, but from different points of view.

And that's what it was: an inferno. Not a bonfire, or a burning warehouse, or even a thousand-acre forest fire. This was a wall of never-ending fire, a whole *world* of fire, a fire which would consume everything – people, houses, forests, even the sky – and go on burning for ever. This was hell.

Ruth remained locked in her chair, her hands clasped together in her lap, with Martin's fingertips pressed to one side of her forehead and Amelia's fingertips pressed to the other. She wanted to stand up. She wanted to break the circle, but her body simply wouldn't obey her. She looked through the transparent flames at Doctor Beech, but Doctor Beech's eyes were unfocused and she appeared to be lost in some kind of hypnotic trance.

'*Doctor Beeeechhhhh!*' she called out, but her voice came out slow and blurry, like a soundtrack played at a quarter speed. '*Doctor Beeeechhhhh!*'

It was obvious, however, that Doctor Beech couldn't hear her, or else she was unable to respond, because her eyes remained unfocused, and she seemed to be whispering something to herself, something quick and urgent. *Whisper-whisper-whisper, like sand, when the wind blows it.*

Ruth turned back to Amelia. Amelia was still staring down at the glittering glass ball, her eyes unfocused like Doctor Beech, and she was whispering, too. So – when she looked at him – was Martin. Ruth began to hear whispering herself, too soft and hurried for her to make much sense of it, but it sounded like the same words being repeated over and over: '*– have to settle it – have to make it right – have to settle it – fingers on fire – eyes on fire – have to settle it—*'

She frowned, trying to hear this garbled, sibilant whisper more clearly. As she did so, she gradually became aware that there was an object lying on the floor of Doctor Beech's consulting-room. She could see it only in the extreme left-hand corner of her field of vision, but she could see that it was almost spherical, and about the size of a soccer-ball, and it was *white*.

She had to use all of her strength to turn her head a little way around, and she could actually hear her neck muscles creaking as she did so. The white object was lying in the corner, close to the skirting-board. Even though she couldn't work out what it was, its appearance filled her with dread, as if it signified that something terrible was about to happen.

She tried to turn back again, so that she could call out to Doctor Beech. Whatever this white object was, she thought it was important that Doctor Beech should see it. It might give her some vital understanding of Amelia's and Martin's shared illusion, and help her to treat them, if they needed treatment. But she had managed to move her head only a fraction of an inch when the white object on the floor slowly rotated on its axis and tilted upward a little and she saw what it was: a deathly-white mask, with a pointed nose – a mask whose expression was fixed in frenzied, triumphant laughter, as if it had just told the greatest joke of all time.

The mask stared back at her for six long heartbeats. She was sure that she could see eyes glistening inside it. All the time, the whispering continued: '– *have to settle it – have to make it right – eyes on fire – face on fire – have to settle it—*'

Ruth had never felt so frightened in her life. Was this just a mask, or did it have a decapitated head inside it? If so, how had it appeared here, on Doctor Beech's floor, and how did it move? Maybe it was just an illusion, a magic trick, like the ghostly flames that were still leaping up in the center of their circle. But it continued to stare at her, and she couldn't take her eyes off it. Its malevolence was almost palpable. If she had been able to get out of her chair and cross the room and pick it up to see what it really was, she would have done, but then again she didn't know if she was brave enough. After all, it might be a real decapitated head.

She squeezed her eyes tight shut and strained as hard as she could to turn away from it. *There's nothing there. This is just some figment of Ammy's imagination, or Martin's, or both of them.*

But then, over the persistent whispering, she heard a thick voice say, 'Don't you remember me, Ruth, baby? Don't tell me you *forgot* me already! It wasn't *that* long ago, surely? Don't you remember the Markland?'

She felt as if thousands of woodlice were pouring down her back. She recognized that voice. *She knew who it was.*

'*You!*' she said, and tried to rear up out of her chair. But the white mask rolled away and knocked against the skirting-board, and then it dropped down into the carpet and vanished, as completely as if it had fallen into a dark-green pond.

Ruth twisted herself around. The flames were still flickering. They were barely visible now, but Amelia and Martin and Doctor Beech were still sitting as they had been before, staring fixedly at the sparkling glass ball.

'*Ammy*,' said Ruth.

But now the whispering grew louder and louder, until it was almost deafening.

'– *settle it, settle it, settle it – make it right – eyes on fire – fingers on fire – settle it, settle it, settle it—*'

The consulting-room door burst open, and dozens of people poured in. They were so smudgy and faint that it was impossible to see what they looked like, or exactly how many there were. They rushed through the room quickly and jerkily, like characters in a speeded-up movie. Ruth's immediate instinct was to throw herself across to Amelia and hold her tight, but she still found it impossible to rise from her chair.

Most of the people who were crowding in were black-faced and charred, and dressed in blackened rags, although they were hurrying around the room so rapidly that Ruth couldn't focus on them to see how seriously they had been burned. They kept criss-crossing in front of the window so that the daylight flickered, and each of them was trailing a swirl of strong-smelling smoke. Even more of them jostled in through the door, and several of these newcomers were still alight, with flames crowning their heads instead of hair, and rippling cloaks of orange fire.

'*Ammy!*' screamed Ruth, or thought she did. '*Ammy, wake up!*'

The room was a riot of whispers and shuffling feet and strobo-scopic images of half-incinerated men and women, and children, too. As more and more burning people came in, the smoke began to thicken, until Ruth's eyes were watering so much that she could hardly see. She coughed, and coughed again, and the stench was so pervasive that she could actually *taste* it – seared flesh and friz-zled hair and smoldering wool.

'*Ammy! Martin! Wake up!*'

It was then that the loose-weave drapes caught alight, and flames leaped up on either side of the window. The temperature climbed rapidly, and Ruth knew that it would only be a matter of seconds before the soft furnishings ignited. If that happened, and they were all unable to leave their chairs, they would be dead from toxic smoke inhalation within less than twelve minutes.

'– *eyes on fire – fingers on fire – settle it, settle it – faces on fire – make it right – settle it, settle it—*'

Ruth tried to shake her head from side to side, to break the contact with Amelia's and Martin's fingertips, but she could only move her head an inch or so in either direction, and their fingertips were pressing against her temples too hard and too persistently. Amelia and Martin were both completely caught up in what Doctor Beech had called the fairground carousel of remembered images, unable or unwilling to get off.

She bent forward in her chair as far as she could manage. She took a deep breath, coughed, then snatched another breath and flung herself backward in her chair as hard as she could. It wasn't enough. The chair remained upright. Meanwhile, the drapes were flaring up to the ceiling, and the black leather on Doctor Beech's chair was starting to shrivel, as if it were growing prematurely old.

By now, the entire consulting-room was thronged with burned and burning people. Some of them were not much more than shadows, rushing from one side of the room to the other, like the panicking audience in a burning movie theater. But, for split-seconds only, Ruth glimpsed people moving more slowly – people with faces stained black as photographic negatives; people whose bodies were so contorted in agony that they looked like hunchbacks. She saw people whose legs had been completely consumed by fire up to their knees and whose arms had been burned to their elbows; people without ears or eyelids or noses or lips, yet who still stared out at the world in pain and desperation, longing for life as it was before they burned, but also longing for it all to be over.

Ruth bent forward again. She took another deep breath and tightened her throat so that she wouldn't cough. She counted to three, and then she threw herself backward again.

There was a moment when her chair teetered on its back legs, and she was sure that she was going to tilt forward again. But then she fell backward, on to the carpet, knocking her head. She would probably have a bruise, but the circle was broken.

The crowds of burned and burning people completely vanished, as if they had never existed. But the drapes were still alight and the consulting-room was thick with smoke, and all four of them started to cough.

Ruth climbed to her feet and gave Amelia a hug. 'Come on, Ammy, come on sweetheart, out of here, now! You too, Martin. And you, Doctor Beech. Where's your fire extinguisher?'

Doctor Beech was still sitting in her chair, looking bewildered. 'What? What happened? Where did all those people go?'

'You're back in the real world, Doctor Beech. All you have to do is get the hell out of here, before you breathe in hydrogen cyanide gas.'

Doctor Beech stood up unsteadily, and Martin came across to take her elbow and support her.

'That was some party trick, Zelda,' he told her.

At that moment, the sprinkler system switched itself on and they were deluged in cold water. Amelia screamed and flapped her hands. The blazing drapes were extinguished almost immediately, and the acrid brown smoke began to shudder like a beaten dog and sink down to floor level.

'Come on,' said Doctor Beech, 'let's get out of here.'

'Look at us,' Martin laughed. 'We look like four drowned rats!'

Doctor Beech said, 'Dora! Call nine-one-one, please, and ask for the Fire Department.'

'I already did that, Doctor,' Dora replied, in a testy voice. 'I did it as soon as I saw smoke coming out from under the door.'

'The door was *closed*?' Martin asked her.

'Yes, sir. It's been closed all the time you've been in there, except when I brought in your coffees.'

'I don't get it. Nobody else came in or out?'

'I think I would have seen them if they had, sir,' said Dora. She was being sarcastic, because her desk was only about four feet away from Doctor Beech's door, on the right-hand side.

Ruth took a quick look back into Doctor Beech's consulting-room, just to make sure that there were no signs of the fire springing into life again. The blackened tatters of the drapes hung from the rail over the window like a row of vampire bats, and all the files and papers on Doctor Beech's desk had been soaked, but apart from that there was no serious damage.

Doctor Beech came up behind her, raking back her wet hair with her fingers. 'How could the drapes have caught fire?' she said. 'Those people – they weren't actually here. They only exist inside of Amelia and Martin's minds.'

Ruth looked up. There was a brown flower-shaped smoke stain

on the ceiling, directly above their circle of chairs. It looked like a giant chrysanthemum, almost six feet in diameter.

'What do you make of that, then?' she asked Doctor Beech. 'If that fire we saw was only inside of their minds, how come it left smoke residue on the ceiling?'

Martin joined them. 'It was all real, that's why. The fire, the people. Amelia and I, we haven't been imagining this stuff, these people coming through from underneath. They *are* coming through, or they're trying to, and we've both been able to sense it. You know, the same way some animals can sense when there's an earthquake coming.'

'Well, Martin,' Ruth told him, 'I have to say that I'm almost inclined to believe you.'

'Really?' Martin raised one eyebrow. 'That's a dramatic change of heart.'

'I know,' she said. 'But even if I can question my own reliability as a witness, I can't argue with the evidence. Those drapes didn't set themselves on fire, and this smoke stain on the ceiling didn't appear by magic. And there was something else. I saw a head on the floor, right over there, in the corner.'

'A *head*?'

'It was covered with a white mask, with a laughing expression on its face. I'm not sure how to describe it to you.'

'Just a head?'

Ruth nodded. 'That was all. A man's head. But he was alive. He spoke to me, and he knew who I was. What was more, I knew who *he* was, too.'

'Go on.'

'His name is Pimo Jackson. The last time I saw him was three years ago, at Indiana State Prison in Michigan City. He's a serial arsonist. He started a fire at the Markland Motel here in Kokomo and eleven people died, including three children. Twenty-seven other people had to be treated for smoke inhalation or serious burns.'

'Jesus.'

'Yes, Jesus. But there's one thing more. Pimo Jackson himself was one of the casualties. That's how we caught him. He was splashing accelerant around so wildly that he almost burned his own face off.'

EIGHTEEN

Dora brought them towels to dry themselves off, and then Ruth went out to her car to let Tyson out. It had stopped raining, but the sky was still thunderously dark, and she could see sheets of rain falling high over Greentown, to the east.

Tyson could smell fire on her straight away, and he snuffled and whined and strained at his leash. Ruth gave him a chance to relieve himself next to a fence-post, and then she took him inside the clinic. About a half-mile away she could hear the honking and whooping of a fire truck.

'What's with the dog?' asked Martin, as she led Tyson into Dora's office.

'His name's Tyson and he's pretty famous around here. He's an arson dog, trained to detect accelerants.'

'But *you* know what caused those drapes to catch fire, and it certainly wasn't arson.'

'Sure, I know it and you know it, but I still have to do it by the book. If you're trying to prove that something unnatural happened, first of all you have to establish that nothing *natural* happened. How do we know that Doctor Beech didn't surreptitiously soak those drapes in lighter fluid, and set fire to them just to impress us?'

'Because she didn't. And we saw *people*, Ruth. We saw scores of people and some of them were burning. That's what caused it.'

Tyson looked up at Martin and gave a deep growl in the back of his throat.

Ruth said, 'You're right. We did see people. But how can we prove it, and where are they now?'

'They're back, for the time being, anyhow. They're back underneath, in hell, or Purgatory, or whatever you want to call it. But they're not going to stay there very much longer. That's what this is all about.'

Through the window, Ruth saw Engine Number Two pull up outside, an International-Pierre Contender, red and silver, followed by a white Ford Expedition with its red lights flashing. A few seconds later Bob Kowalski, the battalion chief, came striding in, his face even more florid than usual.

'Hi there, Ruthie!' he greeted her. 'Where's the fire?'

'Bob! You didn't have to come out here in person. It was only a set of drapes, and they're out now.'

'Hey, I didn't have anything else to do. Apart from that, I was playing pinochle with Gary and Keith and Jim The Spaceman, and I was getting creamed.'

Ruth unclipped Tyson's leash and he trotted into Doctor Beech's clinic and sniffed around. Ruth and Bob Kowalski followed him.

'So what happened here?' Bob Kowalski asked her, reaching up and tugging at the tattered remains of the drapes. 'Somebody get careless with a cigarette?'

Ruth pointed at the brown chrysanthemum-shaped stain on the ceiling. 'We were holding what you might call a group therapy session. I can't exactly explain what happened. I *saw* things. We all did. They could have been hallucinations. They could have been real. But this is what happened.'

Bob Kowalski stared at the stain for a long time, thoughtfully pulling at his upper lip, as if he were wondering whether to grow a moustache. 'You saw things and then the drapes caught fire?'

'That's right.'

'I'm finding this kind of hard to follow, Ruthie. What kind of things?'

'We saw flames, and then we saw people. I believe they might be connected with the Julie Benfield fire, and the Tilda Frieburg fire, and the Spirit of Kokomo bus fire.'

'*People*? What people? Where people?'

'They were fire victims,' said Ruth. 'Some of them were still burning. I guess that's how the drapes caught alight.'

Martin came forward. 'Excuse me, Chief. We call them PMVs. Post-mortem visitations. Their existence has been verified by some very respectable researchers.'

Bob Kowalski's eyes narrowed. 'You're talking dead folks?'

'If that's what you want to call them, yes.'

'So you were having a group therapy session and some dead folks showed up and torched the drapes?'

'That's about the size of it, yes.'

Bob Kowalski looked at Ruth. 'What kind of therapy was this exactly?'

'It's for Amelia,' Ruth told him. 'She's been having anxiety attacks.'

'I see.'

Martin said, 'You don't, I'm afraid. You think this was mass hysteria, Chief, but I can absolutely assure you that it wasn't. You have a very dangerous situation building up here.'

'You want to tell me who you are, sir?' Bob Kowalski demanded.

Martin held out his hand, which Bob Kowalski ignored. 'My name's Martin Watchman, and I've come down here today to help Amelia to deal with her anxiety attacks. At Doctor Beech's request, may I add, and with Ruth's explicit approval.'

Bob Kowalski looked at Ruth, as if he expected her to deny it, but Ruth nodded. 'Martin has been having exactly the same kind of attacks as Ammy. Well, not so much attacks as visions, or premonitions. I don't really know what to call them.'

'I think you and me need to talk about this back at headquarters,' said Bob Kowalski. 'Meanwhile, do you want to handle this yourself, or do you want Jack to come out here and take over?'

'Bob, this is serious. Something very strange is happening and we can't ignore it.'

'Did I say I was going to ignore it? You've all had a very disturbing experience this afternoon, I can understand that. But don't let's start getting all mystical here. Whatever set these drapes on fire, it's explicable. Every fire has a physical cause and this one is no exception.'

'But that's the whole point,' Martin interrupted him. 'The cause *was* physical, not mystical. PMVs might seem supernatural to you, but they're not. In their own way, in their own space and time, they're just as real as you are.'

'What, you're trying to tell me that I'm some kind of ghost?'

'Of course not. But if people still have problems to sort out, after they're dead, they have the ability to come back and sort them out, if they need to. For God's sake, have you never watched *Ghost Whisperer*? It's only fiction, of course. You don't really go into any light when you die, you go into total goddamned darkness, excuse my French, and that's it. Goodbye for ever. But Ruth saw these people and I saw these people and so did Doctor Beech, and it was these people who set fire to the drapes and could have killed all four of us, if Ruth hadn't had her wits about her.'

Amelia came up and took hold of Ruth's hand. 'I saw them,

too, Uncle Bob. I saw the people and I saw the fire that burned the ceiling.'

Bob Kowalski laid his hand on Amelia's shoulder, as if he forgave her for supporting her mother. 'We'll get to the bottom of this, sweetheart, don't you worry. I know it seems confusing and scary, but that's what shock does to you. Give it some time and it'll start to make sense. How about it, Ruthie? Let me call Jack for you. Why don't you take Amelia home?'

At that moment, however, Tyson let out a single loud bark. Ruth called out, 'Hold on, boy!' and went back into Doctor Beech's consulting room to see what had excited him. He was sniffing around the blackened fibers that had fallen from the drapes. He was circling around and around and his tail was drumming furiously against the air-conditioning unit.

Ruth hunkered down beside him. 'What is it, Tyson? What did you find?'

Tyson sniffed again, and then sneezed. Ruth picked up some of the fibers and rubbed them between finger and thumb. There was something else mixed in with them: not fiber, but gritty gray ash. In fact, not ash at all, but what looked like cremated remains.

'Bob!' she said. 'Come here, take a look at this!'

Bob Kowalski came into the room, but as he did so Tyson let out another bark, and bundled past him, out of the door, almost tripping him up.

'*Tyson*! Where are you going? Tyson, come back here!'

Tyson had never disobeyed her before, but now he hurtled out of the front door of the clinic, down the steps and across the parking area. Ruth said, 'Sorry about this, Bob,' and went after him.

Outside, the sky was gloomier than ever, and it was starting to rain again. Tyson ran across the parking area, jumping over the chain-link fence that surrounded it, and headed for a small stand of silver birch trees, off to the left.

'*Tyson*! Slow down!' Ruth ordered him. She stepped over the chain-link fence and crossed the grass. 'Tyson! Come here, you disobedient mutt!'

But it was then that she saw what Tyson had been tracking. Or rather, *who*. Underneath the overhanging trees, his face luminously white, his curly hair tousled, stood the Creepy Kid. Without hesitation Tyson ran right up to him and the boy knelt down and put his arms around Tyson's neck and held him close. Tyson, for his part, whined like he did when he wanted food, or a walk, or affection. He even licked the boy's cheek.

Ruth approached the Creepy Kid very cautiously. 'Tyson,' she said. 'Heel, Tyson.'

'He wants a cuddle,' said the Creepy Kid. His voice was high and defiant. Although he didn't say it, the implication was 'he wants a cuddle so what are you going to do about it?'

'*Heel, Tyson!*' Ruth snapped at him. Tyson turned his head around and looked at her with guilty, bulging eyes, but he stayed where he was. The Creepy Kid was tugging rhythmically at his ears now, just the way he liked it.

'What are you doing here, kid?' Ruth demanded.

'Maybe I should ask you the same darn question,' the boy retorted.

'I want you to let go my dog now, you got it?'

'He'll come when he's good'n ready. You'll see.'

'I said, leave him alone!'

The boy said, 'You didn't leave *me* alone, did you? Even though I asked you nice as pie.'

'You threatened me with trouble. You call that "nice as pie"?'

'Depends what kind of a pie takes your fancy. There's all kinds of pie. There's blueberry pie, for sure, and cherry pie. But then there's trouble pie, poison pie, and stab-you-in-the-eye pie.'

'Tyson, come here!' Ruth shouted. Tyson made a jerking move to come toward her, but the boy held on to him tight.

'Let go my dog!' Ruth told him.

'I *told* you,' the boy insisted. 'He'll come when he's good'n ready, not before. And I want to make sure that *you're* good'n ready, too.'

'What are you talking about? Let him go!'

She went right up to the boy and seized Tyson's collar. The boy held on to Tyson even tighter, and stared up at her with those odd, wide-apart eyes, like something staring at her out of a fishbowl. The expression on his face was frighteningly triumphant.

'I told you to leave me be, didn't I? I told you. What I gotta do I gotta do, and I don't want you interferin' none because there's souls to be saved and all manner of mis'ry that needs to be attended to. It ain't your right to let other folks suffer in eternal torment, now is it? It ain't your place. So you promise me now that you're going to back away and leave me be, and everything's going to be fine and dandy, lickerish candy.'

'Let go my dog, you little bastard. I mean it.'

The Creepy Kid grinned. His teeth were unnaturally small, as if he still had his milk-teeth. 'You got to promise me first. All them fires was acts of God, that's all. So don't you go pokin' into them no further, less'n you want to take on more trouble than you ever knew that one person could suffer.'

Ruth pulled at Tyson's collar again, harder, so that Tyson made a strangling noise in his throat, but still the boy wouldn't release him.

She stood up straight. It was raining harder now, and the raindrops were pattering through the leaves of the silver birches. She turned around and saw Bob Kowalski walking toward her, closely followed by Martin Watchman.

'Ruthie? What's going on here?' asked Bob Kowalski. 'Are you OK?'

'Not really. I'm having a little problem with this young man here. He's holding on to Tyson and he won't let him go.'

Bob Kowalski came up to them and said, 'Come on, kid. Let the dog loose.'

The boy shook his head vigorously. 'He wants a cuddle.'

'Well, I'm afraid he's not a cuddling kind of a dog, kid. He's a working dog and right now he needs to be working.'

'I don't want him to be workin'. I want him to stop snifflin' around and leave me be.'

'What's your name, kid? You shouldn't be here, this is private property. Do your folks know you're here?'

'My folks are dead. And I can go any darn place I want.'

Martin leaned close to Ruth and murmured, 'Is this him? Is this the Creepy Kid?'

Ruth nodded.

'It's the same kid who was hanging around outside my house,' Martin told her. 'You need to be very careful, take my word for it. Whatever you do, don't upset him. Like I told you, he's a catalyst.'

'What you two mumblin' about?' the boy called out. 'You got somethin' to say to me, you say it out loud so's I can hear it!'

Martin stepped up to him. Tyson twisted uncomfortably in the boy's arms, but still he wouldn't let go.

'Remember me, son?' said Martin. He spoke so quietly that Ruth could hardly hear him over the rustling of the rain.

The boy blinked up at him. 'Should I?'

'Not necessarily. But I know who you are. More to the point, I know *what* you are, too, and I know why you're here and I know what you want.'

'So what are *you*?' the boy retorted. 'Some kind of ever-livin' smartass?'

'Not at all. I just happen to know what's what, that's all. Now, if this lady promises to file a report saying that all of those recent fires were caused by natural phenomena – how about you let the dog go?'

The boy frowned. 'What's a natural fermonima?'

'It means that those fires were nobody's fault. They were caused by lightning, maybe, or a short-circuit, or a chemical spill, something like that. That way, the investigations get closed, and nobody will come looking for you.'

'No dogs snifflin'?'

'No dogs. No cops. No children's services. Nobody from the Fire Department. Nobody.'

Martin stepped back. The boy looked up at Ruth and said, 'Would you do that?'

Out of the corner of his mouth, Martin said, '*For Christ's sake, say yes. You don't have to mean it.*'

Ruth cleared her throat. 'Yes, OK,' she said, loud and clear. 'I'd do that.'

'You promise? Swear to God and spit in the sky?'

'I promise.'

'Swear to God and spit in the sky?'

But Bob Kowalski said, 'Hold up a tootin' minute here! We're talking about three serious cases of probable arson, with multiple fatalities. We can't make no promises like that. These fires, they're going to be investigated thoroughly and we're not going to let up until we find out how the hell they started and who's responsible, just like we always do.'

'Chief . . .' said Martin, and made a patting gesture in the air which meant that he should hold it down. 'We have a very special situation here, Chief, if you understand what I mean.'

'Excuse me? You might be Ruthie's friend, sir, but I don't think that you're in any position to decide what's a special situation and what isn't, or how we're going to respond to it, even if it is. Officers of the Kokomo Fire Department don't make no promises to cover up potential cases of deliberate fire-setting, not for nobody, and under no circumstances, not ever.'

Ruth crossed over to Bob Kowalski, turning her back on the Creepy Kid so that he couldn't see her face. 'Bob,' she said, and her voice was low and urgent. 'Please go along with this. Please. I need him to let Tyson go.'

'Ruthie – you don't have to promise this kid nothing. He's only a kid, and a skinny kid at that. I can take him apart with one hand.'

'Are you *mumblin'* again?' the boy protested. 'I told you I didn't want you to do no *mumblin'*!'

Ruth turned around to face him. 'I've made you a promise. Now let my dog go.'

'You never said swear to God and spit in the sky.'

At that moment, Bob Kowalski's cellphone made a siren noise. He flipped it open and said, 'B.C. Kowalski. What the hell is it? I'm tied up right now.'

But then he raised one hand, as if to stop Ruth and Martin from saying or doing anything more, at least until he had finished talking. He listened for a long time, his hand still raised, and then he said, 'When did this happen? What? *What*? How many?'

He listened again. The Creepy Kid said, 'You didn't promise yet. Not properly.'

'All right,' said Ruth. 'Swear to God and spit in the sky.'

But Bob Kowalski suddenly said, 'Christ on crutches, you're kidding me! OK, Jim. I'll be there in ten. Who's attending from Fire and Arson? OK, great. I have Ruthie with me, too. Yes, she's here. I'll bring her along.'

He snapped his cellphone shut and his face was grim.

'What is it?' Ruth asked him.

'Charles Gardner's daughter, Nadine, out at Weatherfield Stables. Looks like she slaughtered seven of their own horses, cut their throats.'

'Nadine Gardner? I can't believe it. She's such a lovely girl. Do they know why she did it?'

'We don't know the full details, not yet. Nadine's dead. Seems like she was trying to ride away from the stables on her favorite horse, but they caught alight.'

'*What*? What do you mean "they caught alight"?'

'Pretty much cremated, that's what Jim said. Rider *and* horse. Charles Gardner was coming home and he ran right into them. Turned into his driveway and they were galloping hell-for-leather right toward him, like a four-legged fireball.'

Ruth looked across at Martin, and then at the Creepy Kid. Martin said, 'Easy, Ruth.'

But Ruth stalked up to the Creepy Kid and snatched Tyson's collar again and pulled him. 'You let my dog go!' she screamed at him. 'I made you a promise so you let my dog go!'

'*No!*' the boy shouted back at her. 'I don't trust you, not one bit! You think I started *that* fire, too, don't you? You think I set fire to that woman and that horse!'

'So you had nothing to do with it, did you? Just like you had nothing to do with any of those other fires? How do you even know about it? *How*? And how can a woman and a horse catch on fire? How can that possibly happen?'

'It was an act of God. They was *all* acts of God.'

'*God*? God had nothing to do with this, did He? It was *you*. I don't know how you do it, not yet, but let me tell you this: if I'm going to make any promises here today, I promise to find out, and when I do find out I promise to hand my evidence over to the cops, and I promise to see you locked up in the Howard County Juvenile Detention Facility for as long as the law will allow. Swear to God and spit in the sky.'

As she shouted at him, the boy began to shuffle himself away from her, on his backside, still with his arms tight around Tyson. Tyson himself was wriggling and struggling, but only spasmodically. He seemed to find it impossible to break free, as if he had lost all of his strength, or couldn't decide any longer where his loyalty lay.

'Give me my dog, you little runt!' Ruth shouted at him, as the boy retreated. 'Give me my dog or I'll twist your goddamned ears off!'

'Ruth!' Martin called after her. 'Ruth – *don't*!'

But Ruth was too angry to take any notice. She stalked up to the boy and seized Tyson's collar again. '*Give – me – my – fucking – dog*!' she shouted at him, right in his face.

At that instant, while he was still clutching Tyson tight to his chest, the boy detonated into a mass of fire. Orange flames burst

out all over him, as if he had been drenched in gasoline and somebody had struck a match. He let out a panicky howl of pain, and
Tyson screamed in a way that Ruth had never heard a dog scream
before, almost like a human baby. She half-jumped, half-stumbled
backward, both of her hands scorched.

'*Tyson*!' she screamed, but even though Tyson was scrabbling
wildly to get himself free, the burning boy still wouldn't release
him.

'*Foam*!' Bob Kowalski bellowed at the fire crew who were
standing around the pumper. 'Keiller! McKay! We need some
goddamned foam here! Like, *now*!'

Ruth stripped off her coat and bundled it around her hands to
protect them. Bob Kowalski said, 'Ruthie! Don't even think about
it!' The boy was already blazing fiercely, in a column of flame
that was over six feet high. The fire burned faster and hotter with
every second, with a soft roaring noise like a giant blowtorch.

Ruth held her arms up to shield her face, but all the same
she could feel the heat against her legs, right through her jeans. She
approached the boy as close as she could, and made a desperate lunge to drag Tyson out of his arms. But Tyson, too, was
on fire. All of his black fur had been singed off, so that his skin
was red-raw. He was jerking convulsively from side to side, like
a cockroach on a hotplate. Right in front of Ruth's eyes, his
spine burst out of the skin on his back.

'*Tyson*!' she wept. '*Oh God, Tyson*!'

Tyson turned his head round and stared at Ruth in agony, but the
fire was far too hot for her to pull him out of it, at least 700 degrees
Celsius, probably more. She knew there was nothing she could do
for him, nothing to spare him from his pain, and that she had no
choice but to watch him die. She tried to see the boy's face through
the flames, but by now it was nothing more than a blackened voodoo
mask, with flames pouring out of his empty eye-sockets, and even
as she looked at him, his jaw dropped open and fire gushed out of
his mouth.

'Tyson, oh God, Tyson. Oh, God.' The heat was so intense that
Ruth had to step even further back. Three firefighters were running
over from the pumper, reeling out a long hose behind them. They
started to blast the fire with high-pressure foam, and within a few
seconds it was noisily extinguished, leaving nothing but a wide
black mark on the ground, and a small clutter of smoking bones.

Ruth could see Tyson's ribcage, and it reminded her so much of the rack of barbecued ribs that she had eaten at the Windmill Grill last week that her mouth was flooded with sour-tasting vomit. She turned away and bent double and retched. She had seen scores of people and animals with horrifying burns, but they had never sickened her as much as this. Tyson had been hers. He had expected her to take care of him and protect him. She found it as devastating as if she had seen her own child burned alive in front of her.

Martin came up to her and without any hesitation put his arm around her shoulders. 'Ruth? Are you OK?' he asked her. 'It wasn't your fault, believe me.' Smoke was drifting past them and it smelled strongly of burned hair and flesh.

Ruth looked up at him, her eyes blurred with tears. 'What do you mean? You warned me not to, didn't you?' She unwrapped her coat and saw that all of her fingers were blistered. 'God, this hurts. I can't imagine what poor Tyson must have gone through.'

Martin said, 'Ruth, it wasn't your fault. That boy has been doing everything he can to discourage you from investigating these fires any further. He's on a mission from hell, Ruth, and he doesn't want you interfering. I told you, your best option is for you and your family to get as far away from here as possible.'

'If he's trying to stop me from interfering, why didn't he burn *me*, instead of Tyson?'

'I wish I could tell you, but I don't know for sure. There's still so much about the afterlife that we don't understand. And we won't be able to, until we die. By which time it will be too goddamned late, won't it? Excuse my French.'

Ruth walked over to the edge of the charred patch under the trees where Tyson and the Creepy Kid had caught fire. The grass and the leaves and the undergrowth had been completely burned away, leaving nothing but blackened, smoking soil. In the center of the patch lay Tyson's skeleton, with his dog-tags and the steel studs from his collar scattered around it.

Bob Kowalski came up beside her, and sniffed, as if he could smell mischief, as well as smoke. 'Real sorry for Tyson, Ruthie. What a hell of a thing to happen.'

Ruth said, 'It was that boy. That Creepy Kid. He's like something out of a nightmare.'

'He just caught fire, for Chrissakes. No accelerant, nothing. Not even a goddamned Zippo.'

'It's like I told you, Bob. It's like some really bad dream, and now you've seen it for yourself. Julie Benfield, Tilda Frieburg, the Spirit of Kokomo bus. Nadine Gardner, too, by the sound of it. How do a woman and a horse both catch fire? Now poor Tyson, too.'

'So what are you saying to me, Ruthie? All this stuff you were telling me about dead folks, you really think it's true?'

'I don't know. But I think we have to keep an open mind. All of these fires are way beyond our normal experience. I mean, you know how Jack and me work. We always stick to the evidence. But something totally unnatural is happening here, and so far none of the evidence is enough to explain what it is.'

The fire crew had brought out two tungsten floodlights, and set them up on metal poles to illuminate the razed area of soil. Bob Kowalski shaded his eyes with his hand and peered at Tyson's remains. 'Hate to say this, but where's the kid at? Like, where are *his* bones?'

Ruth said, 'Wait.' She stepped carefully across the burned patch, until she reached Tyson's skeleton. His back legs and his tail had been less seriously burned, and were still intact, and when she saw them she felt sick rising up in her throat again. She took three deep breaths, and then she hunkered down and gently brushed the soil around his skeleton. It was covered with heaps of gritty gray powder, some of it damp and lumpy from the firefighters' foam. She carefully picked up a lump between finger and thumb and carried it back to Bob Kowalski.

'What's this?' he asked her.

'What does it look like? It's the Creepy Kid. What's left of him, anyhow.'

'You're kidding me! I witnessed that fire for myself, with my own eyes. You don't get remains like this, not even from a fire as hot as that. You only get remains like this when you've been cremated in a proper crematorium, and your bones have been all crushed up in the old crembola.'

'That's right, Chief,' said Martin.

'So how in hell–?'

At that moment, however, Ruth saw that Amelia was crossing the parking lot toward them. 'Excuse me, Bob,' she said. 'There's no way I want Amelia to see this. She adored Tyson.'

She hurried back and managed to intercept Amelia just as she was stepping over the chain-link fence. She took hold of both of Amelia's hands and said, 'I'm so sorry, sweetheart. There's been an accident. Tyson got burned.'

'What happened to your *fingers*?' asked Amelia.

'It was the fire. I was trying to pull him out, but I couldn't. It was much too hot.'

Amelia's eyes were glistening with tears. 'It was that Creepy Kid, wasn't it? I felt him. I knew he was there.'

Ruth nodded. 'I'm so sorry. We'll give Tyson a proper burial at the pet cemetery.'

'But they're together now. Tyson and the Creepy Kid.'

'What do you mean, together?'

'They're underneath, but they're going to come back. I know it. I can feel it.'

'Ammy, Tyson's dead.'

Amelia shook her head furiously. 'No, he's not. They're together. Him and that Creepy Kid. And they're going to come back, I promise you.'

NINETEEN

'I could seriously use a drink,' said Ruth.

Amelia rummaged in her purple woven bag and produced a bottle of Gatorade No Excuses. 'Here you are, Mommy. It's a bit warm, but it's wet.'

'Very sweet of you, sweetheart, but I need a *drink* drink.'

Her eyes flicked up to her rear-view mirror.

'Is he keeping up with us?' asked Amelia, twisting around in her seat.

Ruth nodded. 'I just hope we're doing the right thing, inviting him home.'

'Mom, he's telling the *truth*, I swear it. You saw those people yourself, all burning. *And* that mask. *And* that Creepy Kid.'

'I still find it really hard to believe. Dead people coming back from hell? There has to be some other explanation.'

'You told Martin that you believed it.'

'I told Martin that I *almost* believed it.'

'But *I* believe it, and you believe *me*, don't you?'

Ruth looked at her. 'Yes,' she said. 'I believe you, sweetheart. But I genuinely wish that I didn't.'

Martin had made himself a reservation at the Courtyard Hotel on Kentucky Drive, but Ruth had insisted that he come back to the Cutter house for a family supper. He was a stranger in a strange city, after all, and whatever his motives he had come a very long way to help them.

More than that, though, she badly needed to talk to him about what had happened at the clinic. She needed to understand where all those burning people had come from, and why the Creepy Kid had punished her by setting fire to Tyson, and himself. She needed to find out why that hysterically-laughing white mask had spoken to her in the voice of Pimo Jackson.

She had no way of knowing for sure if Martin was genuine, or if Professor Frederick Solway really existed, or if the Nine Circles of Hell were any more real than Middle Earth. Martin could be nothing more than a con artist. He could be certifiably insane.

But even after all of the forensic tests that she and Jack had carried out, none of the material evidence from any of the fires that they were investigating made any scientific sense whatsoever. As far-fetched as it was, Martin's was the only theory that so far fitted all or at least most of the facts.

But there was something else, too. Martin and Amelia seemed to have developed an unspoken but almost tangible affinity, exchanging looks that made any words unnecessary. And she had to admit that she herself found Martin's presence strangely reassuring, as if he was an old college friend she had known for years. Maybe that was what made him a good con artist. Just for tonight, though, she didn't really care.

When they turned into the driveway, Ruth saw that Craig was already home. Out of habit, she went around to the back of her Windstar and was about to open up the tailgate when she realized that Tyson was no longer sitting in the back, snuffling impatiently to be let out, and never would be. She looked at Amelia and Amelia looked sadly back at her.

Martin had parked his battered silver Taurus by the curb, and he followed them up to the porch.

'This *is* going to be OK, isn't it?' he asked. 'I mean, your husband won't have his nose put out of joint if I join you for supper?'

'Of course not. Why should he?'

Martin shrugged. 'Some men are pretty skeptical about the afterlife, that's all. More than women.'

Ruth unlocked the front door. 'We saw what we saw, Martin. Maybe they were dead people coming back from hell, maybe they weren't. But we can't pretend that we didn't see them, and we can't pretend that Tyson wasn't burned to death in front of our eyes. We have to talk this over, no matter what anybody else thinks about it.'

Craig was pacing around and around the living-room, talking on the phone.

'I know, Roger. I know that. But I can't cut the price any lower than seventy-eight-five. I have to break even, at the very least.' He paused, and then he said, 'OK. Get back to me. But you know that I can give you a top-quality job. Far better than Hausmann's, any day.'

He hung up. There were bags under his eyes, and his hair was all mussed up.

'Roger Letterman,' he said. 'I think I just lost out on six kitchens out on Cottonwood Drive. I don't know how anybody else could fit them any cheaper. Not unless they make their worktops out of compressed horse-manure. Still – the Logansport contract is going ahead OK, touch wood and whistle.'

Ruth said, 'Craig, honey, this is Martin Watchman.' She hesitated. Her throat was so constricted that she could barely speak. Craig looked blank, and so she said, 'You know – the gentleman who came down from Chicago today to help with Ammy's anxiety attacks.'

'Oh – OK,' said Craig, and held out his hand. 'Pleased to meet you, Martin. How did it go today? Make any progress?'

'Tyson's dead,' said Ammy. Her cheeks were shining with tears. She rushed over to Craig and put her arms around him.

'*What*?' said Craig. 'What the hell happened?'

Ruth could only speak in a choking staccato. 'It was terrible. The whole thing was terrible. Those visions that Ammy's been having, I saw them too. We all saw them. And then that Creepy Kid showed up. He put his arms around Tyson and they both burned up. They caught *fire*.' The word *fire* came out only as a throaty squeak.

'*What*?' said Craig.

Martin said, 'Your wife has had a bad shock, Mr Cutter. I think she could use a drink.'

They sat around the kitchen table with a bottle of wine and talked for almost an hour. Gradually, Ruth and Amelia and Martin explained to Craig about the Liébault experiment at Doctor Beech's clinic, and the horrifying images it had conjured up.

'And these what-d'you-call-'ems – these PMVs – they actually set the drapes on fire?'

'They're not ghosts, Craig. They're not holograms. They're real people.'

'But they're dead, right?'

'Dead, yes,' said Martin, 'but not at rest. They're a split-second ahead of us in time, that's all. It's just like somebody walking down the street about twenty yards ahead of you. If you're both walking at the same speed, you're never going to catch them up, right? But if they turn around and start walking back toward you, then you're going to meet up with them pretty quick, because your closing speed is doubled.'

Craig turned to Ruth. 'What's he talking about? Do you know what he's talking about?'

'Craig,' Ruth appealed to him. 'Please try to understand. I don't know if Martin's theory about hell is true or not. I don't have any way of proving it. But then again, I don't have any way of *dis*proving it, either.'

'*Andie's ashes*,' Amelia whispered.

'Excuse me?' said Martin.

'Andie's ashes. Somebody just whispered "*Andie's ashes*" into my ear.'

Craig tilted back his chair and drummed his fingers on the table. 'You know, I don't want to be the party-pooper here. But it seems to me like a classic case of mass hysteria. Like, you're all working each other up into such a state that you're beginning to believe that it's really happening. But, let's be logical here for a moment, how *can* it be?'

Martin said, 'Ruth gave me to understand that you believe in the afterlife.'

'I do. I believe that when we die we're judged by God and we get our just desserts. If we've tried our best to live a good and honest life, we get admitted to heaven. But if we've been purposely and unrepentantly wicked, we get sent to hell.'

'So what's your problem, Craig? You believe in some kind of continuing existence after death, and that's exactly what we're talking about here.'

'I know. And I do believe in life after death. But I don't believe that dead people come back, wherever they've been sent to. And I certainly don't believe that they set fire to innocent people.'

'Not just people,' Amelia put in. 'Dogs, too.'

'People, dogs, whatever. I don't believe it. That's no way for a soul to get absolution, is it, however sinful they might have been when they were alive, or whatever problems they might have left behind them?'

'You think that because you're a monotheist,' said Martin.

'Say what?'

'You believe in only the one God. And to some extent, yes, you're right. He *is* the Supreme Being, although He's not quite the whiskery old senior sitting on a storm-cloud that Michelangelo painted.'

Craig lifted his hand. 'Don't let's get blasphemous here, Martin.'

'No blasphemy intended, Craig. What you have to realize is that, apart from this one Supreme Being, there are many other lesser gods, who carry out the day-to-day administrative stuff. That's what Professor Solway thinks, anyhow. He believes that there are gods of happiness, gods of grief, gods who console you when everything in your life seems to be going down the crapper, excuse my French.

'You've heard about people in very dangerous situations, who have sworn blind that there was somebody next to them, kind of a third presence, who helped them out of it. Shackleton believed there was somebody walking next to his party, when they were stranded at the South Pole, somebody who guided them to safety. And there was a guy on the seventy-sixth floor of the World Trade Center on September eleventh who was sure that there was a stranger close beside him who told him to run headlong into the flames, even though that was the last thing his natural instinct would have told him to do.

'Those are the lesser gods, Craig. But not all of them are sweetness and light. In the case of these fires, I think we're probably dealing with the gods of retribution or the gods of ill fortune.'

Craig stood up. 'I'm sorry, Martin. But I really think that this is baloney. How about another drink and then we change the subject?'

Martin was unfazed. 'Craig,' he said, 'what evidence do you have for the existence of God? Absolutely none, do you? None at all. Yet you believe in Him absolutely. So at least try to have an open mind about lesser gods. Professor Solway is sure that there are gods or spirits or elemental forces which can save the souls of the damned from everlasting torture. The damned can do a deal with them, if you like. If they perform a ritual sacrifice which finally resolves the problems they left unfinished before they died, then the gods will allow them to have peace.'

'This is such shit,' Craig protested.

Ruth said, '*Craig*!' but Craig waved his hand dismissively.

'Why do you think that, Craig?' Martin persisted. 'The Holy Communion is a re-enactment of the Last Supper, isn't it? And Catholics believe in transubstantiation . . . that when they drink that communion wine and eat that communion wafer, they are actually ingesting the blood and the flesh of Christ. If that's not a ritual sacrifice, I don't know what it is.'

'But these fires have killed totally innocent people. God wouldn't allow that.'

Martin shrugged. 'If God didn't allow the death of innocent people, this would be a very happy world indeed. But also a very dull one.'

Ruth said, 'Is anybody hungry? How about some three-cheese pie, and a little salad?'

'That sounds very tempting, Ruth,' Martin smiled at her.

But Craig shook his head and said, 'No, thanks. Not hungry. I had a burger with Mike Watterson at A&W's.'

At that moment, the front door opened and Jeff came in, his hair sticking up on end, wearing a black T-shirt with *Cattle Decapitation* lettered on the front. He was closely followed by Detective Ron Magruder and Detective Sandra Garnet.

'Met these guys outside,' said Jeff.

'Sorry to intrude, Ruth,' said Detective Magruder. 'We heard about Tyson. You don't know how sorry we are. He was one hell of a dog, Tyson. One hell of a dog.'

'We're all going to miss him so much,' said Detective Garnet. 'Especially you.'

Ruth said, 'Yes, I am. I saw him die right in front of me, but I still can't believe he's gone.'

Amelia piped up, 'He *hasn't* gone! I *told* you! He's coming back!'

Ruth put her arm around Amelia's shoulders and said, 'Let's talk about that later, sweetheart. Right now I think Detective Magruder has something he wants to say to me.'

Jeff picked up a slice of three-cheese pie in his fingers and started to eat it. Then he went to the fridge and took out a can of Dr Pepper. 'Dad? I thought we were going to pick up my new car this evening,' he said.

'Yes – yes, of course,' said Craig. 'In fact now might be a good time. Ruth, honey – Jeff and I are going over to Gus Probert's house to pick up that Grand Prix. He only lives out on Meadow Drive, by the golf course, so we shouldn't be more than forty-five minutes, tops. Jeff, do you want to call a taxi?'

Jeff said, '*Yesssss!*' and clenched his fist.

Ruth introduced Martin. 'Martin's come down from Chicago, to help with Ammy's therapy.'

Detective Magruder and Detective Garnet shook his hand and said, 'Pleased to meet you, sir. Any friend of Ruth's . . .'

'Have you been out to Weatherfield Stables yet?' Ruth asked them.

'Yes, we did,' said Detective Magruder. 'Jack's still out there, along with Val Minelli. You never saw anything like it in your life.' He nodded his head toward Martin and said, 'Is it all right if we talk about this now?'

'Absolutely,' Ruth assured him. 'Martin's been helping us to make sense of all this. But Ammy, sweetheart – why don't you take your pie upstairs to your room? I don't think you want to hear any of this horrible stuff.'

'I saw Tyson on fire, didn't I?' Amelia protested.

'Yes you did, and I wish you hadn't. I don't want you having nightmares.'

'Tyson's coming back,' Amelia told Detective Magruder, with complete confidence.

'Oh, really? Well – I guess that dogs have souls, too, don't they?'

'No, they don't. But he's still coming back.'

'Ammy, please,' said Ruth. 'I need to talk to Detective Magruder without you being here. There's a good girl.'

'O-K,' sighed Amelia, and picked up her plate and went upstairs.

'She's such a character,' said Detective Garnet.

'Oh, she's much more than that,' Martin put in. 'She's a genuine sensitive. Because of her William's Syndrome, she can pick up all kinds of disturbances in the atmosphere that none of the rest of us are aware of. If anybody can help us to find out who's been causing all of these fires, then she can.'

Detective Magruder said, '*Amelia*? You really think so?'

'I've been having some of the same feelings myself, but nothing like as clearly as Ammy. Did you hear her, just now? She said that somebody had whispered "Andie's ashes" in her ear, but none of the rest of us heard it. She's amazing.'

'Sit down,' said Ruth. 'Tell me about Nadine Gardner. Do you have any idea what happened?'

Detective Garnet sat down and took out her notebook. 'A KPD patrol car answered a nine-one-one call and went out to Weatherfield Riding Stables on Isaac Walton Road, where they found Mr Charles Gardner, the owner of the stables, in a state of severe shock. He said that he had been turning into his driveway when a horse and rider had come galloping toward him, both of them blazing, and had collided with his SUV.

'Horse and rider were both explosively dismembered by the impact. Mr Gardner said it was like a bomb going off. There were pieces of both horse and rider scattered over a thirty-foot area, but Mr Gardner found a human forearm lying on the driveway close to his SUV and it was wearing a silver charm bracelet that he and his wife had given to their daughter Nadine to celebrate her graduating from vet college.'

'Oh, God,' said Ruth. 'I met Nadine quite a few times at charity horse shows. She was *such* a sweet girl.'

Detective Garnet flipped over a page, and then said, 'The attending officers went to the Gardner house where they interviewed the housemaid Cora Wilkins and the handyman Duncan Scruggs. Neither of them had seen or heard anything prior to the collision between Nadine Gardner and her horse and Mr Gardner's SUV.

'The attending officers then went to the stable-block where they found that seven out of a total of eighteen horses had been slaughtered by having their throats cut open. There were bloody handprints all over the horses' stalls and the officers also discovered a large bloodstained knife which was almost certainly the weapon used to kill them. We're still waiting for a fingerprint match, but there was no indication that anybody apart from Nadine Gardner was present in the stable-block at that time, and the handprints were described by the attending officers as "small, likely to be female".

'Incidentally, they found all of Nadine Gardner's clothes on the floor of the stable, including her underwear, so it was likely that she was naked at the time of the incident.'

Ruth slowly shook her head. 'So it looks like Nadine killed seven of her family's horses and then somehow climbed up on to another one and set fire to the both of them?'

'Looks that way, on the face of it.'

'Was there any stress between Nadine and her family? Anything that might have triggered this off?'

'Not that her father and mother can think of. They both say that Nadine seemed to be blissfully happy. Her whole life was horses, and riding, and she loved working for the stables. She had no other issues that they could think of. No boyfriend trouble because she didn't have a steady boyfriend. No drug problems, no drink problems, no psych problems. Nothing to explain why she would have flipped like that.'

'*But*?' said Martin.

Ruth turned to him, and Martin said, 'I'm sorry, but I sense a "but".'

'Well, you're right,' said Detective Magruder. 'There is a "but". When I interviewed Charles Gardner he said that what had happened was "just like the Flying X". I didn't know what he meant, but of course he's in the horse business so he knew all about it. It seems like, three years ago, a young woman who worked for a riding stables outside of Scottsdale, Arizona, did almost exactly the same thing. She cut the throats of seven horses and then she set the stables alight. She suffered seventy-five per cent burns and died in hospital about four days later.'

Detective Garnet said, 'After we'd finished up at the Gardner place we went back to headquarters and checked with the Scottsdale PD. They sent us a PDF file on the Flying X. Before she died, the young woman gave the police a statement. She alleged that she had been kept as a virtual prisoner at the riding stables and repeatedly abused by its owner and his two grown-up sons, who were both in their twenties. She had slaughtered their horses and set fire to their stables as an act of revenge.'

'So what happened to the owner and his sons?'

'Nothing,' said Detective Garnet. 'There was no evidence against them, and no witnesses, apart from the owner's thirteen-year-old son, who told police that his father and his brothers had treated the young woman "mean". However, the boy was evaluated by a police psychiatrist and judged to have a very low IQ, and to be prone to making up fantastic stories.'

Martin had been listening to all of this attentively, with his hand pressed over his mouth. But now he sat up straight and said, 'I thought so. Just like I told you, it was a ritual sacrifice.'

'Excuse me?' said Detective Magruder.

'That young woman in Scottsdale, whoever she was, she died of her burns, but she still had unfinished business in the world of the living. What she did – cutting those horses' throats, setting fire to herself – it all had to be re-enacted so that her pain would finally be over and she could find peace.'

'A ritual sacrifice?' Detective Magruder repeated. He glanced at Detective Garnet and raised his eyebrows. 'I see.'

'I don't really expect you to understand what I'm talking about,' said Martin. 'Even if you do, I don't expect you to go along with it. But that doesn't matter. What does matter is that you've given me the confirmation that I've been looking for, that certain PMVs are coming back from the Ninth Circle of Hell, and that they're playing out the circumstances in which they died.'

'So that they can find peace?' said Detective Magruder. Ruth had to admire the way that he kept any hint of sarcasm out of his voice.

'You got it,' said Martin. 'All they want is to end their agony, and go back into the darkness, and they don't care what they do or who they hurt. Let's put it this way: if you were suffering unbearable pain – all day, every day – with no prospect of it ever ending, would *you* care what it took to relieve it? Would you care if some stranger died, so long as it stopped?'

'I'm not too sure I'm following any of this,' said Detective Magruder. 'But don't get me wrong, I want to find out who's causing these fires, and why, and I don't have any preconceptions about any of the evidence that we've collected so far, because so far it doesn't amount to a hill of mixed beans.'

Ruth said, 'You're right, Ron. All of these fires have been pyrotechnically inexplicable, and none of them bears any relation to any of the others. So far, Martin's explanation is the only one we have. And I have to tell you that I've seen these post-mortem visitations for myself, these PMVs. I have, and Amelia, and Martin, and Doctor Beech, too.'

She told the detectives about the Liébault session. While she did so, Detective Garnet frowned at her intently, as if she wanted to tell Ruth that she had a speck of spinach on her front tooth, but didn't want to interrupt; while Detective Magruder constantly cleared his throat and jiggled his left leg.

'Well,' said Detective Magruder, when she had finished by telling them how Tyson had been burned to death. 'Stranger than fiction, huh? Gee-whiz. I don't really know what to say.'

'Is there any way you can check on Pimo Jackson?' Ruth asked him. 'He should still be in prison, right? They gave him eleven consecutive life sentences, after all.'

Detective Magruder jotted a note in his notebook. 'Sure, I'll check on him for you. But if he's only a talking mask I don't think you have too much to worry about.'

Ruth said, 'Ron, this is serious! I know it sounds totally crazy, but it really happened and we all saw it.'

'Correct me if I'm wrong, Ruth, but you saw what was going on inside of Amelia's and Martin's heads. A whole lot goes on inside of *my* head, too, but that doesn't make it real. If it did, you wouldn't be able to see me for the crowds of lap-dancers all around me.'

'Your lap-dancers don't set fire to your drapes,' Ruth retorted. 'And your lap-dancers don't bring some creepy kid along with them – a boy who burns your dog to death.'

'Like I've been telling you right from the beginning,' said Martin, 'the boy is the key. He's the catalyst, the fire starter. He's the angel of death.'

'But if he burned up when Tyson burned up, that's the end of him, right?'

'He was probably burned up years ago,' Martin told him. 'He died, and he was properly cremated, but he keeps coming back. He left his ashes at the clinic, and Ruth tells me that she found similar ashes at all the other fires, so the chances are that they *all* belong to him.'

'That sounds like one hell of a lot of ashes,' said Detective Magruder. 'Exactly how big *was* this kid?'

Martin said, 'He only *looks* like the same kid. But each time he reappears, he's somebody else, another PMV. That's what I think, anyhow. I may be wrong. But as far as I can work out, that's the only way he can be constantly reincarnated, in the flesh, and leave so many ashes when he burns up.'

'All right then, answer me something else. Why is he appearing *here*, in Kokomo? That Flying X business was in Arizona.'

'Don't ask me. But from what Professor Solway says, hell is everywhere and nowhere, both at the same time. I don't think PMVs have the same sense of location as we do. The only place they know is pain.'

'OK.' Detective Magruder tucked his notebook into his inside pocket. 'So what do you think we ought to do now? Any suggestions?'

'I'm not sure. There's no pattern to these fires, so we can't predict where the Creepy Kid is going to strike next. Somehow we have to close off the way through from hell, and I'm not at all sure how we're going to do that. Or even if we can.'

'Ruth?' asked Detective Magruder.

Ruth said, 'That's something we'll have to put our minds to, isn't it? How do you close off the way through from hell when you don't even know if it exists, or even if it *does* exist, where to find it? But – sure – we'll give it a try.

'That doesn't mean that Jack and I won't be carrying on with all of our routine computer models and all of our forensics. Maybe these fires *do* have some supernatural cause, but I still want to understand the science behind them. Even if it's weird science.'

'OK,' said Detective Magruder. 'We'll catch you tomorrow, right? Don't have too many bad dreams. Personally, I think I'm going to.'

The two detectives left. Ruth and Martin sat down together and Ruth poured them both another glass of wine. Upstairs, Ruth could hear Amelia singing one of her songs.

'*I knew the rain would come before the morning*
I knew that he would leave before it came.'

'I should be going after this,' said Martin.

'You can stay over if you want to.'

'No, thanks all the same. I sense that your husband doesn't altogether approve of me. Besides, I need to do some serious thinking about how we can close the way through, and that means I have to pace up and down, and maybe make some phone calls, too.'

'Do you believe it's possible? Do you think we *can* close the way through?'

'I have no idea. I don't have any real conception of what it is, or *where* it is, or what it looks like – if it looks like anything at all. It might be a shining archway, or a mirror, or a window. It might be nothing more than a thin slit between two walls, or a crack between two floorboards. Even if we do manage to find it, I don't have any idea how to seal it off. There's no instruction manual – *How To Keep The Living Dead Out Of Your House.*'

'What about your Professor Solway? Do you think that he might have some idea?'

'Professor Solway? He's away right now. I'm not exactly sure where.'

They sat in silence for a while. Ruth felt exhausted, both

physically and emotionally, but she still felt guilty that she wasn't over on West Superior Street, helping Jack to analyze the remains from the Weatherfield Riding Stables fire. She kept thinking that she ought to feed Tyson, too, and take him for his evening walk. His dark blue Sunday-best leash was hanging on the hat-rack by the front door, next to Craig's fishing-hat and her own red beret.

'Can I ask you a personal question?' said Ruth.

'Of course. Anything.'

'How did you manage to put your Susan to rest?'

'What do you mean?'

'Well, I told you about my colleague Jack, who scattered his wife's remains on her favorite gardens. After that, he never saw her again, so he guessed that she must have passed over and found peace.'

'Sure, yes. But I never tried to put Susan to rest.'

'You didn't? You mean – you mean she still comes back to you?'

He nodded. 'I guess you think that's very selfish. But I find it impossible to let her go.'

'But isn't she *suffering*, wherever she is? She drowned, didn't she? Doesn't she feel like she's *still* drowning, twenty-four-seven?'

'I don't know, Ruth. I don't think so. She never gives me the impression that she's distressed. She just clings on to me as if she doesn't want to let *me* go, either.'

'So every time you take a bath, or a shower, or go swimming—?'

'She doesn't come to me every time. But whenever I go near water, I'm conscious that she's there. Or at least she *could* be there.'

Ruth didn't know what to say. Today she had seen for herself that the everyday world which she had always taken for granted was only one reality in a maze of countless realities. There were dead people everywhere, whispering behind walls, walking through gardens, floating in the darkest lakes. There were people who had been strangled, or burned, or drowned, or suffered heart seizures, breathing their last desperate breath in hospital wards. And they were always whispering, *whisper-whisper-whisper*, because they wanted to come back through, and settle old scores, or see their loved ones one last time, or stay for ever, if they could.

Whatever Martin said, Ruth found it hard to believe that *all* of them wanted that seamless darkness, that eternal silence, that absolute emptiness called death.

Martin finished his glass of wine and stood up to leave. 'I'll call you tomorrow morning, shall I?'

'Yes. You can catch me at the Fire Department any time after nine. Here, I'll write the number down for you. Four-five-seven, two-six-three-six.'

'About today—'

She took hold of his hand. 'Don't let's talk about today until tomorrow, OK? I'm still trying to take it all in.'

He looked at her for a long moment without saying anything. Then he said, 'I hope you realize that I'm no expert when it comes to all of this afterlife stuff. Nobody is. But I know for a fact that not everybody goes quietly, because I can hear them, and I can see them, the same way that Amelia does.'

He leaned forward and kissed her cheek. 'I'll see you in the morning,' he said, and left. Ruth stood by the open front door watching his car turn around in the street, and then drive off.

When she closed the door she found that Amelia was close behind her, her face crumpled and her eyes filled with tears.

'Poor Tyson,' she wept. 'I miss him so much.'

Ruth hugged her and shushed her. 'Shush, sweetheart. He's in a much better place now.'

'That's the trouble,' sobbed Amelia. 'He's not. He's in *hell*.'

TWENTY

'What do you think?' Craig shouted, as they drove back into the city on South Washington Street. Jeff had brought one of his Pig Destroyer CDs with him, and was playing 'Fourth Degree Burns' at maximum volume, so that the window frames buzzed at every beat.

'Fucking amazing!' Jeff shouted back.

'Don't swear!' Craig retorted.

'Sorry, Pops! But it's so fucking fantastic!'

The Grand Prix was in surprisingly good condition for a ten-year-old car, although the knob was missing from the gear shift and the corner of the passenger seat was heavily stuck with duct tape where the tan-colored vinyl had split. As far as Jeff was concerned, however, it was the greatest ride ever. He was driving with his dad, so he was not only observing the speed limit, he was stopping at all the red traffic signals, even if there was nothing coming, and religiously using his indicators, even if there was nobody behind him. But in his mind his car was already crowded with all of his friends, and the music was pumping so loud that they couldn't hear themselves think, and he was revving up the 3.1-liter engine until it screamed.

They turned off South Washington on to West Sycamore.

'Wait until Lennie sees this!' said Jeff. 'He's going to, like, *die* of jealousy! He's going to sob like a girl!'

'Well, I'm glad you like it,' grinned Craig.

'Like it? You are absolutely the best dad ever!'

'Thanks. I do what I can.'

'I got to get one of those Dyno-Max exhausts, though. They got that real deep *throb*, if you know what I mean. You can pull the girls even when you're stopped at the traffic signals.'

'Sure,' said Craig. 'I know exactly what you mean. But as far as I'm concerned, it all happened a long time ago, on a planet far, far away.'

As they drove along West Sycamore, Jeff glanced in his rear-view mirror and said, 'Look at this guy. If there's one thing I hate, it's people who tailgate. Like, the street is totally deserted, dude! If you want to overtake, overtake!'

Craig turned his head around. An elderly black Buick Riviera was driving so close up behind them that he couldn't even see its radiator grille.

'What's his problem?' he said. 'Slow down, Jeff, and wave him past.'

Jeff said, 'OK,' although Craig could tell that he really wanted to step on the gas pedal and leave the Buick way behind him.

Jeff reduced his speed to a crawl, and waved his left arm out of the window as if he were swimming, but the Buick continued to follow them, only a few inches behind their rear bumper.

'Overtake, asshole!' Jeff shouted. 'How fucking slow do you want me to go?'

'Turn the music off,' said Craig. Jeff did as he was told, and suddenly the loudest sound they could hear was the menacing burble of the Buick's engine. Craig shielded his eyes with his hand, trying to see who was driving it. Every street light they passed was reflected from its windshield, so that he could only see the driver intermittently, but he appeared to have a dead white face – more like a mask than a face – and his front-seat passenger had a dead white face, too.

Jeff was driving at less than five miles an hour, but the Buick stayed close up behind them, and now Craig knew that they were in some kind of trouble.

'Stop,' he told Jeff. 'Pull into the curb and stop. And put up your window.'

'Who the hell *are* these guys?' said Jeff, staring at them in his mirror. 'Do you think you should call nine-one-one?'

Craig patted the pockets of his windbreaker. 'I forgot my cell. How about you?'

'I didn't bring mine either. My battery's dead.' He frowned up at his mirror again. 'Like, what do they *want*?'

'I don't know. But stay ready. If I say go, then put your foot right down to the floor and *go*.'

'Dad – maybe you should drive.'

'Unh-hunh. I don't think that either of us should get out of the car. But if I do say go, take a left on South Western Avenue, and then another left on West Superior, then a right on South Philips.'

Jeff steered the Grand Prix into the side of the road and stopped.

Immediately, the Buick shunted their rear bumper, pushing them forward three or four feet and giving both of them a spine-jerking jolt.

'Jesus!' said Jeff. 'This guy's totally psycho!'

'Put on your parking-brake,' Craig told him.

'I already did! I already did!'

The Buick backed up about ten feet and then collided with them again, much harder this time.

'Shit!' said Jeff. 'What are we going to do, Dad?'

'Just hold tight,' said Craig. 'They're probably drug addicts. All we need to do is stay calm.'

'Calm?' Jeff screamed at him. Because now, with a hideous grinding and squeaking of metal and plastic, the Buick forced itself right up against their rear bumper. The driver kept gunning his engine, and inch by inch they were pushed along the street, even though their wheels were locked and their tires were screeching in a high, hysterical chorus.

'*Reverse!*' shouted Craig. '*Put it in reverse!*'

Jeff pulled back the gear-shift to R, and pressed the gas pedal down to the floor. The Grand Prix's rear wheels spun, and clouds of rubbery blue smoke billowed across the street, but the Buick weighed nearly two-and-a-half tons and had an engine that developed more than 300 horsepower, and it relentlessly edged them forward.

For a split-second, Craig wondered if they ought to jump out of the car and make a run for it on foot, but maybe that was exactly what these goons wanted them to do. Besides, this Grand Prix was much more than just a car. This was his way of showing his family that he was still capable of providing for them, and taking care of them. He wasn't going to let some crackhead morons in masks take it away from him, less than fifteen minutes after he had picked it up.

As the Grand Prix was rammed further and further along the street, the grating of metal and the shrieking of tires grew deafening. Jeff tried stamping on the gas pedal in bursts, but the Buick was unstoppable. Craig turned around again to look at its occupants, and he was sure that the front seat passenger was laughing.

'Right,' he said. 'Let's get the hell out of here. Remember – when I say go, give it everything you've got. And don't hesitate.

Not for a moment. Keep going as fast as you can until I say it's OK.'

Jeff nodded. He released the parking-brake and shifted gear into D1, but kept his foot pressed hard on the brake pedal.

The Riviera backed away, only nine or ten feet, but then its engine bellowed and it collided with them yet again. It backed away once more, even further, nearly three car-lengths, and the driver was obviously preparing to ram them even harder. Its headlights filled the interior of the Grand Prix with blinding white light.

'*Go!*' said Craig, and they slewed away from the curb and sped along the street.

Craig looked around again, and he could see that the Buick was coming after them, but they had a two-block start, at least, and in this part of Kokomo there were scores of criss-crossing streets and avenues where they could shake it off.

'Keep going! Keep going!' he shouted. 'Left at South Western Avenue – *there*!'

The Grand Prix's tires howled as Jeff steered them around the corner. The rear end of the car snaked from side to side, and for a moment Craig thought that they were going into a 180-degree skid, which would have left them facing back to West Sycamore Drive, and the Buick that was chasing them. But with his hands flailing at the steering wheel, Jeff managed to straighten them out, and they roared off southward, faster and faster. South Western Avenue was only a quiet suburban street, lined with trees and single-story houses, but by the time they were halfway down it they were touching sixty-five miles an hour.

Craig turned around. He could see the Buick's headlights as it turned into the avenue after them. His heart seemed to be beating three times faster than it ought to be.

'Next left!' he panted. 'Here – West Superior! *Go!*'

Jeff steered the Grand Prix in a wide screeching semicircle, and again Craig thought that he was close to losing it. With a resonating bang, their nearside rear wheel hit the curb, and the whole car joggled and bounced. They ended up sideways across the street, with the engine stalled.

'Shit!' said Jeff, and punched the steering wheel in panic and frustration. 'Shit! Shit! Shit!'

'Shift into neutral,' Craig told him, trying to keep his voice steady. 'That's it. Now restart the engine. Brilliant. Now put it into drive, and go.'

West Superior was only a short street, but they hadn't even reached the end of it before the Buick came around the corner in pursuit, its suspension dipping, black and battered like a malevolent old shark. Craig said, '*Right*! Go right here, into South Philips – then right again – then left!'

His plan was to lead the Buick and its occupants into the intricate maze of roads and crescents next to the railroad lines, so that he could loop around and double back and leave them comprehensively lost. He just hoped that they didn't know where he lived, and follow them home, but once he and Jeff made it back they could call the cops. Besides that, he had his own gun – a Glock, in the left-hand drawer of his desk.

They turned right into West Carter Street and then immediately left into Conradt Avenue. 'Now – switch off your lights,' said Craig.

Jeff's confidence was growing now. Conradt Avenue was narrow and heavily overshadowed by trees, and there were cars parked all along the right-hand side, but he put his foot down and by the time they were only halfway down it they were nudging forty-five. Turning around again, Craig saw the Buick miss the turning from West Carter Street and carry on speeding westward.

'We lost 'em!' he said, triumphantly. 'They didn't see us come down here!'

Jeff lifted his hand and gave him a high-five. 'Wahoo! Nobody messes with the Cutters! No-bod-ee! Way to go, Dad!'

At that instant, Jeff realized that there was somebody standing in the middle of the road, about a hundred feet in front of them, under a street light. A young boy, not moving, not making any attempt to jump out of the way. Jeff stood on the brakes and the Grand Prix went into a long screaming skid.

Craig saw the boy coming nearer and nearer, as if he were watching a slow-motion movie. He could see the boy's face with unnerving clarity, pale and unsmiling, with wide-apart eyes and lips as pink as a girl's. He could hear a high-pitched squealing noise, a squealing that went on and on, but as the boy drew closer he realized that it was Jeff, making the sound of brakes, as if that could somehow bring the car to a stop any sooner.

The Grand Prix stopped so close to the boy that he was able to raise his right hand and rest it on top of the hood.

'Holy shit,' said Jeff. 'Holy shit that was close. I could of killed him.'

He reached for the door handle, but Craig grabbed hold of his arm and said, 'Wait.'

'What? The kid was standing right in the middle of the road and I could have knocked him down. I just want to make sure he's OK.'

'No. Wait. This is the Creepy Kid your mom was talking about.'

'*What*?'

'I'm sure of it. Pale face, dark curly hair. Washed-out black T-shirt, red jeans.'

'OK. So what's he doing out here, trying to get himself knocked down by a car? Doesn't he have a home to go to?'

'Mom says he killed Tyson. Burned him alive, and himself, too. I know it sounds crazy.'

Jeff pulled a disbelieving face. 'He doesn't look very burned alive to me.'

'I know. I know that. But I think the best thing we can do is just get out of here.'

'He's a kid, Dad. That's all. You're not scared of some *kid*?'

'Jeff – your mom has gotten herself involved in some pretty weird stuff lately. I'm not saying that I believe in any of it, but I think we'd be wiser to play this safe.'

The boy was still standing in front of the car, staring at them. Not smiling, not moving, but keeping one hand on the hood, as if he wanted to stop them from leaving.

'Let me just ask him if he's OK,' Jeff suggested. 'There can't be any harm in that. I mean, look at him. He can't weigh more than sixty pounds.'

'Your average pit-bull terrier weighs less than sixty pounds, but it can still tear your throat out. Come on, let's go.'

Jeff shifted the gear-shift into drive, and waited.

'What are you waiting for?' Craig asked him.

'He's not moving out of the way, is he? I can't just run him over.' He waved his hand and called out, 'Hey, get out of here! Get lost, kid! Scram!' But the boy stayed where he was, with his hand still resting on the Grand Prix's hood.

'The only thing you can do is back up,' said Craig.

'OK,' said Jeff, and engaged reverse. When he turned around in his seat, however, he said, 'Oh, shit. Look.'

Craig turned around, too. Coming slowly toward them down the street was the black Buick Riviera, with its lights out. It stopped about fifty feet away, its engine running, and smoke blowing out of its exhaust. Craig could see the white-faced driver and the white-faced front-seat passenger, but now he could see that there was another passenger, in the back seat, and that he had a white face, too.

'What the fuck's going on?' said Craig. 'Like, who *are* these guys?'

The Buick's doors opened and the three men climbed out. Apart from their white masks, they were all wearing long black overcoats, so that they looked like three gunfighters from a Sergio Leone movie. They came right up to the Grand Prix and the man in the laughing mask rapped on Craig's window with his knuckles.

'Get out of the car!' he said, in a loud but muffled voice.

With a tight feeling around his heart, Craig was suddenly reminded of the laughing mask that Ruth had seen in Doctor Beech's clinic, except that this man was more than just a disembodied head.

'Get out of the car!' the man repeated.

Another man rapped at Jeff's window. This man had no expression on his mask at all. 'You heard what he said. Don't pretend you didn't. Get out of the car!'

Craig vigorously shook his head. 'I don't know what you want, but whatever it is you're not getting it! I've called the cops, they're going to be here any second.'

'Are you deaf? I said get out of the car. I have a message for your wife and daughter.'

'*What*? What message?'

The laughing man stepped away from the car, tugging at his black leather gloves. 'I'm not telling you until you get out!'

'Dad!' said Jeff. 'Let's just go!'

Craig looked around. The Buick was effectively blocking the street behind them, and the Creepy Kid was still standing right in front of them.

The laughing man rapped on Craig's window again. 'You getting out, fella, or what? You really need to give your wife and daughter this message. Otherwise we might have to give it to them personal. Hand-deliver it, so to speak.'

'Dad!' said Jeff. 'They're bluffing, I'll bet you anything! They just want us to get out of the car so they can jack it!'

'They're going to all of this trouble for a 'ninety-nine Pontiac? I don't believe it!'

'Then what *do* they want?'

'I don't know. It looks like I'll just have to get out of the car and find out.'

'Dad – *don't*!'

'Listen, Jeff. Stay calm. If they had wanted to kill us, they would have shot us through the windows by now.'

The laughing man called out, 'Are you coming out, or what? We can do this any way you want. But your wife and your daughter, they need to get this message one way or another.'

'All right!' Craig shouted back at him. 'I'm coming out!'

He opened the car door and stepped out on to the road. The laughing man came up to him and said, 'There . . . that wasn't so hard, was it?' Inside his mask his voice was thick and breathy, as if he had a heavy cold.

'Who the hell are you?' Craig demanded. 'What do you think you're trying to do, rear-ending us like that, and chasing after us? Are you some kind of psycho? What have we done to you?'

'You personally have done nothing,' said the laughing man. 'Me and my friends, we don't have any bones to pick with you. But your dearly beloved wife seems to be suffering from selective deafness. My little friend here has told her to drop her investigation more than once, but for some reason she doesn't seem to be listening.'

'Listen,' said Craig, 'I don't have any idea what this is all about, but if you have a problem why don't you take it up with the Fire Department?'

The laughing man prodded Craig in the chest. 'I don't need to take it up with the Fire Department because I'm telling *her*. And I'm telling that daughter of yours, the one who thinks she can see things and hear things.'

'You leave my daughter out of this.'

The laughing man shook his mask from side to side. 'Can't do that, my friend. Your daughter knows what's happening, that's why. Your daughter's got the sensitivity. But if she wants my advice she should stick to singing her songs, and drawing her pretty pictures, and forget about people coming through from underneath.'

'Why?' Craig challenged him. 'Why should she? What in God's name is this all about?'

The laughing man came up closer. He was at least four inches taller than Craig, but Craig stood his ground. The laughing man said, 'Deals have been done, my friend. Undertakings have been given. We can't have anybody upsetting the apple-cart, not now. You need to tell your dearly beloved wife that all of the fires she's been looking into recently, they were all started by natural causes, so she can close her files and turn her attention to something less con-*trov*-ershul. And you need to advise your dearly beloved daughter that if she happens to hear whispering, or doors opening and closing, then all she has to do is turn up the music to drown them out, and forget she ever heard them.'

'Why don't you tell them yourself?'

'Because I'm asking *you* to do it, that's why.'

'OK. Supposing I tell you to go screw yourself?'

'You wouldn't, because you're a decent churchgoing man who doesn't hold with language like that.'

Now the Creepy Kid came around from the front of the car, and stared up at Craig with undisguised hostility.

'Your wife, she needs to mind her own beeswax,' he piped up. 'I thought I taught her enough of a lesson already, burning her dog.'

'Oh, that *was* you, was it?'

'Sure it was. That was to teach her a lesson. That was to teach her to mind her own beeswax.'

'If that was you, how come *you* didn't get burned?'

'Maybe I *did* get burned,' the boy snapped at him. 'Maybe I got burned to nothing but ashes. But what do you know? You don't know nothing about nothing! You don't know comings and you don't know goings. You don't know dying and you don't know pain. People never made you promises and then double-crossed you. You were never burned alive on account of the fact that nobody cared squat about you, even your own mother. I came out of her, didn't I? How come everybody was allowed back inside of her, except me?'

Craig was shaking. He didn't understand any of this encounter, or who these people were, but he was determined that he wasn't going to allow them to intimidate him. He had been crushed enough in the past eighteen months – by banks, by developers, by credit agencies, by the IRS. He wasn't going to take any more, especially not from some snot-nosed kid with a face like a flatfish and three bozos in carnival masks.

'You listen to me,' he told them. 'We're leaving now, my son and me. You characters – you can do whatever you darn well please. You don't scare me and I won't allow you to threaten my family.'

'I don't think that you quite understood me,' said the laughing man. 'You have to tell your wife that her investigations into all of those recent fires are finished. You have to tell your daughter to close her eyes and close her ears and above all to close her mouth. And you can tell that so-called psychic to go back home, too.'

'Or what?' Craig challenged him.

'Do you really want to find out?'

'Like I said,' Craig told him. 'Go screw yourself.'

He climbed back into the Grand Prix and slammed the door. Jeff was staring at him half in admiration and half in bewilderment.

'That's it,' said Craig. He was pumped up with adrenaline and his heart was thumping against his ribcage. 'Let's just get out of here. Go straight ahead. You can take a left at the end of the street, and then another left, and we'll be back on South Philips.'

Jeff started the engine and drove off. Neither the Creepy Kid nor any of the three masked men made any attempt to stop them. As they reached the end of Conradt Avenue, Craig turned around and saw that they were still standing in the road, watching them.

'That was unreal,' said Jeff.

'You think so? It was too darn real for my liking.'

'You want to go to police headquarters and report it?'

'No, let's go home first. I want to make sure that your mom and Ammy are OK.'

As they passed West Carter Street, Craig took a good look to the left to make sure that the Buick hadn't turned around to follow them, but the street was deserted, apart from lines of parked cars and a man walking a Dalmatian.

'What was that about a message?' asked Jeff.

'I'm not too sure. But it seems like they want Mom to drop all of those arson investigations she's been handling lately, and they want Ammy to stop going on about people coming through from underneath.'

'How the hell did they know about *that*?'

'Don't ask me. Maybe Ammy told one of her friends at school about it and her friend told somebody else and somehow those freaks got to hear about it, although I don't see why it should matter to them. But believe me, I'm going to find out who they are and I'm going to make sure that they all get locked up.'

They were only half-a-dozen blocks away from home now, and Craig was beginning to calm down.

'Come on, Jeff, you don't have to drive so fast. It's all over now.'

But Jeff said, 'That Creepy Kid. Shit. He's like *beyond* creepy, man. He just stood in the road, right in front of me, and I must have been doing forty-five, easy. Didn't even flinch. Didn't even fucking *blink*. What if I'd hit him? He'd be dead, and I'd be up for vehicular manslaughter.'

Craig said, 'He knew about Tyson, that's what I don't understand. If he didn't do it, how did he know about it? There hasn't been anything about it on TV. But he wasn't burned at all, was he? Your mom said that he and Tyson, they both burned up together. They were practically *cremated*.'

Jeff shook his head. 'He sure didn't look dead to me. But whether he's dead or not – I could have been in jail now, charged with killing him.'

'Maybe he's a twin,' said Craig. 'I don't know, maybe he's even sextuplets.'

'Hard to work it out, ain't it?' said a reedy voice, close to Craig's left ear.

Craig twisted around in shock. Sitting in the back of the car, his thin elbows resting on the back of Craig's seat, was the Creepy Kid. Jeff turned his head and saw him too and the Grand Prix lurched violently sideways.

The boy's eyes were black and glittering and his bright pink lips were moist, as if he had been licking them. He looked grubby, as if he hadn't had a bath in a very long time, and he smelled like the inside of a charity clothing store.

'How in the name of God did *you* get in here?' Craig barked at him. 'Jeff, stop the car! He gets out right now!'

'No! Don't stop yet!' said the Creepy Kid. 'You have to give a message to your dearly beloved wife, and your dearly beloved daughter, and I'm here to make sure that you do.'

'Jeff! Stop the darn car!'

Jeff drew the car into the curb and stopped, but the Creepy Kid stayed where he was. Suddenly, unexpectedly, he smiled at them, first at Jeff and then, even more winningly, at Craig. 'Don't you want to find out what's really going on? Don't you want to know who my friends are? They're real scary, aren't they? I think they're the scariest friends I've ever had. You never know what expression they've got on their faces under those masks. Brrrrrr! Don't that just give you the willies?'

Craig said, 'Get the hell out of this car before I drag you out.'

'Don't you think your dearly beloved wife will want to know what's going on? If you throw me out now, she'll never ever know. Unless she's a stupid dumb bitch, of course, and carries on trying to find out for herself.'

Craig took a deep breath. Every muscle in his body was tensed up, ready to jump out of the car, open the rear door, and throw the boy bodily on to the sidewalk. But he knew that Ruth was desperate to find out why and how all of those people had been incinerated, and how Tyson had died. If the Creepy Kid could give her some clue, maybe it would bring her some closure, even if it never led to any arrests.

'OK,' he said, so quietly that the Creepy Kid obviously didn't hear him.

'I'll get out then, shall I?' the Creepy Kid asked him. 'Just don't blame me for what happens next, man. My friends . . . they don't have much in the way of self-control, if you understand what I'm saying.'

'I said, *OK*!' Craig repeated. 'You can come back home with us and you can explain to my wife who's been causing these fires, and why. Then you can listen while I give her your friend's message about closing her investigation, and while I tell my daughter to ignore any noises or voices or whatever makes her think that people are coming through from underneath. Will that satisfy you?'

'It might. It depends.'

'Will you then go away and leave us alone and stop hanging around outside of our house?'

'I might. It depends.'

Craig looked across at Jeff. Jeff made a face which meant that he didn't really know what to think.

'Come on,' said Craig. 'Let's go home and sort this out once and for all.'

Jeff drove very slowly along the next three blocks, reluctant to reach home. The Creepy Kid sat perched on the edge of the back seat with both elbows on the front seats and whistled 'Lazy Bones' in a breathy, high, irritating pitch.

At last they reached the Cutter house and turned into the driveway, parking next to Ruth's Windstar.

Craig said, 'You wait here, you got it? I'll go fetch Ruth. There's no way I want you in the house.'

The Creepy Kid smiled and said, 'That's OK. I understand. Lots of my friends' moms didn't want me in their houses. They said I smelled funny.'

'That's because you do,' said Jeff.

The Creepy Kid lowered his head. 'It weren't my fault. She never gave me a bath or washed me none. Only Belinda ever did that, until Belinda went away and never came back.'

Craig said, 'I won't be a minute.' He went up to the porch and opened the front door and called out, 'Ruth! Ruth, do you want to come out here?'

Ruth appeared, still rubbing moisturizing cream on her hands. 'You got Jeff's car! That's wonderful! But you were such a long time. What happened?'

Craig took hold of her arm to stop her from pushing her way past him. 'Hold up just a second, honey. We ran into some trouble.'

Ruth frowned, and tried to look over his shoulder. 'Trouble? What kind of trouble?'

'We were almost home when we got rear-ended by this Buick. We tried to lose them because we thought they were crackheads trying to jack the car.'

'Go on,' said Ruth. She didn't like the sound of this at all.

'We gave them the slip, but we had to stop because there was some kid standing in the middle of the road and Jeff would have hit him otherwise.'

Ruth said nothing, waiting for him to continue.

'Actually,' said Craig, 'it wasn't just any kid. It was *him*.'

Ruth felt as if she were sinking very fast in a high-speed elevator. 'Oh, my God. So he's back already. Martin was right. He gets burned up, but then he comes back, over and over. There's no getting rid of him.'

'There's more than that, Ruth. When we stopped, the Buick caught up with us, and there were three guys in it. They were all wearing white masks, with different expressions. The one who spoke to me, he had a laughing mask.'

'Like the mask I saw at Doctor Beech's clinic?'

'That's exactly what *I* thought, yes.'

'What did he say? Did he tell you who he was?'

'No, he didn't. But he said I should give you a message. You and Ammy, both.'

Ruth said, 'What message? What's going on, Craig? What's Jeff doing?'

'He's sitting in the car, waiting.'

'What's wrong, Craig? Something's wrong, isn't it?'

'Yes. It's the Creepy Kid. He's in the car, too.'

Ruth stared at him, aghast. 'My God, Craig, you have to get Jeff out of there!'

She forced her way past him and out on to the driveway. Jeff was still sitting in the driver's seat and the Creepy Kid had his hand on his shoulder.

'Jeff, get out!' Ruth shouted at him. 'Get out of the car right now!'

Jeff tried to open his door but it seemed to be locked. He stared out through the windshield and shook his head. Ruth went around to the side of the car and yanked at the handle, but she couldn't open the door either.

'*Craig!*' she shouted. 'Help me get the doors open!' Then she hammered on the window with her fist and said, 'Let him out, you little bastard! Do you hear me? Let him out!'

Craig tried the doors on the passenger side of the car, but they were locked, too. Jeff turned around in his seat and tried to punch the Creepy Kid, but the Creepy Kid kept ducking, and when Jeff turned the other way, he grabbed a handful of Jeff's hair and jerked his head back.

Ruth hammered on the window again. 'Let him out, or so help me . . .'

'You want to see him *burn*?' the Creepy Kid screamed at her. Ruth could only just hear him. 'You want to see him burn the same way your dog did? 'Cause if you don't, you'd better *back off*!'

At that moment, Amelia came out on to the porch, wearing her pale blue bathrobe and fluffy slippers, her hair tied up in pale blue ribbons. '*Mom?*' she said. Then she shaded her eyes with her hand and peered into the interior of the Grand Prix and said, 'I thought he was here. I thought I heard him.'

'Ammy,' said Craig, putting his arm around her, 'you'd better get inside. Call nine-one-one and tell them we have an emergency.'

'No,' said Ammy, vigorously shaking her head. 'We mustn't do that. If the police show up, there's no telling what he'll do.'

Ruth said, 'Craig, break the windows. I'm going to drag out that little runt and strangle him myself.'

'No, Mommy, no!' said Amelia. 'He wants to *talk* to us, that's all.'

'If he wants to talk to us, this is not exactly the way to go about it, is it? *Let my son out of there, you miserable little bastard! Do you hear me?*'

Craig went over to his SUV, lifted the tailgate and took out his tire-iron. He went back to the passenger side of the Grand Prix and lifted up the tire-iron so that the Creepy Kid could see it.

'You got three!' Craig shouted. 'Then I'm coming in to get you!'

The Creepy Kid gave him a slow, sly smile. He kept his grip on Jeff's hair, but he stretched forward with his left hand so that he could put down the driver's-side window.

'Jeff?' asked Ruth. 'Are you OK?'

'Kid's stronger than he looks,' Jeff panted, and said, 'Ow! Fuck!' as the boy gave his hair another sharp tug.

'Try opening the door again,' Ruth told him.

Jeff jiggled the handle but the door remained locked.

'All right,' said Ruth. 'My daughter says you have something to say. Let's hear it.'

The boy was still smiling. 'Your dearly beloved husband has to give you a message first.'

Craig came around and stood next to her. 'The guy in the laughing mask said that he wanted you to drop all of your recent arson investigations. Put them all down to natural causes, and close the book on them.'

'Now why would he want me to do that?' asked Ruth. She was trembling with anger, but she was trying very hard to control herself. She had seen what the Creepy Kid could do, if he was crossed.

'Because people are sufferin', Ruth, and they sorely need their sufferin' to come to a close.'

'Maybe they do. But they're dead. Just like *you're* dead. And you can't expect to relieve one person's pain by killing another.'

'Sorry, Ruth. That's the deal. It's been like that for ever and ever amen. Some people get good fortune, others get ill. That's the nat'ral way of things. But bargains can be struck, and the gods don't mind *whose* life they take, so long as the books stay straight. Life and fate, they're all about numbers, Ruth. And those people I take, they don't suffer none. They don't go to hell. They're innocent, after all. That's the whole point.'

'Are you going to take *more*?' Ruth demanded.

'Of course I am. But when I do, you're going to put all of *them* down to natural causes, too.'

'But what about the people coming through from underneath?' said Ammy. 'There are *hundreds* of them.'

'That's right. I showed them the way through and now they're all getting themselves ready to follow. Not just kids, like me. But anybody who got burned in a fire and can't find any peace. People who died because of other people's carelessness. People who were burned up in auto wrecks. People who fell into acid, or got scaldified by superheated steam. Old people whose beds caught fire and burned them alive. They're on the move, Ruth. They're all in desp'rate agony and they all want an end to it, no matter how they get it.'

'What's your name?' Amelia asked him. Her tone was surprisingly gentle. 'Are you Andie?'

The boy looked away, and then he looked back again, but he didn't answer.

'Andie's ashes,' Amelia persisted. 'Are they *your* ashes?'

But the boy pulled at Jeff's hair harder and said, 'I need to hear you promise. Both of you.'

'All right,' said Ruth. 'I promise.'

'Me, too,' said Amelia.

'Swear to God and spit in the sky?'

'Yes.'

'*Say* it, then. Swear to God and spit in the sky.'

At that instant, Craig swung his tire-iron back and smashed the car's rear window. Immediately, he lunged inside and made a grab for the Creepy Kid's arm. The Creepy Kid let out a shrill whinny and twisted away from him, but he still wouldn't relinquish his grip on Jeff's hair. Craig pulled him across the passenger seat but he clung on.

Jeff yelled, 'Jesus, man! You're pulling all of my fucking hair out!'

Ruth tugged frantically at the driver's door handle. 'Jeff! Get out of there! Unlock the door!'

Jeff scrabbled to find the locking switch on the armrest, and jabbed at it frantically, but it had no effect. It was then that the boy burst into flames. There was a soft, explosive thump, and for five searing seconds the whole interior of the car was filled with billowing orange fire. Craig toppled backward on to the rockery with both of his shirtsleeves alight, knocking the back of his head on a lump of red granite. He lay there for a few moments, stunned, but then he managed to roll over on to his side and struggle up on to his knees, clapping at his sleeves to beat out the sparks.

Ruth was shouting, '*No*! *No*! *Open the door!*'

Although he was blazing, the Creepy Kid had put up the driver's window again, sealing himself and Jeff inside the car.

'*Jeff*! *Get out of there*! *Jeff*! *Get out!*' Ruth screamed at him, and Ammy was screaming, too, in a voice so high it was almost a whistle. Lights were going on in bedroom windows all the way along the street.

Craig picked up the tire-iron, climbed up on to his feet, and lurched around the back of the Grand Prix. He pushed Ruth away from the driver's door and hit the window as hard as he could. Inside, Jeff was staring at him wildly, his hair blazing, his face blistering, and his mouth stretched wide open in agony. His entire seat was shriveling. The foam headrest was alight, and dripping molten plastic on to his shoulders. Behind him, the back seat was filled with a mass of fire, in the middle of which Craig could vaguely make out the figure of the Creepy Kid, both arms raised as if he were a drumming monkey.

Craig struck the window again, and this time it shattered. Flames gushed out of it like a dragon breathing fire, scorching Craig's face and singeing the front of his hair. But in spite of the intense heat, he plunged both hands into the car, unbuckled Jeff's red-hot seat-belt, and grasped him under the armpits. Shouting with pain and effort, he heaved Jeff's shoulders through the window, and then managed to grab his belt and manhandle him out on to the driveway. One of Jeff's sneakers tumbled, smoking, down toward the street.

Jeff lay face-down on the red-brick paving, his face blackened and his T-shirt smoldering. He was quaking with pain.

'Craig! We have to get him away from here!' Ruth shouted. 'That car is going to blow up any second! Ammy – call nine-one-one, now! And when you've done that, bring out some blankets!'

Both of Craig's hands were a mass of blisters, but he managed to heave Jeff over on to his back. All of Jeff's hair was burned down to his scalp and his ears were curled up like two bacon-rinds. Craig took his arms and Ruth took his legs, and between the two of them they managed to shuffle him across the driveway and lay him down on the grass, sheltered from the blazing Grand Prix by Craig's Explorer.

'We have to cool him down!' said Ruth. 'Craig! Listen! Open up the garage and bring out the hose!' She knew that Craig was hurting, too, and already showing the first signs of shock, but Jeff was so badly burned that he needed immediate first aid if he wasn't going to die.

Craig opened the door of his SUV and pressed the remote control which lifted the garage door. He limped inside and turned on the garden hose which was fixed to the wall. Then he reeled it out across the grass, soaking his pants and his shoes.

Ruth was kneeling beside Jeff, shushing him and reassuring him that help was coming. She took the hose with trembling hands and adjusted it to a fine spray, waving it slowly up and down so that he was drenched from head to foot in cold water. Jeff groaned and murmured, 'What are you doing, dude? That really *hurts.*'

Amelia came hurrying back out of the house, carrying a large blue honeycomb blanket. 'I called them!' she said. 'The ambulance, and the Fire Department, both.'

She looked over at the Grand Prix. The flames were leaping so high that it looked like a monstrous Fourth of July bonfire. Several neighbors had begun to gather in the street, although sensibly they were keeping their distance.

'Ammy, keep down!' said Ruth, and almost as soon as she did so, the Grand Prix's gas tank exploded with a deafening bang, and a lurid orange fireball rolled up into the sky. The wreckage of the Grand Prix was blown clear over the rockery and on to the lawn, where it lay on its side underneath the basswood tree, burning so fiercely that the lower branches caught fire.

Craig sank down on to his knees, holding up his hands as if he were begging for mercy from an unforgiving god. Ruth looked over at him, and knew how much pain he was suffering, but all she could do was pray that the paramedics wouldn't take too much longer.

Amelia, though, was standing at the side of the lawn, her hands by her sides, looking slowly to the left and then to the right, and frowning.

'Ammy!' Ruth shouted at her. 'Ammy, are you OK?'

'I can hear them!' Amelia called back. 'I can hear them! They're coming closer! They're all coming through from underneath! Hundreds of them! Hundreds and hundreds!'

TWENTY-ONE

Ruth and Amelia had to wait until two thirty in the morning before the doctor came into the waiting-room to see them. Amelia was curled up on one of the couches, although she hadn't slept, and had spent the night whispering her songs to herself, songs about boys and rain and unfulfilled love affairs. Ruth stared at her own reflection in the night-blackened window and thought how tired she looked, and how lonely.

They heard the doctor's sneakers squelching along the corridor before he eventually appeared. He was in his early forties, swarthy, balding, with thick-lensed eyeglasses and black bushy eyebrows, and fuzzy black hair on his forearms.

'Mrs Cutter? I'm Doctor Bercow. I'm in charge of the team who have been taking care of your son, Jeff.'

'How is he? Can I see him?'

'Not just yet, I'm afraid. We're keeping him in a totally sterile environment because of the extent of his burns. His airway was damaged by the flames so he's on a respirator at the moment, and we're giving him fluids to keep him from going into hypovolemic shock. He's suffered second- and third-degree burns to his face and hands, and first-degree burns to a further twenty per cent of his body surface area.'

'Oh, God,' said Ruth. She paused, and then she said, 'He's not going to *die*, is he?'

Doctor Bercow took off his glasses. There were plum-colored bags under his eyes and he looked as if he hadn't had a good night's sleep in a month. 'So long as Jeff doesn't contract any serious bacterial infection, I'm pretty confident that he's going to pull through. I won't try to pretend that it isn't going to be touch-and-go. He's going to need extensive skin-grafting, once he's stable. But he was comparatively lucky that your husband pulled him out of that car so quick. His burns could have been a whole lot worse.'

'How about my husband? Is he OK?'

'Your husband, yes. We've treated his hands with antibiotic

cream and we've given him some heavy-duty painkillers. He's asleep right now. When his hands heal, he'll probably have some scarring, and maybe some stiffness in the fingers of his left hand, but apart from that he should make a complete recovery.'

'Thank you,' said Ruth. She sat down again, suddenly exhausted. 'You will keep us posted, won't you?'

'Of course I will, Mrs Cutter. Right now, though, it's just a question of wait and see. If I were you, I'd take your daughter back home and get some sleep. I doubt if things will change very much in the next eight hours. Come back around eleven.'

'You're right. That's a good idea. Come on, Ammy. How about it?'

Amelia abruptly sat up and stared at Ruth, with her eyes very wide. 'They're talking much louder now!'

Doctor Bercow said, 'Excuse me?'

'They're not whispering any more. They're jabbering. *Jabber-jabber-jabber*. Like they're really excited!'

Ruth put her arm around Amelia's shoulders and gave her a squeeze. 'She's over-tired, that's all. It's been a very traumatic night.'

'I know *you* can't hear them,' said Amelia. 'But *I* can, and Martin can – although Martin can't hear them nearly as clear as me.'

'That's enough, Ammy. Tell me about it when we get home.'

'But there's hundreds of them. *Hundreds!*'

Ruth took Amelia's arm and led her out. Doctor Bercow opened the doors for them and said, 'Don't worry, Mrs Cutter. I promise you that if there are any developments, we'll call you right away.'

'Thank you.'

'By the way,' he said, as he walked them to the hospital entrance. 'Do you have any idea how your son's vehicle caught fire like that? He doesn't have any burns that I would normally associate with any kind of accelerant. Gasoline, or kerosene, or any kind of chemical.'

'I don't know what caused it – no, not yet. Maybe an electrical fault. One of my colleagues from the arson unit will be taking a look at it over the next few days.'

'It was *him*,' said Amelia, in a low, conspiratorial voice. '*He* did it, that Creepy Kid. And now he's going to let them all through. "Come through! Come through!" That's what he's telling them! "Come through!"'

Ruth gave Doctor Bercow a weary smile. 'Time for a glass of warm milk and bed, don't you think?'

Doctor Bercow nodded. 'Sounds like a plan to me. If only. I have a six-year-old boy to attend to, with thirty-five per cent burns. He thought he could be like the Human Torch, in *X-Men*. Soaked himself in barbecue-lighting fluid and struck a match.'

They drove back to St Joseph's Hospital at eleven forty-five the following morning. The clouds were inky black as they drove along West Sycamore. The rain drummed furiously on the roof of Ruth's car and hammered on the streets and sidewalks, throwing up a fine mist of spray, through which pedestrians walked like ghosts with umbrellas.

Jeff had been moved from the emergency operating theater to one of the fifteen beds in the intensive care unit, so Ruth and Amelia were able to see him through a window in the side of his room. His face was charred black and scarlet, and glistening with antibiotic ointment. He was still on a respirator to help him breathe, and he was hooked up to a drip of lactated Ringer's solution to replace the bodily fluids that were weeping out of his burns.

A red-haired nurse with a saintly, medieval face said, 'The first twenty-four hours are always the most critical. But your Jeff seems to be a real fighter.'

Ruth didn't know what to say. She could only stand there looking at Jeff with her hand pressed over her mouth and tears in her eyes. Amelia touched her shoulder and said, 'He'll get better, Mom. I know he will. I can *feel* it.'

They went in to see Craig, who was propped up in bed, both hands bundled up in white gauze. His fringe was prickly where it had been singed by the fire, and his eyebrows had gone, which gave him an oddly surprised look.

'Ruth! Hi, honey! Hi, Ammy! Did you see Jeff yet?' His voice was slurred and he seemed to find it hard to focus, but the nurse had already warned Ruth that he was doped up with morphine.

Ruth sat down beside his bed. 'The doctors seem to think that he has a real good chance of pulling through. But, oh – his poor face. He's going to be scarred for life.'

'It's all my fault,' said Craig. 'I never should have listened to that Creepy Kid. I should have tossed him out of the car as soon as he showed his face. I don't even know how he got in there.

How did he get in there? Between Conradt Street and West Sycamore, we never stopped once.'

'Come on, Craig. You couldn't have known what he was going to do.'

'I should of known. In fact I *did* know. He burned Tyson to death, didn't he? And you *told* me that he was connected to all of those fires. But I left Jeff in the car with him. How darned stupid was that?'

'Craig, honey, he would only have found another way to hurt us. He wants me to quit investigating these fires, and I don't think he's going to give me any peace until I do.'

'So *are* you going to quit?'

'I don't know, Craig. It's my job. It's my duty. And how many other innocent people are going to get burned to death, unless I find a way to stop him?'

'So what's next?' Craig wanted to know. He waved one of his huge gauze-bandaged hands toward Amelia. 'You're going to let him incinerate Ammy? Then you?'

'You have mummy hands,' said Amelia.

'Mummy hands?'

'Like the priests started to make you into a mummy, but after they wrapped up your hands they decided they were bored with it and stopped.'

Craig gave her a wry smile. But then he said, 'Ammy – listen to me. You have to forget about all of this stuff about people coming through from underneath. If you think you hear them, put on your iPod and turn it up loud. I don't understand who these people are or what they want, but I don't want the same thing happening to you that's happened to Jeff.'

'The Creepy Kid won't hurt me,' said Amelia, emphatically. 'He won't hurt Mommy either.'

'How can you possibly know that?'

'Because he loves us.'

'He *loves* us?' Ruth asked her, in total surprise. 'If he loves us – jeez, he has a funny way of showing it. He killed poor Tyson, he almost burned Jeff to death, and look what he's done to your daddy's hands. How can you possibly imagine that he *loves* us?'

Amelia slowly turned to stare at the opposite side of the room, as if the Creepy Kid were standing in the corner, invisible to every-body except her. Outside the hospital, off to the north-east, they heard a crumbling rumble of thunder, like a department store collapsing. 'The Creepy Kid doesn't have a mommy and he doesn't have a sister and he wants us. He thinks that *we'll* take care of him.'

'Why does he think that?'

'Because I can see pictures of what goes on inside of his head. They're like scratchy old movies. And sometimes I can hear him crying. I think I know what he wants. He wants us to love him. He thinks everybody should love him, and he doesn't understand why they don't. He doesn't know how creepy and horrible he is. He doesn't know how bad he *smells*. He wants to do dirty things. But he wants everybody to love him, which is why he burns people.'

Craig looked at Ruth and pulled a face to show that he couldn't follow any of this. Amelia said, 'Ask Martin. He knows more about it than me.'

The red-haired saintly nurse came in and said, 'I'm sorry, but Mr Cutter needs to have his fluids and his blood pressure checked now, and then he should get some rest. You can come back around three this afternoon, if you like.'

Ruth kissed Craig on the forehead. 'I still haven't told you how brave you were, pulling Jeff out of that car. You were amazing.'

'No, I wasn't,' Craig protested, in a drowsy voice. 'I should never have allowed it to happen in the first place.'

'Daddy,' Amelia whispered. 'It wasn't your fault.'

'Of course it was. It was totally my fault.'

'No! The Creepy Kid doesn't care how many people he hurts. He's real, but he isn't real. He burns up, but then he isn't burned up at all. He's dead, but he's still alive. There was no way in the whole wide world you could have stopped him.'

'Maybe not, sweetheart. But I didn't even try.'

Amelia kissed him. 'You did better than that, Daddy. You rescued Jeff when he could have died. You saved my brother's life. We can make him well again, you'll see. We'll all work together and we'll make him well.'

Craig looked up at her. 'Where did you come from, Ammy? You're a gift from heaven.'

When they walked out of the emergency unit they found Detective Magruder sitting in the reception area, the shoulders of his raincoat still sparkling with raindrops.

'Hey, how's Jeffrey?' he asked them, standing up.

'We're hoping and we're praying,' Ruth told him. 'There's not much else we can do. The doctors seem to be pretty optimistic. But he's not out of the woods yet, not by a long way. He could still go into shock, or get an infection.'

'Listen, Ruth, I'm sure he's going to make it,' said Detective Magruder. 'It's amazing how they can treat burns these days. I saw a TV program about it a couple of weeks ago. They can even grow artificial skin, in case a burns victim doesn't have enough spare skin of his own.'

'So how are things going?' Ruth asked him. 'Has Jack been in touch with you about Nadine Gardner, and the way she and her horse got burned up?'

'Yes, he has, and he's going to call you about that. He said something about remains. "*More of the same*," he said, whatever that means.'

Ruth nodded. 'I know what that means. I think I do, anyhow.'

'But you ought to see what *I've* dug up,' said Detective Magruder. He held up a black leather document case, as triumphantly as if it were a baseball trophy. 'This is the main reason I came here to see you.'

'Oh, yes? I thought you had that eager-puppy look on your face.'

'Say what you like – you really need to hear this. Yesterday I called the superintendent's office at the Indiana State Prison, and asked about your friend Pimo Jackson. It turns out that six weeks ago Pimo was sent from the ISP to the burns unit at Carmel Hospital for extensive plastic surgery on his face. But while he was being prepped for his surgery, he escaped.'

'You're kidding me! There was nothing about it on the news. Not that *I* saw, anyhow.'

'The federal authorities sat on it, that's why. Apparently, the corrections officer who was supposed to have been guarding him decided to take some unofficial time out while Pimo was on the operating table. He wanted to play doctors and nurses with a couple of nurses. And they weren't female nurses, either.'

'So . . . Pimo's on the lam.'

'Not just Pimo, either. Six days after he escaped, a prison bus was taking Pimo's two brothers back to the federal penitentiary at Terre Haute from a rehab center in Indianapolis when it was ambushed by a man in a white mask. The bus driver was shot in the cheek and seriously injured. Pimo's two brothers and three other unrelated inmates got clear away.'

'I didn't know that Pimo *had* any brothers.'

'Oh, yes. Freddie and Karlo. And this is where it gets really interesting. When they were in their late teens and early twenties, they all used to live with their mother Velma in a house on South Home Avenue.'

'I see. And?'

'And their mother was a hopeless junkie, who used to sell herself two or three times a day to pay for her habit. But Pimo and Freddie and Karlo were whacked out of their heads, too, most of the time, and they used to have regular sex with her themselves – sometimes two brothers at a time, sometimes all three of them. She would do *anything,* their mother, or so it seems. Things that would really turn your stomach if a woman did them with a stranger, let alone her own sons.'

'Jesus. How did you find this out?'

'Social services. Kelly Wulwik told me, so long as I promised on my life not to mention her name. She owes me big time after that Catholic school business.'

'How come none of this ever came to court?'

'Simple. Some of Mrs Jackson's clients were prominent members of the Kokomo civic and business community. We're talking chamber of commerce here. You think they wanted the lurid details of all of their perverted little antics to be plastered all over the *Tribune*? And, like I say, we're talking about *very* perverted, not just whips and handcuffs and Johnson's baby oil.'

Ruth glanced to one side to make sure that Amelia wasn't listening to any of this, but Amelia was kneeling down by the tropical aquarium on the far side of the reception area, talking solemnly to the angel fish. 'What's it *like* in there? What's it *like* in that water? Can you see me?'

'OK,' said Ruth, 'we're talking drug addiction, prostitution and incest. But what does that have to do with any of these fires?'

Detective Magruder unzipped his document case and pulled out a green cardboard file. 'Mrs Jackson had a *fourth* son, Andrew, who was thirteen at the time Kelly was detailed to look into the Jackson family. Andrew's school attendance record was very poor, and his teachers had reported that he appeared to be undernourished and unwashed, and that he regularly turned up at school with bruises on his face and arms.

'The Jacksons' neighbors had complained about the constant coming and going of strange men at all hours of the day and night, and also the loud music and laughter and screaming. Because Andrew was underage, and he was missing so many days at school, social services were able to send Kelly around to the family home to see what was going on.

'Kelly talked to Mrs Jackson, who was totally high and very abusive. Kelly said that the whole house stank to high heaven. The kitchen sink was filled up with dirty dishes and there were take-out boxes everywhere, with moldy noodles still inside them, crawling with cockroaches. There were stains on the walls and stains on the furniture and stains on the rugs, and Kelly said she didn't even dare to imagine what they were.

'She interviewed Andrew out in the yard, which was cluttered up with shopping carts and rusty auto parts and a dog kennel that she couldn't pluck up enough courage to look into, because there was something hairy and *collapsed* inside it, that's exactly the word she used – but she didn't know what it was.

'Andrew told her that he was unhappy because his mother didn't love him. She didn't feed him properly or wash his clothes or take proper care of him. Worse than that, though, she had regular sex with his older brothers but she wouldn't allow him to do it. He used to stand in his room with the door ajar, watching his mother and his brothers performing every kind of sex act you can think of, and quite a few that you can't, and he didn't feel disgusted or outraged or anything like that. He simply felt excluded.'

'God almighty,' said Ruth. 'I think I need to sit down.'

She sat down on a couch underneath a large impressionistic painting of poppies by one of the Hoosier Group. Detective Magruder sat down beside her.

'I don't mean to upset you, Ruth. Especially not now. But what happened in the Jackson house, I think it's really significant.'

'Significant?' Ruth had never heard Ron Magruder use a word like that before. She looked at him closely and she realized that he was beginning to show some gray hairs. She thought: *How each day leaves us, one day after the other, like overnight guests slipping out of the front door at dawn, and very quietly closing the door, so as not to wake us.*

'Kelly tried desperately to have Andrew removed from the Jackson household, but she found her recommendation blocked at every turn. Of course it was being stonewalled by the same local bigwigs who wanted to make sure that none of their visits to Mrs Jackson became public knowledge.

'One afternoon, about three weeks after Kelly's visit, Andrew came back early from school to find his mother lying in bed, stark naked and stoned out of her brain. The forensic evidence indicated that Andrew took advantage of the situation by taking off his clothes and having sex with her, in all the same ways that he had seen his brothers doing it.

'When he was through, he lay next to his mother and hugged her and made the mistake of falling asleep. Freddie and Karlo came home, both of them high, and when they saw Andrew lying next to their mother, they went berserk. They went out to the back yard, lugged in a jerrycan of gasoline, and splashed gallons of it all over the bed. All they intended to do was to set the bed alight. They were so high that they genuinely thought they were doing nothing more than teaching Andrew a lesson. But there was so much gasoline vapor in the air that the whole bedroom exploded, and Freddie and Karlo both suffered severe facial burns. Freddie was blinded in one eye and Karlo lost his nose.

'Needless to say, Andrew and Mrs Jackson were both burned to death. Freddie said that Andrew ran round and around the bedroom, naked and in flames, screaming like a cat that Freddie had once set fire to when he was eight years old. Mrs Jackson was so drugged up that she was cremated alive without ever regaining consciousness. Least, that's what Freddie said.'

'So the fire at South McCann Street—'

'I know that I was skeptical about it before, Ruth, and I'm sorry. But I'm prepared to believe that your friend Martin could be at least half-right. The burning of Julie Benfield was a ritual of some kind, just like the fire that killed Tilda Frieburg, and the Spirit of Kokomo bus fire, and the fire that killed Nadine Gardner at Weatherfield Stables. Like, they were all re-enactments. Don't ask me if there was any supernatural element involved; supernatural doesn't come within my remit. But look at these pictures – these are what convinced me.'

Out of the cardboard file he produced two photographs, both of young women. One of them was holding the reins of a chestnut horse and smiling, one eye closed against the sunshine. The other was sitting on a porch swing, with autumnal trees behind her.

'I had the Scottsdale PD email me this picture of Helen McTighe, who was the girl who killed all of those horses at the Flying X. And this is Nadine Gardner.'

'My God,' said Ruth. 'They could almost be the same girl. Or sisters, anyhow.'

'Now take a look at these,' said Detective Magruder, and handed her two more photographs. One of them was a black-and-white Police Department mug shot, showing a woman with scraggly hair and puffy eyes and a bruise at the side of her mouth. The other one showed a laughing woman in a park someplace, with swings and roundabouts in the background.

'On your left, Velma Jackson, prostitute and crackhead and mother of Pimo, Freddie, Karlo and Andrew. On your right, Julie Benfield, wife and mother and respectable personal assistant at the Harris Bank. But there's no question, is there? Apart from a distinct difference in personal grooming, they could be the same woman.'

Ruth looked at the photographs again. Four women from totally different backgrounds, but all of them born to be sisters in a grisly and agonizing death.

She was still looking at them when Detective Magruder handed her another photograph. A pasty-faced boy, with unkempt curls and wide-apart eyes, and strangely cherubic lips.

'Andrew Jackson,' he said. 'This picture was taken in the fifth grade at Maple Crest Middle School. He was one of almost thirty-eight per cent of pupils who qualified for free or reduced-price lunch.'

Ruth felt as if she couldn't get enough air. 'It's him,' she said. 'It's the Creepy Kid. You saw him too, didn't you, at South McCann Street?'

Detective Magruder nodded.

'Have you shown this to Bob Kowalski yet?' Ruth asked him.

'Not yet. I want to wrap this whole case up first. Right now, Sandra's using the NCIC database to see if she can locate any suspicious fires that involved the deaths of six or more senior citizens, and also any fires in which a single woman was burned to death in a bathtub. I may be wrong, but I think we can tie all of these fires together with irrefutable forensic evidence.'

Ruth said, '*Andie's ashes.*'

'Excuse me?'

'Ammy keeps hearing somebody whispering in her ear. *Andie's ashes. Andie's ashes.* The cremated remains we found in the burned mattress at South McCann Street, they must have belonged to Andrew Jackson. But the cremated remains we found in Tilda Frieburg's bathtub and in the Spirit of Kokomo bus, they had the same DNA. And I'll bet that Jack found cremated remains at Weatherfield Stables, too – that's what he meant by "more of the same". And he'll find them in the back seat of Jeff's Grand Prix. And they'll both match the same genetic code.'

Detective Magruder tugged at his prickly little moustache. 'So you think that this Creepy Kid is the late Andrew Jackson, but somehow he's more than Andrew Jackson? He's, like, *generic*? He's every abused thirteen-year-old boy rolled into one?'

'Yes. Yes, I do.'

'So he's Billy McTighe, too – who was Helen McTighe's brother at the Flying X. And he's the same kid who killed Tyson, and the same kid who set fire to Jeffrey's car? His brothers burned Andrew Jackson up, and then what was left of him was professionally cremated, but he keeps on coming back, time after time, and he can set light to anything and anyone?'

Ruth stared at him, unblinking, and then shook her head, disbelievingly, and smiled. 'Didn't I hear you just say that supernatural doesn't come within your remit?'

'No, Ruth. It absolutely *does not*. I'm asking you what *you* think, is all. I still prefer to believe that for some obscure reason those cremated remains were deliberately left at the crime scenes by some human perpetrator. Maybe some religious nut.'

'There was far too much, Ron. Even the remains of a fully-grown man rarely weigh as much as three kilos.'

'Well, I'm damned if I know. Maybe he was twins. Maybe he was triplets, even, all with the same DNA. Let me finish up my investigation first.'

Ruth said, 'OK. But I should really go now. You'll let me know if you find out anything from NCIC, won't you?'

'I surely will. And I hope that Jeffrey gets over this real quick. And Craig, too. Give him our best.'

Ruth and Amelia hurried down the hospital steps and ran across the rainswept parking lot. As soon as they had climbed into the car and slammed the doors, Amelia said, 'We have to do some-thing, Mommy!'

'What do you mean, we have to do something? Like *what*?'

Amelia put down her rain-hood and clamped both hands over her ears. 'They're going to come through! I can hear them all the time now! They don't want to wait any longer!'

'You mean those people we saw at Doctor Beech's clinic? Those people who were all on fire?'

Amelia turned to her and her face was miserable and fright-ened. 'They won't wait any longer. They say it's their turn.'

'Listen, sweetheart, don't worry. I know that the past couple of days have been really horrible, but we have to be strong. You said so yourself, didn't you? We have to stick together, and not allow ourselves to be intimidated. You know what your grandpa used to say? "I'm not scaredified. Not of nobody nor nothing, not never."'

She switched on her cellphone, and it warbled almost imme-diately. It was a voice message from Martin.

'*Ruth? What's happening? I've been trying to call you all morning. I tried the Fire Department but they wouldn't tell me where you were. Ruth – I think it's urgent. I think it's all hell let loose.*'

TWENTY-TWO

Martin arrived outside the house a few minutes after one. The sky was beginning to clear, as if a dark curtain were being dragged away, and a fresh wind was blowing, but there were still unsettled rumblings in the distance. Jeff's burned-out Grand Prix had been taken away by the Fire Department, although the front of the house was still cordoned off with yellow crime-scene tapes that bounced and flapped in the wind. The red bricks of the driveway were scorched and cracked, as if a meteorite had landed there, and the lower branches of the basswood tree looked like the blackened fingers of an arthritic witch.

'What happened?' Martin asked her, as soon as Ruth opened the front door.

'What do you think? The Creepy Kid happened.'

'Oh, God. Tell me.'

'The Creepy Kid set himself alight inside of Jeff's new car. He just caught fire, like a thermic lance. Jeff has forty per cent burns and Craig's hands were burned, too, when he was pulling him out.'

'Oh, Ruth, Jesus. I'm so sorry.'

'It wasn't your fault, Martin. You did warn me, didn't you? You warned me once and you warned me twice.'

'I know. I know I did. But I never thought that he'd come after you so quickly. Mind you, I think that things are coming to a head.'

Ruth led Martin through to the living-room. Amelia came out of the kitchen, wearing a sloppy orange sweater with a cowl neck and overlong sleeves, her hair tied up in bunches. 'Hi, Martin! I'm making some iced chocolate with chocolate flaky bits. Do you want some?'

Martin smiled but shook his head. 'I think I'll pass on that, thanks, Amelia.' Ruth thought that he was looking bloodless and tired, as if he hadn't slept well. His hair was mussed up and he hadn't shaved.

'How about something stronger?' she asked him. 'I could use a drink myself, to tell you the truth.'

'Jeffrey and Craig . . . where are they now?' Martin asked her, as she poured them each a large glass of Goosecross Merlot.

'St Joseph's emergency unit. Jeff's airway was burned so he's still on a respirator. They're giving him fluids and trying to keep him free from infection. There isn't a whole lot more they can do, not just yet. Craig – well, his hands are badly blistered, but they think that he should make a ninety per cent recovery.'

'Ruth – I can't tell you how sorry I am. I should have realized what was happening a whole lot sooner.'

Amelia came out of the kitchen tinkling her glass of iced chocolate with a spoon. 'They're coming through soon, aren't they, Martin? I hear them all the time now. They're jabbering, like jabberwockies. *Jabber-jabber-jabber*! We're coming through, we're coming through!'

'I can hear them, too,' said Martin, wearily. 'That's why I wanted to see you. We have to find *where* they're going to come through, and how, and we have to try and stop them. This is serious, Ruth. It sounds to me like the whole nine circles of hell are in a turmoil.'

'"*We're all coming through*! *We're all coming through*"!' Amelia repeated, vigorously nodding her head. '"*You can't stop us now*! *We're all coming through*!"'

Martin reached across and took hold of Amelia's hand to quieten her. 'I think I understand what's happening. I may be completely wrong, but if Amelia can hear the same voices that I can, then at least I know that I'm not the only one who's crazy.'

'Before you go on,' said Ruth, 'you'd better know what Ron Magruder's found out.' She told him about Velma Jackson and her four sons, and how Velma and Andrew had been burned to death. She also told him about Helen McTighe, and her brother Billy. She told him about the photographs, and how Velma Jackson and Julie Benfield had looked just like sisters.

'I guessed as much,' said Martin. 'Especially Pimo and his brothers. It's all beginning to make sense.'

'Well, I'm glad it's making sense to you.'

Martin set down his wine glass. 'Right from the beginning I thought that the Creepy Kid was somebody who had made a deal with a lesser god. God, angel, I'm not really sure. But your Detective Magruder, God bless him, has pretty much proved it for me. When he was burned to death, young Andrew Jackson would have been sent to the ninth circle of hell because of what he did to his mother, and because of the unresolved feelings of revenge that he still had for his brothers. He would have burned and burned, day after day, night after night. Unendurable pain, twenty-four-seven, for ever. Think about it. Wouldn't you sell your soul to be free of it, even for a minute?'

'But why *him*? And how can he keep burning up to nothing but ashes and then come back to life again?'

Martin said, 'I can't tell you why he was chosen in the first place. Maybe the gods sensed that he was ready to do what they wanted. Maybe he had sinned so badly that he needed redemption more than any other boy they could find. Whatever it was, they would have made a deal with him. They would have taken his immortal soul, in exchange for giving him darkness and peace. But once they possessed his soul they would have been able to resurrect his earthly remains. They would have been able to take his ashes and recreate him exactly as he was on the day that he died.

'One morning, five years ago, Andrew Jackson woke up in the morning and put on his black T-shirt and his red jeans and went to school. He ate his free lunch and then he went home, and that's the boy you can still see today. Except that he's not that boy. He's an angel of death, like I said. He's a god, in a child's body. And as far as I can work out, he's going to go on taking revenge for every thirteen-year-old boy who ever got abused or mistreated, even if he's doing it by proxy. He's using Pimo and his two brothers to set up scenarios as near to their original abuse as possible – even if he's burning up innocent people who just happen to look like his abusers.

'Every time one of those innocent people dies, the angel of death gets to take possession of their soul. As far as I can make out, none of them suffer. Julie Benfield, Tilda Frieburg – nor any of those seniors who got burned on the bus. They didn't go to hell to burn for ever, the way that Andrew Jackson did, and those people we saw in Doctor Beech's clinic. They got that wall-to-wall blackness that all of us long for, in the end. They got absolute nothingness. And that's what Andrew Jackson got, too, for surrendering his soul and allowing the angel to use his ashes. He got *peace*.'

'But why do these gods *want* all of these people's souls?'

'You'd have to ask Professor Solway about that. But I think he would tell you that life in heaven and hell is not so very different from life on earth. The more human souls that any god can gather around him, the more influence he has. It's spiritual politics. It's all about the power, and the glory. All of those stories about the war in heaven, with Lucifer finally getting cast out, they're true, in their way, although nobody knows what a god or an angel really is, or what they really look like.'

'I'm trying to get my head around this, believe me,' said Ruth. 'But I'm not finding it easy.'

Martin said, 'I know. It's like all wars, you only know half the story until it's all over, and somebody's lost or won. But we don't have much time. Those voices that Ammy and I have been hearing, they're people from the ninth circle of hell who think that if *they* start ritualistic fires, if *they* re-enact their own deaths, they could end their suffering, too.'

'But if what you said about Andrew Jackson is true, they have to make a deal with this angel first, the way *he* did. They have to get Pimo or somebody like him to set everything up.'

'They should, and they probably won't find peace if they don't. But they're in agony, Ruth, and they don't want to wait any longer. They just want to come through and set fire to everything. Worse than that, though – if the people from the ninth circle of hell can find a way back to the living world, they'll *all* want to come back, from every other circle – plague victims, crash victims, drowning victims, all of them.'

'You're not serious.'

'Ruth – Jeff is in the hospital fighting for his life and you think I'm not serious? This could happen everywhere. Every single person who went to hell with unfinished business with the living, they could all come back through from underneath and make sure that they finish it.'

Ruth called Jack. She told him that Jeff was stable and that Craig was making good progress. Then she said, 'Ron Magruder gave me your message about the remains from Weatherfield Stables – "more of the same". I presume you meant cremated remains.'

'You presumed right, Boss. I sent them over to Aaron Scheinman and he put a rush on them for me. Lo and behold, the DNA is identical to the other samples. That means we now have enough cremated remains from one individual to make two individuals and possibly half of a third. Impossible, of course. But true.'

'Martin's here. He's explained it to me. I don't really understand it, and even if I could, I don't think I would believe it. But so far it's still the only explanation that makes any sense.'

'You're not talking to a totally closed mind here, Ruth. Remember Lois.'

'Did they bring Jeff's car in yet?'

'The Grand Prix? Yes, it's in the garage. I'll be getting down there as soon as I've finished the computer model from the Walters Clinic. I've only just received Tyson's necropsy from the vet.'

'Thanks, Jack. Call me as soon as you have any news, won't you?'

'Of course. And, Ruth – take it easy, huh? You've had some pretty serious shocks in the past forty-eight hours, and you're only human, like the rest of us.'

'Thanks, Jack.'

She hung up the phone, but almost immediately it warbled again.

'Hi, Ruth. It's Sandra Garnet. Ron just had to go out to a hold-up at the Speedway gas station out on West Jefferson, but he asked me to call you asap.'

'You've had some results from the NCIC?'

'That's right. I found one case of arson that was just like the Spirit of Kokomo fire, and another just like Tilda Frieburg's. And guess what? In *both* cases, there was a thirteen-year-old boy involved.'

'Go on.'

Sandra cleared her throat. 'In May 2007, there was a serious fire at a mental hospital in Kenosha, Wisconsin. Seven elderly patients were burned to death, as well as a hospital porter and the thirteen-year-old grandson of one of the inmates.'

'What happened?'

'According to the medical examiner, all of the patients had been prone to violent outbursts so they had been put on a new drug called Occus-Ex to keep them calm and sociable. Unfortunately, it seems like the drug had exactly the opposite effect on them. One afternoon, with no apparent provocation, they beat up on each other and tore each other's clothes off and then they deliberately set fire to their day-room. The hospital porter was stabbed and wounded as he tried to put the flames out, and the boy was knocked unconscious when he tried to rescue his grandfather. They both died of second-degree burns and smoke inhalation.

'The NCIC have sent me pictures of five of the deceased. At least one of them has a very strong resemblance to a woman called Ida Mae Lutz who died in the Spirit of Kokomo bus fire. The boy's name was Ricky Billings. They sent me his picture, too, and apart from his freckles and his fair hair he's the spitting image of Andrew Jackson.'

Ruth looked across at Martin. She covered the phone with her hand and said, 'It's the police.' Then, to Sandra Garnet, 'What about the Tilda Frieburg fire?'

'OK . . . in the past three years there were two separate and unrelated incidents of girls being burned alive in bathtubs, one in Fort Lauderdale, Florida, and the other in Champaign, Illinois. In both cases they were doused in accelerants and set alight, but the girl in Fort Lauderdale was black, and very thin, and lived with her boyfriend, while the girl in Champaign was white and over-weight, like Tilda Frieburg. and lived alone.

'Her name was Belinda Cusack. Until she was seventeen she lived with her mother and her kid brother on West Eureka Street, but her mother was a hopeless drunk and Belinda had to cook and clean and find a way to pay the rent, too. From the age of fifteen she brought men home to supplement her income. The family wouldn't have survived, otherwise. She wasn't pretty so she had to let men do whatever they liked to her, and some of what they liked was really repulsive, I can tell you.

'In the end Belinda couldn't take it any more and she packed up and left home. But she went back one evening to find out if her brother was OK. Her brother wasn't there, but her mother was. They had a fierce argument about money and her mother attacked her and hit her over the head with a steam-iron, and knocked her cold.

'Her mother thought that Belinda was dead, so she took off her clothes and dragged her into the bathroom. She poured a quart of potato vodka all over her and set her alight. She never admitted it, but it seems like she was trying to make it look as if one of her clients had murdered her.

'Belinda must have woken up when she started burning, because the neighbors heard her screaming, although – surprise, surprise – not one of them came to find out if there was anything wrong. But it was then that her young brother came home. He tried to save his sister, but while he was trying to put out the flames his mother hit him with the steam-iron, too, four or five times, and killed him.'

'That's terrible,' said Ruth. 'God, that's terrible.'

Detective Garnet said, 'Sometimes, the things people do to each other, it makes it hard to believe in God, don't it?'

By four p.m., Amelia was growing more and more agitated. She kept pacing backward and forward across the living-room, holding her hands over her ears, and saying, 'Stop! Stop! I don't *care* if you're coming through! Just stop!'

Ruth tried to put her arms around her and calm her down, but she pulled herself away and started to walk from room to room, into the kitchen and through to the dining-room and back out to the living-room, talking to herself higher and higher.

'*Stop*! *I don't care if you're coming through*! *Leave me alone*!'

Martin said, 'Ruth, listen to me – we have to do something, and we have to do it now. We don't want Ammy to have a break-down.'

'Maybe I should call Doctor Feldstein, or Doctor Beech.'

'Ammy doesn't need a doctor, Ruth. She needs to face up to these people who are coming back from hell. I can hear them myself, although Ammy can obviously hear them much louder than I can. They're growing more and more hysterical, and if we don't stop them – well, who else is going to stop them, except us? Nobody else believes in them.'

Ruth watched Amelia as she stalked out of the kitchen and back into the living-room, her hands still pressed over her ears, her eyes darting from side to side. She kept jerking, and sniffing, and colliding against the walls, as if she were having a fit.

'What can we do, then?' asked Ruth. 'Come on, Martin, tell me what the hell we can *do*!'

Martin laid his hand on her shoulder. 'More than anything else, we mustn't panic. OK? We need to keep our heads because the people who are coming through, they're going to be out of their minds with pain. They're going to be hurting and they're going to be disoriented and above all they're going to be angry. But we need to find out *where* they're going to come through. Once we've done that, we can go there and send them back.'

'But how can we do that?'

'They're *burning*, aren't they? They're all on fire. You work for the Fire Department. Can't you call on a couple of fire trucks? If they come through but they can't set anything alight, what choice will they have? They're dead. They'll have to go back to hell.'

'This is madness,' said Ruth.

'Of course it's madness. Life is madness. Death is madness. Before we're born, we're nothing at all, we're not even conscious. Then we wake up and we live out these lives full of happiness and light. Then we're gone again. Click, finished. Lights off. If that's not madness, then I don't know what is.'

'But you can understand why these people want to come back, can't you? These people who got burned, or drowned, or caught some terrible disease? Don't you think they feel cheated?'

Martin looked down at the carpet. 'Yes. I know they feel cheated. Susan's told me that.'

'You've felt her again?'

Martin said nothing, but Ruth said, 'You *have* felt her again, haven't you? You felt her last night.'

Martin nodded. 'Felt her. Heard her. This disturbance in the ninth circle of hell . . . it's spreading to all of the other circles, like a ripple effect. Susan, she's in the eighth circle, with all of the drowning victims like her. I was in the shower last night and she came to me. She came to me, and she held me very close – closer than she has for a long, long time. She said she was frightened, because the waters are getting all churned up, and people are screaming, and it's just like a dam's going to burst. They want to be saved, those people. Not from death, because they know that they're dead already. They just want to be saved from drowning.'

Ruth looked at him. She was tempted to reach out and touch his lips with her fingertips, as if to console him for what he had said. In another life, if she hadn't been married to Craig, and if she hadn't been Jeff and Amelia's mother, maybe she would have done. She had that unreal feeling that she had met a soulmate at the wrong time, under all the wrong circumstances, and all she could do was to watch him, and talk to him, and keep her hands and her feelings to herself.

'So what are we going to do?' she asked him. 'How are we going to find out where these people are coming through?'

'I think Ammy can do it, if I guide her. We can do one of those Liébault sessions – just you and me and her, together. They're close, Ruth, and they're coming closer. This time, when they come through, we won't be able to stop them just by breaking the circle. This time it's going to be some kind of war.'

TWENTY-THREE

The three of them sat cross-legged in the middle of the living-room. Outside it was growing gloomy again and the wind was rising, so that they could see leaves whirling wildly around the yard. They didn't have a rotating glass ball on which they could focus, like Doctor Beech's, but Ruth managed to find a candleholder with a globe-shaped crystal shade. It had been given to them as a wedding gift by one of Craig's sisters, and Ruth had kept it in the back of the dining-room sideboard and never used it.

Now, however, she fitted a candle in it and lit it, and it sparkled with prismatic colors, almost as glittery as Doctor Beech's ball.

Martin said, 'OK . . . let's make contact.' He reached out and touched his fingertips against Amelia's forehead, and Amelia touched her fingertips to Ruth's forehead. Ruth hesitated for a moment, and Martin glanced at her as if he knew why she was hesitating, but then she touched her fingertips to his forehead, too.

'Let's look at the colors,' said Martin. 'Let's see what kind of pictures they make. Let's empty our minds and see what images we can conjure up.'

They sat in silence for over three minutes. Rain began to clatter against the living-room window, and broken twigs, too, and a strong draft began to seethe under the door, as if a monstrous animal were trying to smell if they were in there.

The colored lights began to shimmer and dance in front of Ruth's eyes. She was sure she could hear the crackling of fire, and when she looked up she saw that flames were reflected on Amelia's face.

'*Ammy,*' she said, but the fire-crackle was so loud that she didn't think Amelia could hear her. Yet when Amelia started to whisper, Ruth could hear that clearly enough.

'"*We're coming through,*"' said Amelia. Her voice was harsh and high, and even though her lips were moving, it didn't sound like Amelia at all. '"*We're coming through and there's nothing you can do to stop us. Not now.*"'

Martin closed his eyes. Ruth turned to him and there were flames reflected on his face, too. 'I can feel you. I can hear you, too. What do you want?'

'"*Have to settle it,*"' said Amelia. '"*Eyes on fire, fingers on fire. Have to settle it.*"'

'How many of you are coming through?' Martin asked her.

'"*Hundreds,*"' said Amelia. '"*Hundreds and hundreds. And you can't stop us now. Have to settle it. Fingers on fire. Eyes on fire. Hair on fire. The pain the pain we can't bear the pain! We can't bear the pain for a minute longer!*"'

Martin looked at Ruth. Then he turned toward the window. 'She's right,' he said. 'They *are* coming through. I can feel them, too.'

'But *where*?' asked Ruth.

'"*Here,*"' said Amelia, but this time her voice was different again. Softer, less panicky.

Ruth looked at Amelia and saw that her face was altering. It was almost as if she were wearing a transparent mask made of fluid, constantly-shifting light. She could still see Amelia's elfin features underneath, but she was wearing another face, too. A face that looked unnervingly familiar. It could have been Ruth herself, except that it wasn't.

It was the woman in the photograph on Amelia's desk – the photograph that she had found in her bedroom closet when they first moved in.

'*Here*?' said Ruth. Her throat was so tight that she barely recognized her own voice.

Amelia nodded, and her ghostly superimposed face looked at Ruth with infinite regret in her eyes.

'"*They're looking for me. I used to live in this house once. My husband, and me, and our young son Paul.*"'

'Who are you?' asked Martin. 'What's your name?'

'"*Jennifer Steadman. The late Jennifer Steadman.*"'

'Why are they coming here, these people? Why are they looking for you?'

'"*Because of what I did,*"' said Amelia, in the same soft voice. '"*One day my husband Peter found out that I had been having an affair with his brother Greg. I told him it had been over for more than a year but he still couldn't forgive me, and he beat up on me so bad he broke my fingers. I took Paul with me and I got*' *into my truck and I left. I was drunk. I was angry. I was in pain. I didn't know where I was going."'*

Ruth wanted to hold Amelia's hand, but she knew that if she took her fingertips away from her forehead, the Liébault circle would be broken.

'What happened?' she asked.

'*"There was a pile-up on Route Thirty-five. Some girl had jumped off the overpass and three or four cars had all collided. I wasn't looking where I was going and I drove straight into them. My truck caught fire. My door was wedged tight, and Paul's seat-belt was jammed. All we could do was sit next to each other and scream."'*

'My God,' said Ruth. 'That sounds like the accident that Doctor Beech was telling us about.'

'*"We've been burning ever since,"'* said Amelia, although her words were fuzzier now, like a badly-tuned radio. '*"Paul and me, we've been sitting in those seats together for day after day, week after week, month after month, burning. It has to end, please. You have to let us go."'*

The rippling mask of light that covered Amelia's face now faded away, and Ruth was sure that she could feel Jennifer Steadman's spirit slip past her, only a few inches away, the faintest warm current in the air. Amelia opened her eyes wide and looked at Ruth and then at Martin and said, '*What?*'

At that instant, however, they heard tornado sirens wailing, all across the city.

Ruth immediately broke the circle and stood up and went to the window. 'What the hell is going on? This isn't tornado season.'

Martin and Amelia came up behind her, and Amelia put her arm around Ruth's waist and hugged her tight. Off to the east, toward the center of Kokomo, Ruth could see an orange glow in the sky. A few seconds later, she saw flames leaping up – flames that must have been at least a hundred feet high. The tornado sirens continued to wail, and then she heard fire trucks honking and warbling, and police squad cars scribbling, and the panicky *whoop-whoop-whoop* of paramedics.

'It looks like the whole goddamned city's on fire,' said Martin. He didn't even say 'excuse my French'.

'They've come through,' said Amelia. 'They've come through and they're coming this way. Hundreds of them.'

Even as they watched, the flames rose higher and higher into the sky, waving in the wind like gigantic banners of fire. It looked to Ruth as if a fifty-block area in the center of the city was burning, including Main Street and Union Street and City Hall. A thick column of smoke was rising up into the darkness, infested with orange sparks.

As they watched, they saw what looked like people carrying torches, walking along the road toward them. It was only when they came nearer that Ruth realized what they were: not people carrying torches, but people who were burning. These were the same people who had appeared to them as a vision in Doctor Beech's clinic, but now they were no longer a vision. They were real, and they had returned from hell, and they were all on fire.

'Jesus,' she said. 'Hell pays us a house call.'

There must have been over 200 of them, probably more. Men with their clothes on fire, their faces reddened, their eyelids burned off. Women with flames instead of hair. Children charred by electrical fires or blinded by chemicals. They trailed cloaks of smoke behind them, and when the wind gusted across the street, clouds of fine gray ash blew up from their shoulders.

'Martin – why have they come here?' said Ruth. 'What do they want with *us*?'

But Amelia suddenly clutched her arm and said, 'Look! He's arrived! This is why!'

She pointed across the driveway. Standing underneath the basswood tree was Andrew Jackson, the Creepy Kid. His face looked even paler than it had before, and his curly hair was standing up in a fright wig. His lips, however, were a bright red bow, and he was smiling.

Close behind him stood three men. They were all wearing long black coats and white papier mâché masks: one of them expressionless, one of them angry, the third one laughing hysterically.

'What do we do now?' asked Ruth. The street was filling up with more and more burning people. The smell of burning flesh began to blow in under the door, and Ruth covered her face with her hand. The sickening thing was that it smelled almost appetizing, like a hundred hog-roasts.

Amelia said, 'He wants Jennifer. I know he does. He wants to take Jennifer out for a drive, on Route Thirty-five."

'He wants *you*, Ruth,' said Martin. 'He's not Andrew Jackson any more, even though he's made up of Andrew Jackson's ashes. He's Paul – the boy who used to live here – and he needs to punish his mother for burning him alive. You live here, you look like Jennifer. He wants a ritual re-enactment, so that he can have peace, and his mother can too.'

Ruth stood by the window, staring out at the Creepy Kid and his three older brothers. Further along the street, she saw that two houses were alight. Flames were licking out from under the eaves, and thick smoke was pouring out of their chimneys. She could hear shouting and screaming and glass breaking. Another house caught fire, and then another. The people from hell were taking their revenge, even if it was going to do them no good.

'Mommy,' said Amelia. 'I'm so scared!'

'You and me both, sweetheart,' Ruth told her. But then she turned to Martin and said, '*What* did your Susan tell you?'

Martin frowned. 'I don't understand. What does that have to do with anything?'

'Didn't she say something about the water being churned up, and all the drowned people screaming to be saved?'

'Yes, she did.'

'Do you think you could talk to her again? Do you think you could talk to her *now*?'

'I guess I could. But why?'

'Couldn't you tell her that she could come through, and that everybody who had ever drowned, they could come with her?'

'I don't know. Maybe. But if that happened, it would be just like a dam bursting. The eighth circle of hell, it's like an ocean, with thousands of people drowning in it. The whole city would be flooded.'

'Yes,' said Ruth. 'Exactly.'

'I hope you realize what you're asking me to do. Drowning isn't any less unpleasant than burning, believe me.'

'Let's take that chance, shall we?' said Ruth. 'We can swim, can't we? But none of us are fireproof.'

'I'll need to fill up the bathtub,' said Martin.

'Then fill it up! We don't have very much time.'

Martin ran upstairs. Outside the window, flaming embers were drifting across the driveway, and some of the branches of the basswood tree had already caught alight. It wouldn't be long before the roof caught fire, and they would be trapped.

Amelia said, 'They're outside! They're standing in the porch! Oh, Mommy, they're right outside!'

As soon as she had said it, there was a thunderous knocking on the door.

'Open up, Ruth!' shouted a hoarse, catarrhal voice. 'Come on, Ruth, baby, don't keep us waiting! You know what we want! We want your body, baby! And this young boy here, he wants your soul!'

Amelia's eyes were wide with terror. 'What shall we do?' she whispered. 'What shall we do?'

Ruth said, 'You go upstairs, see how Martin's getting on. Go on, there's a good girl.'

'I don't want to! I want to stay with you!'

'Ammy – do as you're told! Just this once! Please!'

Amelia gave Ruth a hug, and then she reluctantly climbed up the stairs. When she reached the landing, she turned around and said, 'Don't let them hurt you, Mommy! Please don't let them hurt you!'

Ruth blew Amelia a kiss with the fingertips of both hands. She waited for a moment, until she was sure that she had gone through to join Martin in the bathroom. Then she went across to Craig's desk, took the key out of the ceramic ink-pot, and unlocked the left-hand drawer. Inside, neatly wrapped in a chamois leather, was Craig's Glock 17 semi-automatic.

Pimo Jackson hammered at the front door yet again.

'Ruth, baby! If you don't open up this door right this minute then me and my brothers, we're going to bust it down! You hear me!'

Ruth unwrapped the pistol, picked up the magazine that was lying next to it, and loaded it. Then she took off the safety catches and approached the front door, carrying it in both hands.

'This is your very last chance, Ruth, baby! We're going to be coming in there whether you like it or not, and we're going to give you the time of your life, believe you me! The time of your life!'

'Don't panic, Pimo!' Ruth called out. 'I'm coming!'

'You will be, baby, you will be!'

Ruth reached out with her left hand and unlatched the front door. She opened it just a few inches and the wind whirled in, smelling of smoke.

There was a long pause, and then Pimo cautiously pushed the door wide open. He was standing on the Welcome doormat in his white laughing mask, with Freddie on his left and Karlo on his right, one expressionless and one angry.

Ruth said nothing at all, but raised the Glock two-handed and pointed it directly at Pimo's mask.

'Hallo, Pimo,' she said. 'What are you laughing about?'

'Hey, Ruth, you wouldn't,' said Pimo, and he started to cough. 'That would be manslaughter, at the very least.'

'Not really,' Ruth retorted. 'Manslaughter is when you kill a human being.'

She squeezed the trigger. There was a deafening bang and Pimo flew backward and landed in the middle of the porch with a thump. Ruth had blown his laughing mask apart, and it lay in two empty pieces on either side of his head. Underneath, his face was a patch-work quilt of beige skin transplants, with a lumpy nose fashioned out of fat from his buttocks and a dragged-down mouth.

Freddie stumbled toward the open door, and Ruth glimpsed a knife flash. She took one step back and shot him between the eyes. He spun around and tumbled down the steps, all arms and legs.

Karlo was already running back down the driveway. The Creepy Kid was still standing under the basswood tree, pale-faced, motionless, watching him. Ruth took a shallow breath, held it, and shot Karlo in the head. There was nothing more than a small nine-millimeter hole in the back of his mask, but his brains came blasting out of his eyeholes like a cartoon character. He fell forward, twitched, and then lay still.

Ruth stood in the open doorway. Almost every house in the street was burning now, and the road was crowded with smoldering people. In the distance, the tornado sirens were still groaning, but there was no sound of fire trucks or police cars.

Smoke blew across the driveway and Ruth realized that it was coming from her own roof.

The Creepy Kid walked toward her. He was smiling.

'What have you done, Jennifer?' he piped up. 'You were supposed to be taking care of me, weren't you? You'll have to pay the price for that, believe me.'

'I thought you loved me. My daughter thinks you love me. My daughter thinks you love both of us.'

'I do, Jennifer. I surely do. I wouldn't hurt you, not for the world. Not my sister, neither. I want you to take care of me. I need taking care of, like you never did before. But first you have to pay the price.'

'You don't want me, do you? You don't want my daughter, either. All you want is our souls.'

'Oh come on, Jennifer. Don't let's go splittin' cows' hairs.'

Ruth said, 'I'm not Jennifer. But I know who you are. More to the point, I know who you're *not*. You're not a real boy. You're not Andie or Billy or Paul or any of those kids. They're all dead. And you – what are you? Who knows. Nothing but a greedy spirit, who wants as many human souls as he can gather together.'

The Creepy Kid said, 'You don't know nothin' about heaven, Jennifer, and you know even less about hell.'

'I think I'd prefer to leave it that way, until I get there. Now why don't you take all of these poor souls back to where they came from?'

The Creepy Kid turned around and looked at the burned and burning people in the street. By now, the smoke was choking, and all the trees were on fire, like rows of chandeliers. The Creepy Kid said, 'Don't think they'll really want to, to tell you the truth. All they got to look forward to is pain and suff'rin'. Would *you* go?'

He climbed the steps and stood in the porch.

'What do you want?' Ruth demanded. 'Whatever it is you came for, you're not getting it.'

'Jennifer, you shouldn't say things like that. You should take care of me!'

Ruth slammed the door in his face, locked it and bolted it and slid back the safety-chain.

'Jennifer!' called out the Creepy Kid. 'What you do that for?'

Ruth ignored him and ran upstairs. Martin and Amelia were in the bathroom, both of them kneeling by the bathtub, which was filled to the brim with cold water. Martin had both of his arms in the water, up to his elbows.

'You'll have to hurry,' said Ruth. 'The Creepy Kid's right outside, but I doubt if he'll stay there for long. Apart from that, I think the house is on fire.'

'She's here already,' said Martin. He had tears in his eyes. 'She's here, I can feel her.'

Ruth knelt down by the bathtub, too. She looked into the water, and there, barely visible, she saw a dark-haired young woman lying under the surface. The woman was almost completely transparent, but Ruth could see her brown eyes, and her lips, and the faintest rose-petal smudge of her nipples.

'Susan,' said Martin. 'I've told her that she can come through, and that everybody else in the eighth circle of hell can come through. I don't know if they will. I don't know if they *can*, even. But I've tried my best.'

He leaned over the bathtub and touched his lips to the surface of the water. Susan's glassy face rose up to meet his, and to kiss him. Then, without warning, the water started to churn and splash, as if it were boiling. Martin sat back, and then pulled out the plug.

'Do you think it's going to work?' asked Ruth.

Martin shrugged. 'I have absolutely no idea.' He stood up, and watched the last swirl of water disappear down the waste pipe.

Amelia stood up, too. 'I *know* it's going to work! I can hear them already! The drowning people. They're coming through, too.'

Ruth walked along the landing to the top of the stairs, with Amelia and Martin close behind her. The front door was wide open, and the Creepy Kid was standing at the bottom of the stairs looking up at her.

'Jennifer, that wasn't very nice, shutting the door on me like that. I thought you wanted things back the way they were, when we were happy. Before you went with Greg, and all those other men.'

He took a step up toward her, and then another one. For some reason, he looked larger than he had before, and he seemed to grow with every step upward.

Ruth lifted the Glock and pointed it at him. 'Don't you come up any further. I'll blow your head off.'

The Creepy Kid gave her an absurd falsetto titter, like a girl, and pressed two fingertips to his lips. 'You're going to blow my *head* off? You don't think I'm real, do you, so how could you do that? I'm nothing but ashes, Jennifer! Ashes and memories! Ashes and pain! You can't blow the head off ashes!'

He took another step upward, and then another.

'Shoot him,' said Martin. 'Shoot the little bastard.'

'Go on, then!' said the Creepy Kid. 'Shoot the little bastard! I dare you!'

Now he was more than halfway up the stairs. Ruth had a terrible feeling that shooting him would be the worst mistake of her life; he wasn't a real boy, she was sure of that, but what was he?

'*Shoot him!*' Martin shouted at her.

She fired. The instant she did so, the Creepy Kid burst into flames – flames so hot that Ruth had to back away from the top of the stairs, her arm lifted to protect her face.

'Mommy!' screamed Amelia.

All three of them retreated along the landing as the blazing boy trudged slowly up the stairs. He was gripping the banister rail with his right hand, and every time he touched it, the varnish blistered. On his left side, the pale pink-and-green wallpaper was scorched brown, and beneath his feet, the stair-carpet was burned with black footprints.

He reached the top of the stairs, and by now the flames that poured out of him were roaring so loudly that Ruth couldn't hear what Martin was shouting at her.

He reached across and lifted her gun hand, and it was only then that she realized that he wanted her to shoot the Creepy Kid again. She fired, right into the center of the flames. She saw a momentary flare, but that was all. The Creepy Kid kept on shuffling toward them, and with every step he grew hotter and brighter, until he was incandescent.

Ruth tried to push Amelia into her bedroom, but as she did so she heard a sharp barking sound. She stopped where she was, thinking, *no, it can't be*. But when she turned around she saw a bundle of fire racing up the stairs, and when it reached the landing she could see what it was: Tyson, on fire. His eyes were scarlet and there were flames pouring out of his mouth – a hound from hell – but she could see clearly that it was Tyson. He barked again, and then again, and then he launched himself at the Creepy Kid as if he had been shot out a catapult.

There was a dazzling explosion of fire. The Creepy Kid toppled over the banister-rails with Tyson on top of him, and they both landed in the hallway like a napalm bomb, with shock-waves of flame rolling out across the floor and up the walls. Ruth rushed over to the banister and looked down, and there lay the both of them, blazing furiously.

'Oh, Tyson,' she said. 'Oh, Tyson, you poor, faithful dog! Thank you!'

Amelia snatched her hand. 'I *told* you he wasn't gone for ever, didn't I? I *told* you he was going to come back!'

Martin came up to both of them. He didn't say a word, but he put his arms around them both and held them tight.

He was still holding them when they heard a deep roaring noise out in the street.

'That's not thunder,' said Amelia, cocking her head to one side and listening hard.

Ruth looked at Martin and said, 'She's right. That's *not* thunder. What the hell is it?'

They went downstairs and out through the front door. Most of the houses were still on fire, and thick gray smoke was billowing out of the shingles of their own roof. But the crowds of burning people were milling around in confusion, as if they could sense that something apocalyptic were about to happen. Some of them were screaming, and other were spinning around and around with their arms out wide, blazing like Catherine-wheels.

Amelia said, in one of her breathy, knowing whispers, 'It's *Susan*!'

The roar was growing louder and louder, and the wind was suddenly ten degrees colder. Ruth peered toward the east, and all she could see was darkness. The flames had died down, and the lurid orange glow that had lit up the city had faded into black. And then she saw a dim white line approaching, a line that stretched all the way across the street.

At first she didn't realize what it was, but then she saw that it was foam, and that it was carrying all kinds of debris with it: trees and bicycles and park benches and broken fences. It was a massive wall of water – all of the water from the eighth circle of hell.

It thundered along the street, so fast that none of the burning people had any chance of escaping it. Their flames were extinguished and they were all swept away, hundreds and hundreds of them, along with automobiles and bushes and street-signs and living people screaming for help. The water was impenetrably dark – dark, boiling green. It rose higher and higher, and as it did so it brought with it another raft of debris: boats and lifebelts and shattered oars, as well as hundreds more bodies, all clogged together in a vast, sodden archipelago.

The water rapidly began to rise up the driveway, and Ruth

and Amelia and Martin retreated to the porch. In less than five minutes, however, it was flooding right into the house and across the living-room carpet. With a sharp, complicated fizzle, it extinguished the last smoking remains of the Creepy Kid, and Tyson's bones, too.

Ruth and Amelia and Martin climbed the stairs up to the landing and sat there watching as the water swirled in. They could also hear crackling in the attic as the roof smoldered.

'Let's hope we don't have to build ourselves an ark,' said Martin, as the water rose halfway up the stairs. 'I was never any good at woodwork.'

They sat on the landing for more than five hours. Amelia softly sang her songs, and Ruth went to sleep with her head against Martin's shoulder.

At last, at dawn, the water began to gurgle away, taking the cremated remains of the Creepy Kid, and Tyson's skull, and all of the hundreds of people who had tried to come back from hell. It was a slow, funereal current that emptied itself down drains and sewers, and it left the streets of Kokomo littered with debris. No bodies, though, except the bodies of the living who had been drowned in it. The bodies of the dead returned to the afterlife.

When Ruth and Amelia and Martin emerged from the house, a watery sun was shining. Dozens of houses were still smoking, with smoke-stained windows, and the roof of the Cutter house had been burned right down to the rafters, but the asphalt street was so bright that they were dazzled.

Ruth said, 'All of those people. Are they really going to suffer all that pain, for ever and ever, amen?'

Martin lifted his hand, as if he wanted to touch her hair.

'Everything we do, Ruth, it's always for ever and ever, amen.'

Three days later, when she was staying with her friend Margaret in Lafayette, she had a phone call from St Vincent's Hospital in Carmel, where Jeff had been taken after the floods.

'Mrs Cutter? This is Doctor Petersen. I'm sorry to have to tell you this, Mrs Cutter, but about an hour ago your son Jeffrey suffered an acute myocardial infarction. We did everything possible, Mrs Cutter, but I'm afraid to say that he's passed.'

'Passed?' said Ruth. She was looking out of the window at Amelia, playing with Margaret's five-year-old son in the yard outside. He looked so much like Jeff, when he was little. She could even hear him laughing.

'I'm sorry,' said Dr Petersen. 'I really am.'

Three months later, when Ruth went up to Amelia's room to say goodnight, Amelia said, 'I hope Jeff isn't hurting.'

Ruth had been looking at the framed picture of Jennifer Steadman on Amelia's desk – that wistful, unfocused smile. 'Oh. Sweetheart. Of course he's not hurting. Jeff's at peace. It's only unhappy people who go to hell when they die.'

'I don't know. Sometimes I think that I can hear him. Just when I'm falling asleep, I can hear him whispering "Ammy".'

'You miss him is all.'

Ruth went to the window, took hold of the drapes, and she was about to draw them together when she saw somebody standing under the basswood tree. A tall teenage boy, with unkempt hair. Not moving, just staring at the house.

She frowned at him. He was wearing black jeans and a black T-shirt. On the front of the T-shirt she could make out the red letters *Cattle Decapitation*.

She raised her hand, but he didn't acknowledge her, and she couldn't be sure that he had seen her.

'Mommy?' frowned Amelia. 'What's wrong? Aren't you going to draw the drapes?'

Ruth went out on to the landing. 'Craig!' she called. 'Craig!'

Craig came out into the hallway and looked up. He was still wearing white cotton gloves to protect his hands.

'What is it, honey?'

Ruth hesitated. She couldn't think how to tell him that their son had come back.